IN A U...... ....RIFE,
DANGER TAKES ON MANY FORMS

2/97

She is a hardened soldier and pilot with a reputation throughout the system for fast reflexes and little patience. But now Morgan must confront a gargantuan, mechanized threat from a distant, unfeeling, alien presence—and her years of training and experience might not be enough. . . .

What are Fomalhautians like? In addition to having two heads and four arms, most of them—as a hapless driving instructor on planet Cassiopeia 43-G discovers—seem to foster dreams of conquest. . . .

Harbin had spent a lifetime dodging shots and taking lives in a solar system gone mad with warring corporations. Now, on a distant asteroid, he must face a challenge that will make his past seem simple by comparison. . . .

And other tales of
INTERGALACTIC
MERCENARIES

INTERGALACTIC
MERCENARIES

Edited by
Sheila Williams
and
Cynthia Manson

A ROC BOOK

ROC
Published by the Penguin Group
Penguin Books USA Inc., 375 Hudson Street,
New York, New York 10014, U.S.A.
Penguin Books Ltd, 27 Wrights Lane,
London W8 5TZ, England
Penguin Books Australia Ltd, Ringwood,
Victoria, Australia
Penguin Books Canada Ltd, 10 Alcorn Avenue,
Toronto, Ontario, Canada M4V 3B2
Penguin Books (N.Z.) Ltd, 182–190 Wairau Road,
Auckland 10, New Zealand

Penguin Books Ltd, Registered Offices:
Harmondsworth, Middlesex, England

First published by Roc, an imprint of Dutton Signet,
a division of Penguin Books USA Inc.

First Printing, November, 1996
10 9 8 7 6 5 4 3 2 1

CONTENTS

ACKNOWLEDGMENTS

We would like to thank Sharah Thomas, Scott L. Towner, and Kathleen Halligan, who helped us with the detail work; George Schumacher, who cleared the permissions; and Jack McDevitt, John Webha, and Gardner Dozois for their suggestions. Special thanks are due our own editor, Amy Stout.

INTRODUCTION

by Sheila Williams

"To be a successful soldier you must know history," wrote General George S. Patton to his son. "What you must know is how man reacts. Weapons change but man who uses them changes not at all. To win battles you do not beat weapons—you beat the soul of man of the enemy man." The battles in this anthology of stories by some of science fiction's most honored and outstanding authors thrust warriors into future conflicts that are often fought on distant planets. Yet those soldiers have much in common with their antecedents. Whether the battles are waged at Salamis or Arbela, Hastings or Lepanto, Gettysburg or Midway, the motives are the same. Wars are fought to save or promote a society, a people, or a way of life. Though they will describe who they are and what they are fighting for in different words, future generations of soldiers will fight for the same reasons.

Those who sign on for the long haul, for whom the war becomes a way of life, become known as the mercenaries. The mercenary volunteers for action. He may fight for his own country or for another. He may fight for money, for glory, for a greater good, or for a multinational corporation. Though he serves another master, it is often in ways that further his own interests. Whether his battles are to be fought on Earth, in the Asteroid Belt, near Cassiopeia 43-G, or on planets named Jackson's Whole and Kirsi, his deeds may change the lives of thousands. They will almost certainly change him.

As Patton said, the weapons change—many a World War I veteran would be amazed to learn that coherent light can produce the deadly effect of the laser, and the sophisticated armaments of the future, so stunningly depicted in this anthology, would astound us in just the same way. The issues change—yesterday we tried to make the world safe for democracy, tomorrow we will try to make the universe safe for humanity. But certain factors remain constant.

The purpose of battle will still be to disable, dismantle, and when necessary, kill the opposition. The goal of the war will be to win. And the character of the players will be interchangeable with those who have waged war throughout history.

Some will be far-seeing, some will be greedy, some will be self-righteous, some will be honorable, some will be cowardly, some will be pragmatic. The individual who volunteers for duty will, as often as not, be brave. While death is to be avoided, it is also an acceptable risk. Whatever originally convinced the warrior to fight will outweigh the consequences of failure.

The enemies may differ. Some of those featured in this anthology are horrendous fighting machines, some are aliens from Formalhaut and Troft, while others remain all too human. Still, like many historical opponents, they continue to bring out the best and the worst in their adversaries. And when the soldier of the future understands his foe, he, too, can beat the soul of the enemy man, alien, or machine.

In many of the stories assembled here, failure would be a major setback, if not total disaster, for humanity. The battle to save the human race may be waged quietly, as in Gordon R. Dickson's breathtaking classic, "Call Him Lord." It may be waged solemnly, as in Ben Bova's moving "Sepulcher," or accidentally, as in Frederick Pohl's hilarious look at "The High Test."

Some of the battles are personal. Stirring conflicts of this type can be found in "Call Him Lord" and "Sepulcher," and one of the most poignant personal encounters is depicted in Timothy Zahn's wrenchingly honest look at how difficult it can be to reintegrate a highly specialized warrior into society when "Jonny Comes Marching Home."

A tremendous sense of adventure pervades *Intergalactic Mercenaries*. In "Pilots of the Twilight," Edward Bryant offers us an exhilarating tale of all-out battle to save a planet from a relentless adversary. Though published in the eighties, it is a story that can gleefully stand next to any gung-ho space opera from an earlier age. Across the reaches of space, Lois McMaster Bujold takes us along on a dangerous escapade with her hero, Miles, who, like his ancient Greek counterpart, Theseus, must face the monstrous Minotaur and find his way out of his own perilous "Labyrinth."

It's been a pleasure working with the highly professional writers assembled here. Their stories are compelling. Some are straightforward, suspenseful dramas, while others are subtle and philosophical. Together they show us that the soldiers who fought the battles from Greece to Normandy are very like the soldiers who will face the intergalactic enemy of tomorrow.

CALL HIM LORD

by Gordon R. Dickson

The highly respected Hugo and Nebula award-winning author Gordon R. Dickson was born in November 1923 in Edmonton, Alberta, Canada. His father was a mining engineer from Sydney, Australia, and his mother was a teacher from the United States. After his father's death, the family returned to the United States, settling in Minneapolis in 1937. Dickson served in the U.S. Army from 1943 to 1946. After the war he resumed his interrupted studies at the University of Minnesota, where he received a B.A. in Creative Writing in 1948.

Dickson has been a full-time writer since 1950. During his career he has published 52 novels, over 150 shorter works, and a number of collections. More than 25 million copies of his books have sold worldwide. The author's major body of work is called the Childe Cycle. Among the books in this series are *Dorsai!* (1957), *Soldier Ask Not* (1967), *The Final Encyclopedia* (1984), and *Other* (1994). He is about to begin work on *Antagonist,* the ninth Childe novel.

Dickson is a founder of the Science Fiction Writers of America (SFWA) and a past president of that organization. In 1965 he received his first Hugo award, science fiction's highest honor, for the short story version of "Soldier Ask Not." In 1981 he received two more Hugos—for the novella "Lost Dorsai" and the novelette "The Cloak and the Staff" (*Analog,* August 1980). In 1966 SFWA awarded him a Nebula for the brilliant short story, "Call Him Lord" (*Analog,* May 1966), that follows.

He called and commanded me
—Therefore, I knew him;
But later on, failed me; and
—Therefore, I slew him!"
     "Song of the Shield Bearer"

The sun could not fail in rising over the Kentucky hills, nor could Kyle Arnam in waking. There would be eleven hours and forty minutes of daylight. Kyle rose, dressed, and went out to saddle the gray gelding and the white stallion. He rode the stallion until the first fury was out of the arched and snowy neck; and then led both horses around to tether them outside the kitchen door. Then he went in to breakfast.

The message that had come a week before was beside his plate of bacon and eggs. Teena, his wife, was standing at the breadboard with her back to him. He sat down and began eating, rereading the letter as he ate.

". . . The Prince will be traveling incognito under one of his family titles, as Count Sirii North; and should not be addressed as 'Majesty'. *You will call him 'Lord'* . . ."

"Why does it have to be you?" Teena asked.

He looked up and saw how she stood with her back to him.

"Teena—" he said, sadly.

"Why?"

"My ancestors were bodyguards to his—back in the wars of conquest against the aliens. I've told you that," he said. "My forefathers saved the lives of his, many times when there was no warning—a Rak spaceship would suddenly appear out of nowhere to lock on, even to a flagship. And even an Emperor found himself fighting for his life, hand to hand."

"The aliens are all dead now, and the Emperor's got a hundred other worlds! Why can't his son take his Grand Tour on them? Why does he have to come here to Earth—and you?"

"There's only one Earth."

"And only one you, I suppose?"

He sighed internally and gave up. He had been raised by his father and his uncle after his mother died, and in an argument with Teena he always felt helpless. He got up from the table and went to her, putting his hands on her and gently trying to turn her about. But she resisted.

He sighed inside himself again and turned away to the weapons cabinet. He took out a loaded slug pistol, fitted it into the stubby holster it matched, and clipped the holster to his belt at the left of the buckle, where the hang of his leather jacket would hide it. Then he selected a dark-handled knife with a six-inch blade and bent over to slip it into the sheath inside his boot top. He dropped the cuff of his trouser leg back over the boot top and stood up.

"He's got no right to be here," said Teena fiercely to the breadboard. "Tourists are supposed to be kept to the museum areas and the tourist lodges."

"He's not a tourist. You know that," answered Kyle, patiently. "He's the Emperor's oldest son and his great-grandmother was from Earth. His wife will be, too. Every fourth generation the Imperial line has to marry back into Earth stock. That's the law—still." He put on his leather jacket, sealing it closed only at the bottom to hide the slug-gun holster, half turned to the door—then paused.

"Teena?" he asked.

She did not answer.

"Teena!" he repeated. He stepped to her, put his hands on her shoulders and tried to turn her to face him. Again, she resisted, but this time he was having none of it.

He was not a big man, being of middle height, round-faced, with sloping and unremarkable-looking, if thick, shoulders. But his strength was not ordinary. He could bring the white stallion to its knees with one fist wound in its mane—and no other man had ever been able to do that. He turned her easily to look at him.

"Now, listen to me—" he began. But, before he could finish, all the stiffness went out of her and she clung to him, trembling.

"He'll get you into trouble—I know he will!" she choked, muffledly into his chest. "Kyle, don't go! There's no law making you go!"

₁₀He stroked the soft hair of her head, his throat stiff and dry. There was nothing he could say to her. What she was asking was impossible. Ever since the sun had first risen on men and women together, wives had clung to their husbands at times like this, begging for what could not be. And always the men had held them, as Kyle was holding her now—as if understanding could somehow be pressed from one body into the other— and saying nothing, because there was nothing that could be said.

So, Kyle held her for a few moments longer, and then reached behind him to unlock her intertwined fingers at his back, and loosen her arms around him. Then, he went. Looking back through the kitchen window as he rode off on the stallion, leading the gray horse, he saw her standing just where he had left her. Not even crying, but standing with her arms hanging down, her head down, not moving.

He rode away through the forest of the Kentucky hillside. It took him more than two hours to reach the lodge. As he rode down the valleyside toward it, he saw a tall, bearded man, wearing the robes they wore on some of the Younger Worlds, standing at the gateway to the interior courtyard of the rustic, wooded lodge.

When he got close, he saw that the beard was graying and the man was biting his lips. Above a straight, thin nose, the eyes were bloodshot and circled beneath as if from worry or lack of sleep.

"He's in the courtyard," said the gray-bearded man as Kyle rode up. "I'm Montlaven, his tutor. He's ready to go." The darkened eyes looked almost pleadingly up at Kyle.

"Stand clear of the stallion's head," said Kyle. "And take me in to him."

"Not that horse, for him—" said Montlaven, looking distrustfully at the stallion, as he backed away.

"No," said Kyle. "He'll ride the gelding."

"He'll want the white."

"He can't ride the white," said Kyle. "Even if I let

him, he couldn't ride this stallion. I'm the only one who can ride him. Take me in."

The tutor turned and led the way into the grassy courtyard, surrounding a swimming pool and looked down upon, on three sides, by the windows of the lodge. In a lounging chair by the pool sat a tall young man in his late teens, with a mane of blond hair, a pair of stuffed saddlebags on the grass beside him. He stood up as Kyle and the tutor came toward him.

"Majesty," said the tutor, as they stopped, "this is Kyle Arnam, your bodyguard for the three days here."

"Good morning, Bodyguard ... Kyle, I mean." The Prince smiled mischievously. "Light, then. And I'll mount."

"You ride the gelding, Lord," said Kyle.

The Prince stared at him, tilted back his handsome head, and laughed.

"I can ride, man!" he said. "I ride well."

"Not this horse, Lord," said Kyle, dispassionately. "No one rides this horse, but me."

The eyes flashed wide, the laugh faded—then returned.

"What can I do?" The wide shoulders shrugged. "I give in—always I give in. Well, almost always." He grinned up at Kyle, his lips thinned, but frank. "All right."

He turned to the gelding—and with a sudden leap was in the saddle. The gelding snorted and plunged at the shock; then steadied as the young man's long fingers tightened expertly on the reins and the fingers of the other hand patted a gray neck. The Prince raised his eyebrows, looking over at Kyle, but Kyle sat stolidly.

"I take it you're armed good Kyle?" the Prince said slyly. "You'll protect me against the natives if they run wild?"

"Your life is in my hands, Lord," said Kyle. He unsealed the leather jacket at the bottom and let if fall open to show the slug pistol in its holster for a moment. Then he resealed the jacket again at the bottom.

"Will—" The tutor put his hand on the young man's knee. "Don't be reckless, boy. This is Earth and the

people here don't have rank and custom like we do.
Think before you—"

"Oh, cut it out, Monty!" snapped the Prince. "I'll be
just as incognito, just as humble, as archaic and independent as the rest of them. You think I've no memory!
Anyway, it's only for three days or so until my Imperial
father joins me. Now, let me go!"

He jerked away, turned to lean forward in the saddle,
and abruptly put the gelding into a bolt for the gate.
He disappeared through it, and Kyle drew hard on the
stallion's reins as the big white horse danced and tried
to follow.

"Give me his saddlebags," said Kyle.

The tutor bent and passed them up. Kyle made them
fast on top of his own, across the stallion's withers.
Looking down, he saw there were tears in the bearded
man's eyes.

"He's a fine boy. You'll see. You'll know he is!"
Montlaven's face, upturned, was mutely pleading.

"I know he comes from a fine family," said Kyle,
slowly. "I'll do my best for him." And he rode off out
of the gateway after the gelding.

When he came out of the gate, the Prince was nowhere in sight. But it was simple enough for Kyle to
follow, by dinted brown earth and crushed grass, the
marks of the gelding's path. This brought him at last
through some pines to a grassy open slope where the
Prince sat looking skyward through a single-lens box.

When Kyle came up, the Prince lowered the instrument and, without a word, passed it over. Kyle put it to
his eye and looked skyward. There was the whir of the
tracking unit and one of Earth's three orbiting power
stations swam into the field of vision of the lens.

"Give it back," said the Prince.

"I couldn't get a look at it earlier," went on the young
man as Kyle handed the lens to him. "And I wanted to.
It's a rather expensive present, you know—it and the
other two like it—from our Imperial treasury. Just to
keep your planet from drifting into another ice age. And
what do we get for it?"

"Earth, Lord," answered Kyle. "As it was before men went out to the stars."

"Oh, the museum areas could be maintained with one station and a half-million caretakers," said the Prince. "It's the other two stations and you billion or so free-loaders I'm talking about. I'll have to look into it when I'm Emperor. Shall we ride?"

"If you wish, Lord." Kyle picked up the reins of the stallion and the two horses with their riders moved off across the slope.

". . . And one more thing," said the Prince, as they entered the farther belt of pine trees. "I don't want you to be misled—I'm really very fond of old Monty, back there. It's just that I wasn't really planning to come here at all—*Look at me, Bodyguard!*"

Kyle turned to see the blue eyes that ran in the Imperial family blazing at him. Then, unexpectedly, they softened. The Prince laughed.

"You don't scare easily, do you, Bodyguard . . . Kyle, I mean?" he said. "I think I like you after all. But look at me when I talk."

"Yes, Lord."

"That's my good Kyle. Now, I was explaining to you that I'd never actually planned to come here on my Grand Tour at all. I didn't see any point in visiting this dusty old museum world of yours with people still trying to live like they lived in the Dark Ages. But—my Imperial father talked me into it."

"Your father, Lord?" asked Kyle.

"Yes, he bribed me, you might say," said the Prince thoughtfully. "He was supposed to meet me here for these three days. Now, he's messaged there's been a slight delay—but that doesn't matter. The point is, he belongs to the school of old men who still think your Earth is something precious and vital. Now, I happen to like and admire my father, Kyle. You approve of that?"

"Yes, Lord."

"I thought you would. Yes, he's the one man in the human race I look up to. And to please him, I'm making this Earth trip. And to please him—only to please *him*, Kyle—I'm going to be an easy Prince for you to conduct around to your natural wonders and watering spots and whatever. Now, you understand me—and how this trip is going to go. Don't you?" He stared at Kyle.

"That's fine," said the Prince, smiling once more. "So now you can start telling me all about these trees and birds and animals so that I can memorize their names and please my father when he shows up. What are those little birds I've been seeing under the trees—brown on top and whitish underneath? Like that one—there!"

"That's a Veery, Lord," said Kyle. "A bird of the deep woods and silent places. Listen—" He reached out a hand to the gelding's bridle and brought both horses to a halt. In the sudden silence, off to their right they could hear a silver bird-voice, rising and falling, in a descending series of crescendos and diminuendos that softened at last into silence. For a moment after the song was ended the Prince sat staring at Kyle, then seemed to shake himself back to life.

"Interesting," he said. He lifted the reins Kyle had let go and the horses moved forward again. "Tell me more."

For more than three hours, as the sun rose toward noon, they rode through the wooded hills, with Kyle identifying bird and animal, insect, tree and rock. And for three hours the Prince listened—his attention flashing and momentary, but intense. But when the sun was overhead that intensity flagged.

"That's enough," he said. "Aren't we going to stop for lunch? Kyle, aren't there any towns around here?"

"Yes, Lord," said Kyle. "We've passed several."

"Several?" The Prince stared at him. "Why haven't we come into one before now? Where are you taking me?"

"Nowhere, Lord," said Kyle. "You lead the way. I only follow."

"I?" said the Prince. For the first time he seemed to become aware that he had been keeping the gelding's head always in advance of the stallion. "Of course. But now it's time to eat."

"Yes, Lord," said Kyle. "This way."

He turned the stallion's head down the slope of the hill they were crossing and the Prince turned the gelding after him.

"And now listen," said the Prince, as he caught up. "Tell me I've got it all right." And to Kyle's astonishment, he began to repeat, almost word for word, everything that Kyle had said. "Is it all there? Everything you told me?"

"Perfectly, Lord," said Kyle. The Prince looked slyly at him.

"Could you do that, Kyle?"

"Yes," said Kyle. "But these are things I've known all my life."

"You see?" The Prince smiled. "That's the difference between us, good Kyle. You spend your life learning something—I spend a few hours and I know as much about it as you do."

"Not as much, Lord," said Kyle, slowly.

The Prince blinked at him, then jerked his hand dismissingly, and half-angrily, as if he were throwing something aside.

"What little else there is probably doesn't count," he said.

They rode down the slope and through a winding valley and came out at a small village. As they rode clear of the surrounding trees a sound of music came to their ears.

"What's that?" The Prince stood up in his stirrups. "Why, there's dancing going on, over there."

"A beer garden, Lord. And it's Saturday—a holiday here."

"Good. We'll go there to eat."

They rode around to the beer garden and found tables back away from the dance floor. A pretty, young waitress came and they ordered, the Prince smiling sunnily at her until she smiled back—then hurried off as if in mild confusion. The Prince ate hungrily when the food came and drank a stein and a half of brown beer, while Kyle ate more lightly and drank coffee.

"That's better," said the Prince, sitting back at last. "I had an appetite ... Look there, Kyle! Look, there are five, six .. seven drifter platforms parked over there. Then you don't all ride horses?"

"No," said Kyle. "It's as each man wishes."

"But if you have drifter platforms, why not other civilized things?"

"Some things fit, some don't, Lord," answered Kyle. The Prince laughed.

"You mean you try to make civilization fit this old-fashioned life of yours, here?" he said. "Isn't that the wrong way around—" He broke off. "What's that they're playing now? I like that. I'll bet I could do that dance." He stood up. "In fact, I think I will."

He paused, looking down at Kyle.

"Aren't you going to warn me against it?" he asked.

"No, Lord," said Kyle. "What you do is your own affair."

The young man turned away abruptly. The waitress who had served them was passing, only a few tables away. The Prince went after her and caught up with her by the dance floor railing. Kyle could see the girl protesting—but the Prince hung over her, looking down from his tall height, smiling. Shortly, she had taken off her apron and was out on the dance floor with him, showing him the steps of the dance. It was a polka.

The Prince learned with fantastic quickness. Soon, he was swinging the waitress around with the rest of the dancers, his foot stamping on the turns, his white teeth gleaming. Finally the number ended and the members of the band put down their instruments and began to leave the stand.

The Prince, with the girl trying to hold him back, walked over to the band leader. Kyle got up quickly from his table and started toward the floor.

The band leader was shaking his head. He turned abruptly and slowly walked away. The Prince started after him, but the girl took hold of his arm, saying something urgent to him.

He brushed her aside and she stumbled a little. A busboy among the tables on the far side of the dance floor, not much older than the Prince and nearly as tall, put down his tray and vaulted the railing onto the polished hardwood. He came up behind the Prince and took hold of his arm, swinging him around.

". . . Can't do that here." Kyle heard him say, as Kyle came up. The Prince struck out like a panther—like a trained boxer—with three quick lefts in succession into the face of the busboy, the Prince's shoulder bobbing, the weight of his body in behind each blow.

The busboy went down. Kyle, reaching the Prince, herded him away through a side gap in the railing. The young man's face was white with rage. People were swarming onto the dance floor.

"Who was that? What's his name?" demanded the Prince, between his teeth. "He put his hand on me! Did you see that? *He put his hand on me!*"

"You knocked him out," said Kyle. "What more do you want?"

"He manhandled me—*me!*" snapped the Prince. "I want to find out who he is!" He caught hold of the bar to which the horses were tied, refusing to be pushed farther. "He'll learn to lay hands on a future Emperor!"

"No one will tell you his name," said Kyle. And the cold note in his voice finally seemed to reach through to the Prince and sober him. He stared at Kyle.

"Including you?" he demanded at last.

"Including me, Lord," said Kyle.

The Prince stared a moment longer, then swung away. He turned, jerked loose the reins of the gelding and swung into the saddle. He rode off. Kyle mounted and followed.

They rode in silence into the forest. After a while, the Prince spoke without turning his head.

"And you call yourself a bodyguard," he said, finally.

"Your life is in my hands, Lord," said Kyle. The Prince turned a grim face to look at him.

"Only my life?" said the Prince. "As long as they don't kill me, they can do what they want? Is that what you mean?"

Kyle met his gaze steadily.

"Pretty much so, Lord," he said.

The Prince spoke with an ugly note in his voice.

"I don't think I like you, after all, Kyle," he said. "I don't think I like you at all."

"I'm not here with you to be liked, Lord," said Kyle.

"Perhaps not," said the Prince, thickly. "But I know *your* name!"

They rode on in continued silence for perhaps another half hour. But then gradually the angry hunch went out of the young man's shoulders and the tightness out of his jaw. After a while he began to sing to himself, a song in a language Kyle did not know; and as he sang, his cheerfulness seemed to return. Shortly, he spoke to Kyle, as if there had never been anything but pleasant moments between them.

Mammoth Cave was close and the Prince asked to visit it. They went there and spent some time going through the cave. After that they rode their horses up along the left bank of the Green River. The Prince seemed to have forgotten all about the incident at the beer garden and be out to charm everyone they met. As the sun was at last westering toward the dinner hour, they came finally to a small hamlet back from the river, with a roadside inn mirrored in an artificial lake beside it, and guarded by oak and pine trees behind.

"This looks good," said the Prince. "We'll stay overnight here, Kyle."

"If you wish, Lord," said Kyle.

They halted, and Kyle took the horses around to the stable, then entered the inn to find the Prince already in the small bar off the dining room, drinking beer and charming the waitress. This waitress was younger than the one at the beer garden had been; a little girl with soft, loose hair and round brown eyes that showed their delight in the attention of the tall, good-looking, young man.

"Yes," said the Prince to Kyle, looking out of the corners of the Imperial blue eyes at him, after the waitress had gone to get Kyle his coffee, "This is the very place."

"The very place?" said Kyle.

"For me to get to know the people better—what did

you think, good Kyle?" said the Prince and laughed at him. "I'll observe the people here and you can explain them—won't that be good?"

Kyle gazed at him, thoughtfully.

"I'll tell you whatever I can, Lord," he said.

They drank—the Prince his beer, and Kyle his coffee—and went in a little later to the dining room for dinner. The Prince, as he had promised at the bar, was full of questions about what he saw—and what he did not see.

". . . But why go on living in the past, all of you here?" he asked Kyle. "A museum world is one thing. But a museum people—" he broke off to smile and speak to the little, soft-haired waitress, who had somehow been diverted from the bar to wait upon their dining-room table.

"Not a museum people, Lord," said Kyle. "A living people. The only way to keep a race and a culture preserved is to keep it alive. So we go on in our own way, here on Earth, as a living example for the Younger Worlds to check themselves against."

"Fascinating . . ." murmured the Prince; but his eyes had wandered off to follow the waitress, who was glowing and looking back at him from across the now-busy dining room.

"Not fascinating. Necessary, Lord," said Kyle. But he did not believe the younger man had heard him.

After dinner, they moved back to the bar. And the Prince, after questioning Kyle a little longer, moved up to continue his researches among the other people standing at the bar. Kyle watched for a little while. Then, feeling it was safe to do so, slipped out to have another look at the horses and to ask the innkeeper to arrange a saddle lunch put up for them the next day.

When he returned, the Prince was not to be seen.

Kyle sat down at a table to wait; but the Prince did not return. A cold, hard knot of uneasiness began to grow below Kyle's breastbone. A sudden pang of alarm sent him swiftly back out to check the horses. But they were cropping peacefully in their stalls. The stallion whickered, low-voiced, as Kyle looked in on him, and turned his white head to look back at Kyle.

"Easy, boy," said Kyle and returned to the inn to find the innkeeper.

But the innkeeper had no idea where the Prince might have gone.

". . . If the horses aren't taken, he's not far," the innkeeper said. "There's no trouble he can get into around here. Maybe he went for a walk in the woods. I'll leave word for the night staff to keep an eye out for him when he comes in. Where'll you be?"

"In the bar until it closes—then, my room," said Kyle.

He went back to the bar to wait, and took a booth near an open window. Time went by and gradually the number of other customers began to dwindle. Above the ranked bottles, the bar clock showed nearly midnight. Suddenly, through the window, Kyle heard a distant scream of equine fury from the stables.

He got up and went out quickly. In the darkness outside, he ran to the stables and burst in. There in the feeble illumination of the stable's night lighting, he saw the Prince, pale-faced, clumsily saddling the gelding in the center aisle between the stalls. The door to the stallion's stall was open. The Prince looked away as Kyle came in.

Kyle took three swift steps to the open door and looked in. The stallion was still tied, but his ears were back, his eyes rolling, and a saddle lay tumbled and dropped on the stable floor beside him.

"Saddle up," said the Prince thickly from the aisle. "We're leaving." Kyle turned to look at him.

"We've got rooms at the inn here," he said.

"Never mind. We're riding. I need to clear my head." The young man got the gelding's cinch tight, dropped the stirrups and swung heavily up into the saddle. Without waiting for Kyle, he rode out of the stable into the night.

"So, boy . . ." said Kyle soothingly to the stallion. Hastily he untied the big white horse, saddled him, and set out after the Prince. In the darkness, there was no way of ground-tracking the gelding; but he leaned for-

ward and blew into the ear of the stallion. The surprised
horse neighed in protest and the whinny of the gelding
came back from the darkness of the slope up ahead and
over to Kyle's right. He rode in that direction.

He caught the Prince on the crown of the hill. The
young man was walking the gelding, reins loose, and
singing under his breath—the same song in an unknown
language he had sung earlier. But, now as he saw Kyle,
he grinned loosely and began to sing with more emphasis. For the first time Kyle caught the overtones of something mocking and lusty about the incomprehensible
words. Understanding broke suddenly in him.

"The girl!" he said. "The little waitress. Where is
she?"

The grin vanished from the Prince's face, then came
slowly back again. The grin laughed at Kyle.

"Why, where d'you think?" The words slurred on the
Prince's tongue and Kyle, riding close, smelled the beer
heavy on the young man's breath. "In her room, sleeping
and happy. Honored ... though she doesn't know it ...
by an Emperor's son. And expecting to find me there in
the morning. But I won't be. Will we, good Kyle?"

"Why did you do it, Lord?" asked Kyle, quietly.

"Why?" The Prince peered at him, a little drunkenly
in the moonlight. "Kyle, my father has four sons. I've
got three younger brothers. But I'm the one who's going
to be Emperor; and Emperors don't answer questions."

Kyle said nothing. The Prince peered at him. They
rode on together for several minutes in silence.

"All right, I'll tell you why," said the Prince, more
loudly, after a while as if the pause had been only momentary. "It's because you're not *my* bodyguard, Kyle.
You see, I've seen through you. I know whose bodyguard you are. You're *theirs!*"

Kyle's jaw tightened. But the darkness hid his
reaction.

"All right—" The Prince gestured loosely, disturbing
his balance in the saddle. "That's all right. Have it your
way. I don't mind, So, we'll play points. There was that
lout at the beer garden who put his hands on me. But
no one would tell me his name, you said. All right, you

managed to bodyguard him. One point for you. But you didn't manage to bodyguard the girl at the inn back there. One point for me. Who's going to win, good Kyle?"

Kyle took a deep breath.

"Lord," he said, "some day it'll be your duty to marry a woman from Earth—"

The Prince interrupted him with a laugh, and this time there was an ugly note in it.

"You flatter yourselves," he said. His voice thickened. "That's the trouble with you—all you Earth people— you flatter yourselves."

They rode on in silence. Kyle said nothing more, but kept the head of the stallion close to the shoulder of the gelding, watching the young man closely. For a little while the Prince seemed to doze. His head sank on his chest and he let the gelding wander. Then, after a while, his head began to come up again, his automatic horseman's fingers tightened on the reins, and he lifted his head to stare around in the moonlight.

"I want a drink," he said. His voice was no longer thick, but it was flat and uncheerful. "Take me where we can get some beer, Kyle."

Kyle took a deep breath.

"Yes, Lord," he said.

He turned the stallion's head to the right and the gelding followed. They went up over a hill and down to the edge of a lake. The dark water sparkled in the moonlight and the farther shore was lost in the night. Lights shone through the trees around the curve of the shore.

"There, Lord," said Kyle. "It's a fishing resort, with a bar."

They rode around the shore to it. It was a low, casual building, angled to face the shore; a dock ran out from it, to which fishing boats were tethered, bobbing slightly on the black water. Light gleamed through the windows as they hitched their horses and went to the door.

The barroom they stepped into was wide and bare. A long bar faced them with several planked fish on the wall behind it. Below the fish were three bartenders— the one in the center, middle-aged, and wearing an air of authority with his apron. The other two were young and muscular. The customers, mostly men, scattered at the square tables and standing at the bar wore rough working clothes, or equally casual vacationers' garb.

The Prince sat down at a table back from the bar and Kyle sat down with him. When the waitress came they ordered beer and coffee, and the Prince half-emptied his stein the moment it was brought to him. As soon as it was completely empty, he signaled the waitress again.

"Another," he said. This time, he smiled at the waitress when she brought his stein back. But she was a woman in her thirties, pleased but not overwhelmed by his attention. She smiled lightly back and moved off to return to the bar where she had been talking to two men her own age, one fairly tall, the other shorter, bullet-headed and fleshy.

The Prince drank. As he put his stein down, he seemed to become aware of Kyle, and turned to look at him.

"I suppose," said the Prince. "You think I'm drunk?"

"Not yet," said Kyle.

"No," said the Prince, "that's right. Not yet. But perhaps I'm going to be. And if I decide I am, who's going to stop me?"

"No one, Lord."

"That's right," the young man said, "That's right." He drank deliberately from his stein until it was empty, and then signaled the waitress for another. A spot of color was beginning to show over each of his high cheekbones. "When you're on a miserable little world with miserable little people . . . hello, Bright Eyes!" he interrupted himself as the waitress brought his beer. She laughed and went back to her friends. ". . . You have to amuse yourself any way you can," he wound up.

He laughed to himself.

"When I think how my father, and Monty—everybody—used to talk this planet up to me—" he glanced aside at Kyle. "Do you know at one time I was actually scared—well, not scared exactly, nothing scares me . . . say *concerned*—about maybe having to come here, some day?" He laughed again. "Concerned that I wouldn't measure up to you Earth people! Kyle, have you ever been to any of the Younger Worlds?"

"No," said Kyle.

"I thought not. Let me tell you, good Kyle, the worst of the people there are bigger, and better-looking and smarter, and everything than anyone I've seen here. And I, Kyle, I—the Emperor-to-be—am better than any of them. So, guess how all you here look to me?" He stared at Kyle, waiting. "Well, answer me, good Kyle. Tell me the truth. That's an order."

"It's not up to you to judge, Lord," said Kyle.

"Not—? Not up to me?" The blue eyes blazed. "*I'm* going to be Emperor!"

"It's not up to any one man, Lord," said Kyle. "Emperor or not. An Emperor's needed, as the symbol that can hold a hundred worlds together. But the real need of the race is to survive. It took nearly a million years to evolve a survival-type intelligence here on Earth. And out on the newer worlds people are bound to change. If something gets lost out there, some necessary element lost out of the race, there needs to be a pool of original genetic material here to replace it."

The Prince's lips grew wide in a savage grin.

"Oh, good, Kyle—good!" he said. "Very good. Only, I've heard all that before. Only, I don't believe it. You see—I've seen you people, now. And you don't outclass us, out on the Younger Worlds. *We* outclass *you*. We've gone on and got better, while you stayed still. And you know it."

The young man laughed softly, almost in Kyle's face.

"All you've been afraid of, is that we'd find out. And I have." He laughed again. "I've had a look at you; and now I know. I'm bigger, better and braver than any man in this room—and you know why? Not just because I'm the son of the Emperor, but because it's born in me! Body, brains and everything else! I can do what I want here, and no one on this planet is good enough to stop me. Watch."

He stood up, suddenly.

"Now, I want that waitress to get drunk with me," he

said. "And this time I'm telling you in advance. Are you going to try and stop me?"

Kyle looked up at him. Their eyes met.

"No, Lord," he said. "It's not my job to stop you."

The Prince laughed.

"I thought so," he said. He swung away and walked between the tables toward the bar and the waitress, still in conversation with the two men. The Prince came up to the bar on the far side of the waitress and ordered a new stein of beer from the middle-aged bartender. When it was given to him, he took it, turned around, and rested his elbows on the bar, leaning back against it. He spoke to the waitress, interrupting the taller of the two men.

"I've been wanting to talk to you," Kyle heard him say.

The waitress, a little surprised, looked around at him. She smiled. Recognizing him—a little flattered by the directness of his approach, a little appreciative of his clean good looks, a little tolerant of his youth.

"*You* don't, mind do you?" said the Prince, looking past her to the bigger of the two men, the one who had just been talking. The other stared back, and their eyes met without shifting for several seconds. Abruptly, angrily, the man shrugged, and turned about with his back hunched against them.

"You see?" said the Prince, smiling back at the waitress. "He knows I'm the one you ought to be talking to, instead of—"

"All right, sonny. Just a minute."

It was the shorter, bullet-head man, interrupting. The Prince turned to look down at him with a fleeting expression of surprise. But the bullet-headed man was already turning to his taller friend and putting a hand on his arm.

"Come on back, Ben," the shorter man was saying. "The kid's a little drunk, is all." He turned back to the Prince. "You shove off now," he said. "Clara's with us."

The Prince stared at him blankly. The stare was so fixed that the shorter man had started to turn away, back to his friend and the waitress, when the Prince seemed to wake.

"Just a minute—" he said, in his turn.

He reached out a hand to one of the fleshy shoulders below the bullet head. The man turned back, knocking the hand calmly away. Then, just as calmly, he picked up the Prince's full stein of beer from the bar and threw it in the young man's face.

"Get lost," he said, unexcitedly.

The Prince stood for a second, with the beer dripping from his face. Then, without even stopping to wipe his eyes clear, he threw the beautifully trained left hand he had demonstrated at the beer garden.

But the shorter man, as Kyle had known from the first moment of seeing him, was not like the busboy the Prince had decisioned so neatly. This man was thirty pounds heavier, fifteen years more experienced, and by build and nature a natural bar fighter. He had not stood there waiting to be hit, but had already ducked and gone forward to throw his thick arms around the Prince's body. The young man's punch bounced harmlessly off the round head, and both bodies hit the floor, rolling in among the chair and table legs.

Kyle was already more than halfway to the bar and the three bartenders were already leaping the wooden hurdle that walled them off. The taller friend of the bullet-headed man, hovering over the two bodies, his eyes glittering, had his boot drawn back ready to drive the point of it into the Prince's kidneys. Kyle's forearm took him economically like a bar of iron across the tanned throat.

He stumbled backwards choking. Kyle stood still, hands open and down, glancing at the middle-aged bartender.

"All right," said the bartender. "But don't do anything more." He turned to the two younger bartenders. "All right. Haul him off!"

The pair of younger, aproned men bent down and came up with the bullet-headed man expertly hand-locked between them. The man made one surging effort to break loose, and then stood still.

"Let me at him," he said.

"Not in here," said the older bartender. "Take it outside."

Between the tables, the Prince staggered unsteadily to his feet. His face was streaming blood from a cut on his forehead, but what could be seen of it was white as a drowning man's. His eyes went to Kyle, standing beside him; and he opened his mouth—but what came out sounded like something between a sob and a curse.

"All right," said the middle-aged bartender again. "Outside, both of you. Settle it out there."

The men in the room had packed around the little space by the bar. The Prince looked about and for the first time seemed to see the human wall hemming him in. His gaze wobbled to meet Kyle's.

"Outside . . . ?" he said, chokingly.

"You aren't staying in here," said the older bartender, answering for Kyle. "I saw it. You started the whole thing. Now, settle it any way you want—but you're both going outside. Now! Get moving!"

He pushed at the Prince, but the Prince resisted, clutching at Kyle's leather jacket with one hand.

"Kyle—."

"I'm sorry, Lord," said Kyle. "I can't help. It's your fight."

"Let's get out of here," said the bullet-headed man.

The Prince stared around at them as if they were some strange set of beings he had never known to exist before.

"No . . ." he said.

He let go of Kyle's jacket. Unexpectedly, his hand darted in towards Kyle's belly holster and came out holding the slug pistol.

"Stand back!" he said, his voice high-toned. "Don't try to touch me!"

His voice broke on the last words. There was a strange sound, half grunt, half moan, from the crowd; and it swayed back from him. Manager, bartenders, watchers— all but Kyle and the bullet-headed man drew back.

"You dirty slob . . ." said the bullet-headed man, distinctly. "I knew you didn't have the guts."

"Shut up!" The Prince's voice was high and cracking. "Shut up! Don't any of you try to come after me!"

He began backing away toward the front door of the bar. The room watched in silence, even Kyle standing still. As he backed, the Prince's back straightened. He hefted the gun in his hand. When he reached the door he paused to wipe the blood from his eyes with his left sleeve, and his smeared face looked with a first touch of regained arrogance at them.

"Swine!" he said.

He opened the door and backed out, closing it behind him. Kyle took one step that put him facing the bullet-headed man. Their eyes met and he could see the other recognizing the fighter in him, as he had earlier recognized it in the bullet-headed man.

"Don't come after us," said Kyle.

The bullet-headed man did not answer. But no answer was needed. He stood still.

Kyle turned, ran to the door, stood on one side of it and flicked it open. Nothing happened; and he slipped through, dodging to his right at once, out of the line of any shot aimed at the opening door.

But no shot came. For a moment he was blind in the night darkness, then his eyes began to adjust. He went by sight, feel and memory toward the hitching rack. By the time he got there, he was beginning to see.

The Prince was untying the gelding and getting ready to mount.

"Lord," said Kyle.

The Prince let go of the saddle for a moment and turned to look over his shoulder at him.

"Get away from me," said the Prince, thickly.

"Lord," said Kyle, low-voiced and pleading, "you lost your head in there. Anyone might do that. But don't make it worse, now. Give me back the gun, Lord."

"Give you the gun?"

The young man stared at him—and then he laughed.

"Give *you* the gun?" he said again. "So you can let someone beat me up some more? So you can not-guard me with it?"

"Lord," said Kyle, "please. For your own sake—give me back the gun."

"Get out of here," said the Prince, thickly, turning back to mount the gelding. "Clear out before I put a slug in you."

Kyle drew a slow, sad breath. He stepped forward and tapped the Prince on the shoulder.

"Turn around, Lord," he said.

"I warned you—" shouted the Prince, turning.

He came around as Kyle stooped, and the slug pistol flashed in his hand from the light of the bar windows. Kyle, bent over, was lifting the cuff of his trouser leg and closing his fingers on the hilt of the knife in his boot sheath. He moved simply, skillfully, and with a speed nearly double that of the young man, striking up into the chest before him until the hand holding the knife jarred against the cloth covering flesh and bone.

It was a sudden, hard-driven, swiftly merciful blow. The blade struck upwards between the ribs lying open to an underhanded thrust, plunging deep into the heart. The Prince grunted with the impact driving the air from his lungs; and he was dead as Kyle caught his slumping body in leather-jacketed arms.

Kyle lifted the tall body across the saddle of the gelding and tied it there. He hunted on the dark ground for the fallen pistol and returned it to his holster. Then, he mounted the stallion and, leading the gelding with its burden, started the long ride back.

Dawn was graying the sky when at last he topped the hill overlooking the lodge where he had picked up the Prince almost twenty-four hours before. He rode down towards the courtyard gate.

A tall figure, indistinct in the pre-dawn light, was waiting inside the courtyard as Kyle came through the gate; and it came running to meet him as he rode toward it. It was the tutor, Montlaven, and he was weeping as he ran to the gelding and began to fumble at the cords that tied the body in place.

"I'm sorry . . ." Kyle heard himself saying; and was dully shocked by the deadness and remoteness of his voice. "There was no choice. You can read it all in my report tomorrow morning—"

He broke off. Another, even taller figure had appeared in the doorway of the lodge giving on the courtyard. As Kyle turned towards it, this second figure descended the few steps to the grass and came to him.

"Lord—" said Kyle. He looked down into features like those of the Prince, but older, under graying hair. This man did not weep like the tutor, but his face was set like iron.

"What happened, Kyle?" he said.

"Lord," said Kyle, "you'll have my report in the morning .."

"I want to know," said the tall man. Kyle's throat was dry and stiff. He swallowed but swallowing did not ease it.

"Lord," he said, "you have three other sons. One of them will make an Emperor to hold the worlds together."

"What did he do? Whom did he hurt? Tell me!" The tall man's voice cracked almost as his son's voice had cracked in the bar.

"Nothing. No one," said Kyle, stiff-throated. "He hit a boy not much older than himself. He drank too much. He may have got a girl in trouble. It was nothing he did to anyone else." He swallowed. "Wait until tomorrow, Lord, and read my report."

"*No!*" The tall man caught at Kyle's saddle horn with a grip that checked even the white stallion from moving. "Your family and mine have been tied together by this for three hundred years. What was the flaw in my son to make him fail his test, back here on Earth? *I want to know!*"

Kyle's throat ached and was dry as ashes.

"Lord," he answered, "he was a coward."

The hand dropped from his saddle horn as if struck down by a sudden strengthlessness. And the Emperor of a hundred worlds fell back like a beggar, spurned in the dust.

Kyle lifted his reins and rode out of the gate, into the forest away on the hillside. The dawn was breaking.

PILOTS OF THE TWILIGHT

by Edward Bryant

Two-time Nebula award-winning author Edward Bryant, though born in White Plains, New York, grew up on a cattle ranch in southeastern Wyoming. He attended a one-room rural school for four years before starting classes in a small town. He received a B.A. in English in 1967 and an M.A. in the same field in 1968 from the University of Wyoming.

Bryant began writing professionally in 1968 and has published more than a dozen books. Some of his titles include *Among the Dead* (1973), *Cinnabar* (1976), *Phoenix Without Ashes* (with Harlan Ellison, 1975); *Fetish* (1991) and a hardcover edition of his 1981 short story collection, *Particle Theory,* which has been expanded and renamed *Strangeness & Charm,* was released late in 1995. *Flirting with Death,* a major collection of his suspense and horror stories, appears in 1996.

Over the years Bryant has occasionally worked in film and television. He adapted his own stories for *The Twilight Zone* (CBS) and a series pilot for Walt Disney Cable. His stories have also been adapted for *The Hidden Room* (Lifetime Cable) and for independent productions. Bryant has worked as an actor in the films *The Laughing Dead* (1988) and *Ill Met by Moonlight* (1994). His most anthologized suspense story, "While She Was Out," is currently in pre-production as a feature film.

These days Bryant lives with two feline Americans in a century-old house in North Denver along with many, many books.

L isten now.
  This concerns a woman and a man, and a large, extremely hostile machine. It is a tale which has changed

in some details over a generation, but is still true in its essentials. Some tellers have attempted to embroider the story, but nearly always have drawn back. They realized there simply was no need, and I concur.

The tale truly happened, and it took place just this way:

The woman's name was Morgan Kai-Anila. Some around her used the diminutive "Mudgie," though usually not more than once; not unless they were long-time friends or family. Morgan Kai-Anila was fast with a challenge, but even swifter with her customized dueling model of the neuro-humiliatron. People tended to watch their step around her.

Morgan was a remittance woman. Her home had been Oxmare, one of the jeweled estates setting off the green, cleared parklands to the south of the Victorian continent's capital. Now her home was wherever she found employment. The jobs had picked up as the political climate of our world, then called Almira, began to heat considerably. Morgan's partner was her ship, a sleek, deadly fighter called Runagate. Both singly and together, they had achieved a crucial style. They were known by everyone who counted.

The man's strong suit was not style. He was too young and too unmoneyed. The man possessed a baggage of names, a confusing matter not of his doing. The North Terrea villagers who finally had been convinced to accept custody of the boy back from the truculent 'Reen, had christened him Holt Calder. Only the smallest distant voice from the past in the adult Holt Calder's memory recalled his birth-parents' wish to name him Igasho. Then there were the 'Reen, who had mouthed the sequence of furry syllables translating roughly as "He-or-phaned-and-helpless-whom-we-obliged-are-to-take-in-but-why-us?" Son of the largely unspoiled forests, "Holt" was what he eventually learned to respond to.

Holt's ship was not the newest or shiniest model of its class, but it had been modified by instinctual rural geniuses to specifications far superior to the original. The fighter's formal name was Limited North Terrea Com-

munity Venture Partnership One. Holt called his ship
Bob.

Then there was the huge and hostile machine. It had
no name as such, other than the digital coding sequences
which differentiated it from all its brothers. It had no
family roots, electronic of otherwise, located in this planetary system. Its style was as blunt and blocky as its
physical configuration.

It was here only because a randomly ranging scout
had registered sensor readings indicating the existence
of sentient life—the enemy—and had transported those
findings back to an authority that could evaluate them
and take decisive action. The result was this massive
killer popping out of nowhere, safely away from the system's gravity wells.

The scout's intelligence had been incomplete. There
were, the new visitor discovered, two inhabited worlds
in this system. Fine. No problem. Armaments were adequate to the increased task.

The machine swept with bulky grace along the plane
of the ecliptic toward the nearer world, even though that
planet was the enemy sanctuary whose orbit was closer
to the central star. The machine's only reason to opt for
that jungle world first was mere convenience. It was a
target of opportunity. If any complications arose, the assassin's implacable brain could compute new strategy.

A sympathetic human might have considered this a
good day for killing. It didn't occur to the machine that
it was having a good day. Nor was it having a bad day.
It was just having a day.

A small part of the machine's brain checked and con-
firmed the readiness of its weapons. Its unfailing logic
knew the precise time it would reach striking distance.
Electrons spun remorselessly, just as the two inhabited
planets ahead rotated on their axes. Maybe the machine
was having a good day ...

Morgan Kai-Anila's day was going fine. Runagate
screamed down through the airless space around the
moon Fear. Occasional defensive particle beams glittered and sparked as they vaporized bits of debris still

descending slowly from Morgan's last strafing run. The missiles to the defense dome housing the Zaharan computers had done their work well, confusing if not destroying the targets.

"Eat coherent light, Zaharan scum," Morgan muttered, punching the firing stud for the lasers. Her heart really wasn't in it. Some of her best friends were Zaharans. This was only a job.

The lasers flashed away from recessed ports to Runagate's prow with a vibrating, high-pitched *thrumm.* Morgan saw the main Zaharan dome slice open and rupture outward from the pressure differential, spilling dozens of flailing, vac-suited figures into the harsh sunlight on Fear's surface.

"Ha!" Morgan kicked in the auxiliaries and hardbanked Runagate into a victory roll as the ship knifed away from the devastation. The pilot's ears registered the distant rumble of the dome explosion. She hoped the tumbling, suited figures all were watching. Good run.

Runagate climbed quickly away from the rugged, cratered surface of the moon. Within a few seconds, the distance allowed Morgan to see the full diameter of the irregular globe that was Fear.

"Good job, Mudge," said Runagate. The ship was allowed to use variations of Morgan's loathed childhood name. But then, she had programmed Runagate.

"Thanks." Morgan leaned back in the padded pilot's couch and sighed. "I hope nobody got torn up down there."

Runagate made the sound Morgan had learned to interpret as an electronic shrug. "Remember that it's just a job. You know that. So do they. Everybody loves the risks and the bonuses or they wouldn't do it."

Morgan touched the controls on the sound and motion simulation panel; the full-throated roar of Runagate slashing through open space died away. The ship now slid silently through the vacuum. "I just hope the raid did some good."

"You *always* say that," Runagate pointed out. "The raid on Fear was a small domino, but an important one. The Zaharans' bombardment base won't be dumping anything dangerous on Catherine for a while. That will give the Catherinians enough time to build up their defensive systems, so that Victoria can take some of the pressure off the Cytherans before Cleveland II and the United Provinces—"

"Enough," said Morgan. "I'm glad you can keep track of continental alliances. I'm suitably impressed. But will you just prompt me from time to time, and avoid the rote?"

"Of course," Runagate said, the synthesized voice sounding a touch sulky.

Morgan swiveled to face the master screen. "Give me a visual plot for our touchdown at Wolverton, please." The ship complied. "Do you estimate I'll have time for a workout before we hit atmosphere? I'm stiff as a plank."

"If you are quick about it," said Runagate.

"And what about my hair?" Morgan undid the rest of her coif. It had started to come undone during the raid on Fear. Red curls tumbled down onto her shoulders.

"It's one or the other," the ship said. "I cannot do your hair while you are working out."

"Oh, all right," Morgan said mournfully. "I'll take the hair."

The ship's voice said, "Did you have plans for tonight?"

Morgan smiled at the console. "I'm going out."

A bunch of spacers were whooping it up at the Malachite Saloon as they were wont to do any evening when a substantial number had returned safely from freelance missions. It had been a lucky day for most, and now was going to be a good night. The swinging copper portals might as well have been revolving doors. The capering holograms on the windowed upper deck had tonight been combined with live dancers. The effect of the real and unreal forms blurring and merging and separating composed an unnerving but fascinating spectacle outside for the occasional non-spacer passerby.

"Look, Mommy!" said one tourist urchin, pointing urgently at the dance level as a finned holo enveloped a dancer. "A shrake ate that man!"

His mother grabbed a hand of each of her two children and tugged them on. "Overpaid low-life," she said. "Pay no heed."

The older brother looked scornfully at his sibling. "Oneirataxia," he said.

"I do *so* know what reality is," said the younger boy.

Inside the Malachite Saloon, Hot Calder sat alone in the fluxing crowd. He was a reasonably alert and pleasant-looking young man, but he was also the new boy on the block, and spacer bonds took time to form. Holt had fought only a comparative handful of actions, and had truly seen nothing particularly exciting until today.

"Let me tell you, son, you almost cashed it in this afternoon off Loathing." The grizzled woman in black leathers raised her voice to penetrate the throbbing music from upstairs. Her hair was styled in a silver wedge and she wore a patch over her left eye. Without invitation, she pulled up a chair and sat down.

Holt put down the nearly empty glass and stared at her. True, he had realized at the time that it was not a particularly intelligent move to speed out of the moon Terror's shadow and pounce on a brace of more heavily armed Provincial raiders. "I didn't really think about it," he said seriously.

"I suspected as much." The woman shook her head. "Damned lucky for you the Cytherans jumped us before I had a chance to lock you in my sights."

"You?" said Holt. "Me? How did you know—"

"I asked," the woman said. "I checked the registry of your ship. Tonight I made a point of coming to this smoke-hole. I figured I ought to hurry if I wanted to see you while you were still alive."

The young man drained his glass. "Sorry about your partner."

The woman looked displeased. "He was about your age and experience. I thought I had him on track. Idiot had to go and get over-eager. Lucky for you."

Holt felt uncertain about what to do or say next.

The woman thrust out her hand. "The name's Tanzin," she said. "I trust you've heard of me—" Holt nodded. "—but nothing good."

Holt felt it unnecessary and indeed, less than politic, to mention that Tanzin was usually spoken of by other free-lancers in the vocabulary that was also used to name the three moons, especially Fear and Terror. Her grip was strong and warm, quite controlled.

"Couldn't help but notice," said Tanzin, "that you've been slugging them down fairly frequently." She gestured at his empty glass. "Buy you another?"

Holt shrugged. "Thanks. I never drank much. Before tonight. I guess the close call got to me."

"You don't have a mission tomorrow, do you?"

The young man shook his head slowly.

"Fine. Then drink tonight."

There was a commotion at the other end of the long, rectangular room. Holt tried to focus through the smoky amber light as a perceptible ripple of reaction ran through the crowd. Public attention had obviously centered on a woman who had just entered The Malachite. Holt couldn't make out much about her from a distance, other than her height, which was considerable, and her hair, which fell long and glowed like coals.

"Who is that?" said Holt.

Tanzin, trying to signal a server, glanced. "The Princess Elect."

Holt's mouth opened as the Princess Elect and a quartet of presumed retainers in livery neared and swept past. "She's beautiful."

"The slut," said a deep voice from behind him. "Out slumming."

"Her hair . . ." Holt closed his mouth, swallowed, then opened it again.

"It's red. So?" That and a chuckle came from a new speaker, a cowled figure sitting at a small table close by Holt's right in the packed bar.

"You *must* have been out on a long patrol," said Tanzin.

"Hey, *I* like red too," said the same booming voice from behind Holt. He turned and saw two men, each dark-bearded, both dwarfing the chairs in which they sat.

The one hitherto silent turned to his companion. "So why don't you ask her to dance, then?"

The louder one guffawed. "I'd sooner dance with a 'Reen."

Before he realized what he was doing, Holt had jumped to his feet and turned to confront the two men. "Take it back," he said evenly. "I won't have you be insulting."

"The Princess Elect?" said the first man in apparent astonishment.

"The 'Reen."

"Are you crazy?" said Tanzin, reaching up and grabbing one elbow.

"Perhaps suicidal," murmured the hooded figure, taking his other elbow. "Sit back down, boy."

"Don't spoil my fun," said the louder of the large men to the pair restraining Holt. "I'd fly all the way to Kirsi and back without a map, just so's I could pound a 'Reen-lover."

"Big talk," said Tanzin. "You do know who I am?"

The man and his partner both looked at her speculatively. "I think I can take you too," said the first.

"How about me?" With the free hand, the cowled figure threw back her hood. Red curls smoldered in the bar light.

The first big man smirked. "I think I can mop, wax, and buff the floor, using the three of you."

The second large man cautioned him. "Hold on, Amaranth. The small one—that's what's-her-name, uh, the Kai-Anila woman."

Amaranth looked pensive. "Oh, yeah.... The hotshot on the circuit. You got as many confirmeds during the Malina Glacier action as I did all last year combined. Shoot, I don't want to take you apart."

"There's an easy way not to," Tanzin said. "Let's all just settle back. Next round's on me."

Amaranth looked indecisive. His friend slowly sat down and tugged at the larger man's elbow. "How about it, Amaranth? Let's go ahead and have a drink with the rookie and these two deadly vets."

Morgan and Tanzin sat. Still standing, Holt said, "Amaranth. What kind of name is that?"

Amaranth shrugged, a motion like giant forest trees bending slightly as wind poured off the tundra. "It's a translation. Undying flower. My pop, he figured we'd get to emigrate to Kirsi and he ought to name me that as a portent. My mom thought it sounded wrong with my last name, so she politicked for Amaranth—it means the same but doesn't alliterate—and it stuck."

"Good name," Holt said. He introduced himself and put out his hand. Amaranth shook it gravely. The other introductions followed. Amaranth's friend was Bogdan Chmelnyckyj. A server appeared and drinks were ordered.

Holt couldn't help but stare then, when he first looked closely at Morgan.

"The hair really is red." She smiled at him. "Even redder than the Princess Elect's."

Holt shut his mouth and then said, "Uh." He knew he was making a fool out of himself, but there didn't seem to be any help for it. He realized his heart was beating faster. This is ridiculous, he told himself, feeling more than comfortably warm. He could smell her and he liked it. We're all professionals, he admonished himself. Cut out the hormonal dancing.

It didn't do any good. He still stared and stammered and hoped that drool wasn't running off his chin.

The other four seemed oblivious to Holt's situation and were talking shop.

"—something's up," Amaranth was saying, as Holt tried to focus on the words. "I got that from the debriefer after I set down at Wolverton. Wasn't that long ago tonight. I hit up four or five grounders for information, but nobody'd divulge a thing."

"I have the same feeling," Tanzin said. She looked thoughtful. "I called a friend of mine over at the Office of the Elect. Basically, she said 'Yes,' and 'I can't tell you anything,' and 'Keep patience—something'll be announced, perhaps as soon as tonight.' I'm still waiting." She drained a shot of 2-4-McGilvray's effortlessly.

"Maybe not much longer." Bogdan motioned slightly.

The five of them looked down the bar. The Princess Elect had returned from wherever her earlier errand had taken her and now stood talking to one of the Malachite's managers. Then she snapped her fingers and two of the huskier members of her entourage lifted her to the top of the hardwood bar.

For a moment she stood there silently. Her clingy green outfit shone even in the dim light. The Princess Elect tapped one booted foot on the bar. A ripple of silence spread out until only murmurs could be heard. The music from upstairs had already cut off.

"Your world needs you," said the Princess Elect. "I will be blunt. Effective now, the normal political wranglings among Victoria, Catherine, Cythera, and all the rest have ceased. The reason for this is simple—and deadly." She paused for maximum drama.

Amaranth raised a shaggy eyebrow. "Our star's going to go nova," he speculated.

"There is an enemy in our solar system," continued the Princess Elect. "We know little about its nature. Something we can be sure of, though, is that effective local sundown tonight, our colonists on Kirsi found themselves in a state of siege."

The level of volume of incredulous voices all around the room rose and the Princess Elect spread her hands, her features grave. "You all know that the few colonists on Kirsi possess only minimal armament. Apparently the satellite station was overwhelmed immediately. At this moment, the enemy orbits Kirsi, turning the jungles into flame and swamps into live steam. I have no way of ascertaining how many colonists still survive in hiding."

"Who is it?" someone cried out. "Who is the enemy?" The hubbub rose until no one could be heard by a neighbor.

The Princess Elect stamped her foot until order could be restored. "Who is the enemy? I—I don't know." For the first time, her composure seemed to crack just a little. Then it hardened again. Holt had heard the Princess Elect was a tough cookie, in every way a professional, just as he was as a pilot. "I have ordered up a task force to proceed to Kirsi and engage the enemy.

All pilots are to be volunteers. All guilds and governments have agreed to cooperate. I wish I had more information to tell you tonight, but I don't.''

Again Holt thought the Princess Elect looked suddenly vulnerable before the shocked scrutiny of the Malachite crowd. Her shoulders started to slump a bit. Then she gathered herself and the steel was back. "Personnel from the Ministry of Politics will be waiting to brief you back at the port. I wish you all, each and every one, a safe and successful enterprise. I want you all to return safely, after saving the lives of as many of our neighbors on Kirsi as is humanly possible." She inclined her head briefly, then leaped lithely to the floor.

"Hey! Just hold on," someone yelled out. Holt could see only the top of the Princess Elect's head. She paused. "What about bonuses?"

"Yeah." Someone else joined in. "You want us to put our tails on the line, making an inter-planet jump and fighting a whatever-it-is—a boojum—all for regular pay and greater glory?"

"How about it?" a third pilot shouted over the rising clamor.

Holt could tell just from the attitude of the top of the Princess Elect's head that she wasn't pleased. She raised one gloved hand and the decibel level lowered. "Bonuses, yes," she said. "Quintuple fees. And that also goes for your insurance to your kin if you don't come back."

"Bork that," said Amaranth firmly. "*I'm* coming back."

"Does 'quintuple' mean 'suicide'?" said Bogdan slowly. He shrugged.

"Satisfactory?" said the Princess Elect. "Good fortune to all of you then, and watch our tails." Within seconds, the entourage had whisked her away.

The crowd was quieter than Holt would have expected.

"Hell of a damper on the party," Tanzin said.

"I am ready," said Amaranth. "Could have used some sleep, but—" He spread his hands eloquently.

Bogdan nodded. "I, as well."

"We may as well start back," said Tanzin. "I expect all transport will be headed toward the field."

Morgan flipped her hood forward. Holt was saddened to see her beauty abruptly hidden. "Some kind of fun now," she said in a low voice.

"I hope . . ." he said. They all looked at him. Holt felt like a child among a group of adults. He said simply, "Nothing. Let's go."

Midnight in the jungle. Nocturnal creatures shrilled and honked on every side. Overhead the star field shimmered and winked, as a brighter star crawled slowly across the zenith.

Kirsi's moon Alnaba began to edge over the tree-canopied horizon to the east.

Then the night sounds stopped.

The image suddenly tilted and washed out in a flare of silent, brilliant white light.

"That was the ground station at Lazy Faire."

Black. Stars that didn't twinkle.

Something moved.

The image flickered, blurred, then focused in on—something.

"What's the scale?"

"About a kilometer across. At this point, we can't be more exact."

It was a polyhedron that at first one might mistake for a sphere. Then an observer perceived the myriad angles and facets. As the image clarified, angular projections could be seen.

The device reflected little light. In its darkness it seemed a personification of something sinister. Implacable machinery, it looked tough and mean enough to eat worlds.

"We managed to swing the cameras of a surface resources surveyor. These were all the pictures we got."

A spark detached from the distant machine. That spark grew larger, closer, until it filled the entire screen. As with the transmission from Kirsi's surface, the image then flared out.

"That was it for the survey satellite. I think you've

gotten a pretty good idea of the fate of nearly everything on and around Kirsi."

The lights came up and Holt blinked.

"It's gonna be one hell of a job, let me tell you that now," Amaranth said to him.

"I think my enthusiasm is wearing thin already." Tanzin looked glum.

"Beams," said Bogdan. "More wattage than this whole continent. Missiles up the rear. How're we gonna tackle that thing?"

Morgan smiled faintly. "I'd say our work's cut out for us."

"Bravado?" Tanzin covered the younger woman's hand with her own. The five of them sat behind a briefing table in the auditorium. "I agree with the sentiment. I just question how we're going to implement it." Complaining voices, questioning tones spiraled up from the other dozens of tables and scores of seated pilots around the room.

"I know what you're all asking. I'll try to suggest some answers." Dr. Epsleigh was the speaker. She was short, dark, intense, the coordinator chosen by the emergency coalition of governments to set up the task force. She was known for the sharpness of her tongue—and an ingenious ability to synthesize solutions out of unapparent patterns.

Someone from the back of the hall shouted, "Your first answer ought to try to squelch all the rumors. Just what *is* that thing?"

"I heard," said Dr. Epsleigh, "that someone earlier in the evening called our opponent a boojum." She smiled grimly. "That was an astute nomenclature."

"Huh?" said the questioner. "What's a boojum?"

"It's fortunate that classical literacy is not a requirement of a first-rate fighter." Dr. Epsleigh snorted. "The long-range sensors detected an object and coded it as a snark, a possible cometary object. One of our programmer ancestors liked literary allusions . . ."

At the table, Morgan's head jerked and she half-raised one hand toward an ear.

"What's wrong?" said Holt, feeling a start of concern.

"Runagate," she answered. "The ship's link. I've got to turn down the volume. Runagate just shouted in my ear that *he* knows all about snarks and boojums. Quote: 'For the snark *was* a boojum, you see.' "

"So just what is—" he started to say.

Dr. Epsleigh's amplified voice overrode him. "What we shall be fighting, as best can be determined at this time, is an automated destroyer, a deadly relic from an ancient war. It's a sentient machine that has been programmed to terminate all the organic life it encounters."

"So what's it got against us?"

"*That's* a dumb question," someone else pointed out. "Maybe you're not organic intelligence, Boz." The first questioner flushed pink.

"Thank you," said Dr. Epsleigh. "We've been running an historical search for information in the computers. Objects like that machine orbiting Krisi were known when we sought refuge in this planetary system four centuries ago. They were just part of the oppressive civilization our ancestors fled. Our people wanted to be left alone to their own devices. It was assumed that the vastness of the galaxy would protect them from discovery by either the machines or the rest of humanity." Dr. Epsleigh paused. "Obviously the machines were better trackers—or perhaps this is just a chance encounter. We don't know."

"Is there room for negotiation?" That was Tanzin.

Dr. Epsleigh's humorless smile appeared again. "Apparently not. In the past, the machines negotiated only when it was part of a larger strategy against their human targets. The attack on Kirsi was without warning. The machine has not attempted to communicate with any human in the system. Nor has it responded to our overtures. It is merely pounding away at Kirsi with single-minded ferocity. We think it picked that world simply because Kirsi was closer to its entrance point into this system." Dr. Epsleigh's jaw visibly tightened; the tension reflected in her voice. "It's not merely trying to defeat our neighbors. The machine is annihilating them. We're witness to a massacre."

"And we're next?" said Morgan.

"All of Almira," said Dr. Epsleigh. "That's what we anticipate, yes."

"So what's the plan?" Amaranth's voice boomed out.

Holt glanced aside at Morgan, her hair almost glowing in the hall's artificial glare. His job had been to send back fee dividends to North Terrae, the village that had invested in him and his ship. Until only a short time ago, his life had centered around adventure, peril, and profit. Now a new factor had intervened. It seemed there suddenly was another facet of life to consider. Morgan. Maybe it *was* only a crush—he'd never find out if it would work or not. He wanted to explore the possibilities. Instead they'd both fly out with the rest of Kirsi. The machine would kill him. Or her. Or the both of them. It was depressing.

Dr. Epsleigh interrupted his reverie. "We don't know what the defensive capabilities of the machine are. The few ships that investigated from Kirsi didn't even get close enough to test its screens. You'll be more careful. We think you've got considerably more speed and mobility than the machine. The strategy will be to slip a few fighters through the machine's protective screens while the other ships are skirmishing. We're jury-rigging some heavier weapons than standard issue."

"Um," said a pilot off to the left. "What you're saying is, you *hope* some of us can find points of vulnerability on that critter?"

"We're continuing to gather intelligence about the machine," said Dr. Epsleigh. "If a miracle answer comes up, believe me, you'll be the first to know."

"It's borking suicide." Amaranth's voice carried throughout the hall.

"Probably." Dr. Epsleigh's smile heated from grim to wry. "But it's the only borking chance we've got."

"Why even *bother* with quintuple bonuses," someone muttered. "No one'll be around to spend 'em other than the machine."

"How can that boojum thing just want to wipe us all out?" came an overly loud musing from the back of the room.

"Aren't you forgetting us and the 'Reen?" Holt said angrily, also loud. His neighbors stared at him.

"We didn't kill 'em all," said Bogdan mildly.

"Might as well have. For four hundred years, we took their land whenever it suited us. They died when they got in our way."

"Not in *my* way," protested Bogdan. "I've never done anything to those stinking badgers."

"Nor *for* them," said Holt.

"Shut up," said Tanzin. "Squabble later. When the machine bombards Almira, I'm sure it won't distinguish between human and 'Reen." She raised her voice back in the direction of Dr. Epsleigh. "So what happens next?"

"We're outfitting the fighters. It will take some hours. You'll be leaving in successive waves. The ready rooms are prepared. I suggest you all get whatever sleep or food or other relaxation you can manage. I'll post specific departure rosters when I can. Questions?"

There were questions, but nothing startling. Holt drew his courage together and turned toward Morgan. "Buy you a caf?" She nodded.

"Buy us all a caf," said Tanzin, "but get a head start now. We'll meet you later."

Unwelcome satellite, the machine continued to circle Kirsi.

Dust.

Steam.

Death.

Oblivion.

That list pretty much inventoried the status of Kirsi's surface. Orbital weapons probed down to the planet's substrata. The boojum, you see, wanted to be *sure*.

The ready rooms were clusters of variously decorated chambers color-keyed to whatever mood the waiting pilots wished. This dawn, the pilots had tended to gather together in either the darkest, most somber rooms, or else the most garishly painted. Seeking privacy, Holt conducted Morgan to a chamber finished in light wood with neutral, sand-colored carpets.

Holt told the room to shut off the background music. It complied. The man and woman sat opposite one another at a small table and stared across their mugs of steaming caf.

Morgan finally said, "So, are you frightened?"

"Not yet." Holt slowly shook his head. "I haven't had time yet. I expect I will be."

She laughed. "When the time comes, when that machine looms up as sharp and forbidding as the Shraketooth Peaks, then I expect I'll shake from terror."

"And after that?" said Holt.

"And then I'll just do my job."

He leaned toward her over the table and touched her free hand. "I want to do the same." She almost imperceptibly pulled her fingers back.

"I know something of your career," said Morgan. "I pay attention to the stats. I'm sure you'll do fine."

Holt reacted to a nuance in her tone. "I'm not *that* much younger than you. I just haven't had quite as much experience."

"That's not what I meant." This time she touched his hand. "I wasn't making light of your youth. I've watched the recordings of your skill as a young fighter pilot. What I'm wondering about is what it took to get there . . ."

Her words lay in the air as an invitation. Holt started to relax just a little. Their fingers remained lightly touching.

It was rarely simple or easy for Holt to explain how he had been raised in the wild by the 'Reen. A casual listener might toss it off as a joke or an elaborate anecdote. But then Holt rarely talked about his background with anyone. The few hearers invariably were impressed with his sincerity.

He found himself not at all reluctant to tell Morgan.

Simply put, Holt had been set out on a hillside to die, while only an infant, by the North Terrea villagers. In the laissez-faire way of all Almira, no one had wanted to take the rap for doing in the baby. It all had something to do with Holt's parents who had perished under hazy circumstances that had never been explained to their son's satisfaction—but then, that circumspection was part of the eventual pact between Holt and the villagers.

At any rate, following the death of his parents, a very young Holt Calder had been placed on the steep, chilly flank of a small mountain, presumably to perish. Within hours, he was found by a roving band of 'Reen hunters. The 'Reen were a stocky, carnivorous, mammalian, sentient species with mythically (according to the human settlers) nasty temperaments—but in spite of colonists' scare-the-children stories, they didn't eat human babies. Instead the 'Reen hunters hissed and grumbled around the infant for a while, discussing this incredible example of human irresponsibility, and then transported the baby down to North Terrea. Under cover of the night, they sneaked past the sentries and deposited Holt Calder at the threshold of the assembly hall.

North Terrea held a village meeting the next night and again voted—although by a smaller margin than the first time—to set Holt back out on a hillside.

It took longer for a 'Reen band to happen across the infant this time. Holt was nearly dead of exposure. Rather than return him to what the 'Reen presumed would be a barbaric and certain death, they took him into their own nomadic tribe.

For a decade, Holt grew up speaking the rough sibilance of the 'Reen tongue. There were certainly times when he realized he was much less hairy than his fellows in the tribe, that his claws and teeth were far less impressive, and that he didn't possess the distinctive flank stripe, lighter than the surrounding fur. The 'Reen went to pains to keep Holt from feeling too much the estrangement of his differentness. The boy was encouraged to rough-house with his fellow cubs. He enjoyed the love of a mated couple who had lost their offspring to a human trap.

After a certain rotation of long winters, though, the 'Reen determined it would be a kinder thing to return Holt to his original people. The time had come for the 'Reen his age to join the Calling. It was a rite of adulthood, and something the 'Reen suspected Holt would never be capable of. So regretfully they deposited him on his twelfth birthday (though none of them knew it) on the threshold of the North Terrea assembly hall.

Holt had not wanted to go. The humans found him in the morning, trussed warmly and securely in a cured skelk hide. Before sunset, Holt had escaped onto the tundra and found his 'Reen band again. They patiently discussed this matter with him. Then they again made him helpless and spirited him into North Terrea.

This time the villagers put the boy under benevolent guard. That night the assembly met for a special session and everyone agreed to take Holt in.

They taught him humanity, starting with their language. They groomed and dressed him in ways different from how he had previously been groomed and dressed. After a time, he agreed to stay. 'Reen-ness receded; humanity advanced.

The passage of more than a decade had brought about certain social changes in North Terrea. The inhabitants wanted to forget the affair of the elder Calders. They plowed their guilt and expiation into rearing the son. And there were those who feared him.

When Holt reached young manhood, it was readily apparently to all who would notice that he was a superior representative of all the new adults in the community. It only followed that his incorporation into the North Terrea population should be balanced with a magnificent gesture. The assembly picked him to be the primary public investment of the North Terrea community partnership.

And that is why they purchased him the second-hand fighting ship, refurbished it, paid for Holt's training, and sent him out to seek his own way, incidentally returning handsome regular bonus dividends to the investors.

Years after his return to human society, Holt had again essayed a return visit to the 'Reen. The nomads traveled a regular, if wide-ranging, circuit and he had found both the original band and his surviving surrogate parent. But it hadn't been the same.

PereSnik't, the silver-pelted shaman of the band, had

sadly quoted to Holt from the 'Reen oral tradition: "You can't come home again."

"But aren't you curious about what your parents did to trigger their mysterious fate?" said Morgan, somewhat incredulous.

"Of course," Holt said, "but I'd assumed I'd have a lifetime to find out. I didn't suspect I'd wind up zapped into plasma somewhere in Kirsi orbit."

"You won't be." Morgan pressed his fingers lightly. "Neither of us will be."

Holt said nothing. Morgan's eyes were ellipsoid, catlike, and marvelously green.

Morgan met the directness of his look. "What was that about the Calling," she said, "when the 'Reen returned you to North Terrea?"

He shook himself, eyes refocusing on another place and time. "Though the Almiran colonists didn't want to admit it, the 'Reen have a culture. They are as intelligent in their way as we are in ours—but their civilization simply isn't as directed toward technology. It didn't have to progress in that line.

"The 'Reen can manipulate tools if they wish—but usually they choose not to. They are hunters—but they have few hunting weapons. That's where the Calling comes in."

He paused for a drink of caf. Morgan remained silent.

"I'm not an ethnologist, but I've picked up more about the 'Reen by living with them than all the deliberate study by the few humans who showed interest through the centuries." Holt chuckled bitterly. "A formal examination would have led to communication, and that to a de facto acknowledgment of intelligence. And *that* would have brought the ethical issue of human expansionism into the open." He shook his head. "No, far better to pretend the 'Reen mere extraordinarily clever beasts."

"I grew up in Oxmare," said Morgan. "I didn't think much about the 'Reen one way or another."

Holt looked mildly revolted. "Here's what I'll tell you about the Calling. It's one of the central 'Reen rituals.

I'm not sure I understand it at all, but I'll tell you what I know."

It's one of the earliest of my memories.

The 'Reen band was hungry, as they so often were. Shortly before dawn, they gathered in the sheltered lee of the mountain, huddled against the tatters of glacial wind that intermittently dipped and howled about them.

There was little ceremony. It was simply something the band *did.*

The shaman PereSnik't, his pelt dark and vigorous, stood at their fore, supporting the slab of rock between his articulated paws. On the flat surface he had painted a new representation of an adult skelk. The horned creature was depicted in profile. PereSnik't had used warm earth colors, the hue of the skelk's spring coat. All the 'Reen—adult, young, and the adopted one—looked at the painting hungrily.

PereSnik't had *felt* the presence of the skelk. It was in hunting range, in Calling range. He led his people in their chant:

"You are near.

"Come to us,

"As we come to you.

"With your pardon,

"We shall kill you

"And devour you,

"That we, the People,

"Might live."

The chant repeated again and again, becoming a litany and finally a roundelay, until the voices wound together in a tapestry of sound that seemed to hang in the air of its own accord.

PereSnik't laid down the effigy upon the bare ground and the voices stopped as one. The pattern of sound still hung there, stable even as the winds whipped through the encampment. The shaman said, "The prey approaches."

The hunters accompanied him in the direction he indicated. Shortly they encountered the skelk walking stiffly toward them. The hunters cast out in the Calling and perceived, overlaid on the prey's muscular body, the life-force, the glowing network of energy that was the true heart of the animal. With an apology to the beast, Pere-Snik't dispassionately *grasped* that heart, halting the flow of energy as the hunters chanted once more. The skelk stumbled and fell, coughed a final time and died as a thin stream of blood ran from its nostrils. Then the 'Reen dragged the carcass back to the tribe. Everyone ate.

"Sympathetic magic," said Morgan, her eyes slightly narrowed. "That's what it sounds like."

"When I became human—" Holt's voice wavered for just a moment. "—I was taught there is no magic."

"Do you really believe that?" said Morgan. "Call it a form of communal telekinesis, then. It makes sense that the 'Reen wouldn't evolve a highly technological culture. They have no need—not if they can satisfy basic requirements such as food with a rudimentary PK ability."

"I didn't have the power," said Holt. "I couldn't join in the Calling. I could only use my teeth and claws. I couldn't be truly civilized. That's why they finally sent me back."

There was a peculiar tone in his voice, the melancholy resonance of someone who has been profoundly left out. She reached for his hand and squeezed it.

"I would guess," she said. "We've greatly underestimated the 'Reen."

Holt coughed, the sound self-conscious and artificial. "What about you?" he said. "I know you're an extraordinary warrior. But I've also heard people call you the—" He hesitated again. "—the obnoxious little rich kid."

Morgan laughed. "I'm a remittance woman," she said.

He stared at her blankly.

Morgan Kai-Anila had been born and reared, as had been the eight previous generations of her line, in Oxmare. The family redoubt reposed in austere splendor not too many kilometers to the south of Wolverton, capital city of Victoria continent. The glass and wood mansion, built with the shrewdly won fortunes of the Kai-

Anilas, had been Morgan's castle as a girl. Child of privilege, she played endless games of pretend, spent uncountable chilly afternoons reading, or watching recordings of bygone times, and programmed a childhood of adventurous dreams. She expected to grow up and become mistress of the manor. Not necessarily Oxmare. But someone's manor somewhere.

That didn't happen.

When the right age arrived, Morgan discovered there was no one whose manor she wished to manage—and that apparently was because her family had simply reared her to be *too* independent (at least that's what one of her frustrated suitors claimed). Actually Morgan had simply come to the conclusion that she wanted to play out the adventures she had lived vicariously as a child.

Fine, said her family. As it happened. Morgan was the third and last-born of her particular generation of Kai-Anilas. Her eldest sister was in line to inherit the estates. Morgan didn't mind. She knew she should always be welcome on holidays at Oxmare. Her middle sister also found a distinctive course. That one joined the clergy.

And finally Morgan's family gave her a ship, an allowance, and their blessing. The dreamer went into private (and expensive) flight training, and came out the sharpest image of a remittance woman. Now she was a hired soldier. In spite of the source of their riches, her family really wasn't entirely sure of the respectability of her career.

The Kai-Anila family had fattened on aggressive centuries of supplying ships and weapons to the mercenary pilots who fought the symbolic battles and waged the surrogate wars that by-and-large settled the larger political wrangles periodically wracking Almira. Symbolic battles and surrogate wars were just as fatal as any other variety of armed clash to the downed, blasted, or lasered pilots, but at least the civilian populations were mostly spared. Slip-ups occasionally happened, but there's no system without its flaws.

A little leery of societal gossip, the increasingly image-conscious Kai-Anila family started trying to give Morgan more money if she would come home to Oxmare less frequently for holidays. The neighbors—who watched the battlecasts avidly—were beginning to talk. The only problem was that Morgan couldn't be bribed. She was already sending home the bonuses she was earning for being an exemplary warrior. Her nieces and nephews worshiped her. She had a flare for armed combat, and Runagate couldn't have been a better partner in the fighter symbiosis.

Her family did keep trying to find her an estate she could mistress. It didn't work. The woman liked what she was doing. There would always be time later for mistressing, she told her parents and aunts and uncles.

In the meantime, she found another pilot she thought she might love. He turned out to be setting her up for an ambush in a complicated three-force continental brouhaha. She found herself unable to kill him. She never forgot.

Morgan found another person to love, but he accidentally got himself in her sights during a night-side skirmish on the moon Loathing. Runagate was fooled as well, and her lover died. For the time being, then, Morgan concentrated on simply being the best professional of her breed.

Temporarily she gave up on people. After all, she loved her ship.

"I don't think I love Bob," said Holt. "After all, he's just a ship." Holt looked flushed and mildly uncomfortable with the direction of the conversation.

"You haven't lived with him as long as I have with Runagate," said Morgan. "Just wait."

"Maybe it's that you're another generation." Morgan's eyebrows raised and she looked at him peculiarly. He quickly added, "I mean, just by a few years. You spend a lot of time on appearances. Style."

Morgan shrugged. "I can back it up. You mean things like the sound and motion simulators?"

He nodded.

"Don't you have them installed?"

Holt said, "I never turn them on."

"You ought to try it. It's not just style, to come roaring down on your target from out of the sun. It helps the pilot. If nothing else, it's a morale factor. The meds say it's linked to your epinephrine feed, not to mention the old reptile cortex. It can be the edge that keeps you alive."

The man shook his head, unconvinced.

"Soul-baring done?"

They both turned. Tanzin stood in the doorway. Bogdan and Amaranth loomed behind her. "Mind if we bring our caf in here?"

The five of them sat and drank and talked and paced. It seemed like hours later that Dr. Epsleigh walked into the ready room. She handed them data-filled sheets. "The departure rosters," she said.

Amaranth scanned his and scowled. "I'm not blasting for Kirsi until the final wave?"

"Nor I?" said Tanzin.

Nor were Holt and Morgan.

"I'm going," said Bogdan, looking up from his sheet.

"Then I shall join you," Amaranth said firmly. He looked at Dr. Epsleigh. "I volunteer."

The administrator shook her head. "I hadn't wanted to save *all* my seasoned best for the last." She paused and smiled, and this time the smile was warm. "I want reserves who know what they're about—so *both* of you will go later."

The two large men looked dismayed.

"All your ships are still being readied," said Dr. Epsleigh. "Obviously I'm saving some of my best for last. Cheer up, Chmelnyckyj."

Bogdan looked put out. Morgan stared down at the table. Holt and Tanzin said nothing.

"I know the waiting's difficult," said Dr. Epsleigh, "but keep trying to relax. It will be a little while yet. Soon enough I'll send you out with your thimbles and forks and hope."

They looked at her with bewilderment, as she turned to go.

Morgan was the only one who nodded. Runagate

shrilled in her ear, "*I* know, *I* know. It's from that snark poem."

"I hate waiting," Amaranth said toward the departing Dr. Epsleigh. "I should like to volunteer to join the first sortie."

The administrator ignored him. They waited.

Since the machine had no sense of whimsy, it couldn't have cared whether it was called a boojum, a snark, or anything else. It would respond to its own code from its fellow destruction machines or its base, but had no other interest in designation.

It detected the swarm of midges long before they arrived near Kirsi's orbit. The boojum registered the number, velocity, mass, and origin of the small ships, as well as noting the tell-tale hydrogen torches propelling them.

No problem.

The machine was done scouring Kirsi anyway. It registered a sufficiently high probability that no life-form beyond a virus or the occasional bacterium existed anywhere on the planetary surface.

The boojum accelerated out of its parking orbit and calculated a trajectory that would meet the advancing fleet at a precise intermediary point. Weapons systems checks showed no problems.

Time passed subjectively for the pilots of the first wave of Almiran ships.

Counters in the boojum ticked off precise calibrations of radioactive decay, but the machine felt no suspense at all.

The Almirans joined the battle when their ships were still hundreds of kilometers distant from the boojum. Their target was too far away to try lasers and charged beam weapons. Missiles pulled smoothly away from launching bays, guidance computers locking on the unmistakable target. If the guidance comps, in their primitive way, felt any rebellious qualm about firing on their larger cousin, there was no indication—just a few score fire-trails arcing away toward the boojum.

The missiles reached the point in space the machine had picked as the outer limit of its defensive sphere. The boojum used them for ranging practice. Beams speared out, catching half the incoming missiles at once. Dozens of weapons flared in sparkling sprays and faded. The machine erected shields, wavery nets of violet gauze, and most of the remaining missiles sputtered out. A handful of missiles had neared the machine before the nets of energy went up and were already inside the shields. More beams flicked out and the missiles died like insects in a flame. One survivor impacted on the boojum's metal surface. Minor debris mushroomed slowly outward, but the machine did not appear affected.

"That's one tough borker," said the first wave leader to his fellows.

Then the boojum began alternating its protective fields in phase with its offensive weapons. Beams lanced toward the nearing Almirans. Some pilots died instantly, bodies disintegrating with the disrupted structures of their ships. Others took evasive action, playing out complex arabesques with the dancing, killing beams. More missiles launched. More lasers and beam weapons were directed toward the boojum. Fireworks proliferated.

But eventually everyone died. No pilot survived. Information telemetry went back to Almira, so there was a record, but no fighters or pilots of the first wave returned.

The boojum lived.

Its course toward Almira did not alter.

The second wave of Almiran fighters held its position, waiting for counsel, waiting for orders, waiting. The third and final wave sat on the ground.

"I won't say that's what we expected would happen, but it was certainly a possibility we feared." Dr. Epsleigh turned away from the information screens. The others in the room were quiet, deadly silent, as an occasional sob escaped. Faces set in grim lines. Tears pooled in more than a few eyes.

"Now what?" said Tanzin quietly.

Morgan asked, "Will we join the second wave of fighters?"

Most of the hundred pilots in the briefing hall nodded.

Weight shifted. Chairs scraped noisily. Noses were blown into handkerchiefs.

Holt said, "What is the plan now?"

"Bad odds I can live with," said Amaranth, stretching his massive arms, joints cracking. "Assured mortality does not thrill me."

Dr. Epsleigh surveyed the room. "I've conferred with the Princess Elect and every strategist, no matter how oddball, we can round up. Given time, we might be able to rig heavier armaments, plan incredibly Byzantine strategies. There is no time." She stopped.

"So?" said Tanzin.

"We're open to ideas," Dr. Epsleigh looked around the room again, scrutinizing each face in turn.

The silence seemed to dilate endlessly.

Until Morgan Kai-Anila cleared her throat. "An idea," she said. Everyone stared at her. "Not me." She slowly pointed. "Him."

And everyone stared at Holt.

"I don't think it will work," said Holt stubbornly.

"Have you got a better idea?" Morgan said.

The young man shook his head in apparent exasperation. "It's like a bunch of kids trying to mount a colonization flight. They borrow their uncle's barn and start building a starship back behind the house."

Morgan said, "I hope my suggested plan is a bit more realistic."

"*Hope?* That machine out there just killed a whole borking planet!"

The woman said stiffly, "I *know* my plan has a chance."

"But how much of one?"

"Holt, can you come up with better?" Tanzin looked at him questioningly—almost, Holt thought, accusingly. He said nothing, only slowly shook his head. No. "In the final seconds before a combat run," Tanzin said, "you've got to choose a course." She shrugged. "If Occam's razor says your only option is faith, then that's what you fly with. Okay?" With her one good eye, she surveyed the others.

"All right, then." Morgan looked over at Dr. Epsleigh. The four of them had adjourned to a smaller office to consult. "Can you arrange transport? The fighters would be faster, but I doubt there's any place close to set down."

Dr. Epsleigh punched one final key on the desk terminal. "It's already done. There'll be a windhover waiting as soon as you get outside. Is it necessary you all go?"

"I really would like to accompany Holt," said Morgan. She glanced at Tanzin.

"I may as well stay here. If this cockamamie plan works, I can start the preparations from this end. Just keep me linked and informed."

Dr. Epsleigh said, "I'll get a larger transport dispatched to follow you north. If you can make progress and see some future in continuing this scheme, the transport will have plenty of space for your, um, friends."

"Are the villagers expecting us in North Terrea?" said Holt.

Dr. Epsleigh nodded. Her tousled black hair fell into her eyes. She shook it back and blinked. Evidently she had been awake for a long time. "They're under a most extreme request to cooperate. I don't think you'll have any difficulty. Besides, you're the fair-haired local boy who made good, true?"

"See?" Morgan smiled tiredly and took Holt's arm. "You *can* come home again."

"Well," said Morgan, "I admit it's not the sort of jewel that Oxmare is." North Terrea sat in awesome desolation in the middle of a cold and windswept semi-arctic plain. The town was surrounded by ore processors, rolling mills, cracking towers flaring jets of flame, and all manner of rusting heavy machinery.

"It's grown since I was last here," said Holt.

"What brought colonists here first?" Morgan began to decelerate the windhover. The craft skimmed along two meters above frozen earth.

Holt shrugged. "Molybdenum, adamantium, titanium, it's hard to say. These plains used to be one of the 'Reen's great hunting preserves. That ended quickly.

North Terrea was built in a day or so, the 'Reen were driven off, the game mostly left of its own accord. That which stayed either got shot by human hunters or was poisoned by industrial chemicals."

"Self-interest run rampant," mused Morgan. "Did no one ever try to put the brakes on?"

"I suspect a few did." Holt looked vague, almost wistful. "I don't think they got too far. There were livings to be made here, fortunes to be wrested from the ground." His tone turned angry and he looked away from her to the fast-expanding image of North Terrea.

"I'm sorry," she said, words almost too soft to hear.

They were indeed expected. A small group of townspeople waited for them as Morgan set the windhover down at North Terrea's tiny landing field. At first Morgan couldn't tell the gender of the members of the welcoming party. Dressed in long fur coats, they were obscured by falling snow. The great, light flakes drifted slowly down like leaves from autumn trees.

Morgan cut the windhover's fans and opened the hatch to a nearly palpable miasma of ice-cold industrial stench. She squinted against the flakes tickling her face and realized that some of the greeters wore thick beards. Presumably they were the men.

"I hope these coats are synthetics," said Holt, as much to himself as to Morgan, "or dyed skelk."

"I think they are," said Morgan, avoiding passing an expert opinion. They don't have any of the quality and gloss my parents' coats do, she carefully did not say aloud.

The greeting party trudged toward them across the landing pad, packed snow squeaking beneath their boots. Holt and Morgan climbed out of the cockpit and down past the ticking, cooling engine sounds.

"Holt, my boy," said the man in the forefront, opening his arms for an embrace. Holt ignored the gesture and stood quietly, arms at his side. The man tried to recover by gesturing expansively. "It's been a while since we've seen you, son."

"Haven't the checks been arriving?" said Holt.

"Punctually, my boy," said the man. "Our civic for-

tunes rise with boring regularity, thanks to you and that
fey ship of yours." He turned to address Morgan. "I
forget my manners. I'm Kaseem MacDonald, the mayor
hereabouts. The 'cast from Wolverton informed us you'd
be Morgan Kai-Anila, true?"

Morgan inclined her head slightly.

"We've certainly heard of you," said the mayor.
"We're all great fans."

Morgan again nodded modestly.

"There isn't much to do of a winter night other than
to keep tabs on the narrowcast and see what fighters
like you and our boy here are doing." Mayor MacDonald chuckled and clapped Holt on the shoulder. "Sure
hope you two never have to go up against each other."

Holt spoke for the first time since alighting from the
windhover. His voice was low. "I think there are ar-
rangements for refueling us?"

"Plenty of time for that," said the major, head bob-
bingly jovially as though it were on a spring. "Our
grounders'll tank you up during the feast. Heh, grounders." He chuckled again. "We even pick up the talk from
the 'casts."

"What feast?" said Holt and Morgan, almost together.

"We don't have time to fool around," said Morgan.

"I believe the message from the capital was a priority
request," said Holt.

The other North Terreans looked on. Morgan didn't
think they looked either particularly happy or
hospitable.

Mayor MacDonald showed teeth when he grinned.
"You need sustenance just as much as the windhover
does. Besides, you can meet some of my local supporters
and I know they'd love to meet you. I'm running for re-
election again, you know."

"We can't do it," said Holt. "There's no time."

"I'm not saying a long dinner," said the mayor. "Just
time to eat and say hello to the folks and be seen. Everybody can use a little reminder of where those venture
investment checks come from."

"No," said Morgan. "I don't think so. We've got to—"

The mayor interrupted her smoothly. "—to get some

nourishment and relaxation before continuing whatever your urgent mission is."

"No."

"Yes," said the mayor. "It's necessary. You'd be shocked, I'm sure, to learn how erratic the ground crew here can be when *they* aren't working refreshed and rested."

Morgan said, "Why, this is—"

This time it was Holt who interrupted her. "We'll take refreshment," he said, gaze locked on the mayor's. "It will be a brief delay."

Mayor MacDonald beamed. "I'm sure your refueling will be as brief, and extremely complete and efficient."

Holt glanced at Morgan and smiled coldly at the mayor. "Then let's be about it."

The mayor waved toward the terminal building. "It isn't far, and warm transport awaits."

As the group trudged off across the field, it seemed to Morgan that she was feeling something like a sense of capture. The fur-coated North Terreans surrounding her reminded Morgan of great sullen animals. Their fur might be synthetic fiber, but it still stank in the moist fog that hung low over the town.

Starships descending atop stilts of flame.

Cargoes of frozen optimists being sledded into chromed defrosting centers.

Towns and villages carved out of tundra winterscapes.

The occasional city erected in the somewhat more temperate equatorial belt.

A developing world torn from wilderness.

The triumph of a people.

Heaps of slain 'Reen piled beyond the revetments of a fort constructed from ice blocks.

Morgan stared at the lowering starships. "That's not right," she said bemusedly. "The big ships stayed in orbit. The shuttles brought the passengers and supplies down. Then the larger vessels were disassembled and ferried down to be used as raw materials. I learned all that when I was three."

"It's artistic license," Holt answered, his own gaze still

fixed on the scene of the slaughtered 'Reen. "Historical accuracy is not the virtue most prized in North Terrea." In the fresco in front of him, the attackers had outnumbered the beleaguered humans by at least ten to one.

"It's not that good, just as art," said Morgan. The mayor's circular dining room was lined with the sequence of historical frescoes. "And it really doesn't trigger my appetite."

Other dinner guests were filtering into the room and beginning to sit at the semi-circular tables. The mayor was off in the kitchen on some unspecified errand. Holt said, "The good people of North Terrea are pragmatists. When the community decided to pay lip service to culture and proclaim a painter laureate, the choice of frescoes in here rather than any other medium was because the plaster would lend an additional layer of insulation."

"Laying it on with a trowel, eh, boy?" said Mayor MacDonald, coming up behind them. "I hope you both are hungry." Without his long fur coat, the mayor looked almost as bulky, dark signs of hirsuteness curling from sleeve-ends and at his collar. The blue-black beard curled down to mid-sternum. "Skelk steaks, snow oysters, my wife's preserves from last green season, shrake liver paté, barley gruel; let me tell you, it's one extravagant meal."

"We're grateful," said Morgan. "Can we start soon?"

"In a blink, my dear." Both Morgan and Holt felt a heavy, mayoral hand descend on a shoulder. Mayor MacDonald raised his voice and said, "All right, friends, citizens, guild-mates. On behalf of all of us who make up the populace of North Terrea, I want to welcome formally our guests; Holt, here, who I know you all remember fondly—" His hand clamped down; long, powerful fingers paternally crushing Holt's clavicle. "—and Morgan Kai-Anila, the splendid contract pilot so many of us have watched and admired on late-night battlecasts." Warned by the look on Holt's face, Morgan had tensed her shoulder muscles. It was still difficult not to wince.

The scattering of applause around the dining room did not seem over-enthusiastic.

"Our boy here," continued the mayor, "and his friend, are just passing through. As best I can figure, they're hadjing off on some solemn but secret mission for our kind down in Wolverton. Naturally we here in North Terrea are delighted to lend whatever aid we can in this mysterious activity."

Neither Holt nor Morgan decided to pick up the cue.

"Now I have a theory," said Mayor MacDonald, "that all this has something to do with the rumors about someone attacking our neighbor world toward the sun. If that's so, then we all can wish only the best fortune to these two, Pilots Calder and Kai-Anila."

The applause was a bit more prolonged this time.

Servers had started to carry in platters of steaming food. The mayor motioned them toward him. "Let our guests eat first." The food looked and smelled good. Morgan and Holt showed no reluctance to dish themselves respectable portions of steaks, biscuits, and vegetables.

"As we share this food today—" Mayor MacDonald lifted his arms to gesture around the circle of frescoes. "—I hope you'll all reflect for just a moment on our four centuries of hardfought progress on this world. Our ancestors left their friends, sometimes their families, certainly their worlds and indeed their entire human civilization to seek out this planetary system. Our new worlds were remote from the interference and paternalism of the old order." The mayor looked far above them all, focusing on something invisible. "I think we've done well with our self-generated opportunities." He looked back at them then, meeting eyes and smiling. The smile widened to a grin. "Let's eat."

The applause seemed clapped with unabashed sincerity.

"Not the election rhetoric I'd have expected," said Holt in a low voice to Morgan. "He must be waiting to sink in the hook later."

"I'm not hungry!" The voice was loud and angry enough to rise above the dinner hubbub. The speaker was a young woman about Morgan's age. Her dark hair was piled atop her head. Her high collar displayed a delicate spray of lace, but her expression belied her appearance.

By now the mayor had sat down to Morgan's right. Holt sat to her left. "Is something amiss, Meg?" said Mayor MacDonald. He held a piece of meat only slightly smaller than a skelk haunch in one hand.

"Only the company of this meal," said the woman called Meg. Other conversation around the tables died away. "It's one thing entirely to dine with Holt Calder. I might not like it, but I recognize the necessity of letting him eat with us. We're all quite aware where our community's investment bonuses originate." She glared toward Morgan. "No, it's *her* I register an objection to."

Morgan's voice was a bit higher than her usual controlled tone. She half arose from her chair. "What's your objection? I've done nothing to you."

Meg rose from her own chair. "It's who you *are*," said the woman, "not just who sits before us." She pointed. "Aristocrats ... You are a blood-bloated, privileged parasite on the body politic." Meg appeared to savor the words.

Morgan shook her head in astonishment and then sat back down.

The mayor looked unhappy. "I said," he repeated, "let's eat."

Meg stalked out of the dining room. Those around her developed an abiding interest in the serving platters, in gravy and chops.

Holt touched Morgan's shoulder. She flinched away.

"My sympathies," Mayor MacDonald said to her. In a confiding tone, he added, "The external universe is not an easy commodity to sell here. I fear we don't find Holt as comfortable a dining companion as we might wish." He turned back toward the young man. "Just between you and me, lad, I couldn't blame you if you found the world not worth saving." Mayor MacDonald put an index finger to his lips. "Just don't let on to my loyal constituents I said that." He looked at the great hunk of meat in his other hand. "And now," he said, apparently addressing the food, "and now, let us eat."

*　　　*　　　*

The windhover skated across the tundra ground-blizzards with full tanks, barely rocking in the gusts. The pilot and passenger rode with full bellies and an anxious sense of anticipation.

"That's it, isn't it?" said Morgan. "That peak off to the east."

Holt nodded.

"Where now?"

Holt gave her a compass heading.

"How do you know? I thought the bands roamed."

"They do," said Holt. "Back at the field, I stood in the open air. Even with the inversion layer I could tell. I know the season. I can feel the patterns. The temperature, the wind, it's all there." He came close to pressing his nose against the port. "The pieces fit."

Morgan glanced sideways at him. "And is there," she said carefully, "perhaps a little bit of instinct, something unquantifiable in the pattern?"

"No," he said flatly.

"I wonder."

Holt repeated the compass direction.

"Aye, sir." Morgan swung the windhover to a north-by-northwesterly heading. A range of jagged mountains loomed in the distance.

"You weren't particularly friendly back in the town," said Morgan.

"I wasn't feeling cordial. I hope friendship awaits me now." His words were overly formal, a bit stilted, as though a different identity were being overlaid on the young man Morgan had met in Wolverton.

"You know," said Morgan, "aside from being presumably competent and obviously a good fighter, you're quite an attractive young man."

Holt didn't answer. Morgan thought she saw the beginnings of a flush at the tips of his ears. She started to consider the ramifications. She wondered whether her own ears—or anything else—betrayed her.

They found the encampment—or at least *an* encampment—just as Holt had predicted. Morgan circled slowly, to give the 'Reen plenty of warning. "Skins?" she said. "They live in hide tents?"

"Look beyond," Holt answered. "There are openings for the dug-out chambers. Even though they're nomadic for most of the year, the 'Reen open earthen tunnels for the heart of the winter. It's a retreat to an earlier life. They dig the passages with their claws. You'll see."

And so she did. Morgan set the windhover down and cut the fans. The mechanical whine ran down the scale, fading to silence. Holt cracked the hatch and they heard the wind shriek. Heat rushed from the craft, to be replaced with darting, stinging snow and marrow-deep chill.

Morgan glanced out and recoiled slightly. While she had been engaged in shutting down the windhover, a silent perimeter of 'Reen had come to encircle the craft. Not, she reflected, that she could have heard them in this gale anyway.

She had never before seen the 'Reen in the flesh. Films had not done them justice. Morgan squinted against the sudden flurry of snowflakes slapping her face. The 'Reen appeared bulky, not as though they could move quickly at all. The woman knew that perception was utterly wrong. She also knew the 'Reen were equally adept on all fours as upright. These adults were standing erect, as high as her shoulder. Their fur color was rich brown, ranging from deep chocolate to a golden auburn.

The sun abruptly burned through the gray sky and Morgan saw the light glitter from the 'Reen claws. Those claws were long and curved like scimitars. They looked as honed as machined steel. The silence, other than the wind's keening, stretched on.

"It's up to you now, isn't it?" she finally said to Holt.

He made a sound that might have been a sigh; then moved forward through the hatch, dropping down to the intermediate step and then to the snow. She followed as he approached the 'Reen squarely facing the hatch. Wind ruffled the auburn pelt. Obsidian eyes tracked the newcomers.

"Quaag hreet'h, PereSnik't tcho?" Holt's voice, ordinarily a baritone, seemed to drop at least one gruff, uncomfortable octave.

At first the 'Reen seemed to ignore his words, staring

back silent and unmoving. It responded as Holt stepped forward and raised both empty palms facing the 'Reen. The man said something brief Morgan couldn't catch. The 'Reen spoke something in return. Then man and 'Reen embraced roughly.

Morgan thought instantly of how she used to hug her huge stuffed creatures when she was a girl, damped the incongruous response, but said under her breath, "I think this is a good sign."

The 'Reen turned its attention to her, cocking its head back slightly. Morgan stared past the blunt muzzle into unblinking, shiny, black eyes. The 'Reen articulated sounds. Holt replied in kind. Then the man turned toward Morgan.

"His short-form name translates as MussGray. He is an artificer, uh, an artist, apprenticed to PereSnik't, the tribal shaman. He says to tell you he's honored to meet one who is vouched for by He-orphaned-and-helpless-whom-we-obliged-are-to-take-in-but-why-us?"

"That's you?" Morgan couldn't help but smile. "I'd like to hear all *that* in 'Reen."

"You did." Holt didn't smile. "The 'Reen tongue is quite economical."

"*Tcho. PereSnik't tcho.*" The 'Reen called MussGray turned and started to walk toward the nearest hide shelter. Morgan noted that the 'Reen's rounded shoulders hunched forward as he moved. Holt followed. "Follow me," he said back to Morgan, who had hesitated. "It's what we came to do."

"I know, I know," she muttered. "And it was my idea."

The other 'Reen had made what to her ears seemed whuffling noises and dispersed among the hide shelters of the encampment.

MussGray led them through a doorway protected by a heavy flap of cured leather. Inside, the shelter was dimly illuminated by the flicker of a few candles. Morgan saw a thin column of apparent smoke drifting up from the room's center, then realized it was rising from a circular hole in the earthen floor.

"That's where we're going," Holt said to her. "Don't worry."

MussGray vanished into the smoke, into the hole. Holt followed. So did Morgan, discovering the top of a sturdy wooden ladder. She clambered down the rungs, attempting to hold her breath, trying not to cough and choke on the smoke. Beside the foot of the ladder, a low fire was separated from the opening of a fresh-air shaft by an upright stone slab.

This chamber also was lit with candles, only slightly abetted by the dusky fire. The interior seemed rounded and close. The place smelled of fresh earth and wood-smoke and a muskiness Morgan did not find unpleasant. Five 'Reen waited there. Morgan took them to be older adults, pelts silvered to an argent that seemed to glow in the candlelight.

"They honor us," Holt said to her. "The 'Reen are nocturnal. Our greeting party up there tumbled out of warm burrows to meet us."

The 'Reen reclined in the shadows on the luxuriant furs blanketing the chamber's floor. Then the largest and most silvered of the adults stood and embraced Holt for a long time. Morgan heard the man say simply, "PereSnik't."

Later he introduced Morgan. The woman, half-remembering one bit of biological trivia about showing one's teeth, inclined her head a moment, but didn't smile.

Then they all made themselves comfortable on the heaps of autumnal black-and-white skelk hides. "We'll need patience," Holt told Morgan. "Both of us. This will take a while. I have too little vocabulary, too few cognates, so I'm going to have to approximate some language as I go."

"Can I help?"

"Maybe," said Holt. "I don't know. I'm going to be improvising this as I go."

PereSnik't rumbled something.

"He says," Holt translated, "that you smell just fine to him."

Morgan covered her smile.

With MussGray, PereSnik't, and the other four 'Reen listening attentively, Holt told his story. He also used body language and a bit of theater. Morgan could decipher the gestures sufficiently to understand at which points in the narrative the boojum arrived in orbit around Kirsi, destroyed that world, and then advanced on the Almiran fighters. She found herself forcing back tears as Holt's long fingers described the rupture of ship after ship, his expressive features miming the final moments of her friends and comrades. Morgan clamped down on the feelings rigidly. Time enough later to mourn, and there would doubtless be many more to keen dirges for. She wondered whether, indeed, there would be anyone left alive to do the mourning.

At last Holt's monologue ceased and what seemed to be serious discussion began. Morgan hugged her knees, feeling a sense of disconnection. There was nothing now she could do to affect what was happening with the 'Reen. She had acted. If all catalyzed as she hoped, she would act again. But for now, she was reduced to sitting on plush furs and listening.

The interplay between Holt and the 'Reen became much more of a staccato exchange. Morgan thought of a ball hit back and forth across a net. She couldn't tell the content of what she heard, but was sure of the context: questions and answers.

As best Morgan could tell, internecine bickering was igniting among the silvered 'Reen. Growls, timbre sliding low, verging on subsonics, filled the underground chamber. Claws as long as her hand clicked and glittered while the candles began to burn down.

MussGray appeared to be taking a moderating role. He deferred to the older adults, but began to interject his own comments when the others roared at Holt.

These are carnivores, thought Morgan, staring at increasingly exposed teeth. They are predators, and they surely must hate us for all we have done to them. Except for Holt.

The discussion had reached a crescendo, a near-pandemonium.

Holt stood and slipped off his windbreaker as the

'Reen fell silent. He tugged his insulated shirt up over his head. His chest hair was not nearly so impressive as the 'Reen fur. Holt slowly raised his empty hands up and apart, forming the bar of a cross.

Morgan realized the man was exposing the vulnerability of his belly. The 'Reen voices began again to grumble and roar. Moran wondered again if they were about to kill Holt; and after him, her. She had no weapons. Holt had insisted on that. She knew she could neither save him, nor beat a homicidal 'Reen up the central ladder.

Holt had *better* know what he was doing.

MussGray said something. PereSnik't said something else in turn. Holt hesitated, but then nodded his head slowly. Affirmatively. He drew his arms in, then proffered both hands in front of him.

It happened almost too quickly for Morgan to see. PereSnik't extended one paw, flicked out a razored claw, and blood traced a thin line down the inside of Holt's right index finger. The blood, black in candlelight, beaded and dripped for a moment before Holt closed his fist to stop the bleeding.

The 'Reen were silent again. MussGray looked from Holt to Morgan, and then back to the man. Shivering, Holt put his shirt and windbreaker back on. He shook his hand as though it stung.

"Are you all right?" Morgan said.

He answered a different question, one unspoken. "It's done."

"They'll help us?"

"The verdict's not in yet. There have to be ... consultations. We're to wait here."

The 'Reen began to climb up the ladder. PereSnik't ascended without saying anything more to Holt. Muss-Gray was the last to go. He turned back from the ladder and spoke briefly.

"He says that we should enjoy the shelter," said Holt. "There's a storm front passing above us. It shouldn't last long, but he says it will keep us from traveling for a few hours."

The 'Reen disappeared through the ceiling hole.

"Now what?"

"We wait," said Holt.

"Are you optimistic?"

The man shrugged.

"Are you simply tired of talking?"

Holt looked down at the furs around them. "Just . . . tired." Then he again raised his eyes to her face. One of the guttering candles flickered a final time and burned out. A second sputtered. "This is probably entirely too forward," he said, hesitating, and then saying nothing more.

"Yes?" she finally said, prompting him.

He met her gaze levelly. "I feel colder than even the storm warrants. Would you give me some reassurance?"

"Yes," she said, "and a good deal more, if you'd like."

Morgan reached to take him gently as the last of the candles went out and the only light was the lambent flames racing over the coals in the fire.

She hadn't *meant* to sleep, Morgan thought, as she moved and stretched under Holt's welcome weight. Since she couldn't recall when she *had* slept last, that probably explained her drifting off. Holt, not having slept at all, his upper body supported by his elbows, glanced toward the center of the chamber and said something in 'Reen. Someone answered. Morgan turned her head and made out MussGray's form limned by the coals at the foot of the ladder.

Holt gently disengaged himself and got to his knees. Her body tautened for a moment. He softly touched the side of her head with his fingers.

MussGray spoke again.

"We'll be ready," said Holt. "Their decision is made," he said to Morgan.

The two of them dressed quickly, unself-consciously. After all, she thought wryly, we're all soldiers, comrades in arms.

"Are they coming down here?"

"No," Holt said. "We're to go back above."

When they climbed the ladder and emerged from the hide shelter, they found a clear, cold starscape overhead.

MussGray led them back to the windhover. Morgan saw that the skids were now covered with fresh snow.

PereSnik't and the other adult 'Reen, not just the silvered elders, waited. Bulked together in the night, they didn't seem to Morgan either ominous or an outright danger. They were simply at home there, not discomforted by the chill.

The two humans stopped a meter from PereSnik't. MussGray crossed over some intangible boundary and rejoined the tribe. He, too, faced Morgan and Holt.

The streamers of Almira's aurora began to play above the horizon. Ribbons of startling blue crackled into the sky.

PereSnik't said something. To Morgan, it seemed surprisingly brief. Holt let out his breath audibly.

"And—?" she said softly.

"It's done."

"Will they help?"

The dark mass of 'Reen stirred. PereSnik't said something to them over his shoulder.

"They will try to aid us," said Holt. "I *think* they understand what I attempted to get across. I'm more concerned about what *I* don't comprehend."

"I'm not sure I follow."

"They agreed." Holt shook his head. "But the terms of the bargain are open. I don't know the price. I'm not sure they do either."

"How expensive can it be?" Actually she had already begun to speculate. Night thoughts.

The man only smiled. In the shifting, ephemeral light of the aurora, it was not a smile of joy.

The machine swept steadily toward the waiting second wave of Almiran fighters. The ragtag fleet neither advanced nor retreated. The ships hung in position, interposing themselves as a flimsy shield between assassin and victim.

The machine electronically seined the inexorably diminishing distance between. It did not project a definitive probability-model of the humans' intention. It could not. The machine searched its memories for similar human strategies. Nothing quite matched. In its way, the machine considered what it perceived to be all the likely human options, attempting to place itself in its opponents' position. No answers emerged.

Electrons continued to spin in paths weaving patterns that simulated organic intelligence—only it was a mind far more carefully considered, infinitely more ordered than that of humans. There was no primitive animal forebrain here. No conscience. No irrationality. Only a paradox. A holographic representation of oblivion.

The boojum searched for any evidence of human trickery, signs of an ambush, but it could accumulate no empirical support.

It sailed on.

But as much as it was capable of doing, the machine wondered. . . .

"No?" said Morgan. *"No?"*

"No. With regrets." Dr. Epsleigh looked very unhappy. "The word came down from the Princess Elect's office a short time before Holt and you returned. I'd already dispatched the transport to pick up the 'Reen, but now I'll have to call it back."

Dr. Epsleigh's office at the Wolverton landing field was spare and austere. The four of them—Tanzin had been waiting for Holt and Morgan the moment the windhover set down—sat in straight-backed, unpadded chairs around a bare desk.

"But why?" Morgan thought that if she gripped the arms of her chair any more tightly, either the furniture or her fingers would snap.

"Spume," said Dr. Epsleigh.

"I don't understand," said Holt.

"It's the word the Prime Minister used." Dr. Epsleigh shrugged. "Moonfoam. Brainfroth. The point being he thought our plan was the silliest proposal of anything anyone had suggested. That's why the summary turndown."

"I have to admit I can see his position," said Tanzin. She leaned back in her chair and stretched her legs, one boot crossed above the other. "It's akin to me saying,

'Hey, I've got a great idea—I think my pet is telepathic, and he can hypnotize the bird in the birdbath.' Then someone else says, 'Hey, it's so crazy, it might just work.' See the point?"

"I gave Morgan's suggestion preliminary approval," said Dr. Epsleigh angrily. "Are you suggesting this is all a pipe-dream? We're in a desperate situation."

"Just a moment," Morgan said. "Hold on. Does the PM have a plan of his own?"

Dr. Epsleigh turned toward her, shaking her head in disgust. "It's death. I told him that, but he said it was the only rational option."

"Suicide." Tanzin inspected her boots. "Pure and simple."

"You don't like any of the alternatives," said Holt.

"No." Tanzin's voice was somber. "No, I don't."

"Suicide?" said Morgan. "What did the PM *say?*"

Dr. Epsleigh gestured out the dawn-lit window toward the massed ranks of fighting ships. "One massive attack. Those ships carrying all the massed armament and fire-power that can be bonded on during the next few hours. Mass against mass. Brute force against force."

"The machine will win," said Holt.

"The PM knows that, I suspect. I also think he believes the machine will prevail in *any* account. A grand doomed gesture is apparently better than this half-baked scheme from a battle hero and a junior pilot." Dr. Epsleigh slapped her small hands down on the desk top with finality.

"No," said Morgan. They all looked at her. She said to Dr. Epsleigh, "Can you use your phone to get through to the Princess Elect's office? I want the woman herself."

Without a word, the administrator punched out a code.

"What are you doing?" said Holt. "I've heard the Princess Elect doesn't do a thing without the PM's approval."

"Have I given you my lecture on power?" Morgan said, without a pause for an answer to her rhetorical question. "I despise the power one is born to without earning it. I've never used that lever."

Dr. Epsleigh had reached someone on the phone. "Tell her the caller is Morgan Kai-Anila," she said.

"My personal rules are now suspended," Morgan said. "It's time for this 'blood-bloated, privileged parasite on the body politic' to kick some rears."

Dr. Epsleigh handed her the phone.

"Hello?" Morgan said. She forced a smile and let that smile seep into her voice. "Hello, Aunt Thea, dear?"

Steam curled up from the jet nozzles of the dart-shaped fighters. The rows of sleek fuselages formed a chevron, the point of which faced away from the administration complex of the landing field at Wolverton. The sun had sunk close to the western horizon, the twilight glow beginning to soften the peaks of the Shraketooth Range.

Swarms of workers surrounded the fighters, topping off water tanks, tuning each weapon, completing installation of the additional acceleration couches.

The briefing hall had become an auditorium of Babel. Intermixed, humans and 'Reen crowded the room. The sessions had been loud and volatile. Serving as translator, Holt had tried to mediate. The basic problem seemed to be that each group thought it was surrounded by unsavory barbarians.

The overtaxed air purifying system could no longer cope with the sweat and musk. Cheek by jowl, fur against flesh, luxuriant flank stripes juxtaposed with extravagantly theatrical uniforms, the warriors groused and growled as Dr. Epsleigh tried to keep peace.

About the height of the average 'Reen, the administrator had to stand on a chair to be seen by all in the room. Many of the pilots looked distinctly dubious after having listened through the first briefing sessions.

"I *know* you have questions," continued Dr. Epsleigh. "I recognize that we've been asking you to take all this in on faith. I also know I can't order any of you simply to be credulous."

Beside her, Holt translated for the benefit of the 'Reen.

"Just let me wrap it up," said Dr. Epsleigh. "The majority of pilots will have the essential task of harrying the boojum in whatever way and from whichever tangent they can. It will be your job to draw the machine's attention from the score of colleagues who will be ferrying our 'Reen allies as near to the enemy as is—" A wry smile broke across her lips. "—humanly possible."

Amaranth stood in the first row. "Isn't this just as foredoomed as the PM's idiotic plan?"

"If it were, I wouldn't endorse it." Dr. Epsleigh raised her eyes machineward. "It will be dangerous, yes. You'll all be dependent upon your wits and the abilities of your ships."

Amaranth nodded, amused. "It's never been any different."

The 'Reen whuffled and coughed at the translation. For them also, it was a point of commonality.

"We've exhaustively pored over the recordings of our first combat encounter with the machine," said Dr. Epsleigh. "So long as the boojum's missiles and beams are avoided, we're sure that some of our ships can maneuver beyond the protective screens."

"Mighty hard to avoid particle beams, maneuvering in slow motion," someone called out from the floor.

"I expect that's why the rest of us'll be speeding our tails off," someone else answered.

"Precisely right," said Dr. Epsleigh. "The machine won't anticipate seeming irrationality."

"So you think."

"So we think." The uproar threatened to drown out the administrator.

"And then the 'Reen will claw the boojum to death?" someone apparently said jokingly, but too loud.

"In a manner of speaking," Dr. Epsleigh said.

Holt translated that for PereSnik't's benefit. MussGray overheard and both 'Reen growled in amusement.

Dr. Epsleigh shook her head in exasperation and asked Holt to explain the Calling again.

"I still don't think I believe in all that occult crap," a pilot called out.

"Neither do I think," Holt said, "that the 'Reen believe simple light can actually be cohered into a laser."

"But that's different."

The room's noise level got louder again.

Twilight had begun to fuzz into actual night.

In the briefing hall, Holt held up a meter-square sheet of shining alloy so that all could see. A grid of silver lines had been etched, then painted in almost a cloisonné effect. Regular clusters of angular symbols cross-connected the lines. The panel could equally have represented an electronic map or a jewelry design. It was an elaborate and stylized pattern.

"The apprentice MussGray created this," said Holt, "under the direction of the shaman, PereSnik't. It will focus the Calling."

"This is the brain of the boojum," Dr. Epsleigh said.

PereSnik't rumbled something.

"The heart," Holt translated. "Energy. The electrical field."

"The design may not be identical to the primary components in that machine up there," said the administrator, "but it's as close as we can come by guess and extrapolation after ransacking the historical computer memories. When we were part of the rest of human civilization, our ancestors helped dissect some of the boojums. We're hoping that logic circuitry is logic circuitry, even allowing for refinement."

The room fell silent.

"Hey," said Amaranth, voice loud and firm. "I'll give it a shot." His lips spread in a grin, revealing broad, white, gleaming teeth.

The 'Reen muttered approvingly as Holt translated.

"We've placed identical copies of the focus pattern in each ship carrying a 'Reen. To help coordinate the plan, our friends will have their own ship's-link channel." Dr. Epsleigh turned on the chair and looked down at Holt. "You're going to be a busy young man. I understand PereSnik't will ride with no one else."

"He is my father," said Holt. "I am his son."

"Will you be able to handle the translating as well?"

"No one else can." Holt's voice was not so much resigned as it was simply matter-of-fact.

PereSnik't said something. Dr. Epsleigh looked at Holt questioningly; the young man had already growled a brief answer. "He wanted to know if it were the chanting time yet. I told him no. The prey is still too distant."

In the forefront of the pilots, Amaranth restlessly shifted his weight from one leg to the other. "Let's get on with it," he said. "It's getting late and we're all getting curious whether we'll live or die."

That triggered smiles and nods from those around him.

Dr. Epsleigh shrugged. "You've heard what I have to say about tactics. Just do what's necessary to get the 'Reen as close to the machine's surface as possible."

Anything else seemed anticlimactic. Holt led the 'Reen out toward the ships. Tanzin followed with the pilots. They mixed at the doors of the hall. The neat division along species lines no longer seemed as clearcut as at the beginning of the day.

Dr. Epsleigh lingered, waiting by a door. Morgan came up to her. "Sympathetic magic and PK indeed," the administrator said. "Should I have said good luck? Godspeed? I might as well simply admit I *am* sending you all out with thimbles and forks and hope."

Morgan squeezed her hand. "You may be surprised by who all come back." Silently, behind her reassuring smile, she thought, I know *I* will be.

Together they walked toward the field and the ships. The dying sunset looked like blood streaking the sky.

The machine did not overtly react when it detected movement in the distant fleet of fighters. Other craft were rising from the planetary surface and joining the group. The boojum's sensory systems registered each increment of numbers, every measure of expended energy.

The fighters began to disperse toward the machine in no particularly discernible formation. The boojum searched for patterns and found none. Then the machine completed another in its infinite series of weapons system status checks.

The ships in the approaching swarm flared energy.

Everything seemed to be fine. The oblivion within the machine waited to be defined and fulfilled.

Like silver shoals of fish they rose up, the fighter formations rising from Almira's surface. Throttles open, the fighters accelerated. Super-heated steam plumes whirled back from the craft, propelling them into an ever blacker sky where the stars had begun to glitter.

The stage, thought Dr. Epsleigh, watching from her tower window in the Wolverton terminal, is set. The massed scream of the rockets deafened her.

She realized the fingers of her right hand were curled into a fist, and that fist was upraised. Get the bastard!

SHIP'S LINK
CHANNEL CHECKS

Wolverton Control/All Ships: "The Princess Elect says 'Good luck' and bring back a chunk of the boojum for the palace garden."

Amaranth/Wolverton Control: "Stuff that! We're gonna bring back enough scrap so the palace gardeners can make a whole public gazebo."

Bogdan/Wolverton Control: "I like the sound of 'gazebo.' Can we perhaps code the machine that instead of 'boojum'?"

Wolverton Control/Bogdan: "Sorry, fellow. Too late. Boojum, it is."

Anonymous/All Ships: "Bloody hell. Death be what it is.'

Holt/'Reen Channel: *Our Hair-like-Morgan-elected-leader-serving-from-the-ground tells you all 'Good fortune and success in the hunt.'*

PereSnik't/'Reen Channel: *Could not your leader/shaman/provider have initiated so enlightened a sentiment a bit earlier than tonight? As perhaps her forebears could have three or four hundred world journeys ago?*

Various/'Reen Channel: *amusement*

Holt/'Reen Channel: *There were many sad winters . . .*

PereSnik't/'Reen Channel: *Sad winters . . . ? ! Skelk

droppings, son. What we do now is a perversion of the Calling that gives me dismay. This is not food-gathering.*

Holt/'Reen Channel: *It is a greater good.*

PereSnik't/'Reen Channel: *My unthought-out comment is unsuitable for either furred ears or bare.*

Various/'Reen Channel: *amusement*

Holt/'Reen Channel: *I am unthinking. Forgive me.*

PereSnik't/'Reen Channel: *Let us concentrate on our onerous task. Let us pursue it with honor.*

All/'Reen Channel: *anticipation*
                    hunger
                    exultation

Runagate/LNTCVP1-Bob: Ship, is your pilot's survivability index high?

LNTCVP1-Bob/Runagate: He has luck, skill, and courage. My level of confidence is high. Why do you inquire?

Runagate/LNTCVP1-Bob: My pilot's interest level in your pilot is increasing. Her concerns are mine as well.

LNTCVP1-Bob/Runagate: I perceive an equivalent status on the part of Holt. I hold no wish to see him injured in any way.

Runagate/LNTCVP1-Bob: Then we both must survive.

LNTCVP1-Bob/Runagate: The projections do not encourage me.

Runagate/LNTCVP1-Bob: We shall live with them.

LNTCVP1-Bob/Runagate: I will look forward to discussing these matters with you after the battle.

Runagate/LNTCVP1-Bob: Likewise. And with pleasure ... Bob.

Morgan ordered Runagate to adjust the artificial gravity so that a satisfying, but less than debilitating, G-force would trickle through the system and settle both 'Reen passengers and the pilot snugly into their harnesses.

Takeoff acceleration hadn't seemed to bother Muss-Gray at all. The artist had endured the climb up to the stratosphere stoically, listening to the voices on the

'Reen channel. He had not so much as shut his polished jet eyes as the ship shuddered and sang. The 'Reen hunter in him bared his teeth at the screens as they imaged the distant boojum. He unsheathed his claws.

Morgan lay cradled in her pilot's couch and exulted in the profligate power of the torch powering her ship. She restrained herself from putting Runagate into a vertical roll. Time enough soon for fancy maneuvers. But, she thought, the power, the sheer, raw force propelling her into space atop a column of incandescent vapor, was the most intoxicating feeling she had ever known.

Competing information channels buzzed and bleated within her ears: Almira and Wolverton Control, the fleet ahead, her colleagues, the 'Reen, Runagate. Morgan had ordered her ship to monitor all links, including the 'Reen channel, and to mix whatever communications he deemed important.

"That may confuse you a bit," Runagate had said.

"I'll live with it."

For all effective densities, Runagate cleared atmosphere. Morgan ordered on the simulators. Her ears registered the distant rumble of the other fighters. The ship shuddered slightly beneath her and she heard the closer, reassuring roar of knife-edged fins slicing through the vacuum.

Holt glanced at the silver-furred 'Reen bulked in the acceleration couch beside his. His adoptive father looked steadily back at him.

"The boojum is accelerating toward us," said Bob.

"Must be getting impatient."

"Perhaps merely suspicious," said the ship.

"Keep on the direct intercept." Holt sighed and said to PereSnik't, *Was it necessary for us to wrangle before everyone listening over the channel?*

PereSnikt's muzzle creased in a grin. *Are we not still speaking to the rest?*

No. For a short time we can talk in privacy.

The 'Reen paused in obvious deliberation. *My son, I now realize I haven't prodded you enough.*

Holt stared at him questioningly.

I believe I erred in turning you back quite so young to the barbarians in North Terrea.

I could not join the Calling. There was no—

PereSnik't held up a paw, the underside gleaming like well-worn polished leather. *It may be that my judgment was premature. No shame to—*

No! Holt turned away from the 'Reen.

PereSnik't shook his massive head slowly and sadly. *It will grieve me if I must conclude you are less of the People than I suspect.*

I am all too human—"what is it, Bob?" Holt answered the imperative blinking of a console tell-tale.

"Runagate messaging," said Bob. "Morgan would like to speak with you."

Holt's spreading, silly smile was indeed all too human.

Amaranth goosed his ship out of the atmosphere. It was not that he had to be the first fighter in the assault—although he wouldn't have turned the position away—but he also knew he didn't want to place anywhere back in the pack. "First in the hearts of his countrymen," he sang atonally. "First to fight their wa-*orrr*." The last note jangled dissonantly in his own ears.

Tanzin's voice crackled over the ship's link. "Perhaps you could, uh, sing, if that's the precise verb that fits, privately instead of on-channel?"

"She's right." Bogdan's voice.

"It's a war song," said Amaranth. "I'm building morale." He hit another, more than slightly askew, note.

Only a meter away, his 'Reen passenger growled ominously.

Amaranth stopped singing. "You're a critic too, my hirsute colleague?"

Another growl, prolonged, rumbling low in the 'Reen's throat.

"ThunderWalker, that's your name, right?" Amaranth said to the 'Reen hunter. "ThunderWalker, perhaps you'd like to join me in a duet."

The ship's link garbled and jammed as a dozen voices said the same word.

*   *   *

"Um, I . . . never heard anything quite like that said on a ship's link," Holt said. He wondered if the warmth showed on his face.

"And quite probably you won't again." The smile permeated Morgan's voice. "Don't worry, it wasn't public. Runagate and Bob locked in the channel."

"We had better open up that channel." It was Runagate's voice. "Things are heating up considerably with the boojum."

"Channel open," said Bob. "Good luck, everybody."

"Buy you a caf after this is over," Morgan said.

The brain of the machine juggled probabilities, determining whether it should, for the time being, ignore the first ships now violating its zone of effective weaponry, in order to lure the great mass of them into range.

SHIP'S LINK
CHANNEL CHECKS

Amaranth/All Ships: "Well, that was easy."

Holt/'Reen Channel: *Though we are in range of its talons, the prey has not sprung for the bait.*

Tanzin/All Ships: "It's got to be a trap."

LNTCVP1-Bob/Runagate: It is a trap.

PereSnik't/'Reen Channel: *Surely, then, the prey is attempting to gull us.*

Runagate/LNTCVP1-Bob: It is a trap.

Morgan/All Ships: "Okay, let's boost *hard!*"

The machine suddenly came alive, bristling missiles as though they were quills erecting on a Q-beast. The missiles flew just as its enemy shattered into a cloud of wildly varied trajectories. The boojum had three hundred and seventeen separate sentient enemies to contend with now, not to mention the thousands of semi-intelligent missiles erupting from the fighters like insects swarming from a nest.

Skeins of contending particle beams crisscrossed the sphere of defensive space, a traveling net with the machine spidered at the center. The boojum's shields and weapons phased in tandem. Incoming missiles sputtered, fused, and burned luridly. The machine had no program for esthetics, so it could not appreciate the beauty of nuclear flowers blooming brilliantly in the garden of the firmament.

The machine looked for patterns to form as the human ships flew in all directions. It had projected that the battle might be won in the first twenty seconds. That was now clearly impossible.

Victory was still a clear probability, but it would be neither fast nor simple.

SHIP'S LINK
CHANNEL CHECKS

Amaranth/All Ships: "We're in. Dammit, we're in!"

Tanzin/All Ships: "Take it easy. We're just fleas, and it doesn't mean spit if the dog hasn't decided to scratch yet."

Holt/'Reen Channel: *Close, we're close.*

ThunderWalker/'Reen Channel: *Good. The chant will also wipe away the noise of my pilot.*

MussGray/'Reen Channel: *At least your pilot has kept you alive.*

Holt/'Reen Channel: *We are *all* still alive.*

Tanzin/All Ships: "Look out! It's scratch—"

Morgan whirled her ship into a maneuver she could term, but never could have identified as to origin: an Immelman turn. Runagate looped around, rolled, then accelerated as a brace of boojum missiles flashed by.

The woman blinked through the array of images Runagate projected throughout the control space. In the holographic display, the lasers and particle beams were colored bright neon shades for clarity. The webwork patterns danced around the painfully slow midge that was Runagate closing on the boojum. Sparks cascaded around the miniature image of the ship. Some were accelerating missiles. Some were bits of debris from the dead and dying.

Everything seemed to move in slow motion.

Morgan glanced at the 'Reen beside her and did a double-take. The artist MussGray had brought on board a pad Dr. Epsleigh had given him. Grumbling happily, he was staring at the screens, displays, and images, and sketching furiously.

The pilot shook her head and her mind retreated to speed. She slammed Runagate into a full-ahead feint at the growing mass of the boojum.

PereSnik't grunted as the restraining straps dug into his thick shoulders. Bob rolled into a hard zig-zag, and Holt prayed the AG would stand up. It if didn't, the inside of the cockpit would look like it had been spread with berry jam.

"You're within the parameters you requested," said Bob. "Good luck."

Holt scanned the instruments, glanced at the chunk of machine balefully occluding his main screen. No casualties among the 'Reen ships yet.

"Now!" he said into the ship's link. *Now!* he said to the 'Reen.

Hyo came the chorus.

He glanced aside at PereSnik't. The 'Reen shaman held tight to the alloy effigy. Fur glittered, reflected in the stylized circuitry. Holt wanted to touch his father a final time, but he didn't want to alter PereSnik't's concentration.

The 'Reen reached over and clasped Holt's upper arm. *Remember* said PereSnik't. *You are as much of me as of them.*

Holt smiled.

PereSnik't began to chant. His voice rumbled as the others picked up the resonance.

You are near

The ship's skin rumpled slightly. Bob's skeleton creaked. Holt couldn't see it with his eyes, but the instruments told him a charged beam had passed within meters of Bob's wingtip.

Come to us

As we come to you

"Closer!" Holt said into the ship's link to the other pilots. "We've got to get in so close, the machine will take up the whole screen."

PereSnik't's voice filled the ship. The chant filled the
space between ships.

With your pardon
We shall kill you—

Holt prayed that the other ships, the ones not carrying
the 'Reen, could continue to draw the machine's attention and its firepower.

—and devour you

He realized he was chanting too. Part of his mind, his
concentration, his attention, more and more of it, was
drawn into the skein of power. I have to pilot, he told
himself. Careful. Careful—

That we the People

"I'm closer to that son of a bitch than you," said Morgan's voice. "Get in here, love!"

Might live

"I'm even closer," said Tanzin over the link. "Move
it, Holt."

You are near

PereSnik't began the chant again. This time Holt sang
with them from the beginning.

Come to us
As we come to you

The images flashed in front of his eyes. The main
screen swept across what seemed an endless expanse
of machine.

With your pardon

The screen was filled with the images of asymmetric
metal forms. The song, the ship—Holt *meshed*.

We shall kill you—

It all worked. He could be both—

"Hey!" Amaranth's voice yelled. "We're in! Did you
ever—" The transmission cut off. Vacuum filled that
space.

One of the boojum's particle beams punched through
Amaranth's ship transversely. Clubbed by a weapon
moving at light-speed, some things just were there, and
then they were *not*.

The components of the ship's brain instantly stressed
to destruction under the energy over-load and flared into

darkness. The ship died of a thousand electronic aneurisms.

Passing through the cockpit, the beam did far more immediate damage to Amaranth than to ThunderWalker.

As the ship twisted sickeningly and began to break up, Amaranth could look down and see little where his chest had been. The scarlet spray beginning to cloud his eyes told him the AG was going wonky.

He knew it should hurt, but it didn't. Shock. It wouldn't. No time.

Amaranth saw a field of spring flowers, all red and gold and vibrant, in a meadow at the foot of the Shrake-tooths. He died before the season changed.

The particle beam had barely grazed ThunderWalker. That was sufficient to vaporize the 'Reen's shoulder.

We shall kill you—

The chant still reverberated inside ThunderWalker's head. And continued for the hunter.

—and devour you

The ship split into ragged sections. The last air was expelled from the cockpit, ripping from ThunderWalker's lungs. Still held back by the elastic restraints, the 'Reen glared out at the machine that filled his sky.

That we the People

The 'Reen hunter was dying in a sea of debris. He reached and grabbed with his remaining paw. Claws tightened around something substantial and silky—the wrist of his severed arm.

He grinned out at the prey filling his eyes and mind, feeling the chant rise to its climax.

Might live

Expending the last of his fury, ThunderWalker whirled the orphaned limb around his head and then hurled it directly into the face of his prey.

He could do no more.

The smallest segment of the boojum's defensive brain detected the strange object moving toward it from the destroyed ship. Circuits reacted. A beam licked out and turned the arm into a dissipating trace of ionized gasses.

The action was the result of a reasonable judgment on the part of the machine. Had the arm not been there to draw fire, the boojum would have selected another target . . .

Bob flashed across the boojum's surface.

Holt looked at PereSnik't and said, *Now!*

The 'Reen shaman felt the pattern of the magic that had just been worked. This prey was no different from a skelk—just larger and inedible.

The People repeated the sum of the chant.

We shall kill you

And devour you

PereSnik't focused and guided the dispassionate *grasp* out and into the prey. He soared along the guideways and glowing paths of the boojum's mighty heart.

It was too much energy even to imagine. But not so much he couldn't interrupt it. PereSnik't touched the true heart of the machine.

That we the People

One millisecond the electrons spun and flowed in streams; the next, the web of energy surged, staggered, choked—

Might live

—and died. Struck through its heart, the great, dead machine hurtled along its course.

Bob abruptly angled to avoid a desultory defensive missile.

The machine was an inert body in the center of a cloud of angry wasps.

Holt looked at PereSnik't and the 'Reen nodded.

It is done he said into the 'Reen Channel. Holt repeated that in Anglish for the other pilots.

"Amaranth . . ." said Bogdan mournfully.

"We'll count the dead later," said Morgan. Her voice was sober. "The machine—are you sure it's finished?"

PereSnik't growled softly.

"It is dead," Holt said.

"Now to dispose of it," said one of the link voices.

"Into the sun?" The voice was Bogdan's.

"It will probably go for salvage," said Tanzin.

"Drawn, quartered, and dismantled. Where did you think our bonuses were going to come from?"

The link settled down to routine traffic as pilots began to tally the casualties.

Morgan's voice came to the channel. "Holt? When we get back to Almira with the 'Reen ... I don't think things are going to be the same." Holt knew exactly what she meant. Then Morgan said, "Don't forget the cup of caf. I want to see you."

"I want to see you too," said Holt.

Dr. Epsleigh came on the general channel and relayed thanks and congratulations from the PM and the Princess Elect. She tried to say all the right things.

"What about that boojum?" said Bogdan. "Once we take it apart, can we figure out where it came from?"

The administrator on Almira admitted that was possible.

"And then follow the trail back and blow hell out of those machines, now that we have our secret weapon?"

Dr. Epsleigh laughed. "Maybe we will, and maybe we won't."

"We will," said Bogdan.

But Holt, translating for the 'Reen channel, wasn't so sure.

Beside him, PereSnik't grunted in agreement.

Listen now.

I have recounted to you the truth. It was the time of rejoining comradeship with "Holt," as the Other People called him, and the beginning of my learning strange and sometimes wonderful new ways.

Young, young and eager I was in that battle, riding with the woman Kai-Anila, smelling her bravery and her spirit, and attempting to lend my own poor effort.

Now I shall pause for both breath and refreshment.

Just remember, my cubs, my children, my future, that this is the rightful tale of how we at last began to gain our freedom.

SEPULCHER

by Ben Bova

During his seven-year reign at the helm of *Analog Science Fiction and Fact,* Ben Bova won six Hugo awards for Best Editor. In 1978 he left *Analog* and became the editor of *Omni.* He ran that magazine until 1982. In addition to his work as an acclaimed editor, Bova is the author of more than eighty-five futuristic novels and nonfiction books. He has been involved in science and high technology since the very beginnings of the space program. President Emeritus of the National Space Society and a past president of SFWA, Bova is a frequent commentator on radio and television, and a widely popular lecturer.

Bova was born in Philadelphia and worked as a newspaper reporter for several years before becoming a technical editor at Project Vanguard, the first American artificial satellite program. Later, he was the marketing manager for Avco Everett Research Laboratory, where he worked with leading scientists in such fields as high-power lasers, artificial hearts, and advanced electrical power generators. In novels that include *Mars* and *Death Dream,* he combines romance, adventure, and the highest degree of scientific accuracy to explore the impact of future technological developments on individual human beings and on society as a whole. In nonfiction books such as *Welcome to Moonbase* and *Assured Survival,* he shows how modern technology can be used to solve economic, social, and political problems. His various writings have predicted the space race, solar power satellites, virtual reality, video games, the Strategic Defense Initiative (Star Wars), the advent of international peacekeeping forces, and zero-gravity sex.

The author has appeared frequently on *CBS Morning News, Good Morning America,* and the *Today Show.* His work has been published in magazines as diverse as *Psy-*

chology Today, Modern Bride, the *New York Times, Smith-sonian, Penthouse,* and the *Wall Street Journal.*

I was a soldier," he said. "Now I am a priest. You may call me Dorn."

Elverda Apacheta could not help staring at him. She had seen cyborgs before, but this ... person seemed more machine than man. She felt a chill ripple of contempt along her veins. How could a human being allow his body to be disfigured so?

He was not tall: Elverda herself stood several centimeters taller than he. His shoulders were quite broad, though; his torso thick and solid. The left side of his face was engraved metal, as was the entire top of his head: like a skullcap made of finest etched steel.

Dorn's left hand was prosthetic. He made no attempt to disguise it. Beneath the rough fabric of his shabby tunic and threadbare trousers, how much more of him was metal and electrical machinery? Tattered though his clothing was, his calf-length boots were polished to a high gloss.

"A priest?" asked Miles Sterling. "Of what church? What order?"

The half of Dorn's lips that could move made a slight curl. A smile or a sneer, Elverda could not tell.

"I will show you to your quarters," said Dorn. His voice was a low rumble, as if it came from the belly of a beast. It echoed faintly off the walls of rough-hewn rock.

Sterling looked briefly surprised. He was not accustomed to having his questions ignored. Elverda watched his face. Sterling was as handsome as cosmetic surgery could make a person appear: chiseled features, earnest sky-blue eyes, straight of spine, long of limb, athletically flat midsection. Yet there was a faint smell of corruption about him, Elverda thought. As if he were dead inside and already beginning to rot.

The tension between the two men seemed to drain the energy from Elverda's aged body. "It has been a long journey," she said. "I am very tired. I would welcome a hot shower and a long nap."

"Before you see it?" Sterling snapped.

"It has taken us months to get here. We can wait a few hours more." Inwardly she marveled at her own words. Once she would have been all fiery excitement. Have the years taught you patience? No, she realized. Only weariness.

"Not me!" Sterling said. Turning to Dorn, "Take me to it now. I've waited long enough. I want to see it now."

Dorn's eyes, one as brown as Elverda's own, the other a red electronic glow, regarded Sterling for a lengthening moment.

"Well?" Sterling demanded.

"I am afraid, sir, that the chamber is sealed for the next twelve hours. It will be imposs—"

"Sealed? By whom? On whose authority?"

"The chamber is self-controlled. Whoever made the artifact installed the controls, as well."

"No one told me about that," said Sterling.

Dorn replied. "Your quarters are down this corridor."

He turned almost like a solid block of metal, shoulders and hips together, head unmoving on those wide shoulders, and started down the central corridor. Elverda fell in step alongside his metal half, still angered at his self-desecration. Yet despite herself, she thought of what a challenge it would be to sculpt him. If I were younger, she told herself. If I were not so close to death. Human and inhuman, all in one strangely fierce figure.

Sterling came up on Dorn's other side, his face red with barely suppressed anger.

They walked down the corridor in silence, Sterling's weighted shoes clicking against the uneven rock floor. Dorn's boots made hardly any noise at all. Half-machine he may be, Elverda thought, but once in motion he glides like a panther.

The asteroid's inherent gravity was so slight that Sterling needed the weighted footgear to keep himself from stumbling ridiculously. Elverda, who had spent most of her long life in low-gravity environments, felt completely at home. The corridor they were walking through was actually a tunnel, shadowy and mysterious, or perhaps a natural chimney vented through the rocky body by escaping gases eons ago when the asteroid was still molten.

Now it was cold, chill enough to make Elverda shudder. The rough ceiling was so low she wanted to stoop, even though the rational side of her mind knew it was not necessary.

Soon, though, the walls smoothed out and the ceiling grew higher. Humans had extended the tunnel, squaring it with laser precision. Doors lined both walls now and the ceiling glowed with glareless, shadowless light. Still she hugged herself against the chill that the others did not seem to notice.

They stopped at a wide double door. Dorn tapped out the entrance code on the panel set into the wall and the doors slid open.

"Your quarters, sir," he said to Sterling. "You may, of course, change the privacy code to suit yourself."

Sterling gave a curt nod and strode through the open doorway. Elverda got a glimpse of a spacious suite, carpeting on the floor and hologram windows on the walls.

Sterling turned in the doorway to face them. "I expect you to call for me in twelve hours," he said to Dorn, his voice hard.

"Eleven hours and fifty-seven minutes," Dorn replied.

Sterling's nostrils flared and he slid the double doors shut.

"This way." Dorn gestured with his human hand. "I'm afraid your quarters are not as sumptuous as Mr. Sterling's."

Elverda said, "I am his guest. He is paying all the bills."

"You are a great artist. I have heard of you."

"Thank you."

"For the truth? That is not necessary."

I was a great artist, Elverda said to herself. Once. Long ago. Now I am an old woman waiting for death.

Aloud, she asked, "Have you seen my work?"

Dorn's voice grew heavier. "Only holograms. Once I set out to see The Rememberer for myself, but—other matters intervened."

"You were a soldier then?"

"Yes. I have only been a priest since coming to this place."

Elverda wanted to ask him more, but Dorn stopped before a blank door and opened it for her. For an instant she thought he was going to reach for her with his prosthetic hand. She shrank away from him.

"I will call for you in eleven hours and fifty-six minutes," he said, as if he had not noticed her revulsion.

"Thank you."

He turned away, like a machine pivoting.

"Wait," Elverda called. "Please—How many others are here? Everything seems so quiet."

"There are no others. Only the three of us."

"But—"

"I am in charge of the security brigade. I ordered the others of my command to go back to our spacecraft and wait there."

"And the scientists? The prospector family that found this asteroid?"

"They are in Mr. Sterling's spacecraft, the one you arrived in," said Dorn. "Under the protection of my brigade."

Elverda looked into his eyes. Whatever burned in them, she could not fathom.

"Then we are alone here?"

Dorn nodded solemnly. "You and me—and Mr. Sterling, who pays all the bills." The human half of his face remained as immobile as the metal. Elverda could not tell if he was trying to be humorous or bitter.

"Thank you," she said. He turned away and she closed the door.

Her quarters consisted of a single room, comfortably warm but hardly larger than the compartment on the ship they had come in. Elverda saw that her meager travel bag was already sitting on the bed, her worn old drawing computer resting in its travel-smudged case on the desk. Elverda stared at the computer case as if it were accusing her. I should have left it home, she thought. I will never use it again.

A small utility robot, hardly more than a glistening drum of metal and six gleaming arms folded like a praying mantis's, stood mutely in the farthest corner. Elverda stared at it. At least it was entirely a machine; not a self-mutilated human being. To take the most beautiful form in the universe and turn it into a hybrid mechanism, a travesty of humanity. Why did he do it? So he could be a better soldier? A more efficient killing machine?

And why did he send all the others away? she asked herself while she opened the travel bag. As she carried her toiletries to the narrow alcove of the bathroom, a new thought struck her. Did he send them away before he saw the artifact, or afterward? Has he even seen it? Perhaps . . .

Then she saw her reflection in the mirror above the wash basin. Her heart sank. Once she had been called regal, stately, a goddess made of copper. Now she looked withered, dried up, bone thin, her face a geological map of too many years of living, her flight overalls hanging limply on her emaciated frame.

You are old, she said to her image. Old and aching and tired.

It is the long trip, she told herself. You need to rest. But the other voice in her mind laughed scornfully. You've done nothing but rest for the entire time it's taken to reach this piece of rock. You are ready for the permanent rest; why deny it?

She had been teaching at the university on Luna, the closest she could get to Earth after a long lifetime of living in low-gravity environments. Close enough to see the world of her birth, the only world of life and warmth in the solar system, the only place where a person could walk out in the sunshine and feel its warmth soaking your bones, smell the fertile earth nurturing its bounty, feel a cool breeze plucking at your hair.

But she had separated herself from Earth permanently. She had stood at the shore of Titan's methane sea; from an orbiting spacecraft she had watched the surging clouds of Jupiter swirl their overpowering colors; she had carved the kilometer-long rock of The Rememberer. But she could no longer stand in the village of her birth, at the edge of the Pacific's booming surf, and watch the soft white clouds form shapes of imaginary animals.

Her creative life was long finished. She had lived too long; there were no friends left, and she had never had a family. There was no purpose to her life, no reason to do anything except go through the motions and wait. At the university she was no longer truly working at her art but helping students who had the fires of inspiration burning fresh and hot inside them. Her life was one of vain regrets for all the things she had not accomplished, for all the failures she could recall. Failures at love; those were the bitterest. She was praised as the solar system's greatest artist: the sculptress of The Rememberer, the creator of the first great ionospheric painting, The Virgin of the Andes. She was respected, but not loved. She felt empty, alone, barren. She had nothing to look forward to; absolutely nothing.

Then Miles Sterling swept into her existence. A life-time younger, bold, vital, even ruthless, he stormed her academic tower with the news that an alien artifact had been discovered deep in the asteroid belt.

"It's some kind of art form," he said, desperate with excitement. "You've got to come with me and see it."

Trying to control the long-forgotten longing that stirred within her, Elverda had asked quietly, "Why do I have to go with you, Mr. Sterling? Why me? I'm an old wo—"

"You are the greatest artist of our time," he had snapped. "You've *got* to see this! Don't bullshit me with false modesty. You're the only other person in the whole whirling solar system who *deserves* to see it!"

"The only other person besides whom?" she had asked.

He had blinked with surprise. "Why, besides me, of course."

So now we are on this nameless asteroid, waiting to see the alien artwork. Just the three of us. The richest man in the solar system. An elderly artist who has outlived her usefulness. And a cyborg soldier who has cleared everyone else away.

He claims to be a priest, Elverda remembered. A priest who is half machine. She shivered as if a cold wind surged through her.

A harsh buzzing noise interrupted her thoughts. Looking into the main part of the room, Elverda saw that the phone screen was blinking red in rhythm to the buzzing.

"Phone," she called out.

Sterling's face appeared on the screen instantly. "Come to my quarters," he said. "We have to talk."

"Give me an hour. I need—"

"Now."

Elverda felt her brows rise haughtily. Then the strength sagged out of her. He has bought the right to command you, she told herself. He is quite capable of refusing to allow you to see the artifact.

"Now," she agreed.

Sterling was pacing across the plush carpeting when she arrived at his quarters. He had changed from his flight coveralls to a comfortably loose royal blue pullover and expensive genuine twill slacks. As the doors slid shut behind her, he stopped in front of a low couch and faced her squarely.

"Do you know who this Dorn creature is?"

Elverda answered, "Only what he has told us."

"I've checked him out. My staff in the ship has a complete file on him. He's the butcher who led the *Chrysalis* massacre, fourteen years ago."

"He . . ."

"Eleven hundred men, women and children. Slaughtered. He was the man who commanded the attack."

"He said he had been a soldier."

"A mercenary. A cold-blooded murderer. He was working for Toyama then. The *Chrysalis* was their habitat. When its population voted for independence, Toyama put him in charge of a squad to bring them back into line. He killed them all; turned off their air and let them all die."

Elverda felt shakily for the nearest chair and sank into it. Her legs seemed to have lost all their strength.

"His name was Harbin then. Dorik Harbin."

"Wasn't he brought to trial?"

"No. He ran away. Disappeared. I always thought Toyama helped to hide him. They take care of their own, they do. He must have changed his name after-

wards. Nobody would hire the butcher, not even
Toyama."

"His face ... half is body ..." Elverda felt terribly
weak, almost faint. "When ... ?"

"Must have been after he ran away. Maybe it was an
attempt to disguise himself."

"And now he is working for you." She wanted to
laugh at the irony of it, but did not have the strength.

"He's got us trapped on this chunk of rock! There's
nobody else here except the three of us."

"You have your staff in your ship. Surely they would
come if you summoned them."

"His security squad's been ordered to keep everybody
except you and me off the asteroid. He gave those
orders."

"You can countermand them, can't you?"

For the first time since she had met Miles Sterling, he
looked unsure of himself. "I wonder," he said.

"Why?" Elverda asked. "Why is he doing this?"

"That's what I intend to find out." Sterling strode to
the phone console. "Harbin!" he called. "Dorik Harbin.
Come to my quarters at once."

Without even an eyeblink's delay the phone's computer-
synthesized voice replied, "Dorik Harbin no longer exists. Transferring your call to Dorn."

Sterling's blue eyes snapped at the phone's blank
screen.

"Dorn is not available at present," the phone's voice
said. "He will call for you in eleven hours and thirty-
two minutes."

"God-*damn* it!" Sterling smacked a fist into the open
palm of his other hand. "Get me the officer on watch
aboard the *Sterling Eagle.*"

"All exterior communications are inoperable at the
present time," the phone repeated, unperturbed.

Sterling stared at the empty screen, then turned slowly
toward Elverda. "He's cut us off. We're really trapped
here."

Elverda felt the chill of cold metal clutching at her.
Perhaps Dorn is a madman, she thought. Perhaps he is
my death, personified.

"We've got to do something!" Sterling nearly shouted.

Elverda rose shakily to her feet. "There is nothing that we can do, for the moment. I am going to my quarters and take a nap. I believe that Dorn, or Harbin, or whatever his identity is, will call on us when he is ready to."

"And do what?"

"Show us the artifact," she replied, silently adding, I hope.

Legally, the artifact and the entire asteroid belonged to Sterling Enterprises, Ltd. It had been discovered by a family—husband, wife, and two sons, ages five and three—that made a living from searching out iron-nickel asteroids and selling the mining rights to the big corporations. They filed their claim to this unnamed asteroid, together with a preliminary description of its ten-kilometer-wide shape, its orbit within the asteroid belt, and a sample analysis of its surface composition.

Six hours after their original transmission reached the commodities market computer network on Earth—while a fairly spirited bidding was going on among four major corporations for the asteroid's mineral rights—a new message arrived at the headquarters of the International Astronautical Authority, in London. The message was garbled, fragmentary, obviously made in great haste and at fever excitement. There was an artifact of some sort in a cavern deep inside the asteroid.

One of the faceless bureaucrats buried deep within the IAA's multilayered organization sent an immediate message to an employee of Sterling Enterprises, Ltd. The bureaucrat retired hours later, richer than he had any right to expect, while Miles Sterling personally contacted the prospectors and bought the asteroid outright for enough money to end their prospecting days forever. By the time the decision-makers in the IAA realized that an alien artifact had been discovered they were faced with a *fait accompli:* the artifact, and the asteroid in which it resided, were the personal property of the richest man in the solar system.

Miles Sterling was no egomaniac. Nor was he a fool. Graciously he allowed the IAA to organize a team of scientists who would inspect this first specimen of alien existence. Even more graciously, Sterling offered to ferry the scientific investigators all the long way to the asteroid at his own expense. He made only one demand, and the IAA could hardly refuse him. He insisted that he see this artifact himself before the scientists were allowed to view it.

And he brought along the solar system's most honored and famous artist. To appraise the artifact's worth as an art object, he claimed. To determine how much he could deduct from his corporate taxes by donating the thing to the IAA, said his enemies. But over the months of their voyage to the asteroid, Elverda came to the conclusion that buried deep beneath his ruthless business *persona* was an eager little boy who was tremendously excited at having found a new toy. A toy he intended to possess for himself. An art object, created by alien hands.

For an art object was what the artifact seemed to be. The family of prospectors continued to send back vague, almost irrational reports of what the artifact looked like. The reports were worthless. No two descriptions matched. If the man and the woman were to be believed, the artifact did nothing but sit in the middle of a rough-hewn cavern. But they described it differently with every report they sent. It glowed with light. It was darker than deep space. It was a statue of some sort. It was formless. It overwhelmed the senses. It was small enough almost to pick up in one hand. It made the children laugh happily. It frightened their parents. When they tried to photograph it, their transmissions showed nothing but blank screens. Totally blank.

As Sterling listened to their maddening reports and waited impatiently for the IAA to organize its hand-picked team of scientists, he ordered his security manager to get a squad of hired personnel to the asteroid as quickly as possible. From corporate facilities on Titan and the moons of Mars, from three separate outposts among the asteroid belt itself, Sterling Enterprises efficiently brought together a brigade of experienced mercenary security troops. They reached the asteroid long before anyone else could, and were under orders to make certain that no one was allowed on the asteroid before Miles Sterling himself reached it.

"The time has come."

Elverda woke slowly, painfully, like a swimmer struggling for the air and light of the surface. She had been dreaming of her childhood, of the village where she had grown up, the distant snow-capped Andes, the warm night breezes that spoke of love.

"The time has come."

It was Dorn's deep voice, whisper-soft. Startled, she flashed her eyes open. She was alone in the room, but Dorn's image filled the phone screen by her bed. The numbers glowing beneath the screen showed that it was indeed time.

"I am awake now," she said to the screen.

"I will be at your door in fifteen minutes," Dorn said. "Will that be enough time for you to prepare yourself?"

"Yes, plenty." The days when she needed time for selecting her clothes and arranging her appearance were long gone.

"In fifteen minutes, then."

"Wait," she blurted. "Can you see me?"

"No. Visual transmission must be keyed manually."

"I see."

"I do not."

A joke? Elverda sat up on the bed as Dorn's image winked out. Is he capable of humor?

She shrugged out of the shapeless coveralls she had worn to bed, took a quick shower, and pulled her best caftan from the travel bag. It was a deep midnight blue, scattered with glittering silver stars. Elverda had made the floor-length gown herself, from fabric woven by her mother long ago. She had painted the stars from her memory of what they had looked like from her native village.

As she slid back her front door she saw Dorn marching down the corridor with Sterling beside him. Despite his longer legs, Sterling seemed to be scampering like a child to keep up with Dorn's steady, solid steps.

"I *demand* that you reinstate communications with my ship," Sterling was saying, his voice echoing off the corridor walls. "I'll dock your pay for every minute this insubordination continues!"

"It is a security measure," Dorn said calmly, without turning to look at the man. "It is for your own good."

"My own good? Who in hell are you to determine what my own good might be?"

Dorn stopped three paces short of Elverda, made a stiff little bow to her, and only then turned to face his employer.

"Sir: I have seen the artifact. You have not."

"And that makes you better than me?" Sterling almost snarled the words. "Holier, maybe."

"No," said Dorn. "Not holier. Wiser."

Sterling started to reply, then thought better of it.

"Which way do we go?" Elverda asked in the sudden silence.

Dorn pointed with his prosthetic hand. "Down," he replied. "This way."

The corridor abruptly became a rugged tunnel again, with lights fastened at precisely spaced intervals along the low ceiling. Elverda watched Dorn's half-human face as the pools of shadow chased the highlights glinting off the etched metal, like the Moon racing through its phases every half-minute, over and again.

Sterling had fallen silent as they followed the slanting tunnel downward into the heart of the rock. Elverda heard only the clicking of his shoes at first, but by concentrating she was able to make out the softer footfalls of Dorn's padded boots and even the whisper of her own slippers.

The air seemed to grow warmer, closer. *Or is it my own anticipation?* She glanced at Sterling; perspiration beaded his upper lip. The man radiated tense expectation. Dorn glided a few steps ahead of them. He did not seem to be hurrying, yet he was now leading them down the tunnel, like an ancient priest leading two new acolytes—or sacrificial victims.

The tunnel ended in a smooth wall of dull metal.

"We are here."

"Open it up," Sterling demanded.

"It will open itself," replied Dorn. He waited a heart-beat, then added, "Now."

And the metal slid up into the rock above them as silently as if it were a curtain made of silk.

None of them moved. Then Dorn slowly turned toward the two of them and gestured with his human hand.

"The artifact lies twenty-two point nine meters beyond this point. The tunnel narrows and turns to the right. The chamber is large enough to accommodate only one person at a time, comfortably."

"Me first!" Sterling took a step forward.

Dorn stopped him with an upraised hand. The prosthetic hand. "I feel it my duty to caution you—"

Sterling tried to push the hand away; he could not budge it.

"When I first crossed this line, I was a soldier. After I saw the artifact I gave up my life."

"And became a self-styled priest. So what?"

"The artifact can change you. I thought it best that there be no witnesses to your first viewing of it, except for this gifted woman whom you have brought with you. When you first see it, it can be—traumatic."

Sterling's face twisted with a mixture of anger and disgust. "I'm not a mercenary killer. I don't have anything to be afraid of."

Dorn let his hand drop to his side with a faint whine of miniaturized servomotors.

"Perhaps not," he murmured, so low that Elverda barely heard it.

Sterling shouldered his way past the cyborg. "Stay here," he told Elverda. "You can see it when I come back."

He hurried down the tunnel, footsteps staccato.

Then silence.

Elverda looked at Dorn. The human side of his face seemed utterly weary.

"You have seen the artifact more than once, haven't you?"

"Fourteen times," he answered.

"It has not harmed you in any way, has it?"

He hesitated, then replied, "It has changed me. Each time I see it, it changes me more."

"You . . . you really are Dorik Harbin?"

"I was."

"Those people of the *Chrysalis* . . . ?"

"Dorik Harbin killed them all. Yes. There is no excuse for it, no pardon. It was the act of a monster."

"But why?"

"Monsters do monstrous things. Dorik Harbin ingested psychotropic drugs to increase his battle prowess. Afterward, when the battle drugs cleared from his bloodstream and he understood what he had done, Dorik Harbin held a grenade against his chest and set it off."

"Oh my god," Elverda whimpered.

"He was not allowed to die, however. The medical specialists rebuilt his body and he was given a false identity. For many years he lived a sham of life, hiding from the authorities, hiding from his own guilt. He no longer had the courage to kill himself; the pain of his first attempt was far stronger than his own self-loathing. Then he was hired to come to this place. Dorik Harbin looked upon the artifact for the first time, and his true identity emerged at last."

Elverda heard a scuffling sound, like feet dragging, staggering. Miles Sterling came into view, tottering, leaning heavily against the wall of the tunnel, slumping as if his legs could no longer hold him.

"No man . . . no one . . ." He pushed himself forward and collapsed into Dorn's arms.

"Destroy it!" he whispered harshly, spittle dribbling down his chin. "Destroy this whole damned piece of rock! Wipe it out of existence!"

"What is it?" Elverda asked. "What did you see?"

Dorn lowered him to the ground gently. Sterling's feet scrabbled against the rock as if he were trying to run away. Sweat covered his face, soaked his shirt.

"It's . . . beyond . . ." he babbled. "More . . . than anyone can . . . nobody could stand it. . . ."

Elverda sank to her knees beside him. "What has happened to him?" She looked up at Dorn, who knelt on Sterling's other side.

"The artifact."

Sterling suddenly ranted, "They'll find out about me! Everyone will know! It's got to be destroyed! Nuke it! Blast it to bits!" His fists windmilled in the air, his eyes were wild.

"I tried to warn him," Dorn said as he held Sterling's shoulders down, the man's head in his lap. "I tried to prepare him for it."

"What did he see?" Elverda's heart was pounding; she could hear it thundering in her ears. "What is it? What did *you* see?"

Dorn shook his head slowly. "I cannot describe it. I doubt that anyone could describe it—except, perhaps, an artist: a person who has trained herself to see the truth."

"The prospectors—they saw it. Even their children saw it."

"Yes. When I arrived here they had spent eighteen days in the chamber. They left it only when the chamber closed itself. They ate and slept and returned here, as if hypnotized."

"It did not hurt them, did it?"

"They were emaciated, dehydrated. It took a dozen of my strongest men to remove them to my ship. Even the children fought us."

"But ... how could ..." Elverda's voice faded into silence. She looked at the brightly-lit tunnel. Her breath caught in her throat.

"Destroy it," Sterling mumbled. "Destroy it before it destroys us! Don't let them find out. They'll know, they'll know, they'll all know." He began to sob uncontrollably.

"You do not have to see it," Dorn said to Elverda. "You can return to your ship and leave this place."

Leave, urged a voice inside her head. Run away. Live out what's left of your life and let it go.

Then she heard her own voice say, as if from a far distance, "I've come such a long way."

"It will change you," he warned.

"Will it release me from life?"

Dorn glanced down at Sterling, still muttering darkly, then returned his gaze to Elverda.

"It will change you," he repeated.

Elverda forced herself to her feet. Leaning one hand against the warm rock wall to steady herself, she said, "I will see it. I must."

"Yes," said Dorn, "I understand."

She looked down at him, still kneeling with Sterling's head resting in his lap. Dorn's electronic eye glowed red in the shadows. His human eye was hidden in darkness.

He said, "I believe your people say, *Vaya con Dios.*"

Elverda smiled at him. She had not heard that phrase in forty years. "Yes. You too. *Vaya con Dios.*" She turned and stepped across the faint groove where the metal door had met the floor.

The tunnel sloped downward only slightly. It turned sharply to the right, Elverda saw, just as Dorn had told them. The light seemed brighter beyond the turn, pulsating almost, like a living heart.

She hesitated a moment before making that final turn. What lay beyond? What difference, she answered herself. You have lived so long that you have emptied life of all its purpose. But she knew she was lying to herself. Her life was devoid of purpose because she herself had made it that way. She had spurned love; she had even rejected friendship when it had been offered. Still, she realized that she wanted to live. Desperately, she wanted to continue living no matter what.

Yet she could not resist the lure. Straightening her spine, she stepped boldly around the bend in the tunnel.

The light was so bright it hurt her eyes. She raised a hand to her brow to shield them and the intensity seemed to decrease slightly, enough to make out the faint outline of a form, a shape, a person. . . .

Elverda gasped with recognition. A few meters before her, close enough to reach and touch, her mother sat on the sweet grass beneath the warm summer sun, gently rocking her baby and crooning softly to it.

Mama! she cried silently. Mama. The baby—Elverda herself—looked up into her mother's face and smiled.

And the mother was Elverda, a young and radiant

Elverda, smiling down at the baby she had never had, tender and loving as she had never been.

Something gave way inside her. There was no pain; rather, it was as if a pain that had throbbed sullenly within her for too many years to count suddenly faded away. As if a wall of implacable ice finally melted and let the warm waters of life flow through her.

Elverda sank to the floor, crying, gushing tears of understanding and relief and gratitude. Her mother smiled at her.

"I love you, Mama," she whispered. "I love you."

Her mother nodded and became Elverda herself once more. Her baby made a gurgling laugh of pure happiness, fat little feet waving in the air.

The image wavered, dimmed, and slowly faded into emptiness. Elverda sat on the bare rock floor in utter darkness, feeling a strange serenity and understanding warming her soul.

"Are you all right?"

Dorn's voice did not startle her. She had been expecting him to come to her.

"The chamber will close itself in another few minutes," he said. "We will have to leave."

Elverda took his offered hand and rose to her feet. She felt strong, fully in control of herself.

The tunnel outside the chamber was empty.

"Where is Sterling?"

"I sedated him and then called in a medical team to take him back to his ship."

"He wants to destroy the artifact," Elverda said.

"That will not be possible," said Dorn. "I will bring the IAA scientists here from the ship before Sterling awakes and recovers. Once they see the artifact they will not allow it to be destroyed. Sterling may own the asteroid, but the IAA will exert control over the artifact."

"The artifact will affect them—strangely."

"No two of them will be affected in the same manner," said Dorn. "And none of them will permit it to be damaged in any way."

"Sterling will not be pleased with you."

He gestured up the tunnel, and they began to walk back toward their quarters.

"Nor with you," Dorn said. "We both saw him babbling and blubbering like a baby."

"What could he have seen?"

"What he most feared. His whole life had been driven by fear, poor man."

"What secrets he must be hiding!"

"He hid them from himself. The artifact showed him his own true nature."

"No wonder he wants it destroyed."

"He cannot destroy the artifact, but he will certainly want to destroy us. Once he recovers his composure he will want to wipe out the witnesses who saw his reaction to it."

Elverda knew that Dorn was right. She watched his face as they passed beneath the lights, watched the glint of the etched metal, the warmth of the human flesh.

"You knew that he would react this way, didn't you?" she asked.

"No one could be as rich as he is without having demons driving him. He looked into his own soul and recognized himself for the first time in his life."

"You planned it this way!"

"Perhaps I did," he said. "Perhaps the artifact did it for me."

"How could—"

"It is a powerful experience. After I had seen it a few times I felt it was offering me ..." he hesitated, then spoke the word, "salvation."

Elverda saw something in his face that Dorn had not let show before. She stopped in the shadows between overhead lights. Dorn turned to face her, half machine, standing in the rough tunnel of bare rock.

"You have had your own encounter with it," he said. "You understand now how it can transform you."

"Yes," said Elverda. "I understand."

"After a few times, I came to the realization that there must be thousands of my fellow mercenaries, killed in engagements all through the asteroid belt, still lying where they fell. Or worse yet, floating forever in space, alone, unattended, ungrieved for."

"Thousands of mercenaries?"

"The corporations do not always settle their differences in Earthly courts of law," said Dorn. "There have been many battles out here. Wars that we paid for with our blood."

"Thousands?" Elverda repeated. "I knew that there had been occasional fights out here—but wars? I don't think anyone on Earth knows it's been so brutal."

"Men like Sterling know. They start the wars, and people like me fight them. Exiles, never allowed to return to Earth again once we take the mercenary's pay."

"All those men—killed."

Dorn nodded. "And women. The artifact made me see that it was my duty to find each of those forgotten bodies and give each one a decent final rite. The artifact seemed to be telling me that this was the path of my atonement."

"Your salvation," she murmured.

"I see now, however, that I underestimated the situation."

"How?"

"Sterling. While I am out there searching for the bodies of the slain, he will have me killed."

"No! That's wrong!"

Dorn's deep voice was empty of regret. "It will be simple for him to send a team after me. In the depths of dark space, they will murder me. What I failed to do for myself, Sterling will do for me. He will be my final atonement."

"Never!" Elverda blazed with anger. "I will not permit it to happen."

"Your own life is in danger from him," Dorn said.

"What of it? I am an old woman, ready for death."

"Are you?"

"I was . . . until I saw the artifact."

"Now life is more precious to you, isn't it?"

"I don't want you to die," Elverda said. "You have atoned for your sins. You have borne enough pain."

He looked away, then started up the tunnel again.

"You are forgetting one important factor," Elverda called after him.

Dorn stopped, his back to her. She realized now that the clothes he wore had been his military uniform. He had torn all the insignias and pockets from it.

"The artifact. Who created it? And why?"

Turning back toward her, Dorn answered, "Alien visitors to our solar system created it, unknown ages ago. As to why—you tell me: why does someone create a work of art?"

"Why would aliens create a work of art that affects human minds?"

Dorn's human eye blinked. He rocked a step backward.

"How could they create an artifact that is a mirror to our souls?" Elverda asked, stepping toward him. "They must have known something about us. They must have been here when there were human beings existing on Earth."

Dorn regarded her silently.

"They may have been here much more recently than you think," Elverda went on, coming closer to him. "They may have placed this artifact here to *communicate* with us."

"Communicate?"

"Perhaps it is a very subtle, very powerful communications device."

"Not an artwork at all."

"Oh yes, of course it's an artwork. All works of art are communications devices, for those who possess the soul to understand."

Dorn seemed to ponder this for long moments. Elverda watched his solemn face, searching for some human expression.

Finally he said, "That does not change my mission, even if it is true."

"Yes it does," Elverda said, eager to save him. "Your mission is to preserve and protect this artifact against Sterling and anyone else who would try to destroy it— or pervert it to his own use."

"The dead call to me," Dorn said solemnly. "I hear them in my dreams now."

"But why be alone in your mission? Let others help you. There must be other mercenaries who feel as you do."

"Perhaps," he said softly.

"Your true mission is much greater than you think," Elverda said, trembling with new understanding. "You have the power to end the wars that have destroyed your comrades, that have almost destroyed your soul."

"End the corporate wars?"

"You will be the priest of this shrine, this sepulcher. I will return to Earth and tell everyone about these wars."

"Sterling and others will have you killed."

"I am a famous artist, they dare not touch me." Then she laughed. "And I am too old to care if they do."

"The scientists—do you think they may actually learn how to communicate with the aliens?"

"Someday," Elverda said. "When our souls are pure enough to stand the shock of their presence."

The human side of Dorn's face smiled at her. He extended his arm and she took it in her own, realizing that she had found her own salvation. Like two kindred souls, like comrades who had shared the sight of death, like mother and son they walked up the tunnel toward the waiting race of humanity.

THE HIGH TEST

by Frederik Pohl

Multiple Hugo and Nebula award winner Frederik Pohl has been about everything that it is possible to be in the field of science fiction, from consecrated fan and struggling poet to critic, literary agent, teacher, book and magazine editor, and above all, writer. Among his most recent novels are *The World at the End of Time, Outnumbering the Dead, Stopping at Slowyear, The Voices of Heaven,* and *Mining the Oort.* In addition, he recently published a nonfiction book about the problems facing our environment and the political aspects of dealing with them, *Our Angry Earth,* which was completed in collaboration with the late Isaac Asimov in 1991 and reissued in an updated edition in 1993.

Many of Pohl's works have been adapted for radio, television, or film, beginning in 1953 with the two-part Columbia Workshop of the Air version of the classic *The Space Merchants.* A number of his stories have been televised by the BBC and made into films in Europe. The 1981 NBC television film, *The Clone Master,* was based on an original concept of his; and his novels *Man Plus* and *Gateway* are currently in development in the United States. *Gateway* has also been dramatized for live theatrical production, and in 1992 it was made into a computer game by Legend Entertainment. A second game, Gateway II: The Home World, was released in August 1993.

Pohl is a past president of both World SF and the Science Fiction Writers of America (SFWA). In 1993, SFWA awarded him the Grand Master Nebula for lifetime contributions to the field. He currently makes his home in Palatine, Illinois, with his wife and noted SF scholar, Dr. Elizabeth Anne Hull.

2213 12 22 1900ugt

Dear Mom:
    As they say, there's good news and there's bad
news here on Cassiopeia 43-G. The bad news is that
there aren't any openings for people with degrees in
quantum-mechanical astrophysics. The good news is that
I've got a job. I started yesterday. I work for a driving
school, and I'm an instructor.

    I know you'll say that's not much of a career for a
twenty-six-year-old man with a doctorate, but it pays the
rent. Also it's a lot better than I'd have if I'd stayed on
Earth. Is it true that the unemployment rate in Chicago
is up to eighty percent? Wow! As soon as I get a few
megabucks ahead I'm going to invite you all to come
out here and visit me in the sticks so you can see how
we live here—you may not want to go back!

    Now, I don't want you to worry when I tell you that
I get hazardous duty pay. That's just a technicality. We
driving instructors have it in our contracts, but we don't
really earn it. At least, usually we don't—although there
are times like yesterday. The first student I had was this
young girl, right from Earth. Spoiled rotten! You know
the kind, rich, and I guess you'd say beautiful, and really
used to having her own way. Her name's Tonda
Aguilar—you've heard of the Evanston Aguilars? In the
recombinant foodstuff business? They're really rich, I
guess. This one had her own speedster, and she was really sulked that she couldn't drive it on an Earth license.
See, they have this suppressor field; as soon as any vehicle comes into the system, zap, it's off, and it just floats
until some licensed pilot comes out to fly it in. So I took
her up, and right away she started giving me ablation.
"Not so much takeoff boost! You'll burn out the tubes!"
and "Don't ride the reverter in hyperdrive!" and "Get
out of low orbit—you want to rack us up?"

    Well, I can take just so much of that. An instructor is
almost like the captain of a ship, you know. He's the
boss! So I explained to her that my name wasn't "Chow-
derhead" or "Dullwit!" but James Paul Madigan, and it
was the instructors who were supposed to yell at the

students, not the other way around. Well, it was her own speedster, and a really neat one at that. Maybe I couldn't blame her for being nervous about somebody else driving it. So I decided to give her a real easy lesson. Practicing parking orbits—if you can't do that you don't deserve a license! And she was really rotten at it. It looks easy, but there's an art to cutting the hyperdrive with just the right residual velocity, so you slide right into your assigned coordinates. The more she tried the farther off she got. Finally she demanded that I take her back to the spaceport. She said I was making her nervous. She said she'd get a different instructor for tomorrow or she'd just move on to some other system where they didn't have benefacted chimpanzees giving driving lessons.

I just let her rave. Then the next student I had was a Fomalhautian. You know that species: they've got two heads and scales and forked tails, and they're always making a nuisance of themselves in the United Systems? If you believe what they say on the vidcom, they're bad news—in fact, the reason Cassiopeia installed the suppressor field was because they had a suspicion the Fomalhautians were thinking about invading and taking over 43-G. But this one was nice as pie! Followed every instruction. Never gave me any argument. Apologized when he made a mistake and got us too close to one of the miniblack holes near the primary. He said that was because he was unfamiliar with the school ship, and said he'd prefer to use his own space yacht for the next lesson. He made the whole day better, after that silly, spoiled rich brat!

I was glad to have a little cheering up, to tell you the truth. I was feeling a little lonesome and depressed. Probably it's because it's so close to the holidays. It's hard to believe that back in Chicago it's only three days until Christmas, and all the store windows will be full of holodecorations and there'll be that big tree in Grant Park and I bet it's snowing ... and here on Cassiopeia 43-G it's sort of like a steam bath with interludes of Niagara falls.

I do wish you a Merry Christmas, Mom! Hope my gifts got there all right.

Love,
Jim Paul

2213 12 25 late

Dear Mom:

Well, Christmas Day is just about over. Not that it's any different from any other day here on 43-G, where the human colonists were mostly Buddhist or Moslem and the others were—well! You've seen the types that hang around the United Systems building in Palatine—smelled them, too, right? Especially those Arcturans. I don't know whether those people have any religious holidays or not, and I'm pretty sure I don't *want* to know.

Considering that I had to work all day, it hasn't been such a bad Christmas at that. When I mentioned to Tor-klemiggen—he's the Fomalhautian I told you about—that today was a big holiday for us he sort of laughed and said that mammals had really quaint customs. And when he found out that part of the custom was to exchange gifts he thought for a minute. (The way Fomal-hautians think to themselves is that their heads whisper in each other's ear—really grotesque!) Then he said that he had been informed it was against the law for a student to give anything to his driving instructor, but if I wanted to fly his space yacht myself for a while he'd let me do it. And he would let it go down on the books of the school as instruction time, so I'd get paid for it. Well, you bet I wanted to! He has some swell yacht. It's long and tapered, sort of shark-shape, like the TU-Lockheed 4400 series, with radar-glyph vision screens and a cruising range of nearly 1800 l.y. I don't know what its top speed is—after all, we had to stay in our own system!

We were using his own ship, you see, and of course it's Fomalhautian made. Not easy for a human being to fly! Even though I'm supposed to be the instructor and Torklemiggen the student, I was baffled at first. I couldn't even get it off the ground until he explained the controls to me and showed me how to read the instruments. There's still plenty I don't know, but after a few minutes I could handle it well enough not to kill us out of hand. Torklemiggen kept daring me to circle the black holes. I told him we couldn't do that, and he got this kind of sneer on one of his faces, and the two heads sort of whispered together for a while. I knew he was thinking of something cute, but I didn't know what at first.

Then I found out!

You know that CAS 43, our primary, is a red giant star with an immense photosphere. Torklemiggen bragged that we could fly right through the photosphere! Well, of course I hardly believed him, but he was so insistent that I tried it out. He was right! We just greased right through that thirty-thousand-degree plasma, like nothing at all! the hull began to turn red, then yellow, then straw-colored—you could see it on the edges of the radar-glyph screen—and yet the inside temperature stayed right on the button of 40° Celsius. That's 43-G normal, by the way. Hot, if you're used to Chicago, but nothing like it was outside! And when we burst out into vacuum again there was no thermal shock, no power surge, no instrument fog. Just beautiful! It's hard to believe that any individual can afford a ship like this just for his private cruising. I guess Fomalhaut must have some pretty rich planets!

Then when we landed, more than an hour late, there was the Aguilar woman waiting for me. She found out that the school wouldn't let her change instructors once assigned. I could have told her that; it's policy. So she had to cool her heels until I got back. But I guess she had a little Christmas spirit somewhere in her ornery frame, because she was quite polite about it. As a matter of fact, when we had her doing parking orbits she was much improved over the last time. Shows what a first-class instructor can do for you!

Well, I see by the old chronometer on the wall that it's the day after Christmas now, at least by Universal-Greenwich Time it is, though I guess you've still got a couple of hours to go in Chicago. One thing, Mom. The Christmas packages you sent didn't get here yet. I thought about lying to you and saying they'd come and how much I liked them, but you raised me always to tell the truth. (Besides, I didn't know what to thank you for!) Anyway, Merry Christmas one more time from—

Jim Paul

2213 12 30 0200ugt

Dear Mom:

Another day, another kilobuck. My first student today was a sixteen-year-old kid. One of those smart-alecky ones, if you know what I mean. (But you probably don't, because you certainly never had any kids like that!) His father was a combat pilot in the Cassiopeian navy, and the kid drove that way, too. That wasn't the worst of it. He'd heard about Torklemiggen. When I tried to explain to him that he had to learn how to go slow before he could go fast, he really let me have it. Didn't I know his father said the Fomalhautians were treacherous enemies of the Cassiopeian way of life? Didn't I know his father said they were just waiting their chance to invade? Didn't I know—

Well, I could take just so much of this fresh kid telling me what I didn't know. So I told him he wasn't as lucky as Torklemiggen. He only had one brain, and if he didn't use all of it to fly this ship I was going to wash him out. That shut him up pretty quick.

But it didn't get much better, because later on I had this fat lady student who just oughtn't to get a license for anything above a skateboard. Forty-six years old, and she's never driven before—but her husband's got a job asteroid-mining, and she wants to be able to bring him a hot lunch every day. I hope she's a better cook than a pilot! Anyway I was trying to put her at ease, so she wouldn't pile us up into a comet nucleus or something, so I was telling her about the kid. She listened, all sympathy—you know, how teenage kids were getting fresher every year—until I mentioned that what we were arguing about was my Fomalhautian student. Well, you should have heard her then! I swear, Mom, I think these Cassiopeians are psychotic on the subject. I wish Torklemiggen were here so I could talk to him about it— somebody said the reason CAS 43-G put the suppressor system in in the first place was to keep them from invading, if you can imagine that! But he had to go home for a few days. Business, he said. Said he'd be back next week to finish his lessons.

Tonda Aguilar is almost finished, too. She'll solo in a couple of days. She was my last student today—I mean yesterday, actually, because it's way after midnight now. I had her practicing zero-G approaches to low-mass asteroids, and I happened to mention that I was feeling a little lonesome. It turned out she was, too, so I surprised myself by asking her if she was doing anything tomorrow night, and she surprised me by agreeing to a date. It's not romance, Mom, so don't get your hopes up. It's just that she and I seem to be the only beings in this whole system who know that tomorrow is New Year's Eve!

Love,
Jim Paul

2214 01 02 2330ugt

Dear Mom:

I got your letter this morning, and I'm glad that your leg is better. Maybe next time you'll listen to Dad and me! Remember, we both begged you to go for a brand-new factory job when you got it, but you kept insisting a rebuilt would be just as good. Now you see. It never pays to try to save money on your health!

I'm sorry if I told you about my clients without giving you any idea of what they looked like. For Tonda, that's easy enough to fix. I enclose a holo of the two of us which we took this afternoon, celebrating the end of her lessons. She solos tomorrow. As you can see, she is a really goodlooking woman and I was wrong about her being spoiled. She came out here on her own to make her career as a dermatologist. She wouldn't take any of her old man Aguilar's money, so all she had when she got here was her speedster and her degree and the clothes on her back. I really admire her. She connected right away with one of the best body-shops in town, and she's making more money than I am.

As to Torklemiggen, that's harder. I tried to a make

a holopic of him, but he got really upset—you might even say nasty. He said inferior orders have no right to worship a Fomalhautian's image, if you can believe it! I tried to explain that we didn't have that in mind at all, but he just laughed. He has a mean laugh. In fact, he's a lot different since he came back from Fomalhaut on that business trip. Meaner. I don't mean that he's different physically. Physically he's about a head taller than I am, except that he has two of them. Two heads, I mean. The head on his left is for talking and breathing, the one on his right for eating and showing expression. It's pretty weird to see him telling a joke. His jokes are pretty weird all by themselves, for that matter. I'll give you an example. This afternoon he said, "What's the difference between a mammal and a roasted hagensbiffik with murgry sauce?" And when I said I didn't even know what those things were, much less what the difference was, he laughed himself foolish and said, "No difference!" What a spectacle. There was his left-hand head talking and sort of yapping that silly laugh of his, deadpan, while the right-hand head was all creased up with giggle lines. Some sense of humor. I should have told you that Torklemiggen's left-hand head looks kind of like a chimpanzee's, and the right one is a little bit like a fox's. Or maybe an alligator's, because of the scales. Not pretty, you understand. But you can't say that about his ship! It's as sweet a job as I've ever driven. I guess he had some extra accessories put on it while he was home, because I noticed there were five or six new readouts and some extra hand controls. When I asked him what they were for he said they had nothing to do with piloting and I would find out what they were for soon enough. I guess that's another Fomalhautian joke of some kind.

Well, I'd write more but I have to get up early in the morning. I'm having breakfast with Tonda to give her some last-minute run throughs before she solos. I think she'll pass all right. She surely has a lot of smarts for somebody who was a former Miss Illinois!

Love,
Jim Paul

2214 01 03 late

Dear Mom:

Your Christmas package got here today, and it was really nice. I loved the socks. They'll come in real handy in case I come back to Chicago for a visit before it gets warm. But the cookies were pretty crumbled, I'm afraid—delicious, though! Tonda said she could tell that they were better than anything she could bake, before they went through the CAS 43-G customs, I mean.

Torklemiggen is just about ready to solo. To tell you the truth, I'll be glad to see the last of him. The closer he gets to his license the harder he is to get along with. This morning he began acting crazy as soon as we got into high orbit. We were doing satellite-matching curves. You know, when you come in on an asymptotic tractrix curve, just whistling through the upper atmosphere of the satellite and then back into space. Nobody ever does that when they're actually driving, because what is there on a satellite in this system that anybody would want to visit? But they won't pass you for a license if you don't know how.

The trouble was, Torklemiggen thought he already did know how, better than I did. So I took the controls away to show him how, and that really blew his cool. "I could shoot better curves than you in my fourth instar!" he snarled out of his left head, while his right head was looking at me like a rattlesnake getting ready to strike. I mean, mean. Then when I let him have the controls back he began shooting curves at one of the mini-black holes. Well, that's about the biggest no-no there is. "Stop that right now," I ordered. "We can't go within a hundred thousand miles of one of those things! How'd you pass your written test without knowing that?"

"Do not exceed your life-station, mammal!" he snapped, and dived in toward the hole again, his fore hands on the thrust and roll controls while his hind hands reached out to fondle the buttons for the new equipment. And all the time his left-hand head was chuckling and giggling like some fiend out of a monster movie.

"If you don't obey instructions," I warned him, "I will

not approve you for your solo." Well, that fixed him. At least he calmed down. But he sulked for the rest of the lesson. Since I didn't like the way he was behaving, I took the controls for the landing. Out of curiosity I reached to see what the new buttons were. "Severely handicapped mammalian species!" his left head screeched, while his right head was turning practically pale pink with terror. "Do you want to destroy this planet?"

I was getting pretty suspicious by then, so I asked him straight out: "What is this stuff, some kind of weapon?"

That made him all quiet. His two heads whispered to each other for a minute, then he said, very stiff and formal, "Do you speak to me of weapons when you mammals have these black holes in orbit? Have you considered their potential for weaponry? Can you imagine what one of them would do, directed toward an inhabited planet?" He paused for a minute, then he said something that really started me thinking. "Why," he asked, "do you suppose my people have any wish to bring culture to this system, except to demonstrate the utility of these objects?"

We didn't talk much after that, but it was really on my mind.

After work, when Tonda and I were sitting in the park, feeding the flying crabs and listening to the singing trees, I told her all about it. She was silent for a moment. Then she looked up at me and said seriously. "Jim Paul, it's a rotten thing to say about any being, but it almost sounds as though Torklemiggen has some idea about conquering this system."

"Now, who would want to do something like that?" I asked.

She shrugged. "It was just a thought," she apologized. But we both kept thinking about it all day long, in spite of our being so busy getting our gene tests and all—but I'll tell you about that later!

Love,
Jim Paul

2214 01 05 2200ugt

Dear Mom:

Take a good luck at this date, the 5th of January, because you're going to need to remember it for a while! There's big news from CAS 43-G tonight ... but first, as they say on the tube, a few other news items.

Let me tell you about that bird Torklemiggen. He soloed this morning. I went along as check pilot, in a school ship, flying matching orbits with him while he went through the whole test in his own yacht. I have to admit that he was really nearly as good as he thought he was. He slid in and out of hyperdrive without any power surge you could detect. He kicked his ship into a corkscrew curve and killed all the drives, so he was tumbling and rolling and pitching all at once, and he got out of it into a clean orbit using only the side thrusters. He matched parking orbits—he ran the whole course without a flaw. I was still sore at him, but there just wasn't any doubt that he'd shown all the skills he needed to get a license. So I called him on the private TBS frequency and said, "You've passed, Torklemiggen. Do you want a formal written report when we land, or shall I call in to have your license granted now?"

"Now this instant, mammal!" he yelled back, and added something in his own language. I didn't understand it, of course. Nobody else could hear it, either, because the talk-between-ships circuits don't carry very far. So I guess I'll never know just what it is he said, but, honestly, Mom, it surely didn't sound at all friendly. All the same, he'd passed.

So I ordered him to null his controls, and then I called in his test scores to the master computer on 43-G. About two seconds later he started screeching over the TBS, "Vile mammal! What have you done? My green light's out, my controls won't respond. Is this some treacherous warm-blood trick?"

He sure had a way of getting under your skin. "Take it easy, Torklemiggen," I told him, not very friendlily— he was beginning to hurt my feelings. "The computer is readjusting your status. They've removed the temporary license for your solo, so they can lift the suppressor field

permanently. As soon as the light goes on again you'll
be fully licensed, and able to fly anywhere in this system
without supervision."

"Hah," he grumbled, and then for a moment I could
hear his heads whispering together. Then—well, Mom, I
was going to say he laughed out loud over the TBS. But
it was more than a laugh. It was mean, and gloating.
"Depraved retarded mammal," he shouted, "my light is
on—and now all of Cassiopeia is mine!"

I was really disgusted with him. You expect that kind
of thing, maybe, from some spacehappy sixteen-year-old
who's just got his first license. Not from an eighteen-
hundred-year-old alien who has flown all over the Galaxy. It sounded sick! And sort of worrisome, too. I
wasn't sure just how to take him. "Don't do anything
silly, Torklemiggen," I warned him over the TBS.

He shouted back: "Silly? I do nothing silly, mammal!
Observe how little silly I am!" And the next thing you
know he was whirling and diving into hyperspace—no
signal, nothing! I had all I could do to follow him, six
alphas deep and going fast. For all I knew we could have
been on our way back to Fomalhaut. But he only stayed
there for a minute. He pulled out right in the middle of
one of the asteroid belts, and as I followed up from the
alphas I saw that lean, green yacht of his diving down
on a chunk of rock about the size of an office building.

I had noticed, when he came back from his trip, that
one of the new things about the yacht was a circle of
ruby-colored studs around the nose of the ship. Now
they began to glow, brighter and brighter. In a moment
a dozen streams of ruby light reached out from them,
ahead toward the asteroid—and there was a bright flare
of light, and the asteroid wasn't there any more!

Naturally, that got me upset. I yelled at him over the
TBS: "Listen, Torklemiggen, you're about to get yourself in real deep trouble! I don't know how they do
things back on Fomalhaut, but around here that's
grounds for an action to suspend your license! Not to
mention they could make you pay for that asteroid!"

"Pay?" he screeched. "It is not I who will pay, func-
tionally inadequate live-bearer, it is you and yours! You

will pay most dreadfully, for now we have the black holes!" And he was off again, back down into hyperspace, and one more time it was about all I could do to try to keep up with him.

There's no sense trying to transmit in hyperspace, of course. I had to wait until we were up out of the alphas to answer him; and by that time, I don't mind telling you, I was *peeved*. I never would have found him on visual, but the radar-glyph picked him up zeroing in on one of the black holes. What a moron! "Listen, Torklemiggen," I said, keeping my voice level and hard, "I'll give you one piece of advice. Go back to base. Land your ship. Tell the police you were just carried away, celebrating passing your test. Maybe they won't be too hard on you. Otherwise, I warn you, you're looking at a thirty-day suspension plus you could get a civil suit for damages from the asteroid company." He just screeched that mean laughter. I added, "And I told you, keep away from the black holes!"

He laughed some more, and said, "Oh, lower than a smiggs-troffle, what delightfully impudent pets you mammals will make now that we have these holes for weapons—and what joy it will give me to train you!" He was sort of singing to himself, more than to me, I guess. "First reduce this planet! Then the suppressor field is gone, and our forces come in to prepare the black holes! Then we launch one on every inhabited planet until we have destroyed your military power. And then—"

He didn't finish that sentence, just more of that chuckling, cackling, *mean* laugh.

I felt uneasy. It was beginning to look as though Torklemiggen was up to something more than just high jinks and deviltry. He was easing up on the black hole and kind of crooning to himself, mostly in that foreign language of his but now and then in English: "Oh, my darling little assault vessel, what destruction you will wreak! Ah, charming black hole, how catastrophic you will be! How foolish these mammals who think they can forbid me to come near you—"

Then, as they say, light dawned. "Torklemiggen," I shouted, "you've got the wrong idea! It's not just a traffic regulation that we have to stay away from black holes! It's a lot more serious than that!''

But I was too late. He was inside the Roche limit before I could finish.

They don't have black holes around Fomalhaut, it seems. Of course, if he'd stopped to think for a minute he'd have realized what would happen—but then, if Fomalhautians ever stopped to think they wouldn't be Fomalhautians.

I almost hate to tell you what happened next. It was pretty gross. The tidal forces seized his ship, and they stretched it.

I heard one caterwauling astonished yowl over the TBS. Then his transmitter failed. The ship ripped apart, and the pieces began to rain down into the Schwarzschild boundary and plasmaed. There was a quick, blinding flash of fall-in energy from the black hole, and that was all Torklemiggen would ever say or do or know.

I got out of there as fast as I could. I wasn't really feeling very sorry for him, either. The way he was talking there toward the end, he sounded as though he had some pretty dangerous ideas.

When I landed it was sundown at the field, and people were staring and pointing toward the place in the sky where Torklemiggen had smeared himself into the black hole. All bright purplish and orangey plasma clouds—it made a really beautiful sunset, I'll say that much for the guy! I didn't have time to admire it, though, because Tonda was waiting, and we just had minutes to get to the Deputy Census Director, division of Reclassification, before it closed.

But we made it.

Well, I said I had big news, didn't I? And that's it, because now your loving son is

Yours truly,
James Paul Aguilar-Madigan,
the newlywed!

WHEN JONNY COMES MARCHING HOME

by Timothy Zahn

Hugo award-winning author Timothy Zahn was born in Chicago in 1951, and grew up in the western suburb of Lombard. He attended Michigan State University in East Lansing, Michigan, earning a B.S. in physics in 1973, and moved to the University of Illinois in Champaign-Urbana, Illinois, for graduate work. He earned an M.S. degree there in physics in 1975. At the same time he began a new hobby: writing science fiction. At first a strictly spare-time occupation, over the next three years his avocation gradually developed into his career. He sold his first story, "Ernie," to *Analog* in December 1978.

Since then Zahn, who is now very much a full-time author, has published nearly sixty short stories and novelettes, fifteen novels, and three short fiction collections. He received his Hugo award in 1984 for the novella "Cascade Point" (*Analog,* December 1983), and has been nominated twice more. He is best known for his three *Star Wars* books, *Heir to the Empire, Dark Force Rising,* and *The Last Command.* Zahn's most recent novel, *Conquerors' Heritage,* is the second volume of his Conquerors Trilogy. The Zahn family now makes their home on the Oregon coast.

The late-afternoon sunlight glinted whitely off the distant mountains as the shuttle came to rest with only a slight bounce. Army-issue satchel slung over his shoulder, Jonny Moreau stepped out onto the landing pad, eyes darting everywhere. He had never been all that familiar with Horizon City, but even to him it was obvious the place had changed. There were half a dozen new buildings visible from the Port, and one or two older ones had disappeared. Several of the trees and many of

the other nearby plants were imported off-world varie-
ties, clearly holding their own against the native vegetation. But the wind was blowing in from the north, across
the plains and forests that were as yet untouched by
man, and with it came the sweet-sour aroma Jonny remembered so well from childhood. It was that scent that
finally, really convinced him.

He was home.

Taking a deep breath of the perfume, Jonny stepped
off the pad and walked the hundred meters to a long,
one-story building labeled "Horizon Customs: Entry
Point." Opening the outer door, he stepped inside.

A smiling man awaited him by a waist-high counter.
"Hello, Mr. Moreau; welcome back to Horizon. I'm
sorry—should I call you 'Cee-three Moreau'?"

" 'Mister' is fine," Jonny smiled. "I'm a civilian now."

"Of course; of course," the man said. He was still
smiling, but there seemed to be just a trace of tension
behind the geniality. "And glad of it, I suppose. I'm
Harti Bell, head of customs here. Your luggage is being
brought from the shuttle. In the meantime, I wonder if
I might inspect your satchel? Just a formality, really."

"Sure." Jonny slid the bag off his shoulder and placed
it on the counter, hearing the familiar faint hum from
his servos as he did so. Bell took the satchel and pulled,
as if trying to move it a few centimeters closer to him. It
moved maybe a centimeter; Bell nearly lost his balance.
Throwing an odd look at Jonny, he apparently changed
his mind and opened the bag where it lay.

By the time he finished, Jonny's two other cases had
been brought in. Bell went through them with quick efficiency, made a few notations on an official-looking
magcard, and finally looked up again, smile still in place.

"All set, Mr. Moreau," he said. "You're free to go."

"Thanks." Jonny put his satchel over his shoulder
once more and transferred the other two bags from the
counter to the floor. "Is Transcape Rentals still in business? I'll need a car to get to Cedar Lake."

"Sure is, but they've moved three blocks farther east.
Want to call a taxi"

"Thanks; I'll walk." Jonny held out his right hand. "Thanks a lot."

For just a moment the smile slipped. Then, almost warily, Bell took the outstretched hand. He let go as soon as he politely could.

Picking up his bags, Jonny nodded at Bell and the left the building.

Mayor Teague Stillman shook his head tiredly as he hefted the latest land-use proposal from the Cedar Lake city council. He had often thought it impossible for a frontier town of sixteen thousand people to generate as much paperwork as Cedar Lake seemed to do. Either official magforms had learned how to breed or else someone was importing them. Whichever, it was probably a Troftian plot.

There was a tap on his open door, and Stillman looked up to see Councilor Sutton Fraser standing in the doorway. "Come on in," he invited.

Fraser did so, closing the door behind him. "Too drafty for you?" Stillman asked mildly as Fraser sat down on one of the mayor's guest chairs.

"I got a call a few minutes ago from Harti Bell out at the Horizon Spaceport," Fraser began without preamble. "Jonny Moreau's back."

Stillman stared at the other for a moment, then shrugged slightly. "He had to come eventually. The war's over, after all. Most of the soldiers came back weeks ago."

"Yeah, but Jonny's not an ordinary soldier. Harti said he lifted a satchel that must have weighed thirty kilos with one hand. Effortlessly. The kid could probably tear a building apart if he got mad."

"Relax, Sut. I know the Moreau family. Jonny's a very even-tempered sort of guy."

"*Was,* you mean," Fraser said darkly. "He's been a Cobra for three years now, killing Trofts and watching them kill his friends. Who knows what that's done to him?"

"Probably instilled a deep dislike for war, if he's like

most soldiers. Aside from that, it hasn't done too much, I'd guess."

"You know better than that, Teague. The kid's dangerous; that's a simple fact. Ignoring it isn't going to do you any good."

"Calling him 'dangerous' is? What are you trying to do, start a panic?"

"I doubt that any panic's going to need my help to get started. Everybody in town's seen the idiot plate reports on Our Heroic Forces—they all know how badly the Cobras chewed up the Troft occupation forces on Adirondack and Silvern."

Stillman sighed. "Look. I'll admit there may be some problems with Jonny's readjustment to civilian life. Frankly, I would have been happier if he'd stayed in the service like a lot of the other Cobras did. But he didn't. Like it or not, Jonny's home, and we can either accept it calmly or run around screaming doom. He risked his life for three years; the least we can do is to give him a chance to forget the war and vanish back into the general population."

"Yeah. Maybe." Fraser shook his head slowly. "It's not going to be an easy road, though. Look, as long as I'm here, maybe you and I could draft some sort of announcement about this to the press. Try to get a jump on the rumors."

"Good idea. Hey, cheer up, Sut—soldiers have been coming home ever since mankind started having wars. We should be getting the hang of this by now."

"Yeah," Fraser growled. "Except that this is the first time since swords went out of fashion that soldiers have gotten to take their weapons home with them."

Stillman shrugged helplessly. "It's out of our hands. Come on; let's get to work."

Jonny pulled up in front of the modest plastframe house at the edge of town and turned off the car engine with a sigh of relief. The roads between Horizon City and Cedar Lake were rougher than he remembered them, and more than once he'd wished he had spent the extra money to rent a hover, even though the weekly rate was almost double that for wheeled vehicles. But he'd made it, with a minimum of kidney damage, and that was what mattered.

He retrieved his bags from the trunk, and as he set them down on the street a hand fell on his shoulder. He turned and looked five centimeters up into the clearest blue eyes he'd ever known. "Welcome home, Son," the man said.

"Hi, Dader," Jonny said, face breaking into a huge grin as he grasped the other's outstretched hand. "How've you been?"

Pearce Moreau's answer was interrupted by a crash and shriek from the front door of the house. Jonny turned to see his ten-year-old sister Gwen tearing across the lawn toward him, yelling like a banshee with a winning lottery ticket. Dropping into a crouch facing her, he opened his arms wide; and, as she flung herself at him, he grabbed her around the waist, straightened up, and threw her a half meter into the air above him. Her shrill laughter almost masked Pearce's sharp intake of breath. Catching her, Jonny lowered her back to the ground. "Boy, you've sure grown," he told her. "Pretty soon you'll be too big to toss around."

"Good," she panted. "Then you can teach me how to arm wrestle. C'mon and see my room, huh, Jonny?"

"I'll be along in a little bit," he told her. "I want to say hello to Momer first. She in the kitchen?"

"Yes," Pearce said. "Why don't you go on ahead, Gwen. I'd like to talk to Jonny for a moment."

"Okay," she chirped. Squeezing Jonny's hand, she scampered back toward the house.

"She's got her room papered with articles and pictures from the past three years," Pearce explained as he and Jonny collected Jonny's luggage. "Everything she could get hard copies of that had anything to do with the Cobras."

"You disapprove?"

"Of what—that she idolizes you? Good heavens, no. Why?"

"You seem a bit nervous."

"Oh. I guess I was a little startled when you tossed Gwen in the air a minute ago."

"I've been using the servos for quite a while now," Jonny pointed out mildly as they headed toward the house. "I really *do* know how to use my strength safely."

"I know, I know. Hell, I used exo-skeleton gear myself in the Minthistin War, you know, when I was your age. But it was pretty bulky, and you couldn't ever forget you were wearing it. I guess . . . well, I suppose I was worried that you'd forget yourself."

Jonny shrugged. "Actually, I'm probably in better control than you ever were, since I don't have to have two sets of responses—with power amplification and without. The servos and ceramic laminae are going to be with me the rest of my life, and I've long since gotten used to them."

Pearce nodded. "Okay." He paused, then continued, "Look, Jonny, as long as we're on the subject . . . the Army's letter to us said that 'most' of your Cobra gear would be removed before you came home. What did they—I mean, what do you still have?"

Jonny sighed. "I wish they'd just come out and listed the stuff instead of being coy like that. It makes it sound like I'm still a walking tank. The truth is that, aside from the skeletal laminae and servos, all I have is the fire-control nanocomputer—which hasn't got much to do now except assist with the servos—and two small lasers in my little fingers, which they couldn't remove without amputation. And the servo power supply, of course. Everything else—the arcthrower capacitors, the antiarmor laser, and all the sonic weapons—are gone." So was the power pack's self-destruct capability, but that subject was best left alone.

"Okay," Pearce said. "Sorry to bring it up, but your momer and I were a little nervous."

"That's all right."

They were at the house now. Entering, they went to the bedroom Jonny had shared with his younger brother Jame for most of the last nineteen years.

"Where's Jame, by the way?" Jonny asked as he piled his bags by his bed.

"Out at New Persius picking up a spare laser tube for the bodywork welder down at the shop. We've only got one working at the moment and can't risk it going out on us. Parts have been nearly impossible to get lately— a side effect of war, you know." He snapped his fingers. "Say. Those little lasers you have—can you weld with them?"

"I can spot-weld with them, yes. They were designed to work on metals, as a matter of fact."

"Great. Maybe you could give us a hand until we can get parts for the other lasers. How about it?"

Jonny hesitated. "Uh ... frankly, Dader, I'd rather not. I don't ... well, the lasers remind me too much of ... other things."

"I don't understand," Pearce said, a frown beginning to crease his forehead. "You ashamed of what you did? Hell, boy, you should be *proud*. You fought well, protected the Dominion from those invading Troftian devils, and got back alive. That's a record few people can match."

"I'm not ashamed; not really. I mean, I knew pretty much what I was getting into when I joined the Cobras, and I don't really have any regrets. It's just ... this war was different from yours, Dader. You were on a star ship, fighting the Minthisti in space. You never saw any ground action. You didn't have to infiltrate planets the Trofts had taken and fight them face-to-face. You didn't have to look at the bodies of human civilians who'd been caught in the fighting." Jonny took a deep breath and forced his throat muscles to relax. "I'd just like to try and forget all of that, at least for a while."

Pearce remained silent for a moment. Then he laid a hand on his son's shoulder. "You're right, Jonny, I never had to do anything like that. I'm not sure I can ever understand all of what it meant to you. I'll do my best, though. Okay?"

"Yeah, Dader. Thanks."

"Sure. Come on, let's go see your momer. Then you can go take a look at Gwen's room."

Dinner that night was a festive occasion, reminding Jonny of his rare trips back home when he was going to college in New Persius. Irena Moreau had cooked her son's favorite meal—center-fried wild balis—and the conversation was light and frequently punctuated by laughter. The warmth and love seemed to Jonny to fill the room, surrounding the five of them with an invisible defense perimeter. For the first time since his basic training on Asgard he felt truly safe, and tensions he'd forgotten he ever had began to drain slowly from his muscles.

It took most of the meal for the others to bring Jonny up to date on the doings of Cedar Lake's people, so it wasn't until Irena brought out the cahve that conversation turned to Jonny's plans.

"I'm not really sure," Jonny confessed, holding his mug of cahve with both hands, letting that heat soak into his palms. "I suppose I could go back to school and pick up my computer tech certificate. But that would take another year, and I'm not crazy about being a student again. Not now, anyway."

Across the table Jonny's brother Jame sipped cautiously at his mug. "If you went to work, what sort of job would you like?" he asked.

"Well, I'd thought of coming back to the shop with Dader, but you seem to be pretty well settled in there."

Jame darted a glance at his father. "Heck, Jonny, there's enough work in town for three of us. Right, Dader?"

"Sure," Pearce replied with only the barest hesitation.

"Thanks," Jonny said, "but it sounds like you're really too low on equipment for me to be very useful. My thought is that maybe I could work somewhere on my own for a few months until we can afford to outfit the shop for three workers. Then, if there's enough business around, I could come and work for you."

Pearce nodded. "That sounds really good, Jonny. I think that's the best way to do it."

"So back to the original question," Jame said. "What kind of job are you going to get?"

Jonny held his mug to his lips for a moment, savoring the rich, minty aroma. Army cahve had a fair taste and plenty of stimulant, but was completely devoid of the fragrance that made a good scent-drink so enjoyable. "I've learned a lot about civil engineering in the past three years, especially in the uses of explosives and sonic cutting tools. I figure I'll try one of the road construction or mining companies you were telling me about that are working south of town."

"Can't hurt to try," Pearce shrugged. "Going to take a few days off first?"

"Nope—I'll head out there tomorrow morning. I figured I'd drive around town for a while this evening, though; get reacquainted with the area. Can I help with the dishes before I go?"

"Don't be silly," Irena smiled at him. "Relax and enjoy yourself."

"Tonight, that is," Jame amended. "Tomorrow you'll be put out in the salt mines with the rest of the new slaves."

Jonny leveled a finger at him. "Beware the darkness of the night," he said with mock seriousness. "There just may be a pillow out there with your name on it." He turned back to his parents.

"Okay if I take off, then? Anything you need in town?"

"I just shopped today," Irena told him.

"Go ahead, son," Pearce said.

"I'll be back before it gets too late." Jonny downed the last of his cahve and stood up. "Great dinner, Momer; thanks a lot."

He left the room and headed toward the front door. To his mild surprise, Jame tagged along. "You coming with me?" Jonny asked.

"Just to the car," Jame said. He was silent until they were outside the house. "I wanted to clue you in on a couple of things before you left," he said as they set off across the lawn.

"Okay; shoot."

"Number one: I think you ought to be careful about pointing your finger at people, like you did at me a few minutes ago. Especially when you're looking angry or even just serious."

Jonny blinked. "Hey, I didn't mean anything by that. I was just kidding around."

"*I* know that, and it didn't bother me. Someone who doesn't know you as well might have dived under the table."

"I don't get it. Why?"

Jame shrugged, but met his brother's eyes. "They're a little afraid of you," he said bluntly. "Everybody followed the war news pretty closely out here. They all know what Cobras can do."

"*Could* do. Most of my armament's gone. And even if it wasn't, I sure wouldn't use it on anyone. I'm sick of fighting."

"I know. But they won't know that, not at first. I'm not just guessing here, Jonny; I've talked to a lot of kids since the war ended, and they're pretty nervous about seeing you again. You'd be surprised how many of them are scared that you'll remember some old high school grudge and come by to settle accounts."

"Oh, come on, Jame. That's ridiculous!"

"That's what I tell the ones that ask me about it, but they don't seem convinced. And it looks like some of their parents have picked up on the attitude, too, and— heck, you know how news travels around here. I think you're going to have to bend over backwards for a while, be as harmless as a dove with blunted toenails. Prove to them they don't have to be afraid of you."

Jonny snorted. "The whole thing is silly, but okay. I'll be a good little boy."

"Great." Jame hesitated. "Now for number two, I guess. Were you planning to stop by and see Alyse Carne tonight?"

"That thought *had* crossed my mind," Jonny grinned. "Why? Has she moved?"

"No, she's still living out on Blakeley Street. I just thought that maybe you'd better call before you go over there. To make sure she .. isn't busy."

Jonny's grin faded. "What are you getting at? She living with someone?"

"Oh, no, it hasn't gone that far," Jame said quickly.

"But she's been seeing Doane Etherege a lot lately and—well, he's been calling her his girlfriend."

Jonny nodded slowly. "We'll have to break him of that habit, I guess." He forced a smile. "Don't worry, though; I'll steal her back from him in a civilized manner."

"Yeah, well, good luck. I'll warn you, though; he's not the drip he used to be."

"I'll keep that in mind." Jonny slid his hand idly along the smooth metal of the car. The idea of a drive into town had lost a lot of its appeal in the past few minutes. Perhaps he should simply stay home.

Jame seemed to sense the indecision. "You still going out?"

Jonny pursed his lips. "Yeah, I think I'll take a quick look around." Opening the door, he slid in and started the engine. "Don't wait up," he added as he drove off.

After all, he told himself firmly, he had not fought Trofts for three years to come home and hide from his own people.

Nevertheless, the trip through Cedar Lake felt more like a reconnaissance mission than the victorious homecoming he had envisioned. He covered most of the town, but stayed in the car and didn't wave or call to the people he recognized. He avoided driving by Alyse Carne's apartment building completely. And he was home within an hour.

For many years the only ground link between Cedar Lake and the tiny farming community to the southwest, Boyar, was a bumpy, one-and-three-quarters-lane perm-turf road that paralleled the Shard Mountains to the west. It had been considered adequate for so long simply because there was little in or around Boyar that anyone in Cedar Lake would want. Boyar's crops went to Horizon City by way of New Persius; supplies traveled the same route in reverse.

Now, however, all that had changed. A large vein of the cesium-bearing ore pollucite had been rediscovered north of Boyar; and as the mining companies moved in, so did the road construction crews. The facility for extracting the cesium was, for various technical reasons, being built near Cedar Lake, and a multi-lane highway would be necessary to get the ore to it.

Jonny found the road foreman near a large outcrop of granite that lay across the road's projected path. "You Sampson Grange?" he asked.

"Yeah. You?"

"Jonny Moreau. Mr. Oberland told me to check with you about a job. I've had training in lasers, explosives, and sonic blasting equipment."

"Well actually, kid, I—waitaminit. Jonny Moreau the Cobra?"

"*Ex*-Cobra, yes."

Grange shifted his spitstick in his mouth, eyes narrowing slightly. "Yeah, I can use you, I guess. Straight level-eight pay."

That was two levels up from minimum. "Fine. Thanks very much." Jonny nodded toward the granite outcrop. "You need this out of the way?"

"Yeah, but that'll keep. C'mon back here a minute."

He led Jonny to where a group of eight men were struggling to unload huge rolls of pretop paper from a truck to the side of the new road. It took three or four men to handle each roll and they were puffing and swearing with the effort.

"Boys, this is Jonny Moreau," Grange told them. "Jonny, we've got to get this stuff out right away so the truck can go back for another load. Give them a hand, okay?" Without waiting for an answer, he strode off.

Reluctantly, Jonny clambered onto the truck. This wasn't exactly what he'd had in mind. The other men regarded him coolly, and Jonny heard the word "Cobra" being whispered to the two or three who hadn't recognized him. Determined not to let it throw him, he stepped over to the nearest roll and said, "Can someone give me a hand with this?"

Nobody moved. "Wouldn't we just be in the way?" one of them, a husky laborer, suggested with more than a little truculence.

Jonny kept his voice steady. "Look, I'm willing to do my share."

"That seems fair," someone else said sarcastically. "It was our taxes that paid to make you into a superman in the first place. And I figure Grange is paying you enough money for four men. So fine; we got the first eight rolls down and you can get the last five. That fair enough, men?"

There was a general murmur of agreement. Jonny studied their faces for moment, looking for some sign of sympathy or support. But all he saw was hostility, envy, and wariness. "All right," he said softly.

Bending his knees slightly, he hugged the roll of pretop to his chest. Servos whining in his ears, he straightened up and carefully carried the roll to the end of the truck bed. Setting it down, he jumped to the ground, picked it up again and placed it off the road with the others. Then, hopping back into the truck, he went to the next roll.

None of the other workers had moved, but their expressions had changed. Fear now dominated everything else. It was one thing, Jonny reflected bitterly, to watch films of Cobras shooting up Trofts on the plate. It was something else entirely to watch one lift two hundred kilos right in front of you. Cursing inwardly, he finished moving the rolls as quickly as possible and then, without a word, went off in search of Sampson Grange.

He found the other busy inventorying sacks of hardener mix and was immediately pressed into service to carry them to the proper workers. That job led to a succession of similar tasks over the next few hours. Jonny tried to be discreet, but the news about him traveled faster than he did. Most of the workers were less hostile toward him than the first group had been, but it was still like working on a stage, and Jonny began to fume inwardly at the wary politeness and sidelong glances.

Finally, just before noon, he caught on, and once more he tracked down the foreman. "I don't like being maneuvered by people, Mr. Grange," he told the other angrily. "I signed on here to help with blasting and demolition work. Instead, you've got me carrying stuff around like a pack mule."

Grange slid his spitstick to a corner of his mouth and regarded Jonny coolly. "I signed you up at level-eight to work on the road. I never said what you were gonna do."

"That's rotten. You knew what I wanted."

"So what? What the hell—you want special privileges or something? I got guys who have *certificates* in demolition work—I should replace them with a kid who's never even seen a real tape on the subject?"

Jonny opened his mouth, but none of the words he wanted to say would come out. Grange shrugged. "Look, kid," he said, not unkindly. "I got nothing against you. Hell, I'm a vet myself. But you haven't got any training or experience in road work. We can use more laborers, sure, and that super-revved body of yours makes you worth at least two men—that's why I'm paying you level-eight. Other than that, frankly, you aren't worth much to us. Take it or don't; it's up to you."

"Thanks, but no go," Jonny gritted out.

"Okay." Grange took out a card and scribbled on it. "Take this to the main office in Cedar Lake and they'll give you your pay. And come back if you change your mind."

Jonny took the card and left, trying to ignore the hundred pairs of eyes he could feel boring into his back.

The house was deserted when he arrived home, a condition for which he was grateful. He'd had time to cool down during the drive and now just wanted some time to be alone. As a Cobra he'd been unused to flat-out failure; if the Trofts foiled an attack he had simply to fall back and try a new assault. But the rules here were different, and he wasn't getting the hang of them as quickly as he'd expected to.

Nevertheless, he was a long way yet from defeat. Dialing up last night's newssheet, he turned to the employment section. Most of the jobs being offered were level-ten laborer types, but there was a fair sprinkling of the more professional sort that he was looking for. Settling himself comfortably in front of the screen, he picked up the pad and stylus always kept by the phone and began to make notes.

His final list of prospects covered nearly two pages, and he spent most of the rest of the afternoon making phone calls. It was a sobering and frustrating experience; and in the end he found himself with only two interviews, both for the following morning.

By then it was nearly dinner time. Stuffing the pages of notes into a pocket, he headed for the kitchen to offer his mother a hand with the cooking.

Irena smiled at him as he entered. "Any luck with the job hunt?" she asked.

"A little," he told her. She had arrived home some hours earlier and had already heard a capsule summary of his morning with the road crew. "I've got two interviews tomorrow—Svetlanov Electronics and Outworld Mining. And I'm lucky to get even that many."

She patted his arm. "You'll find something. Don't worry." A sound outside made her glance out the window. "Your dader and Jame are home. Oh, and there's someone with them."

Jonny looked out. A second car had pulled to the curb behind Pearce and Jame. As he watched, a tall, somewhat paunchy man got out and joined the other two in walking toward the house. "He looks familiar, Momer, but I can't place him."

"That's Teague Stillman, the mayor," she identified him, sounding surprised. "I wonder why he's here." Whipping off her apron, she dried her hands and hurried into the living room. Jonny followed more slowly, unconsciously taking up a back-up position across the living room from the front door.

The door opened just as Irena reached it. "Hi, honey," Pearce greeted his wife as the three men entered. "Teague stopped by the shop just as we were closing up and I invited him to come over for a few minutes."

"How nice," Irena said in her best hostess voice. "It's been a long time since we've seen you, Teague. How is Sharene?"

"She's fine, Irena," Stillman said, "although she says *she* doesn't see me enough these days, either. Actually,

I just stopped by to see if Jonny was home from work yet."

"Yes, I am," Jonny said, coming forward. "Congratulations on winning your election last year, Mr. Stillman. I'm afraid I didn't make it to the polls."

Stillman laughed and reached out his hand to grasp Jonny's briefly. He seemed relaxed and friendly . . . and yet, right around the eyes, Jonny could see a touch of the caution that he'd seen so often in the road workers. "I'd have sent you an absentee ballot if I'd known exactly where you were," the mayor joked. "Welcome home, Jonny."

"Thank you, sir."

"Shall we sit down?" Irena suggested.

They moved into the living room proper, Stillman and the Moreau parents exchanging small talk all the while. Jame had yet to say a word, Jonny noted, and the younger boy took a seat in a corner, away from the others.

"The reason I wanted to talk to you, Jonny," Stillman said when they were all settled, "was that the city council and I would like to have a sort of 'welcome home' ceremony for you in the park next week. Nothing too spectacular, really; just a short parade through town, followed by a couple of speeches—you don't have to make one if you don't want to—and then some fireworks and perhaps a torchlight procession. What do you think?"

Jonny hesitated, but there was no way to say this diplomatically. "Thanks, but I really don't want you to do that."

Pearce's proud smile vanished. "What do you mean, Jonny? Why not?"

"Because I don't want to get up in front of a whole bunch of people and get cheered at. It's embarrassing and—well, it's embarrassing. I don't want any fuss made over me."

"Jonny, the town wants to honor you for what you did," Stillman said soothingly, as if afraid Jonny was becoming angry.

That thought was irritating. "The greatest honor it

could give me would be to stop treating me like a freak," he retorted.

"Son—" Pearce began warningly.

"Dader, if Jonny doesn't want any official hoopla, it seems to me the subject is closed," Jame spoke up unexpectedly from his corner. "Unless you all plan to chain him to the speakers' platform."

There was a moment of uncomfortable silence. Then Stillman shifted in his seat. 'Well, if Jonny doesn't want this, there's no reason to discuss it further." He stood up, the others quickly following suit. "I really ought to get home now."

"Give Sharene our best," Irena said.

"I will," Stillman nodded. "We'll have to try and get together soon. Goodby, all; and once more, welcome home, Jonny."

"I'll walk you to your car," Pearce said, clearly angry but trying to hide it.

The two men left. Irena looked questioningly at Jonny, but all she said before disappearing back into the kitchen was, "You boys wash up and call Gwen from her room; dinner will be ready soon."

"You okay?" Jame asked softly when his mother had gone.

"Yeah. Thanks for backing me up." Jonny shook his head. "They don't understand."

"I'm not sure I do, either. Is it because of what I said about people being afraid of you?"

"Oh, no, that had nothing to do with it." Jonny sighed. "Look. Horizon is all the way across the Dominion from where the war was fought. You weren't within fifty light-years of a Troft even at their deepest penetration. How can I accept the praise of people who have no idea what they're cheering for? It'd just be going through the motions." He turned his head to stare out the window. "The people of Adirondack had a big ceremony after our Cobra teams forced the Trofts off their planet. There was nothing of duty or obligation about it—when they cheered, you could tell they knew *why* they were doing so. And they also knew who they were there to honor. Not those of us who were on the stage, but those who weren't. Instead of a torchlight procession, they sang a requiem." He turned back to face Jame. "How could I watch Cedar Lake's fireworks after that?"

Jame touched his brother's arm and nodded silently. "I'll go call Gwen," he said a moment later.

Pearce came back into the house. He said nothing, but flashed Jonny a glare that looked to be at least fifty percent disappointment. Then he disappeared into the kitchen. Sighing, Jonny went to wash his hands.

Dinner was very quiet that evening.

The interviews the next morning were complete washouts, with the two prospective employers clearly seeing him just out of politeness. Gritting his teeth, Jonny returned home and dialed up the newssheet once again. He lowered his sights somewhat this time, and his new list came out to be three and a half pages long. Doggedly, he began making the calls.

By the time Jame came to bring him to dinner he had exhausted all the numbers on the list. "Not even any interviews this time," he told Jame disgustedly as they walked into the dining room where the others were waiting. "News really does travel in this town, doesn't it?"

"Come on, Jonny, there has to be *someone* around who doesn't care that you're an ex-Cobra," Jame said.

"Perhaps you should lower your standards a bit," Pearce suggested. "Working as a laborer wouldn't hurt you any."

"Or maybe you could be a patroller," Gwen spoke up. "That would be neat."

Jonny shook his head. "I've tried being a laborer, remember? The men on the road crew were either afraid of me or thought I was trying to show them up."

"But once they got to know you, things would be different," Irena said.

"Or maybe if they had a better idea of what you'd done for the Dominion they'd respect you more," Pearce added.

"No, Dader." Jonny had tried explaining to his father why he didn't want Cedar Lake to honor him publicly, and the elder Moreau had listened and said he understood. But Jonny doubted that he really did, and Pearce clearly hadn't given up trying to change his son's mind. "I probably would be a good patroller, Gwen," he added to his sister, "but I think it would remind me too much of some of the things I had to do in the army."

"Well, then, maybe you should go back to school," Irena suggested.

"No!" Jonny snapped with a sudden flash of anger.

A stunned silence filled the room. Inhaling deeply, Jonny forced himself to calm down. "Look, I know you're all trying to be helpful, and I appreciate it. But I'm twenty-four years old now and capable of handling my own problems." Abruptly, he put down his fork and stood up. "I'm not hungry. I think I'll got out for a while."

Minutes later he was driving down the street, wondering what he should do. There was a brand-new pleasure center in town, he knew, but he wasn't in the mood for large groups of people. He mentally ran through a list of old friends, but that was just for practice; he knew where he really wanted to go. Jame had suggested he call Alyse Carne before dropping in on her, but Jonny was in a perverse mood. Turning at the next corner, he headed for Blakeley Street.

Alyse seemed surprised when he announced himself over her apartment building's security intercom, but she was all smiles as she opened her door. "Jonny, it's good to see you," she said, holding out her hand.

"Hi, Alyse." He smiled back, taking her hand and stepping into her apartment, closing the door behind him. "I was afraid you'd forgotten about me while I was gone."

Her eyes glowed. "Not likely," she murmured . . . and suddenly she was in his arms.

After a long minute she gently pulled away. "Why don't we sit down?" she suggested. "We've got three years to catch up on."

"Anything wrong?" he asked her.

"No. Why?"

"You seem a little nervous. I thought you might have a date or something."

She flushed. "Not tonight. I guess you know I've been seeing Doane."

"Yes. How serious is it, Alyse? I deserve to know."

"I like him," she said, shrugging uncomfortably. "I suppose I started going with him to insulate myself from pain in case you . . . didn't come back. I didn't expect it to grow like it did, though. . . ." Her voice trailed off.

"You don't have to make any decisions tonight," Jonny said after a moment. "Except whether or not you'll spend the evening with me."

She smiled. "That one's easy. Have you eaten yet, or shall I just make us some cohve?"

They talked until nearly midnight, and when Jonny finally left he had recaptured the contentment he'd felt on first arriving at Cedar Lake. Doane Etherege would soon fade back into the woodwork, he was sure, and with Alyse again at his side, there was nothing he couldn't accomplish. His mind was busy with plans for the future as he let himself into the Moreau house and tiptoed to his bedroom.

"Jonny?" a whisper came from across the room. "You okay?"

"Fine, Jame—just great," Jonny whispered back.

"How is Alyse?"

Jonny chuckled. "Go to sleep, Jame."

"That's nice. Good night, Jonny."

One by one, the great plans crumbled.

With agonizing regularity, employers kept turning Jonny down, and he was eventually forced into a succession of the level-nine and -ten manual jobs he had hoped so desperately to avoid. None of the jobs lasted very long; the resentment and fear of his fellow workers invariably generated an atmosphere of sullen animosity which Jonny found hard to take for more than a few days at a time.

As his search for permanent employment faltered, so did his relationship with Alyse. She remained friendly and willing to spend time with him, but there was a distance between them that hadn't existed before the war. To make matters worse, Doane refused to withdraw gracefully from the field, and aggressively competed with him for Alyse's time and attention.

But worst of all, from Jonny's point of view, was the unexpected trouble his problems had brought upon the rest of the family.

His parents and Jame, he knew, could stand the glances, whispered comments, and mild stigma that went with being related to an ex-Cobra. But it hurt him terribly to watch Gwen retreat into herself from the half-unintentional cruelty of her peers. More than once Jonny considered leaving Horizon and returning to active service, freeing his family from the cross-fire he had put them into. But to leave now would be to admit defeat, and that was something he couldn't bring himself to do.

And so matters precariously stood for three months, until the night of the accident. Or the murder, as some called it.

Sitting in his parked car, watching the last rays from the setting sun, Jonny let the anger and frustration drain out of him and wondered what to do next. He had just stormed out of Alyse's apartment after their latest fight, the tenth or so since his return. Like the job situation, things with Alyse seemed to be getting worse instead of better. Unlike the former, he could only blame himself for the problems in his love life.

The sun was completely down by the time he felt capable of driving safely. The sensible thing would be to go home, of course. But the rest of the Moreau family was out to dinner, and the thought of being alone in the house bothered him for some reason. What he needed, he decided, was something that would completely take his mind off his problems. Starting the car, he drove into the center of town where the Raptopia, Cedar Lake's new pleasure center, was located.

Jonny had been in pleasure centers on three other worlds while in the army, and by their standards the Raptopia was decidedly unsophisticated. There were fifteen rooms and galleries, each offering its own combination of sensual stimuli for customers to choose from. The choices seemed limited, however, to permutations of the traditional recreations: music, food and drink, mood drugs, light shows, games, and thermal booths. The extreme physical and intellectual ends of the pleasure spectrum, personified by prostitutes and professional conversationalists, were conspicuous by their absence.

Jonny wandered around for a few minutes before settling on a room with a loud music group and wildly flickering light show. Visibility under such conditions was poor, and as long as he kept his distance from the other patrons, he was unlikely to be recognized. Finding a vacant area of the contoured softfloor, he sat down.

The music was good, if dated—he'd heard the same songs three years ago in the pleasure centers on Asgard—and he began to relax as the light and sound swept like a cleansing wave over his mind. So engrossed did he become that he didn't notice the group of teenaged kids that came up behind him until one of them nudged him with the tip of his shoe.

"Hi there, Cobra," he said as Jonny looked up. "What's new?"

"Uh, not much," Jonny replied cautiously. There were seven of them, he noted; three girls and four boys, all dressed in the current teen-age styles so deplored by Cedar Lake's more conservative adults. "Do I know you?"

The girls giggled. "Naw," another of the boys drawled. "We just figured everybody ought to know there's a celebrity here. Let's tell 'em, huh?"

Slowly, Jonny rose to his feet to face them. From his new vantage point he could see that all seven had the shining eyes and rapid breathing of heavy stim-drug users. "I don't think that's necessary," he said.

"You want to fight about it?" the first boy said, dropping into a caricature of a fighting stance. "C'mon, Cobra. Show us what you can do."

Wordlessly, Jonny turned and walked toward the door, followed by the giggling group. As he reached the exit the two talkative boys pushed past him and stood in the doorway, blocking it.

"Can't leave 'til you show us a trick," one said.

Jonny looked him in the eye, successfully resisting the

urge to bounce the smart-mouth off the nearest wall. Instead, he picked up both boys by their belts, held them high for a moment, and then turned and set them down to the side of the doorway. A gentle push sent them sprawling onto the softfloor. "I suggest you all stay here and enjoy the music," he told the rest of the group as they stared at him with wide eyes.

"Turkey hop," one of the smartmouths muttered. Jonny ignored the apparent insult and strode from the room, confident that they wouldn't follow him. They didn't.

But the mood of the evening was broken. Jonny tried two or three other rooms for a few minutes each, hoping to regain the relaxed abandonment he'd felt earlier. But it was no use, and within a quarter hour he was back outside the Raptopia, walking through the cool night air toward his car, parked across the street a block away.

He had covered the block and was just starting to cross the road when he became aware of the low hum of an idling car nearby. He turned to look back along the street—and in that instant a car rolling gently along the curb suddenly switched on its lights and, with a squeal of tires, hurtled directly toward him.

There was no time for thought or human reaction, but Jonny had no need of either. Acting with a will of its own, his body launched itself into a flat, ten-meter dive that took him to the walkway on the far side of the street. He landed on his right shoulder, rolling expertly to absorb the impact, but crashed painfully into a building before he could stop completely. The car roared past; and as it did so two needles of light flashed from Jonny's little fingers to the car's two right-hand tires. The double blowout was audible even over the engine noise. Instantly out of control, the car swerved violently, bounced off two parked cars, and finally crashed broadside into the corner of a building.

Aching all over, Jonny got to his feet and ran to the car. Ignoring the gathering crowd, he worked feverishly on the crumpled metal, and had the door open by the time a rescue unit arrived. But his effort was in vain.

The car's driver was already dead, and his passenger died of internal injuries on the way to the hospital.

They were the two teen-aged boys who had accosted Jonny in the Raptopia.

The sound of his door opening broke Mayor Stillman's train of thought, and he turned from his contemplation of the morning sky in time to see Sutton Fraser closing the door behind him. "Don't you ever knock?" he asked the city councilor irritably.

"You can stare out the window later," Fraser said, pulling a chair close to the desk and sitting down. "Right now we've got to talk."

Stillman sighed. "Jonny Moreau?"

"You got it. It's been over a week now, Teague, and the tension out there's not going down. People in my district are still asking why Jonny's not in custody."

"We've been through this, remember? The legal department in Horizon City has the patroller report; until they make a decision we're treating it as self-defense."

"Oh, come on. You know the kids would have swerved to miss Jonny. That's how that stupid turkey hop is played—okay, okay, I realize Jonny didn't know that. But did *you* know he fired on the car *after* it had passed him? I've got no less than three witnesses now that say that."

"So have the patrollers. I'll admit I don't understand that part. Maybe it's something from his combat training."

"Great," Fraser muttered.

Stillman's intercom buzzed. "Mayor Stillman, there's a Mr. Vanis D'arl to see you," his secretary announced.

Stillman glanced questioningly at Fraser, who shrugged and shook his head. "Send him in," Stillman said.

The door opened and a slender, dark-haired man entered and walked toward the desk. His appearance, clothing, and walk identified him as an offworlder before he had taken two steps. "Mr. D'arl," Stillman said as he and Fraser rose to their feet, "I'm Mayor Teague

Stillman; this is Councilor Sutton Fraser. What can we do for you?"

D'arl produced a gold ID pin. "Vanis D'arl, representing the Central Committee of the Dominion of Man." His voice was slightly accented.

Out of the corner of his eye Stillman saw Fraser stiffen. His own knees felt a little weak. "Very honored to meet you, sir. Won't you sit down?"

"Thank you." D'arl took the chair Fraser had been sitting in. The councilor moved to a seat farther from the desk, possibly hoping to be less conspicuous there.

"This is mainly an informal courtesy call, Mr. Stillman," D'arl said. "However, all of what I'm going to tell you is to be considered confidential Dominion business." He waited for both men to nod agreement before continuing. "I've just come from Horizon City, where all pending charges against Reserve Cobra-Three Jonny Moreau have been ordered dropped."

"I see," Stillman said. "May I ask why the Central Committee is taking an interest in this case?"

"Cee-three Moreau is still technically under army jurisdiction, since he can be called into active service at any time. Hence our authority."

"Are you familiar with the incident that Mr.—uh, Cee-three Moreau was involved in?"

"Yes, and I understand the doubts both you and the planetary authorities have had about the circumstances. However, Moreau cannot be held responsible for his actions at that time. He was under attack and acted accordingly."

"His combat training is that strong?"

"Not precisely." D'arl hesitated. "I dislike having to tell you this, as it has been a military secret up until recently. But you need to understand the situation. Have you ever wondered what the name 'Cobra' stands for?"

"Why . . ." Stillman floundered, caught off guard by the question. "I assumed it referred to the Terran snake."

"Only secondarily. It's an acronym for 'Computerized Body Reflex Armament.' I'm sure you know about the ceramic laminae on Moreau's bones and the servo network connected to it, as well as the various weapon systems. You may also know about the nanocomputer implanted just under his brain. This is where the ... problem ... originates.

"You must understand that a soldier, especially a guerrilla in enemy-held territory, needs a good set of combat reflexes if he is to survive. Training can give him some of what he needs, but this takes a long time and has its limits. Therefore, since a computer was going to be necessary for equipment monitoring and fire control anyway, a set of combat reflexes was also programmed in,"

Stillman's eyes narrowed. "What exactly are you implying, Mr. D'arl?"

"I am *saying,* not implying, that Moreau will react instantly, and with very little conscious control, to any deadly attack launched at him. In this particular case the pattern shows clearly that this is what happened. He evaded the initial attack, but was left in a vulnerable position—off his feet and away from cover—and was thus forced to counterattack. Without specific programming his computer didn't know how to disable the car and so aimed, by default, for the wheels. Part of its job is to monitor the weapon systems, so it knew the metalwork lasers were all it had left. So it used them."

A deathly silence filled the room. "Let me get this straight," Stillman said at last. "The Army made Jonny Moreau into an automated fighting machine who will react lethally to anything that even *looks* like an attack? And then let him come back to us without making any attempt to change that?"

"The system was designed to defend a soldier in enemy territory," D'arl said. "It's not nearly as hair-trigger as you seem to imagine. And as for 'letting' him come back like that, there was no other choice. The computer cannot be reprogrammed or removed without risking brain damage."

"What the *hell*!" Fraser had apparently forgotten he was suppose to be courteous to Dominion representatives. "What damn idiot came up with *that* idea?"

D'arl turned to face the councilor. "The Central Committee is tolerant of criticism, Mr. Fraser." His voice was even, but had an edge to it. "But your tone is unacceptable."

Fraser refused to shrivel. "Never mind that. How did you expect us to cope with him when he reacts to attacks like that?" He snorted. "*Attacks,* Two kids playing a game!"

"Use your head," D'arl snapped. "We couldn't risk having a Cobra captured by the Trofts and sent back to us with his computer reprogrammed. The Cobras were soldiers, first and foremost, and every tool and weapon they had made perfect sense from a military standpoint."

"Didn't it occur to anyone that the war would be over someday? And that the Cobras would be going home to civilian life?"

"Less powerful equipment might well have cost the dominion the war, and would certainly have cost many more Cobras their lives. At any rate, it's done now, and you'll just have to learn to live with it like everyone else."

Stillman frowned. " 'Everyone else?' How widespread is this problem?"

D'arl turned back to face the mayor, looking annoyed that he'd let that hint slip out. "It's not good," he admitted. "We tried to keep as many Cobras as possible in the service after the war, but all were legally free to leave and several hundred did so. Most of those are having trouble of one kind or another. We're trying to help them, but it's difficult to do. People are afraid of them, and that hampers our efforts."

"Can you do anything to help Jonny?"

D'arl shrugged slightly. "I don't know. He's an unusual case, in that he came back to a small home town where everyone knew what he was. I suppose it might help to move him to another planet, maybe give him a new name. But people would eventually find out. Cobra strength is hard to hide for long."

"So are Cobra reflexes," Stillman nodded grimly. "Besides, Jonny's family is here. I don't think he'd like leaving them."

"That's why I'm not recommending his relocation,

though that's the usual procedure in cases like this,"
D'arl said. "Most Cobras don't have the kind of close
family support he does. It's a strong point in his favor."
He stood up. "I'll be leaving Horizon tomorrow morning, but I'll be within a few days' flight of here for the
next month. If anything happens I can be reached
through the Dominion governor-general's office in Horizon City."

Stillman rose from his chair. "I trust the Central Committee will be trying to come up with some kind of solution to this problem."

D'arl met his gaze evenly. "Mr. Stillman, the government is far more concerned about this situation than
even you are. You see one minor frontier town; we see
seventy worlds. If an answer exists, we'll find it."

"And what do we do in the meantime?" Fraser
asked heavily.

"Your best, of course. Good day to you."

Jame paused outside the door, took a single deep
breath, and knocked lightly. There was no answer. He
raised his hand to knock again, then thought better of
it. After all, it was *his* bedroom, too. Opening the door,
he went in.

Seated at Jame's writing desk, hands curled into fists
in front of him, Jonny was staring out the window. Jame
cleared his throat.

"Hello, Jame," Jonny said, without turning.

"Hi." The desk, Jame saw, was covered with official-
looking magforms. "I just dropped by to tell you that
dinner will be ready in about fifteen minutes." He nodded at the desk. "What're you up to?"

"Filling out some college applications."

"Oh. Decided to go back to school?"

Jonny shrugged. "I might as well."

Stepping to his brother's side, Jame scanned the magforms. University of Rajput, Bomu Technical Institute
on Zimbwe, University of Aerie. All off-planet. "You're
going to have a long way to travel when you come home
for Christmas," he commented. Another fact caught his

eye: all three applications were filled out only up to the space marked *Military Service.*

"I don't expect to come home very often," Jonny said quietly.

"You're just going to give up, huh?" Jame put as much scorn into the words as he could.

It had no effect. "I'm retreating from enemy territory," Jonny corrected mildly.

"The kids are dead, Jonny. There's nothing in the universe you can do about it. Look, the town doesn't blame you—no charges were brought, remember? So quit blaming yourself. Accept the fact of what happened and let go of it."

"You're confusing legal and moral guilt. Legally, I'm clear. Morally? No. And the town's not going to let me forget it. I can see the disgust and fear in people's eyes. They're even afraid to be sarcastic to me any more."

"Well ... it's better than not getting any respect at all."

Jonny snorted. "Thanks a lot," he said wryly. "I'd rather be picked on."

A sign of life at last. Jame pressed ahead, afraid of losing the spark. "You know, Dader and I have been talking about the shop. You remember that we didn't have enough equipment for three workers?"

"Yes—and you still don't."

"Right. But what stops us from having *you* and Dader run the place while *I* go out and work somewhere else for a few months?"

Jonny was silent for a moment, but then shook his head. "Thanks, but no. It wouldn't be fair."

"Why not? That job used to be yours. It's not like you were butting in. Actually, I'd kind of like to try something else for a while."

"I'd probably drive away all the customers if I was there."

Jame's lip twisted. "That won't fly, and you know it. Dader's customers are there because they like him and his work. They don't give two hoots who handles the actual repairs as long as Dader supervises everything. You're just making excuses."

Jonny closed his eyes briefly. "And what if I am?"

"I suppose it doesn't matter to you right now whether or not you let your life go down the drain," Jame gritted. "But you might take a moment to consider what you're doing to Gwen."

"Yeah. The other kids are pretty hard on her, aren't they?"

"I'm not referring to them. Sure, she's lost most of her friends, but there are a couple who're sticking by her. What's killing her is having to watch her big brother tearing himself to shreds."

Jonny looked up for the first time. "What do you mean?"

"Just what I said. She's been putting up a good front for your sake, but the rest of us know how much it hurts her to see the brother she adores sitting in his room and—" He groped for the right words.

"Wallowing in self-pity?"

"Yeah. You owe her better than that, Jonny. She's already lost most of her friends; she deserves to keep her brother."

Jonny looked back out the window for a long moment, then glanced down at the college magforms. "You're right." He took a deep breath, let it out slowly. "Okay. You can tell Dader he's got himself a new worker," he said, collecting the magforms together into a neat pile. "I'll start whenever he's ready for me."

Jame grinned and gripped his brother's shoulder. "Thanks," he said quietly. "Can I tell Momer and Gwen, too?"

"Sure. No; just Momer," He stood up and gave Jame a passable attempt at a smile. "I'll go tell Gwen myself."

The tiny spot of bluish light, brilliant even through the de-contrast goggles, crawled to the edge of the metal and vanished. Pushing up the goggles, Jonny set the laser down and inspected the seam. Spotting a minor flaw, he corrected it and then began removing the fender from its clamps. He had not quite finished the job when a gentle buzz signaled that a car had pulled into the drive.

Grimacing, Jonny took off his goggles and headed for the front of the shop.

Mayor Stillman was out of his car and walking toward the door when Jonny emerged from the building. "Hello, Jonny," he smiled, holding out his hand with no trace of hesitation. "How are you doing?"

"Fine, Mr. Stillman," Jonny said, feeling awkward as he shook hands. He'd been working here for three weeks now, but still didn't feel comfortable dealing directly with his father's customers. "Dader's out right now; can I help you with something?"

Stillman shook his head. "I really just dropped by to say hello to you and to bring you some news. I heard this morning that Wyatt Brothers Contracting is putting together a group to demolish the old Lamplighter Hotel. Would you be interested in applying for a job with them?"

"No, I don't think so. I'm doing okay here right now. But thanks for mentioning—"

He was cut off by a dull thunderclap. "What was that?" Stillman asked, glancing at the cloudless sky.

"An explosion," Jonny said curtly, eyes searching the southwest sky for evidence of fire. For an instant he was back on Adirondack. "A big one, southwest of us. There!" He pointed to a thin plume of smoke that had suddenly appeared.

"The cesium extractor, I'll bet," Stillman muttered. "Damn! Come on, let's go."

The déjà vu vanished. "I can't go with you," Jonny said.

"Never mind the shop. No one will steal anything." Stillman was already getting into his car.

"But—" There would be *crowds* there! "I just can't."

"This is no time for shyness," the mayor snapped. "If that blast really *was* all the way over at the extraction plant, there is probably one hell of a fire there now. They might need our help. Get *in*, damn it!"

Jonny obeyed. The smoke plume, he noted, was growing darker by the second.

Stillman was right on all accounts. The four-story cesium extraction plant was indeed burning furiously as they roared up to the edge of the growing crowd of spectators. The patrollers and firemen were already there, the latter pouring a white liquid through the doors and windows of the building. The flames, Jonny saw as he and the mayor pushed through the crowd, seemed largely confined to the first floor. The *entire* floor was burning, however, with flames extending even a meter or two onto the ground outside the building. Clearly, the fire was being fueled by one or more liquids.

The two men had reached one of the patrollers now. "Keep back, folks—" he began.

"I'm Mayor Stillman," Stillman identified himself. "What can we do to help?"

"Just keep back—no, wait a second, you can help us string a cordon line. There could be another explosion any time and we've got to keep these people back. The stuff's over there."

The "stuff" consisted of thin, bottom-weighted poles and bright red cord to string between them. Stillman and Jonny joined three patrollers who were in the process of setting up the line.

"How did it happen?" Stillman asked as they worked, shouting to make himself heard over the roar of the flames.

"Witnesses say a tank of iaphanine got ruptured somehow and ignited," one of the patrollers shouted back. "Before they could put it out the heat set off another couple of tanks. I guess they had a few hundred kiloliters of the damned stuff in there—it's used in the refining process—and the whole lot went up at once. It's a wonder the building's still standing."

"Anyone still in there?"

"Yeah. Half a dozen or so—third floor."

Jonny turned, squinting against the light. Sure enough, he could see two or three anxious faces at a partially open third-floor window. Directly below them cedar Lakes's single "skyhooker" fire truck had been driven to within a cautious ten meters of the building and was extending its ladder upwards. Jonny turned back to the cordon line—

The blast was deafening, and Jonny's built-in reflexes

reacted by throwing him flat on the ground. Twisting around to face the building, he saw that a large chunk of wall a dozen meters from the working firemen had been disintegrated by the explosion. In its place was now a solid sheet of blue-tinged yellow flame. Fortunately, none of the firemen seemed to have been hurt.

"Oh, hell," a patroller said as Jonny scrambled to his feet. "Look at that."

A piece of the wall had apparently winged the skyhooker's ladder on its way to oblivion. One of the uprights had been mangled, causing the whole structure to sag to the side. Even as the firemen hurriedly brought it down the upright snapped, toppling the ladder onto the ground.

"Damn!" Stillman muttered. "Do they have another ladder long enough?"

"Not when it has to sit that far from the wall," the patroller gritted. "I don't think the Public Works tall-trucks can reach that high either."

"Maybe we can get a hover-plane from Horizon City," Stillman said, a hint of desperation creeping into his voice.

"They haven't got time." Jonny pointed at the second-floor windows. "The fire's already on the second floor. Something has to be done right away."

The firemen had apparently come to the same conclusion and were pulling one of their other ladders from its rack on the skyhooker. "Looks like they're going to try to reach the second floor and work their way to the third from inside," the patroller muttered.

"That's suicide," Stillman shook his head. "Isn't there any place they can set up airbags close enough to let the men jump?"

The answer to that was obvious and no one bothered to voice it: if the firemen could have done that, they would have already done so. Clearly, the flames extended too far from the building for that to work.

"Do we have any strong rope?" Jonny asked suddenly. "I'm sure I could throw one end of it up to them."

"But they'd slide down into the fire," Stillman pointed out.

"Not if you anchored the bottom end fifteen or twenty meters away; tied it to one of the fire trucks, say. Come on, let's go talk to one of the firemen."

They found the fire chief in the group trying to set up the new ladder. "It's a nice idea, but I doubt if all of the men up there could make it down a rope," he frowned after Jonny had sketched his plan. "They've been in smoke and terrific heat for nearly a quarter hour now and are probably getting close to collapse."

"Do you have anything like a breeches buoy?" Jonny asked. "It's like a sling with a pulley that slides on a rope."

The chief shook his head. "Look, I haven't got any more time to waste here. We've got to get our men inside right away."

"You can't send men into that," Stillman objected. "The whole second floor must be on fire by now."

"That's why we have to hurry, damn it!"

Jonny fought a brief battle with himself. But, as Stillman had said, this was no time to be shy. "There's another way. I can take a rope to them along the *outside* of the building."

"What?" "How?" the chief and Stillman asked simultaneously.

"You'll see. I'll need at least thirty meters of rope, a pair of insulated gloves, and about ten strips of heavy cloth. *Now!*"

The tone of command, once learned, was not easily forgotten. Nor was it easy to resist; and within a minute Jonny was climbing up the ladder the firemen had placed on the second-floor window ledge. The rope, tied firmly around his waist, trailed behind him, kept just taut enough to stay out of the flames.

It was a lot hotter than Jonny had expected it to be, but he pushed onward, reaching the window without any obvious burns. A fresh blast of heat greeted him as his head topped the ledge. Clearly, the second floor was uninhabitable. Climbing the last few rungs quickly, Jonny stepped onto the ledge and moved to its farthest edge where the wall—hot though it was—provided him some protection from the blast-furnace effect.

Twisting his head, he looked up. Two meters above him was his target window. This kind of vertical jump was tricky—it was easy to add in too much horizontal component—but he knew how to do it. Carefully flexing his knees, he leaped and caught the ledge, pulling himself over it and through the half-open window in one smooth motion.

The fire chief's guess about the heat and smoke had been correct. The seven men lying or sitting on the floor of the small room were so groggy they weren't even startled by Jonny's sudden appearance. Three were already unconscious. A quick check showed they were alive, but just barely. He would have to move fast.

The first task was to get the window completely open. It was designed, Jonny saw, to only open halfway, the metal frame of the upper section firmly joined to the wall. The pane itself was an unbreakable plastic which would, nevertheless, probably yield to a Cobra-strength kick. But that would leave jagged edges, something Jonny didn't want. So instead of breaking the window, he turned his lasers onto the frame. A few carefully placed shots into the heat-softened metal did the trick, and a single kick popped the pane neatly and sent it tumbling to the ground.

Moving swiftly now, Jonny untied the rope from his waist and fastened it to a convenient stanchion, tugging three times on it to alert the firemen below to take in the slack. Hoisting one of the unconscious men to a more or less vertical position, he tied a strip of cloth to the man's left wrist, tossed the other end over the slanting rope, and tied it to the man's right wrist. With a quick glance outside to make sure the firemen were ready, he lifted the man through the window and let him slide down the taut rope into the waiting arms of the firemen. Jonny didn't wait to watch them cut him loose, but went immediately to the second unconscious man.

Parts of the floor were beginning to smolder by the time the last man disappeared out the window. Tossing one more cloth strip over the rope, Jonny gripped both ends with his right hand and jumped. The wind of his passage felt like an arctic blast on his sweaty skin and he found himself shivering as he reached the ground. Letting go of the cloth, he stumbled a few steps away— and heard a strange sound.

The crowd was cheering.

He turned to look at them, wondering, and finally it dawned on him that they were cheering for *him*. Unbidden, an embarrassed smile crept onto his face, and he raised his hand shyly in acknowledgment

And then Mayor Stillman was at his side, gripping Jonny's arm and smiling broadly. "You did it, Jonny; you did it!" he shouted over the all the noise.

Jonny grinned back. With half of Cedar Lake watching he'd saved seven men, and had risked his life doing it. They'd seen that he wasn't a monster, that his abilities could be used constructively and—most importantly— that he *wanted* to be helpful. Down deep, he could sense that this was a potential turning point. Maybe—just maybe—things would be different for him now.

Stillman shook his head sadly. "I really thought things would be different for him after the fire."

Fraser shrugged. "I'd hoped so, too. But I'm afraid I hadn't really counted on it. Even while everybody was cheering for him you could see that nervousness still in their eyes. That fear of him was never gone, just covered up. Now that the emotional high has worn off that's all that's left."

"Yeah," Lifting his gaze from the desk, Stillman stared for a moment out the window. More and more lately the office had begun to feel like a prison cell, to the point where he sometimes half-expected to see bars on the window. "So they treat him like an incurable psychopath. Or a wild animal."

"You can't really blame them. They're scared of what his strength and lasers could do if he went berserk."

"He doesn't *go* berserk, damn it!" Stillman flared, slamming his fist down on the desk.

"*I* know that!" the councilor shot back. "Fine—so you want to tell everyone the truth? Even assuming Vanis D'arl didn't jump down our throats for doing it, would you *really* want to tell people Jonny has no control whatsoever over his combat reflexes? You think that would help?"

Stillman's flash of anger evaporated. "No," he said quietly. "It would just make things worse." He stood up and walked over to the window. "Sorry I blew up, Sut. I know it's not your fault. It's just ..." He sighed. "We've lost it, Sut. That's all there is to it. We're never going to get Jonny reintegrated into this town now. If becoming a bona fide hero didn't do it, then I have no idea what else to try."

"It's not your fault either, Teague. You can't take it personally." Fraser's voice was quiet. "The government had no business doing what it did to Jonny, and then dropping him on us without any preparation. The Cobras were a new breed of soldier and *someone* should have recognized there were going to be special problems when they came home. Obviously, no one did. But they're not going to be able to ignore the problem. You remember what D'arl said—the Cobras are having trouble all over the Dominion. Sooner or later the government's going to have to do something about it. We've done our best; it's up to them now."

Stillman's intercom buzzed. Walking back to his desk, the mayor tapped the key. "Yes?"

"Sir, Mr. Do-sin just called from the press office. He says there's something on the DOM-Press line that you should see."

"Thank you." Sitting down, Stillman turned on his plate and dialed the proper channel. The last three news items were still visible, the top one marked with a star, indicating its importance. Both men hunched forward to read it.

DOMINION JOINT MILITARY COMMAND HQ, ASGARD:

A MILITARY SPOKESMAN ANNOUNCED TODAY THAT ALL RESERVE COBRAS WILL BE RECALLED INTO ACTIVE SERVICE BY THE END OF NEXT MONTH. THIS MOVE IS DESIGNED TO COUNTER A MINTHISTIN BUILD-UP ALONG THE DOMINION'S ANDROMEDA BORDER. AS YET NO REGULAR ARMY OR

FLEET RESERVES ARE BEING RECALLED, BUT ALL OPTIONS
ARE BEING KEPT OPEN.

"I don't believe it," Fraser shook his head. "Are those
damn Minthisti going to try it *again*? I thought they
learned their lesson the last time we stomped them."

Stillman didn't reply.

Vanis D'arl swept into Mayor Stillman's office with
the air of a man preoccupied by more important business. He nodded shortly at the two men who were waiting there for him and sat down without invitation. "I
trust this is as vital as your message implied," he said to
Stillman. "I postponed an important meeting to detour
to Horizon. Let's get on with it."

Stillman nodded, determined not to be intimidated,
and gestured to the youth sitting quietly by his desk.
"May I present Jame Moreau, brother of Cobra-Three
Jonny Moreau. He and I have been discussing the Reserve call-up set for later this month in response to the
alleged Minthistin threat."

"Alleged?" D'arl's voice was soft but there was a
warning under it.

Stillman hesitated, suddenly aware of the risk they
were taking with this confrontation. But Jame stepped
into the gap. "Yes, *alleged*. We know this whole thing
is a trumped-up excuse to pull all the Cobras back into
the service and ship them off to the border where they'll
be out of the way."

D'arl looked keenly at Jame, as if seeing him for the
first time. "You are concerned about your brother, of
course; that's only natural," he said at last. "But your
allegations are unprovable and come perilously close to
sedition. The Dominion makes war only in self-defense.
Even if your claim was true, what would such an action
gain us?"

"That is precisely our point," Jame said calmly, showing a self-control and courage far beyond his nineteen
years. "The government is trying to solve the Cobra
problem, clearly. But this isn't a solution; it's merely a
postponement."

"And yet, the Cobras were generally unhappy in their new civilian roles," D'arl pointed out. "Perhaps this will actually be better for them."

Jame shook his head, his eyes still holding D'arl's. "No. Because you can't hold them there forever, you see. You either have to release them again someday— in which case you're right back where you started—or else you have to hope that the problem will ... work itself out."

D'arl's face was an expressionless mask. "What do you mean by that?"

"I think you know." For just a second Jame's control cracked, and some of the internal fire leaked out. "But don't you see? It won't *work*. You can't kill off all the Cobras, no matter how many wars you put them through, because the Army will be making new ones as fast as the old ones die. They're just too damn useful for the brass to simply drop the project."

D'arl looked back at Stillman. "If this is all you wanted, to throw out ridiculous accusations, then you've wasted my time. Good day to you." He stood up and headed toward the door.

"It isn't," Stillman said. "We think we've come up with an alternative."

D'arl stopped and turned back to face them. For a moment he measured them with his eyes, then slowly came and sat down again. "I'm listening."

Stillman leaned forward in his chair, willing calmness into his mind. Jonny's life was riding on this. "The Cobra gear was designed to give extra speed, weaponry, and reflexes to its owners; and according to Jame here, Jonny told him that the original equipment included vision and auditory enhancers as well." D'arl nodded once, and Stillman continued, "But warfare isn't the only area where these things would be useful. Specifically, how about new planet colonization?"

D'arl frowned, but Stillman hurried on before he could speak. "I've done some reading on this in the last few weeks, and the usual procedure seems to involve four steps. First, an initial exploration team goes in to confirm the planet is habitable. Then a more extensive scientific party is landed for more tests; after that you usually need a precolony group to go in with heavy machinery for clearing land and starting settlements. Only then does the first main wave of colonists arrive. The whole process takes a year or more and is very expensive, mainly because you need a small military there the whole time to protect the explorers from unknown dangers. That means feeding a few hundred men, transporting weapons and lots of support gear—"

"I know what it involves," D'arl interrupted. "Get to your point."

"Sending in Cobras instead of regular soldiers would be easier and cheaper," Stillman said. "Their equipment is self-contained and virtually maintenance-free, and they can both act as guards and help with the other work. True, a Cobra probably costs more to equip than the soldiers and workers he'll replace—but you've already *got* the Cobras."

D'arl shook his head impatiently. "I listened this long because I hoped you might have come up with something new. The Central Committee considered this same idea months ago. Certainly, it would save money—but only if you've got some place to use it. There are no more than a half-dozen habitable worlds left within our borders and all have had a preliminary exploration. We are hemmed in on all sides by alien empires; to gain more worlds we would have to go to war for them."

"Not necessarily," Jame said. "We could go *past* the aliens."

"What?"

"Here's what we had in mind," Stillman said. "The Trofts just lost a war to us, and they know that we're still strong enough to really tear into their empire if we decided to invade. So it shouldn't be too hard to talk them into ceding us a corridor of space through their territory, for non-military transport only. All the charts show there's at least *some* unclaimed space on the far side of their territory; that's where we set up the colony."

D'arl was gazing into space, a thoughtful look on his

face. "What if there aren't any habitable planets out there?"

"Then we're out of luck," Stillman admitted. "But if there *are*, look at what you've gained. New worlds, new resources, maybe new alien contacts and trade—it would be a far better return on the Cobra investment than you'd get by killing them off in a useless war."

"Yes. Of course, we'd have to put the colony far enough past the border that the Trofts wouldn't be tempted to sneak out and destroy it. With that kind of long-distance transport, using Cobras instead of an armor battalion makes even more sense. We'd still need to give it enough armament to defend itself. . . ." He pursed his lips. "And as the colony gets stronger it should help keep the Trofts peaceful—they know better than to start a two-front war. The Army might be interested in that aspect."

Jame leaned forward. "Then you agree with us? You'll suggest this to the Central Committee?"

Slowly, D'arl nodded. "I will. It makes sense and is potentially profitable for the Dominion—a good combination. I'm sure the . . . trouble . . . with the Minthisti can be handled without the Cobras." Abruptly, he stood up. "I expect both of you to keep silent about this," he cautioned. "Premature publicity would be harmful. I can't make any promises; but whatever decision the committee makes will be quick."

He was right. Less than two weeks later the announcement was made.

The big military shuttle was surrounded by a surprisingly large crowd, considering that only twenty-odd people would be accompanying Jonny from Horizon to the new colonist training center on Asgard. At least ten times that many people were at the Port, what with family, friends, and general well-wishers seeing the emigrants off. Even so, the five Moreaus and Stillman had little trouble working their way through the mass. For some it seemed to be fear that moved them out of the way of the red and black diamond-patterned Cobra dress uniform; but for others—the important ones—it was genuine respect. Pioneers, Jonny reflected, probably had a different attitude toward powerful men than the general populace. Not really surprising; it was on just those men that their lives would soon be depending.

"Well, Jonny, good luck," Stillman said as they stopped near the inner edge of the crowd. "I hope things work well for you."

"Thanks, Mr. Stillman," Jonny replied, gripping the mayor's outstretched hand firmly. "And thanks for—well, for your support."

"You'll write before you leave Asgard, won't you?" Irena asked, her eyes moist.

"Sure, Momer," Jonny hugged her. "Maybe in a couple of years you'll all be able to come out and visit me."

"Yeah!" Gwen agreed enthusiastically.

"Perhaps," Pearce said. "Take care, son."

"Watch yourself, Jonny," Jame seconded.

And with another round of hugs it was time to go. Picking up his satchel, Jonny stepped aboard the shuttle, pausing once on the steps to wave before entering. The shuttle was empty, but even as he chose a seat the other colonists began coming in. Almost, Jonny thought, as if his boarding had been the signal they'd been waiting for.

That thought brought a bittersweet smile to his lips. From social outcast in his own home town to a leader on a new world! Few men were ever granted a new chance like this one, and he knew well he'd never receive another. But that was all right. Where they were going there were only two options: success or death. And for Jonny, either was preferable to failure.

Still smiling, he leaned back in his seat and waited peacefully for takeoff.

LABYRINTH

by Lois McMaster Bujold

Lois McMaster Bujold is the second multiple Nebula and Hugo award winner to appear in *Intergalactic Mercenaries*. Bujold's first Nebula came for her novel *Falling Free* in 1988. She picked up another Nebula and her first Hugo for her May 1989 *Analog* novella, "The Mountains of Mourning." That same year the excellent novella that begins on the next page, "Labyrinth" was the winner of the Analytical Laboratory—*Analog's* readers' awards poll. Since then Bujold has won Hugos for her novels *Barrayar* and *Mirror Dance*.

Bujold was born in Columbus and remained in Ohio for much of her life. The author graduated from Ohio State University in 1972, and went to work as a pharmacy technician at the University Hospitals until she quit to start a family. Her daughter, Anne, was born in 1979 and her son, Paul, was born in 1981. Like Timothy Zahn, she began writing as a hobby, but soon learned that it was too demanding and draining to justify as an avocation. Determining that only serious professional recognition would satisfy her, she began to do whatever had to be done in terms of writing, rewriting, cutting, editorial analysis, and trying again. Her first book, *Shards of Honor,* was completed in 1983. She wrote two more novels in quick succession, and they eventually sold to Baen Books. Baen released all three novels in 1986, "leading the uninitiated to imagine that I wrote a book every three months." Bujold's latest novel, *Cetaganda,* was recently published in hardcover, and another book, tentatively titled *Memory,* is due out next winter.

Bujold now lives with her children in Minneapolis, Minnesota.

Miles contemplated the image of the globe glowing above the vid plate, crossed his arms, and stifled queasiness. The planet of Jackson's Whole, glittering, wealthy, corrupt ... Jacksonians claimed their corruption was entirely imported—if the galaxy was willing to pay for virtue what it paid for vice, the place would be a pilgrimage shrine. In Miles's view this seemed rather like debating which was superior—maggots or the rotten meat they fed off. Still, if Jackson's Whole didn't exist, the galaxy would probably have had to invent it. Its neighbors might feign horror, but they wouldn't permit the place to exist if they didn't find it a secretly useful interface with the sub-economy.

The planet possessed a certain liveliness, anyway. Not as lively as a century or two back, to be sure, in its hijacker-base days. But its cutthroat criminal gangs had evolved into Syndicate monopolies, almost as structured and staid as little governments. An aristocracy, of sorts. Naturally. Miles wondered how much longer the major Houses would be able to fight off the creeping tide of integrity.

House Dyne, detergent banking—launder your money on Jackson's Whole. House Fell, weapons deals with no questions asked. House Bharaputra, illegal genetics. Worse, House Ryoval, whose motto was "Dreams Made Flesh," surely the damnedest—Miles used the adjective precisely—procurer in history. House Hargraves, the galactic fence, prim-faced middlemen for ransom deals— you had to give them credit, hostages exchanged through · their good offices came back alive, mostly. And a dozen smaller syndicates, variously and shiftingly allied.

Even we find you useful. Miles touched the control and the vid image vanished. His lip curled in suppressed loathing, and he called up his ordnance inventory for one final check of his shopping list. A subtle shift in the vibrations of the ship around him told him they were matching orbits—the fast cruiser *Ariel* would be docking at Fell Station within the hour.

His console was just extruding the completed data disk of weapons orders when his cabin door chimed, followed by an alto voice over its comm, "Admiral Naismith?"

"Enter." He plucked off the disk and leaned back in his station chair.

Captain Thorne sauntered in with a friendly salute. "We'll be docking in about thirty minutes, sir."

"Thank you, Bel."

Bel Thorne, the *Ariel's* commander, was a Betan hermaphrodite: man/woman descendant of a centuries-past genetic-social experiment every bit as bizarre, in Miles's private opinion, as anything rumored to be done for money by House Ryoval's ethics-free surgeons. A fringe effort of Betan egalitarianism run amok, hermaphroditism had not caught on, and the original idealists' hapless descendants remained a minority on hyper-tolerant Beta Colony. Except for a few stray wanderers like Bel. As a mercenary officer Thorne was conscientious, loyal, and aggressive, and Miles liked him/her/it—Beta custom used the neuter pronoun—a lot. *However* . . .

Miles could smell Bel's floral perfume from here. Bel was emphasizing the female side today. And had been, increasingly, for the five days of this voyage. Normally Bel chose to come on ambiguous-to-male, soft short brown hair and chiseled, beardless facial features counteracted by the grey-and-white Dendarii military uniform, assertive gestures, and wicked humor. It worried Miles exceedingly to sense Bel soften in his presence.

Turning to his computer console's holovid plate, Miles again called up the image of the planet they were approaching. Jackson's Whole looked demure enough from a distance, mountainous, rather cold—the populated equator was only temperate—ringed in the vid by a lacy schematic net of colored satellite tracks, orbital transfer stations, and authorized approach vectors. "Have you ever been here before, Bel?"

"Once, when I was a lieutenant in Admiral Oser's fleet," said the mercenary. "House Fell has a new baron since then. Their weaponry still has a good reputation, as long as you know what you're buying. Stay away from the sale on neutron hand grenades."

"Heh. For those with strong throwing arms. Fear not, neutron hand grenades aren't on the list." He handed the data disk to Bell.

Bel sidled up and leaned over the back of Miles's station chair to take it. "Shall I grant leaves to the crew while we're waiting for the baron's minions to load cargo? How about yourself? There used to be a hostel near the docks with all the amenities: pool, sauna, great food ... " Bel's voice lowered. "I could book a room for two."

"I'd only figured to grant day passes." Necessarily, Miles cleared his throat.

"I *am* a woman, too," Bel pointed out in a murmur.

"Among other things."

"You're so hopelessly monosexual. Miles."

"Sorry." Awkwardly, he patted the hand that had somehow come to rest on his shoulder.

Bel sighed and straightened. "So many are."

Miles sighed, too. Perhaps he ought to make his rejection more emphatic—this was only about the seventh time he'd been around with Bel on this subject. It was almost ritualized by now, almost, but not quite, a joke. You had to give the Betan credit for either optimism or obtuseness. ... or, Miles's honesty added, genuine feeling. If he turned around now, he knew, he might surprise an essential loneliness in the hermaphrodite's eyes, never permitted on the lips. He did not turn around.

And who was he to judge another, Miles reflected ruefully, whose own body brought him so little joy? Crippled in a congenital accident, all his home-world's medical resources had only half-healed him. At full growth he had only achieved 4 foot 9. Oversized head, face pale and sharp-featured against his dark hair; short neck, twisted spine, brittle bones. Mismatched with a soul's passion for soldiering that would not be denied. He glanced down at the grey Dendarii officer's uniform he wore. The uniform he had won. *If you can't be seven feet tall, be seven feet smart.* His reason had so far failed to present him with a solution to the problem of Thorne, though.

"Have you ever thought of going back to Beta Colony, and seeking one of your own?" Miles asked seriously.

Thorne shrugged. "Too boring. That's why I left. It's so very safe, so very narrow. . . ."

"Mind you, a great place to raise kids." One corner of Miles's mouth twisted up.

Thorne grinned. "You got it. You're an almost perfect Betan, y'know? Almost. You have the accent, the in-jokes. . . ."

Miles went a little still. "Where do I fail?"

Thorne touched Miles's cheek; Miles flinched.

"Reflexes," said Thorne.

"Ah."

"I won't give you away."

"I know."

Bel was leaning in again. "I could polish that last edge. . . ."

"Never mind," said Miles, slightly flushed. "We have a mission."

"Inventory," said Thorne scornfully.

"That's not a mission," said Miles, "that's a cover."

"Ah ha." Thorne straightened up. "At last."

"At last?"

"It doesn't take a genius. We came to purchase ordnance, but instead of taking the ship with the biggest cargo capacity, you chose the *Ariel*—the fleet's fastest. There's no deader dull routine than inventory, but instead of sending a perfectly competent quartermaster, you're overseeing it personally."

"I do want to make contact with the new Baron Fell," said Miles mildly. "House Fell is the biggest arms supplier this side of Beta Colony, and a lot less picky about who its customers are. If I like the quality of the initial purchase, they could become a regular supplier."

"A quarter of Fell's arms are Betan manufacture, marked up," said Thorne. "Again, ha."

"And while we're here," Miles went on, "a certain middle-aged man is going to present himself and sign on to the Dendarii Mercenaries as a medtech. At that point all Station passes are canceled, we finish loading cargo as quickly as possible, and we leave."

Thorne grinned in satisfaction. "A pick-up. Very good. I assume we're being well paid?"

"Very. If he arrives at his destination alive. The man happens to be the top research geneticist of House Bharaputra Laboratories. He's been offered asylum by a planetary government capable of protecting him from the long arms of Baron Luigi Bharaputra's enforcers. His soon-to-be-former employer is expected to be highly irate at the lack of a month's notice. We are being paid to deliver him to his new masters alive and not, ah, forcibly debriefed of all his trade secrets.

"Since House Bharaputra could probably buy and sell the whole Dendarii Free Mercenary Fleet twice over out of petty cash, I would prefer we not have to deal with Baron Luigi's enforcers either. So we shall be innocent suckers. We'll just say, All we did was hire a bloody medtech, sir. And we shall be irate ourselves when he deserts after we arrive at fleet rendezvous off Escobar."

"Sounds good to me," conceded Thorne. "Simple."

"So I trust," Miles sighed hopefully. Why, after all, shouldn't things run to plan, just this once?

The purchasing offices and display areas for House Fell's lethal wares were situated not far from the docks, and most of House Fell's smaller customers never penetrated further into Fell Station. But shortly after Miles and Thorne placed their order—about as long as needed to verify a credit chit—an obsequious person in the green silk of House Fell's uniform appeared, and pressed an invitation into Admiral Naismith's hand to a reception in the Baron's personal quarters.

Four hours later, giving up the pass cube to Baron Fell's major domo at the sealed entrance to the station's private sector, Miles checked Thorne and himself over for their general effect. Dendarii dress uniform was a grey velvet tunic with silver buttons on the shoulders and white edging, matching grey trousers with white side piping, and grey synthasuede boots—perhaps just a trifle effete? Well, he hadn't designed it, he'd just inherited it. Live with it.

The interface to the private sector was highly interesting. Miles's eye took in the details while the majordomo scanned them for weapons. Life-support—in fact, all sys-

tems—appeared to be run separately from the rest of
the station. The area was not only sealable, it was de-
tachable. In effect, not Station but Ship—engines and
armament around here somewhere, Miles bet, though it
could be lethal to go looking for them unescorted. The
majordomo ushered them through, pausing to announce
them on his wrist comm: "Admiral Miles Naismith, commanding, Dendarii Free Mercenary Fleet. Captain Bel
Thorne, commanding the fast cruiser *Ariel*, Dendarii
Free Mercenary Fleet." Miles wondered who was on the
other end of the comm.

The reception chamber was large and gracefully ap-
pointed, with iridescent floating staircases and levels cre-
ating private spaces without destroying the illusion of
openness. Every exit (Miles counted six) had a large
green-garbed guard by it, trying to look like a servant
and not succeeding very well. One whole wall was a
vertigo-inducing transparent viewport overlooking Fell
Station's busy docks and the bright curve of Jackson's
Whole bisecting the star-spattered horizon beyond. A
crew of elegant women in green silk saris rustled among
the guests offering food and drink.

Grey velvet, Miles decided after one glance at the
other guests, was a positively demure choice of garb. He
and Bel would blend right into the walls. The thin scattering of fellow privileged customers wore a wide array
of planetary fashions. But they were a wary bunch, little
groups sticking together, no mingling. Guerrillas, it appeared, did not speak to mercenaries, nor smugglers to
revolutionaries; the Gnostic Saints, of course, spoke only
to the One True God, and perhaps to Baron Fell.

"Some party," commented Bel. "I went to a pet show
with an atmosphere like this once. The high point was
when somebody's Tau Cetan beaded lizard got loose and
ate the Best-In-Show from the canine division."

"Hush," Miles grinned out of the corner of his mouth.
"This is business."

A green-sari'd woman bowed silently before them, offering a tray. Thorne raised a brow at Miles—*do we*? . . .

"Why not?" Miles murmured. "We're paying for it,
in the long run. I doubt the baron poisons his customers,

it's bad for business. Business is emperor, here. *Laissez-faire* capitalism gone completely over the edge." He selected a pink tid-bit in the shape of a lotus and a mysterious cloudy drink. Thorne followed suit. The pink lotus, alas, turned out to be some sort of raw fish. It squeaked against his teeth. Miles, committed, swallowed it anyway. The drink was potently alcoholic, and after a sip to wash down the lotus he regretfully abandoned it on the first level surface he could find. His dwarfish body refused to handle alcohol, and he had no desire to meet Baron Fell while either semi-comatose or giggling uncontrollably. The more metabolically fortunate Thorne kept beverage in hand.

A most extraordinary music began from somewhere, a racing rich complexity of harmonics. Miles could not identify the instrument—instruments, surely. He and Thorne exchanged a glance, and by mutual accord drifted toward the sound. Around a spiraling staircase, backed by the panoply of station, planet, and stars, they found the musician. Miles's eyes widened. *House Ryoval's surgeons have surely gone too far this time. . . .*

Little decorative colored sparkles defined the spherical field of a large null-gee bubble. Floating within it was a woman. Her ivory arms flashed against her green silk clothes as she played. *All four* of her ivory arms . . . She wore a flowing, kimono-like belted jacket and matching shorts, from which the second set of arms emerged where her legs should have been. Her hair was short and soft and ebony black. Her eyes were closed, and her rose-tinted face bore the repose of an angel, high and distant and terrifying.

Her strange instrument was fixed in air before her, a flat polished wooden frame strung across both top and bottom with a bewildering array of tight gleaming wires, soundboard between. She struck the wires with four felted hammers with blinding speed, both sides at once, her upper hands moving at counterpoint to her lowers. Music poured forth in a cascade.

"Good God," said Thorne, "it's a quaddie."

"It's a what?"

"A quaddie. She's a long way from home."

"She's—not a local product?"

"By no means."

"I'm relieved. I think. Where the devil does she come from, then?"

"About two hundred years ago—about the time hermaphrodites were being invented," a peculiar wryness flashed across Thorne's face, "there was this rush of genetic experimentation on humans, in the wake of the development of the practical uterine replicator. Followed shortly by a rush of laws restricting such, but meanwhile, somebody thought they'd make a race of free fall dwellers. Then artificial gravity came in and blew them out of business. The quaddies fled—their descendants ended up on the far side of nowhere, way beyond Earth from us in the Nexus. They're rumored to keep to themselves, mostly. Very unusual, to see one this side of Earth. H'sh." Lips parted, Thorne tracked the music.

As unusual as finding a Betan hermaphrodite in a free mercenary fleet, Miles thought. But the music deserved undivided attention, though few in this paranoid crowd seemed to even be noticing it. A shame. Miles was no musician, but even he could sense an intensity of passion in the playing that went beyond talent, reaching for genius. An evanescent genius, sounds woven with time and, like time, forever receding beyond one's futile grasp into memory alone.

The outpouring of music dropped to a haunting echo, then silence. The four-armed musician's blue eyes opened, and her face came back from the ethereal to the merely human, tense and sad.

"Ah," breathed Thorne, stuck its empty glass under its arm, raised hands to clap, then paused, hesitant to become conspicuous in this indifferent chamber.

Miles was all for being inconspicuous. "Perhaps you can speak to her," he suggested by way of an alternative.

"You think?" Brightening, Thorne tripped forward, swinging down to abandon the glass on the nearest handy floor and raising splayed hands against the sparkling bubble. The hermaphrodite mustered an entranced, ingratiating smile. "Uh . . ." Thorne's chest rose and fell.

Good God, Bel, tongue-tied? Never thought I'd see it.
"Ask her what she calls that thing she plays," Miles supplied helpfully.

The four-armed woman tilted her head curiously, and starfished gracefully over her boxy instrument to hover politely before Thorne on the other side of the glittering barrier. "Yes?"

"What do you call that extraordinary instrument?" Thorne asked.

"It's a double-sided hammer dulcimer, ma'am—sir. . . ." her servant-to-guest dull tone faltered a moment, fearing to give insult, "Officer."

"Captain Bel Thorne," Bel supplied instantly, beginning to recover accustomed smooth equilibrium. "Commanding the Dendarii fast cruiser *Ariel*. At your service. How ever did you come to be here?"

"I had worked my way to Earth, I was seeking employment, and Baron Fell hired me." She tossed her head, as if to deflect some implied criticism, though Bel had offered none.

"You are a true quaddie?"

"You've heard of my people?" Her dark brows rose in surprise. "Most people I encounter here think I am a *manufactured* freak." A little sardonic bitterness edged her voice.

Thorne cleared its throat. "I'm Betan, myself. I've followed the history of the early genetics explosion with a rather more personal interest." Thorne cleared its throat again, "Betan hermaphrodite, you see," and waited anxiously for the reaction.

Damn. Bel never waited for reactions, Bel sailed on and let the chips fall anyhow. *I wouldn't interfere with this for all the world.* Miles faded back slightly, rubbing his lips to wipe off a twitching grin as all Thorne's most masculine mannerisms reasserted themselves from spine to fingertips and outward into the aether.

Her head tilted in interest. One upper hand rose to rest on the sparkling barrier not far from Bel's. "*Are* you? You're a genetic too, then."

"Oh, yes. And tell me, what's your name?"

"Nicol."

"Nicol. Is that all? I mean, it's lovely."

"My people don't use surnames."

"Ah. And, uh, what are you doing after the party?"

At this point, alas, interference found them. "Heads up, *Captain*," Miles murmured. Thorne drew up instantly, cool and correct, and followed Miles's gaze. The quaddie floated back from the force barrier and bowed her head over her hands held palm-to-palm and palm-to-palm as a man approached. Miles, too, came to a polite species of attention.

Georish Stauber, Baron Fell, was a surprisingly old man to have succeeded so recently to his position, Miles thought. In the flesh he looked older than the holovid Miles had viewed of him at his own mission briefing. The baron was balding, with a white fringe of hair around his shiny pate, jovial and fat. He looked like somebody's grandfather. Not Miles's, Miles's grandfather had been lean and predatory even in his great age. And the old Count's title had been as real as such things got, not the courtesy-nobility of a Syndicate survivor. Jolly red cheeks or not, Miles reminded himself, Baron Fell had climbed a pile of bodies to attain this high place.

"Admiral Naismith. Captain Thorne. Welcome to Fell Station," rumbled the baron, smiling.

Miles swept him an aristocratic bow. Thorne somewhat awkwardly followed suit. Ah. He must copy that awkwardness next time. Of such little details were cover identities made. And blown.

"Have my people been taking care of your needs?"

"Thank you, yes." So far the proper businessmen.

"So glad to meet you at last," the baron rumbled on. "We've heard a great deal about you here."

"Have you," said Miles encouragingly. The baron's eyes were strangely avid. *Quite a glad-hand for a little tinpot mercenary, eh?* This was a little more stroke than was reasonable even for a high-ticket customer. Miles banished all hint of wariness from his return smile. *Patience. Let the challenge emerge, don't rush to meet what you cannot yet see.* "Good things, I hope."

"Remarkable things. Your rise has been as rapid as your origins are mysterious."

Hell, hell, what kind of bait was this? Was the baron hinting that he actually knew "Admiral Naismith's" real identity? This could be sudden and serious trouble. No—fear outran its cause. Wait. Forget that such a person as Lieutenant Lord Vorkosigan, Barrayaran Imperial Security, ever existed in this body. *It's not big enough for the two of us anyway, boy.* Yet why was this fat shark smiling so ingratiatingly? Miles cocked his head, neutrally.

"The story of your fleet's success at Vervain reached us even here. So unfortunate about its former commander."

Miles stiffened. "I regret Admiral Oser's death."

The baron shrugged philosophically. "Such things happen in the business. Only one can command."

"He could have been an outstanding subordinate."

"Pride is so dangerous," smiled the baron.

Indeed. Miles bit his tongue. *So he thinks I "arranged" Oser's death. So let him.* That there was one less mercenary than there appeared in this room, that the Dendarii were now, through Miles, an arm of the Barrayaran Imperial Service so covert most of them didn't even know it themselves . . . it would be a dull Syndicate baron who couldn't find profit in those secrets somewhere. Miles matched the baron's smile and added nothing.

"You interest me exceedingly," continued the baron. "For example, there's the puzzle of your apparent age. And your prior military career."

If Miles had kept his drink, he'd have knocked it back in one gulp right then. He clasped his hands convulsively behind his back instead. Dammit, the pain lines just didn't age his face enough. If the baron was indeed seeing right through the pseudo-mercenary to the twenty-three-year-old Security lieutenant—and yet, he usually carried it off—

The baron lowered his voice. "Do the rumors run equally true about your Betan rejuvenation treatment?"

So *that's* what he was on about. Miles felt faint with relief. "What interest could you have in such treatments, my lord?" he gibbered lightly. "I thought Jackson's Whole was the home of practical immortality. It's said that there are some here on their third cloned body."

"I am not one of them," said the baron rather regretfully.

Miles's brows rose in genuine surprise. Surely this man didn't spurn the process as murder. "Some unfortunate medical impediment?" he said, injecting polite sympathy into his voice. "My regrets, sir."

"In a manner of speaking." The baron's smile revealed a sharp edge. "The brain transplant operation itself kills a certain irreducible percentage of patients—"

Yeah, thought Miles, *starting with 100 percent of the clones, whose brains are flushed to make room...*

"—another percentage suffer varying sorts of permanent damage. Those are the risks anyone must take for the reward."

"But the reward is so great."

"But then there are a certain number of patients, indistinguishable from the first group, who do not die on the operating table by accident. If their enemies have the subtlety and clout to arrange it. I have a number of enemies, Admiral Naismith."

Miles made a little who-would-think-it gesture, flipping up one hand, and continued to cultivate an air of deep interest.

"I calculate my present chances of surviving a brain transplant to be rather worse than the average," the baron went on. "So I've an interest in alternatives." He paused expectantly.

"Oh," said Miles. Oh, indeed. He regarded his fingernails and thought fast. "It's true, I once participated in an ... unauthorized experiment. A premature one, as it happens, pushed too eagerly from animal to human subjects. It was not successful."

"No?" said the baron. "You appear in good health."

Miles shrugged. "Yes, there was some benefit to muscles, skin tone, hair. But my bones are the bones of an old man, fragile." *True.* "Subject to acute osteo-inflammatory attacks—there are days when I can't walk without medication." *Also true, dammit.* A recent and unsettling medical development. "My life expectancy is not considered good." *For example, if certain parties here ever figure out who "Admiral Naismith" really is, it could go down to as little as fifteen minutes.* "So unless you're extremely fond of pain and think you would enjoy being crippled, I fear I must dis-recommend the procedure."

The baron looked him up and down. Disappointment pulled down his mouth. "I see."

Bel Thorne, who knew quite well there was no such thing as the fabled "Betan rejuvenation treatment," was listening with well-concealed enjoyment and doing an excellent job of keeping the smirk off its face. Bless its little black heart.

"Still," said the baron, "your ... scientific acquaintance may have made some progress in the intervening years."

"I fear not," said Miles. "He died." He spread his hands helplessly. "Old age."

"Oh." The baron's shoulders sagged slightly.

"Ah, there you are, Fell," a new voice cut across them. The baron straightened and turned.

The man who had hailed him was as conservatively dressed as Fell, and flanked by a silent servant with "bodyguard" written all over him. The bodyguard wore a uniform, a high-necked red silk tunic and loose black trousers, and was unarmed. Everyone on Fell Station went unarmed except Fell's men; the place had the most strictly enforced weapons regs Miles had ever encountered. But the pattern of calluses on the lean bodyguard's hands suggested he might not need weapons. His eyes flickered and his hands shook just slightly, a hyperalertness induced by artificial aids—if ordered, he could strike with blinding speed and adrenalin-insane strength. He would also retire young, metabolically crippled for the rest of his short life.

The man he guarded was also young—some great lord's son? Miles wondered. He had long shining black hair dressed in an elaborate braid, smooth dark olive skin, and a high-bridged nose. He couldn't be older than Miles's real age, yet he moved with a mature assurance

"Ryoval," Baron Fell nodded in return, as a man to an equal, not a junior. Still playing the genial host, Fell added. "Officers, may I introduce Baron Ryoval of House Ryoval. Admiral Naismith, Captain Thorne. They

belong to that Illyrican-built mercenary fast cruiser in
dock, Ry, that you may have noticed."

"Haven't got your eye for hardware, I'm afraid, Georish." Baron Ryoval bestowed a nod upon them, of a
man being polite to his social inferiors for the principle
of it. Miles bowed clumsily in return.

Dropping Miles from his attention with an almost audible thump, Ryoval stood back with his hands on his
hips and regarded the null-gee bubble's inhabitant. "My
agent didn't exaggerate her charms."

Fell smiled sourly. Nicol had withdrawn—recoiled—
when Ryoval first approached, and now floated behind
her instrument, fussing with its tuning. Pretending to be
fussing with its tuning. Her eyes glanced warily at Ryoval, then returned to her dulcimer as it if might put some
magic wall between them.

"Can you have her play—" Ryoval began, and was
interrupted by a chime from his wrist comm. "Excuse
me, Georish." Looking slightly annoyed, he turned half-
away from them and spoke into it. "Ryoval. And this
had better be important."

"Yes, m'lord," a thin voice responded. "This is Manager Deem in Sales and Demonstrations. We have a
problem. That creature House Bharaputra sold us has
savaged a customer."

Ryoval's Greek-statue lips rippled in a silent snarl. "I
told you to chain it with duralloy."

"We did, my lord. The chains held, but it tore the
bolts right out of the wall."

"Stun it."

"We have."

"Then punish it suitably when it awakes. A sufficiently
long period without food should dull its aggression; it's
metabolism is unbelievable."

"What about the customer?"

"Give him whatever comforts he asks for. On the
House."

"I . . . don't think he'll be in shape to appreciate them
for quite some time. He's in the clinic now. Still
unconscious."

Ryoval hissed. "Put my personal physician on his case.

I'll take care of the rest when I get back downside, in about six hours. Ryoval out." He snapped the link closed. "Morons," he growled. He took a controlled, meditative breath, and recalled his social manner as if booting it up out of some stored memory bank. "Pardon the interruption, please, Georish."

Fell waved an understanding hand, as if to say, *Business.*

"As I was saying, can you have her play something?" Ryoval nodded to the quaddie.

Fell clasped his hands behind his back, his eyes glinting in a falsely benign smile. "Play something, Nicol."

She gave him an acknowledging nod, positioned herself, and closed her eyes. The frozen worry tensing her face gradually gave way to an inner stillness, and she began to play, a slow, sweet theme that established itself, rolled over, and began to quicken.

"Enough!" Ryoval flung up a hand. "She's precisely as described."

Nicol stumbled to a halt in mid-phrase. She inhaled through pinched nostrils, clearly disturbed by her inability to drive the piece through to its destined finish, the frustration of artistic incompletion. She stuck her hammers into their holders on the side of the instrument with short, savage jerks, and crossed her upper and lower arms both. Thorne's mouth tightened, and it crossed its arms in unconscious echo. Miles bit his lip uneasily.

"My agent conveyed the truth," Ryoval went on.

"Then perhaps your agent also conveyed my regrets," said Fell dryly.

"He did. But he wasn't authorized to offer more than a certain standard ceiling. For something so unique, there's no substitute for direct contact."

"I happen to be enjoying her skills where they are," said Fell. "At my age, enjoyment is much harder to obtain than money."

"So true. Yet other enjoyments might be substituted. I could arrange something quite special. Not in the catalog."

"Her *musical* skills, Ryoval. Which are more than special. They are unique. Genuine. Not artificially augmented in any way. Not to be duplicated in your laboratories."

"My laboratories can duplicate anything, sir." Ryoval smiled at the implied challenge.

"Except originality. By definition."

Ryoval spread his hands in polite acknowledgment of the philosophical point. Fell, Miles gathered, was not just enjoying the quaddie's musical talent, he was vastly enjoying the possession of something his rival keenly wanted to buy, that he had absolutely no need to sell. One-upsmanship was a powerful pleasure. It seemed even the famous Ryoval was having a tough time coming up with a better—and yet, if Ryoval could find Fell's price, what force on Jackson's whole could save Nicol? Miles suddenly realized he knew what Fell's price could be. Would Ryoval figure it out, too?

Ryoval pursed his lips. "Let's discuss a tissue sample, then. It would do her no damage, and you could continue to enjoy her unique services uninterrupted."

"It would damage her uniqueness. Circulating counterfeits always brings down the value of the real thing, you know that, Ry," grinned Baron Fell.

"Not for some time," Ryoval pointed out. "The lead time for a mature clone is at least ten years—ah, but you know that." He reddened and made a little apologetic bow, as if he realized he'd just committed some *faux pas*.

By the thinning of Fell's lips, he had. "Indeed," said Fell coldly.

At this point Bel Thorne, tracking the interplay, interrupted in hot horror. "You can't sell her tissues! You don't own them. She's not some Jackson's Whole construct, she's a freeborn galactic citizen!"

Both barons turned to Bel as if the mercenary were a piece of furniture that had suddenly spoken. Out of turn. Miles winced.

"He can sell her contract," said Ryoval, mustering a glassy tolerance. "Which is what we are discussing. A *private* discussion."

Bel ignored the hint. "On Jackson's Whole, what practical difference does it make if you call it a contract or call it flesh?"

Ryoval smiled a little cool smile. "None whatsoever. Possession is rather more than nine points of the law, here."

"It's totally illegal!"

"Legal, my dear—ah—you are Betan, aren't you? That explains it," said Ryoval. "And illegal, is whatever the planet you are on chooses to call so and is able to enforce. I don't see any Betan enforcers around here to impose their peculiar version of morality on us all, do you, Fell?"

Fell was listening with raised brows, caught between amusement and annoyance.

Bel twitched. "So if I were to pull out a weapon and blow your head off, it would be perfectly legal?"

The bodyguard tensed, balance and center-of-gravity flowing into launch position.

"Quash it, Bel," Miles muttered under his breath.

But Ryoval was beginning to enjoy baiting his Betan interruptor. "You have no weapon. But legality aside, my subordinates have instructions to avenge me. It is, as it were, a natural or virtual law. In effect you'd find such an ill-advised impulse to be illegal indeed."

Baron Fell caught Miles's eye and tilted his head just slightly. Time to intervene. "Time to move on, Captain," Miles said. "We aren't the baron's only guests here."

"Try the hot buffet," suggested Fell affably.

Ryoval pointedly dropped Bel from his attention and turned to Miles. "Do stop by my establishment if you get downside, Admiral. Even a Betan could stand to expand the horizons of his experience. I'm sure my staff could find something of interest in your price range."

"Not any more," said Miles. "Baron Fell already has our credit chit."

"Ah, too bad. Your next trip, perhaps." Ryoval turned away in easy dismissal.

Bel didn't budge. "You can't sell a galactic citizen down there," gesturing jerkily to the curve of the planet beyond the viewport. The quaddie Nicol, watching from behind her dulcimer, had no expression at all upon her face, but her intense blue eyes blazed.

Ryoval turned back, feigning sudden surprise. "Why, Captain, I just realized. Betan—you must be a genuine genetic hermaphrodite. You possess a marketable rarity yourself. I can offer you an eye-opening employment experience at easily twice your current rate of pay. And you wouldn't even have to get shot at. I guarantee you'd be extremely popular. Group rates."

Miles swore he could see Thorne's blood pressure sky-rocketing as the meaning of what Ryoval had just said sunk in. The hermaphrodite's face darkened, and it drew breath. Miles reached up and grasped Bel by the shoulder, hard. The breath held.

"No?" said Ryoval, cocking his head. "Oh, well. But seriously, I would pay well for a tissue sample, for my files."

Bel's breath exploded. "My clone-siblings, to be— be—some sort of sex-slaves into the next century! Over my dead body—or yours—you—"

Bel was so mad it was stuttering, a phenomenon Miles had never seen in seven years' acquaintance, including combat.

"So Betan," smirked Ryoval.

"Stop it, Ry," growled Fell.

Ryoval sighed. "Oh, very well. But it's so easy."

"We can't win, Bel," hissed Miles. "It's time to withdraw." The bodyguard was quivering.

Fell gave Miles an approving nod.

"Thank you for your hospitality, Baron Fell," Miles said formally. "Good day, Baron Ryoval."

"Good day, Admiral," said Ryoval, regretfully giving up what was obviously the best sport he'd had all day. "You seem a cosmopolitan sort, for a Betan. Perhaps you can visit us sometime without your moral friend, here."

A war of words should be won with words. "I don't think so," Miles murmured, racking his brain for some stunning insult to withdraw on.

"What a shame," said Ryoval. "We have a dog-and-dwarf act I'm sure you'd find *fascinating*."

There was a moment's absolute silence.

"Fry 'em from orbit," Bel suggested tightly.

Miles grinned through clenched teeth, bowed, and backed off, Bel's sleeve clutched firmly in his hand. As he turned he could hear Ryoval laughing.

Fell's majordomo appeared at their elbows within moments. "This way to the exit, please, officers," he smiled. Miles had never before been thrown out of any place with such exquisite politeness.

Back aboard the *Ariel* in dock, Thorne paced the wardroom while Miles sat and sipped coffee as hot and black as his own thoughts.

"Sorry I lost my temper with that squirt Ryoval," Bel apologized gruffly.

"Squirt, hell," said Miles. "The brain in that body has got to be at least a hundred years old. He played you like a violin. No. We couldn't expect to count coup on him. I admit, it would have been nice if you'd had the sense to shut up." He sucked air to cool his scalded tongue

Bel made a disturbed gesture of acknowledgment and paced on. "And that poor girl, trapped in that bubble—I had one chance to talk to her, and I blew it—I blithered. . . ."

She really had brought out the male in Thorne, Miles reflected wryly. "Happens to the best of us," he murmured. He smiled into this coffee, then frowned. No. Better not to encourage Thorne's interest in the quaddie after all. She was clearly much more than just one of Fell's house servants. They had one ship here, a crew of twenty; even if he had the whole Dendarii fleet to back him he'd want to think twice about offending Baron Fell in Fell's own territory. They had a mission. Speaking of which, where was their blasted pick-up? Why hadn't he yet contacted them as arranged?

The intercom in the wall bleeped.

Throne strode to it. "Thorne here."

"This is a Corporal Nout at the portside docking hatch. There's a . . . woman here who's asking to see you."

Thorne and Miles exchanged a raised-brows glance. "What's her name?" asked Thorne.

An off-side mumble, then, "She says it's Nicol."

Thorne grunted in surprise. "Very well. Have her escorted to the wardroom."

"Yes, Captain." The corporal failed to kill his intercom before turning away, and his voice drifted back, ". . . stay in this outfit long enough, you see one of *everything*."

Nicol appeared in the doorway balanced in a float chair, a hovering tubular cup that seemed to be looking for its saucer, enameled in a blue that precisely matched her eyes. She slipped it through the doorway as easily as a woman twitching her hips, zipped to a halt near Miles's table, and adjusted the height to that of a person sitting. The controls, run by her lower hands, left her uppers entirely free. The lower body support must have been custom-designed just for her. Miles watched her maneuver with great interest. He hadn't been sure she could even live outside her null-gee bubble. He'd expected her to be weak. She didn't look weak. She looked determined. She looked at Thorne

Thorne looked all cheered up. "Nicol. How nice to see you again."

She nodded shortly. "Captain Thorne. Admiral Naismith." She glanced back and forth between them, and fastened on Thorne. Miles thought he could see why. He sipped coffee and waited for developments.

"Captain Thorne. You are a mercenary, are you not?"

"Yes . . ."

"And . . . pardon me if I misunderstood, but it seemed to me you had a certain . . . empathy for my situation. An understanding of my position."

Thorne rendered her a slightly idiotic bow. "I understand you are dangling over a pit."

Her lips tightened, and she nodded mutely.

"She got herself into it," Miles pointed out.

Her chin lifted, "And I intend to get myself out of it."

Miles turned a hand palm out, and sipped again.

She readjusted her float chair, a nervous gesture ending at about the same altitude it began.

"It seems to me," said Miles, "that Baron Fell is a formidable protector. I'm not sure you have anything to fear from Ryoval's, er, carnal interest in you as long as Fell's in charge."

"Baron Fell is dying." She tossed her head. "Or at any rate, he thinks he is."

"So I gathered. Why doesn't he have a clone made?"

"He did. It was all set up with House Bharaputra. The clone was fourteen years old, full-sized. Then a couple of months ago, somebody assassinated the clone. The baron still hasn't found out for sure who did it, though he has a little list. Headed by his half-brother."

"Thus trapping him in his aging body. What a . . . fascinating tactical maneuver," Miles mused. "What's this unknown enemy going to do next, I wonder? Just wait?"

"I don't know," said Nicol. "The Baron's had another clone started, but it's not even out of the replicator yet. Even with growth accelerators it'd be years before it would be mature enough to transplant. And . . . it has occurred to me that there are a number of ways the baron could die besides ill health between now and then."

"An unstable situation," Miles agreed.

"I want out. I want to buy passage out."

"Then why, he asked," said Miles dryly, "don't you just go plunk your money down at the offices of one of the three galactic commercial passenger lines that dock here, and buy a ticket?"

"It's my contract," said Nicol. "When I signed it back on Earth, I didn't realize what it would mean once I got to Jackson's Whole. I can't even buy my way out of it, unless the baron chooses to let me. And somehow . . . it gets much worse before my time is up."

"How much time?" asked Thorne.

"Five more years."

"Ouch," said Thorne sympathetically.

"So you, ah, want us to help you jump a Syndicate contract," said Miles, making little wet coffee rings on the table with the bottom of his mug. "Smuggle you out in secret, I suppose."

"I can pay. I can pay more right now than I'll be able

to next year. This wasn't the gig I expected when I came here. There was talk of recording a vid demo—it never happened. I don't think it's ever going to happen. I have to be able to reach a wider audience, if I'm ever to pay my way back home. Back to my people. I want . . . *out* of here before I fall down that gravity well." she jerked an upper thumb in the general direction of the planet they orbited. "People go downside here who never come up again." She paused. "Are you *afraid* of Baron Fell?"

"No!" said Thorne, as Miles said, "Yes." They exchanged a sardonic look.

"We are inclined to be careful of Baron Fell," Miles suggested. Thorne shrugged agreement.

She frowned, and maneuvered to the table. She drew a wad of assorted planetary currencies out of her green silk jacket and laid it in front of Miles. "Would this bolster your nerve?"

Thorne fingered the stack, flipped through it. At least a couple thousand Betan dollars worth, at conservative estimate, mostly in middle denominations, though a Betan single topped the pile, camouflaging its value to a casual glance. "Well," said Thorne, glancing at Miles, "and what do we mercenaries think of that?"

Miles leaned back thoughtfully in his chair. The kept secret of Miles's identity wasn't the only favor Thorne could call in if it chose. Miles remembered the day Thorne had helped capture an asteroid mining station and the pocket dreadnought *Triumph* for him with nothing but sixteen troops in combat armor and a hell of a lot of nerve. "I encourage creative financing on the part of my commanders," he said at last. "Negotiate away, Captain."

Thorne smiled, and pulled the Betan dollar off the stack. "You have the right idea," Thorne said to the musician, "but the amount is wrong."

Her hand went uncertainly to her jacket and paused, as Thorne pushed the rest of the stack of currency, minus the single, back to her. "What?"

Thorne picked up the single and snapped it a few times. "This is the right amount. Makes it an official contract, you see." Bel extended a hand to her; after a bewildered moment, she shook it. "Deal," said Thorne happily.

"Hero," said Miles, holding up a warning finger, "beware, I'll call in my veto if you can't come up with a way to bring this off in dead secret. That's my cut of the price."

"Yes, *sir,*" said Thorne.

Several hours later, Miles snapped awake in his cabin aboard the *Ariel* to an urgent bleeping from his comconsole. Whatever he had been dreaming was gone in the instant, though he had the vague idea it had been something unpleasant. Biological and unpleasant. "Naismith here."

"This is the duty officer in Nav and Com, sir. You have a call originating from the downside commercial comm net. He says to tell you it's Vaughn."

Vaughn was the agreed upon code name of their pickup. His real name was Dr. Canaba. Miles grabbed his uniform jacket and shrugged it on over his black T-shirt, passed his hands futiley through his hair, and slid into his console station chair. "Put him through."

The face of a man on the high side of middle age materialized above Miles's vid plate. Tan-skinned, racially indeterminate features, short wavy hair greying at the temples; more arresting was the intelligence that suffused those features and quickened the brown eyes. *Yep, that's my man,* thought Miles with satisfaction. *Here we go.* But Canaba looked more than tense. He looked distraught.

"Admiral Naismith?"

"Yes. Vaughn?"

Canaba nodded.

"Where are you?" asked Miles.

"Downside."

"You were to meet us up here."

"I know. Something's come up. A problem."

"What sort of problem? Ah—is this channel secure?" Canaba laughed bitterly. "On this planet, nothing is secure. But I don't think I'm being traced. But I can't come up yet. I need . . . help."

"Vaughn, we aren't equipped to break you out against superior forces—if you've become a prisoner—"

He shook his head. "No, it's not that. I've . . . lost something. I need help to get it back."

"I'd understood you were to leave everything. You would be compensated later."

"It's not a personal possession. It's something your employer wants very badly. Certain . . . samples, have been removed from my . . . power. They won't take me without them."

Dr. Canaba took Miles for a mercenary hireling, entrusted with minimum classified information by Barrayaran Security. So. "All I was asked to transport was you and your skills."

"They didn't tell you everything."

The hell they didn't. Barrayar would take you stark naked, and be grateful. What was this?

Canaba met Miles's frown with a mouth set like iron. "I *won't* leave without them. Or the deal's off. And you can whistle for your pay, mercenary."

He meant it. Damn. Miles's eyes narrowed. "This is all a bit mysterious."

Canaba shrugged acknowledgment. "I'm sorry. But I *must* . . . Meet with me, and I'll tell you the rest. Or go, I don't care which. But a certain thing must be accomplished, must be . . . expiated." He trailed off in agitation.

Miles took a deep breath. "Very well. But every complication you add increases your risk. And mine. This had better be worth it."

"Oh, Admiral," breathed Canaba sadly, "it is to me. It is to me."

Snow sifted through the little park where Canaba met them, giving Miles something new to swear at if only he hadn't run out of invective hours ago. He was shivering even in his Dendarii-issue parka by the time Canaba walked past the dingy kiosk where Miles and Bel roosted. They fell in behind him without a word.

Bharaputra Laboratories were headquartered in a

downside town Miles frankly found worrisome: guarded shuttleport, guarded Syndicate buildings, guarded municipal buildings, guarded walled residential compounds; in between, a crazy disorder of neglected aging structures that didn't seem to be guarded by anyone, occupied by people who *slunk*. It made Miles wonder if the two Dendarii troopers he'd detailed to shadow them were quite enough. But the slithery people gave them a wide berth; they evidently understood what guards meant. At least during daylight.

Canaba led them into one of the nearby buildings. Its lift tubes were out of order, its corridors unheated. A darkly dressed maybe-female person scurried out of their way in the shadows, reminding Miles uncomfortably of a rat. They followed Canaba dubiously up the safety ladder set in the side of a dead lift tube, down another corridor, and through a door with a broken palm-lock into an empty dirty room, greyly lit by an unpolarized but intact window. At least they were out of the wind.

"I think we can talk safely here," said Canaba, turning and pulling off his gloves.

"Bel?" said Miles.

Thorne pulled an assortment of anti-surveillance detectors from its parka and ran a scan, as the two guards prowled the perimeters. One stationed himself in the corridor, the second near the window.

"It scans clean," said Bel at last, as if reluctant to believe its own instruments. "For now." Rather pointedly, Bel walked around Canaba and scanned him too. Canaba waited with bowed head, as if he felt he deserved no better. Bel set up the sonic baffler.

Miles shrugged back his hood and opened his parka, the better to reach his concealed weapons in the event of a trap. He was finding Canaba extraordinarily hard to read. What were the man's motivations anyway? There was no doubt House Bharaputra had assured his comfort—his coat, the rich cut of his clothing beneath it, spoke of that—and though his standard of living surely would not drop when he transferred his allegiance to the Barrayaran Imperial Science Institute, he would not have nearly the opportunities to amass wealth on the side that he had here. But why work for a place like House Bharaputra in the first place unless greed overwhelmed integrity?

"You puzzle me, Dr. Canaba," said Miles lightly. "Why this mid-career switch? I'm pretty well acquainted with your new employers, and frankly, I don't see how they could out-bid House Bharaputra." There, that was a properly mercenary way to put it.

"They offered me protection from House Bharaputra. Although, if *you're* it . . ." he looked doubtfully down at Miles. Ha. And, hell. The man really was ready to bolt. Leaving Miles to explain the failure of his mission to Chief of Imperial Security Illyan in person. "They bought our services," said Miles, "and therefore you command our services. They want you safe and happy. But we can't begin to protect you when you depart from a plan designed to maximize your safety, throw in random factors, and ask us to operate in the dark. I need full knowledge of what's going on if I'm to take full responsibility for the results."

"No one is asking you to take responsibility."

"I beg your pardon, doctor, but they surely have."

"Oh," said Canaba. "I . . . see." He paced to the window, back. "But will you do what I ask?"

"I will do what I can."

"Happy," Canaba snorted. "God . . ." he shook his head wearily, inhaled decisively. "I never came here for the money. I came here because I could do research I couldn't do anywhere else. Not hedged round with outdated legal restrictions. I dreamed of breakthroughs . . . but it became a nightmare. The freedom became slavery. The things they wanted me to do! . . . Constantly interrupting the things *I* wanted to do. Oh, you can always find someone to do anything for money, but they're second-raters. These labs are full of second-raters. The very best can't be bought. I've done things, unique things, that Bharaputra won't develop because the profit would be too small, never mind how many people it would benefit—I get no credit, no standing for my work—every year, I see in the literature of my field galactic honors going to lesser men, because I cannot publish my results. . . ." he stopped, lowered his head. "I doubtless sound like a megalomaniac to you."

"Ah . . ." said Miles, "you sound quite frustrated."

"The frustration," said Canaba, "woke me from a long sleep. Wounded ego—it was only wounded ego. But in my pride, I rediscovered shame. And the weight of it stunned me, stunned me where I stood. *Do* you understand? Does it matter if you understand? Ah!" He paced away to the wall, and stood facing it, his back rigid.

"Uh," Miles scratched the back of his head ruefully, "yeah, I'd be glad to spend many fascinating hours listening to you explain it to me—on my ship. Outbound."

Canaba turned with a crooked smile. "You are a practical man, I perceive. A soldier. Well, God knows I need a soldier now."

"Things are that screwed up, eh?"

"It . . . happened suddenly. I thought I had it under control."

"Go on," sighed Miles.

"There were seven synthesized gene-complexes. One of them is a cure for a certain obscure enzyme disorder. One of them will increase oxygen generation in space station algae twenty-fold. One of them came from outside Bharaputra Labs, brought in by a man—we never found out who he really was, but death followed him. Several of my colleagues who had worked on his project were murdered all in one night, by the commandos who pursued him—their records destroyed—I never told anyone I'd borrowed an unauthorized tissue sample to study. I've not unraveled it fully yet, but I can tell you, it's absolutely unique."

Miles recognized that one, and almost choked, reflecting upon the bizarre chain of circumstances that had placed an identical tissue sample in the hands of Dendarii Intelligence a year ago. Terrence See's telepathy complex—and the main reason *why* His Imperial Majesty suddenly wanted a top geneticist. Dr. Canaba was in for a little surprise when he arrived at his new Barrayaran laboratory. But if the other six complexes came anywhere near matching the value of the known one,

Security Chief Illyan would peel Miles with a dull knife
for letting them slip through his fingers. Miles's attention
to Canaba abruptly intensified. This side-trip might not
be as trivial as he'd feared.

"Together, these seven complexes represent tens of
thousands of hours of research time, mostly mine, some
of others—my life's work. I'd planned from the beginning to take them with me. I bundled them up in a
viral insert and placed them, bound and dormant, in a
live . . ." Canaba faltered, "organism, for storage. An
organism, I thought, that no one would think to look at
for such a thing."

"Why didn't you just store them in your own tissue?"
Miles asked irritably. "Then you couldn't lose 'em."

Canaba's mouth opened. "I . . . never thought of that.
How elegant. Why didn't I think of that?" His hand
touched his forehead wonderingly, as if probing for systems failure. His lips tightened again. "But it would have
made no difference. I would still need to . . ." he fell
silent. "It's about the organism," he said at last. "The
. . . creature." Another long silence.

"Of all things I did," Canaba continued lowly, "of all
the interruptions this vile place imposed on me, there is
one I regret the most. You understand, this was years
ago. I was younger, I thought I still had a future here
to protect. And it wasn't all my doing—guilt by committee, eh? Spread it around, make it easy, say it was *his*
fault, *her* doing. . . . well, it's mine now."

You mean it's *mine* now, thought Miles grimly. "Doctor, the more time we spend here, the greater the chance
of compromising this operation. Please get to the point."

"Yes . . . yes. Well, a number of years ago, House
Bharaputra Laboratories took on a contract to manufacture a . . . new species. Made to order."

"I thought it was House Ryoval that was famous for
making people, or whatever, to order," said Miles.

"They make slaves, one-off. They are very specialized.
And small—their customer base is surprisingly small.
There are many rich men, and there are, I suppose,
many depraved men, but a House Ryoval customer has
to be a member of both sets, and the overlap isn't as

large as you'd think. Anyway, our contract was supposed to lead to a major production run, far beyond Ryoval's capabilities. A certain subplanetary government, hard-pressed by its neighbors, wanted us to engineer a race of super-soldiers for them."

"What, again?" said Miles. "I thought that had been tried. More than once."

"This time, we thought we could do it. Or at least, the Bharaputra hierarchy was willing to take their money. But the project suffered from too much input. The client, our own higher-ups, the genetics project members, everybody had ideas they were pushing. I swear it was doomed before it ever got out of the design committee."

"A super-soldier. Designed by a committee. Ye gods. The mind boggles." Miles's eyes were wide in fascination. "So then what happened?"

"It seemed to . . . several of us, that the physical limits of the merely human had already been reached. Once a, say, muscle system has been brought to perfect health, stimulated with maximum hormones, exercised to a certain limit, that's all you can do. So we turned to other species for special improvements. I, for instance, became fascinated by the aerobic and anaerobic metabolism in the muscles of the thoroughbred horse—"

"What?" said Thorne, shocked.

"There were other ideas. Too many. I swear, they weren't all mine."

"You mixed human and animal genes?" breathed Miles.

"Why not? Human genes have been spliced into animals from the crude beginnings—it was almost the first thing tried. Human insulin from bacteria and the like. But till now, none dared do it in reverse. I broke the barrier, cracked the codes. . . . It looked good at first. It was only when the first ones reached puberty that all the errors became fully apparent. Well, it was only the initial trial. They were meant to be formidable. But they ended up monstrous."

"Tell me," Miles choked, "were there any actual combat-experienced soldiers on the committee?"

"I assume the client had them. They supplied the parameters." said Canaba.

Said Thorne in a suffused voice, "*I* see. They were trying to reinvent the *enlisted* man."

Miles shot Thorne a quelling glower, and tapped his chrono. "Don't let us interrupt, doctor."

There was a short silence. Canaba began again. "We ran off ten prototypes. Then the client ... went out of business. They lost their war—"

"Why am I not surprised?" Miles muttered under his breath.

"—funding was cut off, the project was dropped before we could apply what we had learned from our mistakes. Of the ten prototypes, nine have since died. There was one left. We were keeping it at the labs due to ... difficulties, in boarding it out. I placed my gene complexes in it. They are there still. The last thing I meant to do before I left was kill it. A mercy ... a responsibility. My expiation, if you will."

"And then?" prodded Miles.

"A few days ago, it was suddenly sold to House Ryoval. As a novelty, apparently. Baron Ryoval collects oddities of all sorts, for his tissue banks—"

Miles and Bel exchanged a look.

"—I had no idea it was to be sold. I came in in the morning and it was gone. I don't think Ryoval has any idea of its real value. It's there now, as far as I know. at Ryoval's facilities."

Miles decided he was getting a sinus headache. From the cold, no doubt. "And what, pray, d'you want us soldiers to do about it?"

"Get in there, somehow. Kill it. Collect a tissue sample. Only then will I go with you."

And stomach twinges. "What, both ears and the tail?"

Canaba gave Miles a cold look. "The left gastrocnemius muscle. That's where I injected my complexes. These storage viruses aren't virulent, they won't have migrated far. The greatest concentration should still be there."

"I see." Miles rubbed his temples, and pressed his eyes. "All right. We'll take care of it. This personal contact between us is very dangerous, and I'd rather not repeat it. Plan to report to my ship in forty-eight hours. Will we have any trouble recognizing your critter?"

"I don't think so. This particular specimen topped out at just over eight feet. I . . . want you to know, the fangs were *not* my idea."

"I . . . see."

"It can move very fast, if it's still in good health. Is there any help I can give you? I have access to painless poisons—"

"You've done enough, thank you. Please leave it to us professionals, eh?"

"It would be best if its body can be destroyed entirely. No cells remaining. If you can."

"That's why plasma arcs were invented. You'd best be on your way."

"Yes." Canaba hesitated. "Admiral Naismith?"

"Yes . . ."

"I . . . it might also be best if my future employer didn't learn about this. They have intense military interests. It might excite them unduly."

"Oh," said Miles/Admiral Naismith/Lieutenant Lord Vorkosigan of the Barrayaran Imperial Service, "I don't think you have to worry about that."

"Is forty-eight hours enough for your commando raid?" Canaba worried. "You understand, if you don't get the tissue, I'll go right back downside. I will not be trapped aboard your ship."

"You will be happy. It's in my contract," said Miles. "Now you'd better get gone."

"I must rely on you, sir." Canaba nodded in suppressed anguish, and withdrew.

They waited a few minutes in the cold room, to let Canaba put some distance between them. The building creaked in the wind; from an upper corridor echoed an odd shriek, and later, a laugh abruptly cut off. The guard shadowing Canaba returned. "He made it to his ground car all right, sir."

"Well," said Thorne. "I suppose we'll need to get hold of a plan of Ryoval's facilities, first—"

"I think not," said Miles.

"If we're to raid—"

"Raid, hell. I'm not risking my men on anything so idiotic. I said I'd slay his sin for him. I didn't say how."

The commercial comconsole net at the downside shuttleport seemed as convenient as anything. Miles slid into the booth and fed the machine his credit card while Thorne lurked just outside the viewing angle and the guards, outside, guarded. He encoded the call.

In a moment, the vid plate produced the image of a sweet-faced receptionist with dimples and a white fur crest instead of hair. "House Ryoval, Customer Services. How may I help you, sir?"

"I'd like to speak to Manager Deem, in Sales and Demonstrations," said Miles smoothly, "about a possible purchase for my organization."

"Who may I say is calling?"

"Admiral Miles Naismith, Dendarii Free Mercenary Fleet."

"One moment, sir."

"You really think they'll just sell it?" Bel muttered from the side as the girl's face was replaced by a flowing pattern of colored lights and some syrupy music.

"Remember what we overheard yesterday?" said Miles. "I'm betting it's *on* sale. Cheap." He must try not to look too interested.

In a remarkably short time, the colored glop gave way to the face of an astonishingly beautiful young man, a blue-eyed albino in a red silk shirt. He had a huge livid bruise up one side of his white face. "This is Manager Deem. May I help you, Admiral?"

Miles cleared his throat carefully. "A rumor has been brought to my attention that House Ryoval may have recently acquired from House Bharaputra an article of some professional interest to me. Supposedly, it was the prototype of some sort of new improved fighting man. Do you know anything about it?"

Deem's hand stole to his bruise and palpated it gently, then twitched away. "Indeed, sir, we do have such an article."

"Is it for sale?"

"Oh, *ye*—I mean, I think some arrangement is pending. But it may still be possible to bid on it."

"Would it be possible for me to inspect it?"

"Of course," said Deem with suppressed eagerness. "How soon?"

There was a burst of static, and the vid image split, Deem's face abruptly shrinking to one side. The new face was only too familiar. Bel hissed under its breath.

"I'll take this call, Deem," said Baron Ryoval.

"Yes, my lord." Deem's eyes widened in surprise, and he cut out. Ryoval's image swelled to occupy the space available.

"So, Betan," Ryoval smiled, "it appears I have something you want after all."

Miles shrugged. "Maybe," he said neutrally. "If it's in my price range."

"I thought you gave all your money to Fell."

Miles spread his hands. "A good commander always has hidden reserves. However, the actual value of the item hasn't yet been established. In fact, its existence hasn't even been established."

"Oh, it exists, all right. And it is . . . impressive. Adding it to my collection was a unique pleasure. I'd hate to give it up. But for you." Ryoval smiled more broadly, "it may be possible to arrange a special cut rate." He chuckled, as at some secret pun that escaped Miles.

A special cut throat is more like it. "Oh?"

"I propose a simple trade," said Ryoval. "Flesh for flesh."

"You may overestimate my interest, Baron."

Ryoval's eyes glinted. "I don't think so."

He knows I wouldn't touch him with a stick if it weren't something pretty compelling. So. "Name your proposal, then."

"I'll trade you even, Bharaputra's pet monster—ah, you should see it, Admiral—for three tissue samples. Three tissue samples that will, if you are clever about it, cost you nothing." Ryoval held up one finger. "One from your Betan hermaphrodite," a second finger, "one from yourself," a third finger, making a W, "and one from Baron Fell's quaddie musician."

Over in the corner, Bel Thorne appeared to be sup-pressing an apopleptic fit. Quietly, fortunately.

"That third could prove extremely difficult to obtain," said Miles, buying time to think.

"Less difficult for you than me," said Ryoval. "Fell knows my agents. My overtures have put him on guard. You represent a unique opportunity to get in under that guard. Given sufficient motivation, I'm certain it's not beyond you, mercenary."

"Given sufficient motivation, very little is beyond me, Baron," said Miles semi-randomly.

"Well, then. I shall expect to hear from you within—say—twenty-four hours. After that time my offer will be withdrawn." Ryoval nodded cheerfully. "Good day, Admiral." The vid blanked.

"Well, then," echoed Miles.

"Well what?" said Thorne with suspicion. "You're not actually seriously considering that —vile proposal, are you?"

"What does he want my tissue sample for, for God's sake?" Miles wondered aloud.

"For his dog and dwarf act, no doubt," said Thorne nastily.

"Now, now. He'd be dreadfully disappointed when my clone turned out to be six feet tall, I'm afraid." Miles cleared his throat. "It wouldn't actually hurt anyone, I suppose. To take a small tissue sample. Whereas a com-mando raid risks lives."

Bel leaned back against the wall and crossed its arms. "Not true. You'd have to fight me for mine. And *hers*."

Miles grinned sourly. "So."

"So?"

"So let's go find a map of Ryoval's flesh pit. It seems we're going hunting."

House Ryoval's palatial main biologicals facility wasn't a proper fortress, just some guarded buildings. Some bloody big guarded buildings. Miles stood on the roof of the lift-van and studied the layout through his nightglasses. Fog droplets beaded in his hair. The cold damp wind searched for chinks in his jacket much as he searched for chinks in Ryoval's security.

The white complex loomed against the dark forested mountainside, its front gardens floodlit and fairy-like in the fog and frost. The utility entrances on the near side looked more promising. Miles nodded slowly to himself and climbed down off the rented lift-van, artistically broken-down on the little mountain side-trail overlooking Ryoval's. He swung into the back, out of the piercing wind.

"All right, people, listen up." His squad hunkered around as he set up the holovid map in the middle. The colored lights of the display sheened their faces: tall Ensign Murka, Thorne's second-in-command, and two big troopers. Sergeant Laureen Anderson was the van driver, assigned to outside back-up along with Trooper Sandy Hereld and Captain Thorne. Miles harbored a secret Barrayaran prejudice against taking female troops inside Ryoval's that he trusted he concealed. It went double for Bel Thorne. Not that one's sex would necessarily make any difference to the adventures that might follow in the event of capture, if even a tenth of the bizarre rumors he'd heard were true. Nevertheless ... Lauren claimed to be able to fly any vehicle made by man through the eye of a needle, not that Miles figured she'd ever done anything so domestic as thread a needle in her life. She would not question her assignment.

"Our main problem remains, that we still don't know where exactly in this facility Bharaputra's creature is being kept. So first we penetrate the fence, the outer courts, and the main building, here and here." A red thread of light traced their projected route at Miles's touch on the control board. "Then we quietly pick up an inside employee and fast-penta him. From that point on we're racing time, since we must assume he'll be promptly missed.

"The key word is quietly. We didn't come here to kill *people,* and we are not at war with Ryoval's employees. You carry your stunners, and keep those plasma arcs and the rest of the toys packed till we locate our quarry. We dispatch it fast and quietly, I get my sample," his hand touched his jacket, beneath which rested the collection case that would keep the tissue alive till they got back to the *Ariel*. "Then we fly. If anything goes wrong before I get that very expensive cut of meat, we don't bother to fight our way out. Not worth it. They have peculiar summary ways of dealing with murder charges here, and I don't see the need for any of us to end up as spare parts in Ryoval's tissue banks. We wait for Captain Thorne to arrange a ransom, and then try something else. We hold a lever or two on Ryoval in case of emergencies."

"*Dire* emergencies," Bel muttered.

"If anything goes wrong after the butcher-mission is accomplished, it's back to combat rules. That sample will then be irreplaceable, and must be got back to Captain Thorne at all costs. Laureen, you sure of our emergency pick-up spot?"

"Yes, sir." She pointed on the vid display.

"Everybody else got that? Any questions? Suggestions? Last-minute observations? Communications check, then, Captain Thorne."

Their wrist comms all appeared to be in good working order. Ensign Murka shrugged on the weapons pack. Miles carefully pocketed the blueprint map cube, that had cost them a near-ransom from a certain pliable construction company just a few hours ago. The four members of the penetration team slipped from the van and merged with the frosty darkness.

They slunk off through the woods. The frozen crunchy layer of plant detritus tended to slide underfoot, exposing a layer of slick mud. Murka spotted a spy eye before it spotted them, and blinded it with a brief burst of microwave static while they scurried past. The useful big guys made short work of boosting Miles over the wall. Miles tried not to think about the ancient pub sport of dwarf tossing. The inner court was stark and utilitarian, loading docks with big locked doors, rubbish collection bays, and a few parked vehicles.

Footsteps echoed, and they ducked down in a rubbish bay. A red-clad guard passed, slowly waving an infrared scanner. They crouched and hid their faces in their infra-red blank ponchos, looking like so many bags of garbage, no doubt. Then it was tiptoe up to the loading docks.

Ducts. The key to Ryoval's facility had turned out to be ducts—for heating, for access to power-optics cables, for the comm system. Narrow ducts. Quite impassable to a big guy. Miles slipped out of his poncho and gave it to a trooper to fold and pack.

Miles balanced on Murka's shoulders and cut his way through the first ductlet, a ventilation grille high on the wall above the loading dock doors. Miles handed the grille down silently, and after a quick visual scan for unwanted company, slithered through. It was a tight fit even for him. He let himself down gently to the concrete floor, found the door control box, shorted the alarm, and raised the door about a meter. His team rolled through, and he let the door back down as quietly as he could. So far so good; they hadn't yet had to exchange a word.

They made it to cover on the far side of the receiving bay just before a red-coveralled employee wandered through, driving an electric cart loaded with cleaning robots. Murka touched Miles's sleeve, and looked his inquiry—*This one?* Miles shook his head, *Not yet.* A maintenance man seemed less likely than an employee from the inner sanctum to know where their quarry was kept, and they didn't have time to litter the place with the unconscious bodies of false trials. They found the tunnel to the main building, just as the map cube promised. The door at the end was locked, as expected.

It was up on Murka's shoulders again. A quick zizz of Miles's cutters loosened a panel in the ceiling, and he crawled through—the frail supporting framework would surely not have held a man of greater weight—and found the power cables running to the door lock. He was just looking over the problem and pulling tools out of his pocketed uniform jacket when Murka's hand reached up to thrust the weapons pack beside him and quietly pull the panel back into place. Miles flung himself to his belly and pressed his eye to the crack as a voice from down the corridor bellowed, "Freeze!"

Swear words screamed through Miles's head. He

clamped his jaw on them. He looked down on the tops of his troopers' heads. In a moment, they were surrounded by half a dozen red-clad, black-trousered armed guards. "What are you doing here?" snarled the guard sergeant.

"Oh, shit!" cried Murka. "*Please,* mister, don't tell my CO you caught us in here. He'd bust me back to private!"

"Huh?" said the guard sergeant. He prodded Murka with his weapon, a lethal nerve disruptor. "Hands up! Who are you?"

"M'name's Murka. We came in on a mercenary ship to Fell Station, but the captain wouldn't grant us downside passes. Think of it—we come all the way to Jackson's Whole, and the sonofabitch wouldn't let us go downside! Bloody pure-dick wouldn't let us see Ryoval's!"

The red-tunic'd guards were doing a fast scan-and-search, none too gently, and finding only stunners and the portion of security-penetration devices that Murka had carried.

"I made a bet we could get in even if we couldn't afford the front door." Murka's mouth turned down in great discouragement. "Looks like I lost."

"Looks like you did," growled the guard sergeant, drawing back.

One of his men held up the thin collection of baubles they'd stripped off the Dendarii. "They're not equipped like an assassination team," he observed.

Murka drew himself up, looking wonderfully offended. "We aren't!"

The guard sergeant turned over a stunner. "AWOL, are you?"

"Not if we make it back before midnight." Murka's tone went wheedling. "Look, m' CO's a right bastard. Suppose there's any way you could see your way clear that he doesn't find out about this?" One of Murka's hands drifted suggestively past his wallet pocket.

The guard sergeant looked him up and down, smirking. "Maybe."

Miles listened with open-mouthed delight. *Murka, if this works I'm promoting you. . . .*

Murka paused. "Any chance of seeing inside first? Not the girls even, just the place? So I could say that I'd seen it."

"This isn't a whorehouse, soldier boy!" snapped the guard sergeant.

Murka looked stunned. "What?"

"This is the *biologicals* facility."

"Oh," said Murka.

"You *idiot,*" one of the troopers put in on cue. Miles sprinkled silent blessings down upon his head. None of the three so much as flicked an eyeball upward.

"But the man in town told me—" began Murka.

"What man?" said the guard sergeant.

"The man who took m'money," said Murka.

A couple of the red-tunic'd guards were beginning to grin. The guard sergeant prodded Murka with his nerve disruptor. "Get along, soldier boy. Back that way. This is your lucky day."

"You mean we get to see inside?" said Murka hopefully.

"No," said the guard sergeant, "I mean we aren't going to break both your legs before we throw you out on your ass." He paused and added more kindly, "There's a whorehouse back in town." He slipped Murka's wallet out of his pocket, checked the name on the credit card and put it back, and removed all the loose currency. The guards did the same to the outraged-looking troopers, dividing the assorted cash up among them. "They take credit cards, and you've still got till midnight. Now move!"

And so Miles's squad was chivvied, ignominiously but intact, down the tunnel. Miles waited till the whole mob was well out of earshot before keying his wristcom. "Bel?"

"Yes," came back the instant reply.

"Trouble. Murka and the troops were just picked up by Ryoval's security. I believe the boy genius has just managed to bullshit them into throwing them out the back door, instead of rendering them down for parts. I'll

follow as soon as I can, we'll rendezvous and regroup
for another try." Miles paused. This was a total bust,
they were now worse off than when they started. Ryoval's security would be stirred up for the rest of the long
Jacksonian night. He added to the comm, "I'm going to
see if I can't at least find out the location of the critter
before I withdraw. Should improve our chances of success next round."

Bel swore in a heartfelt tone. "Be careful."

"You bet. Watch for Murka and the boys. Naismith
out."

Once he'd identified the right cables it was the work
of a moment to make the door slide open. He then had
an interesting dangle by his fingertips while coaxing the
ceiling panel to fall back into place before he dropped
from maximum downward extension, fearful for his
bones. Nothing broke. He slipped across the portal to
the main building and took to the ducts as soon as possible, the corridors having been proved dangerous. He lay
on his back in the narrow tube and balanced the blueprint holocube on his belly, picking out a new and safer
route not necessarily passable to a couple of husky
troopers. And where did one look for a monster? A
closet?

It was at about the third turn, inching his way through
the system dragging the weapons pack, that he became
aware that the territory no longer matched the map. Hell
and damnation. Were these changes in the system since
its construction, or a subtly sabotaged map? Well, no
matter, he wasn't really lost, he could still retrace his
route.

He crawled along for about thirty minutes, discovering
and disarming two alarm sensors before they discovered
him. The time factor was getting seriously pressing. Soon
he would have to—ah, there! He peered through a vent
grille into a dim room filled with holovid and communications equipment. *Small Repairs,* the map cube named
it. It didn't look like a repairs shop. Another change
since Ryoval had moved in? But a man sat alone with
his back to Miles's wall. Perfect, too good to pass up.

Breathing silently, moving slowly, Miles eased his

dart-gun out of the pack and made sure he loaded it with the right cartridge, fast-penta spiked with a paralyzer, a lovely cocktail blended for the purpose by the *Ariel's* medtech. He sighted through the grille, aimed the needle-nose of the dart gun with tense precision, and fired. Bull's-eye. The man slapped the back of his neck once and sat still, hand falling nervelessly to his side. Miles grinned briefly, cut his way through the grille, and lowered himself to the floor.

The man was well dressed in civilian-type clothes—one of the scientists, perhaps? He lolled in his chair, a little smile playing around his lips, and stared with unalarmed interest at Miles. He started to fall over.

Miles caught him and propped him back upright. "Sit up now, that's right, you can't talk with your face in the carpet now, can you?"

"Nooo ..." the man bobbled his head and smiled agreeably.

"Do you know anything about a genetic construct, a monstrous creature, just recently bought from House Bharaputra and brought to this facility?"

The man blinked and smiled. "Yes."

Fast-penta subjects did tend to be literal, Miles reminded himself. "Where is it being kept?"

"Downstairs."

"Where exactly downstairs?"

"In the sub-basement. The crawl-space around the foundations. We were hoping it would catch some of the rats, you see." The man giggled. "Do cats eats rats? Do rats eat cats? ..."

Miles checked his map-cube. Yes. That looked good, in terms of the penetration team getting in and out, though it was still a large search area, broken up into a maze by structural elements running down into the bedrock, and specially set low-vibration support columns running up into the laboratories. At the lower edge, where the mountainside sloped away, the space ran high-ceilinged and very near the surface, a possible break-out point. The space thinned to head-cracking narrowness and then to bedrock at the back where the building wedged into the slope. All right. Miles opened his dart case to find something that would lay his victim out cold and non-questionable for the rest of the night. The man pawed at him and his sleeve slipped back to reveal a wrist-comm almost as thick and complex as Miles's own. A light blinked on it. Miles looked at the device, suddenly uneasy. This room . . . "By the way, who are you?"

"Moglia, Chief of Security, Ryoval Biologicals," the man recited happily. "At your service, sir."

"Oh, indeed you are." Miles's suddenly-thick fingers scrabbled faster in his dark case. Damn, damn, *damn.*

The door bust open. "Freeze, mister!"

Miles hit the tight-beam alarm/self-destruct on his own wrist comm and flung his hands up, and the wrist comm off, in one swift motion. Not by chance, Moglia sat between Miles and the door, inhibiting the trigger reflexes of the entering guards. The comm melted as it arced through the air—no chance of Ryoval security tracing the outside squad through it now, and Bel would at least know something had gone wrong.

The security chief chuckled to himself, temporarily fascinated by the task of counting his own fingers. The red-clad guard sergeant, backed by his squad, thundered into what was now screamingly obvious to Miles as the Security Operations room, to jerk Miles around, slam him face-first into the wall, and begin frisking him with vicious efficiency. Within moments he had separated Miles from a clanking pile of incriminating equipment, his jacket, boots, and belt. Miles clutched the wall and shivered with the pain of several expertly-applied nerve jabs and the swift reversal of his fortune.

The security chief, when un-penta'd at last, was not at all pleased with the guard sergeant's confession about the three uniformed men he had let go with a fine earlier in the evening. He put the whole guard shift on full alert, and sent an armed squad out to try and trace the escaped Dendarii. Then, with an apprehensive expression on his face very like the guard sergeant's during his mortified admission—compounded with sour satisfaction, contemplating Miles, and drug-induced nausea—he made a vid call.

"My lord?" said the security chief carefully.

"What is it, Moglia?" Baron Ryoval's face was sleepy and irritated.

"Sorry to disturb you sir, but I thought you might like to know about the intruder we just caught here. Not an ordinary thief, judging from his clothes and equipment. Strange-looking fellow, sort of a tall dwarf. He squeezed in through the ducts." Moglia held up tissue-collection kit, chip-driven alarm-disarming tools, and Miles's weapons, by way of evidence. The guard sergeant bundled Miles, stumbling, into range of the vid's pick-up. "He was asking a lot of questions about Bharaputra's monster."

Ryoval's lips parted. Then his eyes lit, and he threw back his head and laughed. "I should have guessed. Stealing when you should be buying, Admiral?" he chortled. "Oh, very good, Moglia!"

The security chief looked fractionally less nervous. "Do you know this little mutant, my lord?"

"Yes, indeed. He calls himself Miles Naismith. A mercenary—bills himself as an admiral. Self-promoted, no doubt. Excellent work, Moglia. Hold him, and I'll be there in the morning and deal with him personally."

"Hold him how, sir?"

Ryoval shrugged. "Amuse yourselves. Freely."

When Ryoval's image faded, Miles found himself pinned between the speculative glowers of both the security chief and the guard sergeant.

Just to relieve feelings, a burly guard held Miles while the security chief delivered a blow to his belly. But the chief was still too ill to really enjoy this as he should. "Came to see Bharaputra's toy soldier, did you?" he gasped, rubbing his own stomach.

The guard sergeant caught his chief's eye. "You know, I think we should give him his wish."

The security chief smothered a belch, and smiled as at a beatific vision. "Yes . . ."

Miles, praying they wouldn't break his arms, found himself being frog-marched down a complex of corridors and lift-tubes by the burly guard, followed by the sergeant and the chief. They took a fast lift-tube to the very bottom, a dusty basement crowded with stored and discarded equipment and supplies. They made their way to a locked hatch set in the floor. It swung open on a metal ladder descending into obscurity.

"The last thing we threw down there was a rat," the guard sergeant informed Miles cordially. "Nine bit its head right off. Nine gets very hungry. Got a metabolism like an ore furnace."

The guard forced Miles onto the ladder and down it a meter or so by the simple expedient of striking at his clinging hands with a truncheon. Miles hung just out of range of the stick, eyeing the dimly-lit stone below. The rest was pillars and shadows and a cold dankness.

"Nine!" called the guard sergeant into the echoing darkness. "Nine! Dinner! Come and catch it!"

The security chief laughed mockingly, then clutched his head and groaned under his breath.

Ryoval had said he'd deal with Miles personally in the morning; surely the guards understood their boss wanted a live prisoner. Didn't they? "Is this the dungeon?" Miles spat blood and peered around."

"No, no, just a basement," the guard sergeant assured him cheerily. "The dungeon is for the *paying* customers. Heh, heh, heh." Still chortling at his own humor, he kicked the hatch closed. The chink of the locking mechanism rained down; then silence.

The bars of the ladder bit chill through Miles's socks. He hooked an arm around an upright and tucked one hand into the armpit of his black T-shirt to warm it briefly. His grey trousers had been emptied of everything but a ration bar, his handkerchief, and his legs.

He clung there for a long time. Going up was futile; going down, singularly uninviting. Eventually the startling ganglionic pain began to dull, and the shaking physical shock to wear off. Still he clung. Cold.

It could have been worse, Miles reflected. The sergeant and his squad could have decided they wanted to play Lawrence of Arabia and the Six Turks. Commodore Tung, Miles's Dendarii chief of staff and a certified military history nut, had been plying Miles with a series of classic military memoirs lately. How had Colonel Lawrence escaped an analogous tight spot? Ah, yes, played dumb and persuaded his captors to throw him out in the mud. Tung must have pressed that book-fax on Murka, too.

The darkness, Miles discovered as his eyes adjusted, was only relative. Faint luminescent panels in the ceiling here and there shed a sickly yellow glow. He descended the last two meters to stand on solid rock.

He pictured the newsfax, back home on Barrayar— *Body of Imperial Officer Found in Flesh-Czar's Dream Palace. Death From Exhaustion?* Dammit, this wasn't the glorious sacrifice in the Emperor's service he'd once vowed to risk, this was just embarrassing. Maybe Bharaputra's creature would eat the evidence.

With this morose comfort in mind, he began to limp from pillar to pillar, pausing, listening, looking around. Maybe there was another ladder somewhere. Maybe there was a hatch someone had forgotten to lock. Maybe there was still hope.

Maybe there was something moving in the shadows just beyond that pillar. . . .

Miles's breath froze, then eased again, as the movement materialized into a fat albino rat the size of an armadillo. It shied as it saw him and waddled rapidly away, its claws clicking on the rock. Only an escaped lab rat. A bloody big rat, but still, only a rat.

The huge rippling shadow struck out of nowhere, at incredible speed. It grabbed the rat by its tail and swung it squealing against a pillar, dashing out its brains with a crunch. A flash of a thick claw-like fingernail, and the white furry body was ripped open from sternum to tail. Frantic fingers peeled the skin away from the rat's body as blood splattered. Miles first saw the fangs as they bit and tore and buried themselves in the rat's tissues.

They were functional fangs, not just decorative, set in a protruding jaw, with long lips and a wide mouth; yet the total effect was lupine rather than simian. A flat nose, ridged, powerful brows, high cheekbones. Hair a dark matted mess. And yes, fully eight feet tall, a rangy, tense-muscled body.

Climbing back up the ladder would do no good, the creature could pluck him right off and swing him just like the rat. Levitate up the side of a pillar? Oh, for

suction-cup fingers and toes, something the bioengineer-
ing committee had missed somehow. Freeze and play
invisible? Miles settled on this last defense by default—
he was paralyzed with terror.

The big feet, bare on the cold rock, also had claw-like
toenails. But the creature was dressed, in clothes made
of green lab-cloth, a belted kimono-like coat and loose
trousers. And one other thing.

They didn't tell me it was female.

She was almost finished with the rat when she looked
up and saw Miles. Bloody-faced, bloody-handed, she
froze as still as he.

In a spastic motion, Miles whipped the squashed ration bar from his trouser thigh-pocket and extended it
toward her in his outstretched hand. "Dessert?" he
smiled hysterically.

Dropping the rat's stripped carcass, she snatched the bar
out of his hand, ripped off the cover, and devoured it in
four bites. Then she stepped forward, grabbed him by an
arm and his black T-shirt, and lifted him up to her face.
Her breath was about what he would have guessed. Her
eyes were raw and burning. "Water!" she croaked.

They didn't tell me she talked.

"Um, um—water," squeaked Miles. "Quite. There
ought to be water around here—look, up at the ceiling,
all those pipes. If you'll, um, put me down, good girl,
I'll try and spot a water pipe or something . . ."

Slowly, she lowered him back to his feet and released
him. He backed carefully away, his hands held out open
at his sides. He cleared his throat, and tried to bring his
voice back down to a low, soothing tone. "Let's try over
here. The ceiling gets lower, or rather, the bedrock rises
. . . over near that light panel, there, that thin composite
plastic tube—white's the usual color-code for water. We
don't want grey, that's sewage, or red, that's the power-
optics . . ." No telling what she understood, tone was
everything with creatures. "If you, uh, could hold me up
on your shoulders like Ensign Murka, I could have a go
at loosening that joint there . . ." he made pantomime
gestures, uncertain if anything was getting through to
whatever intelligence lay behind those terrible eyes.

The bloody hands, easily twice the size of his own, grabbed him abruptly by the hips and boosted him upward. He clutched the white pipe, inched along it to a screw-joint. Her thick shoulders beneath his feet moved along under him. Her muscles trembled, it wasn't all his own shaking. The joint was tight—he needed tools—he turned with all his strength, in danger of snapping his fragile finger bones. Suddenly the joint squeaked and slid. It gave, the plastic collar was moving, water began to spray between his fingers. One more turn and it sheared apart, and water arced in a bright stream down onto the rock beneath.

She almost dropped him in her haste. She put her mouth under the stream, wide open, let the water splash straight in and all over her face, coughing and guzzling even more frantically than she'd gone at the rat. She drank, and drank, and drank. She let it run over her hands, her face and head, washing away the blood, and then drank some more. Miles began to think she'd never quit, but at last she backed away and pushed her wet hair out of her eyes, and stared down at him. She stared at him for what seemed like a full minute, then suddenly roared, "Cold!"

Miles jumped. "Ah ... cold ... right. Me too, my socks are wet. Heat, you want heat. Lessee. Uh, let's try back this way, where the ceiling's lower. No point here, the heat would all collect up there out of reach, no good ..." She followed him with all the intensity of a cat tracking a ... well ... rat, as he skittered around pillars to where the crawl space's floor rose to genuine crawl-height, about four feet. There, that one, that was the lowest pipe he could find. "If we could get this open," he pointed to a plastic pipe about as big around as his waist, "it's full of hot air being pumped along under pressure. No handy joints though, this time." He stared at his puzzle, trying to think. This composite plastic was extremely strong.

She crouched and pulled, then lay on her back and kicked up at it, then looked at him quite woefully.

"Try this." Nervously, he took her hand and guided it to the pipe, and traced long scratches around the circumference with her hard nails. She scratched and scratched, then looked at him again as if to say, *This isn't working!*

"Try kicking and pulling again now," he suggested.

She must have weighed three hundred pounds, and she put it all behind the next effort, kicking then grabbing the pipe, planting her feet on the ceiling and arching with all her strength. The pipe split along the scratches. She fell with it to the floor, and hot air began to hiss out. She held her hands, her face to it, nearly wrapped herself around it, sat on her knees and let it blow across her. Miles crouched down and stripped off his socks and flopped them over the warm pipe to dry. Now would be a good opportunity to run, if only there were anywhere to run to. But he was reluctant to let his prey out of his sight. His prey? He considered the incalculable value of her left calf muscle, as she sat on the rock and buried her face in her knees.

They didn't tell me she wept.

He pulled out his regulation handkerchief, an archaic square of cloth. He'd never understood the rationale for the idiotic handkerchief, except, perhaps, that where soldiers went there would be weeping. He handed it to her. "Here. Mop your eyes with this."

She took it, and blew her big flat nose in it, and made to hand it back.

"Keep it," Miles said. "Uh ... what do they call you, I wonder?"

"Nine," she growled. Not hostile, it was just the way her strained voice came out of that big throat. ". . . What do they call you?"

Good God, a complete sentence. Miles blinked. "Admiral Miles Naismith." He arranged himself cross-legged.

She looked up, transfixed. "A soldier? A *real officer*?" And then more doubtfully, as if seeing him in detail for the first time, "You?"

Miles cleared his throat firmly. "Quite real. A bit down on my luck just at the moment," he admitted.

"Me, too," she said glumly, and sniffled. "I don't know how long I've been in this basement, but that was my first drink."

"Three days, I think," said Miles. "Have they not, ah, given you any food, either?"

"No." She frowned; the effect, with the fangs, was quite overpowering. "This is worse than anything they did to me in the lab, and I thought that was bad."

It's not what you don't know that'll hurt you, the old saying went. *It's what you do know that isn't so.* Miles thought of his map cube; Miles looked at Nine. Miles pictured himself taking this entire mission's carefully-worked-out strategy plan delicately between thumb and forefinger and flushing it down a waste-disposal unit. The ductwork in the ceiling niggled at his imagination. Nine would never fit through it. . . .

She clawed her wild hair away from her face and stared at him with renewed fierceness. Her eyes were a strange light hazel, adding to the wolfish effect. "What are you *really* doing here? Is this another test?"

"No, this is real life." Miles's lips twitched. "I, ah, made a mistake."

"Guess I did, too," she said, lowering her head.

Miles pulled at his lip and studied her through narrowed eyes. "What sort of life have you had, I wonder?" he mused, half to himself.

She answered literally. "I lived with hired fosterers till I was eight. Like the clones do. Then I started to get big and clumsy and break things—they brought me to live at the lab after that. It was all right, I was warm and had plenty to eat."

"They can't have simplified you too much if they seriously intended you to be a soldier. I wonder what your IQ is?" he speculated.

"One hundred and thirty-five."

Miles fought off stunned paralysis. "I . . . see. Did you ever get . . . any training?"

She shrugged. "I took a lot of tests. They were . . . OK. Except for the aggression experiments. I don't like electric shocks." She brooded a moment. "I don't like experimental psychologists, either. They lie a lot." Her shoulders slumped. "Anyway, I failed. We all failed."

"How can they know you failed if you never had any proper training?" Miles said scornfully. "Soldiering en-

tails some of the most complex, cooperative learned be-
havior ever invented—I've been studying strategy and
tactics for years, and I don't know half yet. It's all up
here." He pressed his hands urgently to his head.

She looked across at him sharply. "If that's so," she
turned her huge clawed hands over, staring at them,
"then why did they do *this* to me?"

Miles stopped short. His throat was strangely dry. *So,
admirals lie too. Sometimes, even to themselves.* After an
unsettled pause he asked, "Did you never think of
breaking open a water pipe?"

"You're punished for breaking things. Or I was.
Maybe not you, you're human."

"Did you ever think of escaping, breaking out? It's a
soldier's duty, when captured by the enemy, to escape.
Survive, escape, sabotage, in that order."

"Enemy?" She looked upward at the whole weight of
House Ryoval pressing overhead. "Who are my
friends?"

"Ah. Yes. There is that . . . point." And where would
an eight-foot-tall genetic cocktail with fangs run to? He
took a deep breath. No question what his next move
must be. Duty, expediency, survival, all compelled it.
"Your friends are closer than you think. Why do you
think I came here?" *Why, indeed?*

She shot him a silent, puzzled frown.

"I came for you. I'd heard of you. I'm . . . recruiting.
Or I was. Things went wrong, and now I'm escaping.
But if you came with me, you could join the Dendarii
Mercenaries. A top outfit—always looking for a few
good men, or whatever. I have this master-sergeant who
. . . who *needs* a recruit like you." Too true. Sergeant
Dyeb was infamous for his sour attitude about women
soldiers, insisting that they were too soft. Any female
recruit who survived his course came out with her aggression highly developed. Miles pictured Dyeb being
dangled by his toes from a height of about eight feet. . . .
He controlled his runaway imagination in favor of concentrating on the present crisis. Nine was looking—
unimpressed.

"Very funny," she said coldly, making Miles wonder

for a wild moment if she'd been equipped with the telepathy gene complex—no, she predated that—"but I'm not even human. Or hadn't you heard?"

Miles shrugged carefully. "Human is as human does." He forced himself to reach out and touch her damp cheek. "Animals don't weep, Nine."

She jerked, as from an electric shock. "Animals don't lie. Humans do. All the time."

"Not *all* the time." He hoped the light was too dim for her to see the flush in his face. She was watching his face intently.

"Prove it." She tilted her head as she sat cross-legged. Her pale gold eyes were suddenly burning, speculative.

"Uh . . . sure. How?"

"Take off your clothes."

". . . what?"

"Take off your clothes, and lie down with me as *humans* do. Men and women." Her hand reached out to touch his throat.

The pressing claws made little wells in his flesh. "Blrp?" choked Miles. His eyes felt wide as saucers. A little more pressure, and those wells would spring forth red fountains. *I am about to die. . . .*

She stared into his face with a strange, frightening, bottomless hunger. Then abruptly, she released him. He sprang up and cracked his head on the low ceiling, and dropped back down, the stars in his eyes unrelated to love at first sight.

Her lips wrinkled back on a fanged groan of despair. "Ugly," she wailed. Her clawed nails raked across her cheeks leaving red furrows. "Too *ugly* . . . animal . . . you *don't* think I'm human—" She seemed to swell with some destructive resolve.

"No, no, no!" gibbered Miles, lurching to his knees and grabbing her hands and pulling them down. "It's not that. It's just, uh—how old are you, anyway?"

"Sixteen."

Sixteen. God. He remembered sixteen. Sex-obsessed and dying inside every minute. A horrible age to be trapped in a twisted, fragile, abnormal body. God only knew how he had survived his own self-hatred then.

No—he remembered how. *He'd* been saved by one who loved him. "Aren't you a little young for this?" he tried hopefully.

"How old were you?"

"Fifteen," he admitted, before thinking to lie. "But . . . it was traumatic. Didn't work out at all in the long run."

Her claws turned toward her face again.

"Don't *do* that!" he cried, hanging on. It reminded him entirely too much of the episode of Sergeant Bothari and the knife. The Sergeant had taken Miles's knife away from him by superior force. Not an option open to Miles here. "Will you *calm down*?" he yelled at her.

She hesitated.

"It's just that, uh, an officer and gentleman doesn't just fling himself onto his lady on the bare ground. One . . . one sits down. Gets comfortable. Has a little conversation, drinks a little wine, plays a little music . . . slows down. You're hardly warm yet. Here, sit over here where it is warmest." He positioned her nearer the broken duct, got up on his knees behind her, tried rubbing her neck and shoulders. Her muscles were tense, they felt like rocks under his thumbs. Any attempt on his part to strangle her would clearly be futile.

I can't believe this. Trapped in Ryoval's basement with a sex-starved teenage werewolf. There was nothing about this in any of my Imperial Academy training manuals. . . . He remembered his mission, which was to get her left calf muscle back to the *Ariel* alive. *Dr. Canaba, if I survive, you and I are going to have a little talk about this . . . .*

Her voice was muffled with grief and the odd shape of her mouth. "You think I'm too tall."

"Not at all." He was getting hold of himself a bit, he could lie faster. "I adore tall women, ask anyone who knows me. Besides, I made the happy discovery some time back that height difference only matters when we're standing up. When we're lying down it's, ah, less of a problem . . ." A rapid mental review of everything he'd ever learned by trial and error, mostly error, about women was streaming uninvited through his mind. It was harrowing. What did women *want*?

He shifted around and took her hand, earnestly. She stared back equally earnestly, waiting for ... *instruction.* At this point the realization came over Miles that he was facing his first virgin. He smiled at her in total paralysis for several seconds. "Nine, you've never done this before, have you?"

"I've seen vids." She frowned introspectively. "They usually start with kisses, but—" a vague gesture toward her misshapen mouth, "maybe you don't want to."

Miles tried not to think about the late rat. She'd been systematically starved, after all. "Vids can be very misleading. For women—especially the first time—it takes practice to learn your own body responses, woman friends have told me. I'm afraid I might hurt you." *And then you'll disembowel me.*

She gazed into his eyes. "That's all right. I have a very high pain threshold."

But I don't.

This was mad. She was mad. *He* was mad. Yet he could feel a creeping fascination for the—proposition—rising from his belly to his brain like a fey fog. No doubt about it, she was the tallest female thing he was ever likely to meet. More than one woman of his acquaintance had accused him of wanting to go mountain-climbing. He could get that out of his system once and for all. . . .

Damn, I do believe she'd clean up good. She was not without a certain ... charm was *not* the word—whatever beauty there was to be found in the strong, the swift, the leanly athletic, the functioning form. Once you got used to the *scale* of it. She radiated a smooth heat he could feel from here—*animal magnetism*? the suppressed observer in the back of his brain suggested. Power? whatever else it was, it would certainly be *astonishing.*

One of his mother's favorite aphorisms drifted through his head. *Anything worth doing,* she always said, *is worth doing well.*

Dizzy as a drunkard, he abandoned the crutch of logic for the wings of inspiration. "Well then, doctor," he heard himself muttering insanely, "let us experiment."

Kissing a woman with fangs was indeed a novel sensa-

tion. Being kissed back—she was clearly a fast learner—
was even more novel. Her arms circled him ecstatically,
and from that point on he lost control of the situation,
somehow. Though some time later, coming up for air,
he did look up to ask, "Nine, have you ever heard of
the black widow spider?"

"No . . . what is it?"

"Never mind," he said airily.

It was all very awkward and clumsy, but sincere, and
when he was done the water in her eyes was from joy,
not pain. She seemed enormously (how else?) pleased
with him. He was so unstrung he actually fell asleep for
a few minutes, pillowed on her body.

He woke up laughing.

"You really do have the most elegant cheekbones,"
he told her, tracing their line with one finger. She leaned
into his touch, cuddled up equally to him and the heat
pipe. "There's a woman on my ship who wears her hair
in a sort of woven braid in the back—it would look just
great on you. Maybe she could teach you how."

She pulled a wad of her hair forward and looked
cross-eyed at it, as if trying to see past the coarse tangles
and filth. She touched his face in turn. "You are very
handsome, Admiral."

"Huh? Me?" He ran a hand over the night's beard
stubble, sharp features, the old pain lines. . . . *She must
be blinded by my putative rank, eh?*

"Your face is very . . . alive. And your eyes see what
they're looking at."

"Nine . . ." he cleared his throat, paused. "Dammit,
that's not a name, that's a number. What happened to
Ten?"

"He died." *Maybe I will too,* her strange-colored eyes
added silently, before her lids shuttered them.

"Is Nine all they ever called you?"

"There's a long biocomputer code-string that's my actual designation."

"Well, we all have serial numbers," Miles had two,
now that he thought of it, "but this is absurd. I can't
call you Nine, like some robot. You need a proper name,

a name that fits you." He leaned back onto her warm
bare shoulder—she was like a furnace, they had spoken
truly about her metabolism—and his lips drew back on
a slow grin. "Taura."

"Taura?" Her long mouth gave it a skewed and lilting
accent. ". . . it's too beautiful for me!"

"Taura," he repeated firmly. "Beautiful but strong. Full
of secret meaning. Perfect. Ah, speaking of secrets . . ."
Was now the time to tell her about what Dr. Canaba
had planted in her left calf? Or would she be hurt, as
someone falsely courted for her money— or his title—
Miles faltered. "I think, now that we know each other
better, that it's time for us to blow out of this place."

She stared around, into the grim dimness. "How?"

"Well, that's what we have to figure out, eh? I confess,
ducts rather spring to my mind." Not the heat pipe, obviously. He'd have to go anorexic for months to fit in it,
besides, he'd cook. He shook out and pulled on his black
T-shirt—he'd put on his trousers immediately after he'd
woke, that stone floor sucked heat remorselessly from
any flesh that touched it—and creaked to his feet. God.
He was getting too old for this sort of thing already. The
sixteen-year-old, clearly, possessed the physical resil-
ience of a minor goddess. What was it he'd gotten into
at sixteen? Sand, that was it. He winced in memory of
what it had done to certain sensitive body folds and crev-
ices. Maybe cold stone wasn't so bad after all.

She pulled her pale green coat and trousers out from
under herself, dressed, and followed him in a crouch
until the space was sufficient for her to stand upright.

They quartered and re-quartered the underground
chamber. There were four ladders with hatches, all
locked. There was a locked vehicle exit to the outside
on the downslope side. A direct breakout might be sim-
plest, but if he couldn't make immediate contact with
Thorne it was a 27-kilometer hike to the nearest town.
In the snow, in his sock feet—her bare feet. And if they
got there, he wouldn't be able to use the vidnet anyway
because his credit card was still locked in the Security
Ops office upstairs. Asking for charity in Ryoval's town
was a dubious proposition. So, break straight out and be

sorry later, or linger and try to equip themselves, risking recapture, and be sorry sooner? Tactical decisions were such fun.

Ducts won. Miles pointed upward to the most likely one. "Think you can break that open and boost me in?" he asked Taura.

She studied it, nodded slowly, the expression closing on her face. She stretched up and moved along to a soft metal-clad joint, slipped her claw-hard fingernails under the strip, and yanked it off. She worked her fingers into the exposed slot and hung on it as if chinning herself. The duct bent open under her weight. "There you go," she said.

She lifted him up as easily as a child, and he squirmed into the duct. This one was a particularly tight fit, though it was the largest he had spotted as accessible in this ceiling. He inched along it on his back. He had to stop twice to suppress a residual, hysteria-tinged laughing fit. The duct curved upward, and he slithered around the curve in the darkness only to find that it split here into a Y, each branch half-sized. He cursed and backed out.

Taura had her face turned up to him, an unusual angle of view.

"No good that way," he gasped, reversing direction gymnastically at the gap. He headed the other way. This too curved up, but within moments he found a grille. A tightly-fitted, unbudgeable, unbreakable, and with his bare hands, uncuttable grille. Taura might have the strength to rip it out of the wall, but Taura couldn't fit through the duct to reach it. He contemplated it a few moments. "Right," he muttered, and backed out again.

"So much for ducts," he reported to Taura. "Uh ... could you help me down?" She lowered him to the floor, and he dusted himself futilely. "Let's look around some more."

She followed him docilely enough, though something in her expression hinted she might be losing faith in his admiralness. A bit of detailing on a column caught his eye, and he went to take a closer look in the dim light.

It was one of the low-vibration support columns. Two

meters in diameter, set deep in the bedrock in a well of fluid, it ran straight up to one of the labs, no doubt, to provide an ultra-stable base for certain kinds of crystal generation projects and the like. Miles rapped on the side of the column. It rang hollow. *Ah yes, makes sense, concrete doesn't float too well, eh?* A groove in the side outlined . . . an access port? He ran his fingers around it, probing. There was a concealed—something. He stretched his arms and found a twin spot on the opposite side. The spots yielded slowly to the hard pressure of his thumbs. There was a sudden pop and hiss, and the whole panel came away. He staggered, and barely kept from dropping it down the hole. He turned it sideways and drew it out.

"Well, well," Miles grinned. He stuck his head through the port, looked down and up. Black as pitch. Rather gingerly, he reached his arm in and felt around. There was a ladder running up the damp inside, for access for cleaning and repairs; the whole column could apparently be filled with fluid of whatever density at need. Filled, it would have been self-pressure-sealed and unopenable. Carefully, he examined the inner edge of the hatch. Openable from either side, by God. "Let's go see if there's any more of these, further up."

It was slow going, feeling for more grooves as they ascended in the blackness. Miles tried not to think about the fall, should he slip from the slimy ladder. Taura's deep breathing, below him, was actually rather comforting. They had gone up perhaps three stories when Miles's chilled and numbing fingers found another groove. He'd almost missed it, it was on the opposite side of the ladder from the first. He then discovered, the hard way, that he didn't have nearly the reach to keep one arm hooked around the ladder and press both release catches at the same time. After a terrifying slip, trying, he clung spasmodically to the ladder till his heart stopped pounding. "Taura?" he croaked. "I'll move up, and you try it." Not much up was left, the column ended a meter or so above his head.

Her extra arm length was all that was needed, the

catches surrendered to her big hands with a squeak of protest.

"What do you see?" Miles whispered.

"Big dark room. Maybe a lab."

"Makes sense. Climb back down and put that lower panel back on, no sense advertising where we went."

Miles slipped through the hatch into the darkened laboratory while Taura accomplished her chore. He dared not switch on a light in the windowless room, but a few instrument readouts on the benches and walls gave enough ghostly glow for his dark-adapted eyes that at least he didn't trip over anything. One glass door led to a hallway. A heavily electronically monitored hallway. With his nose pressed to the glass Miles saw a red shape flit past a cross-corridor; guards here. What did they guard?

Taura oozed out of the access hatch to the column— it was a tight fit—and sat down heavily on the floor, her face in her hands. Concerned, Miles nipped back to her. "You all right?"

She shook her head. "No. Hungry."

"What, already? That was supposed to be a twenty-four hour rat—er, ration bar." Not to mention the two or three kilos of meat she'd had for an appetizer.

"For you, maybe," she wheezed. She was shaking.

Miles began to see why Canaba had dubbed his project a failure. Imagine trying to feed a whole army of such appetites. Napoleon would quail. Maybe the raw-boned kid was still growing. Daunting thought.

There was a refrigerator at the back of the lab. If he knew lab techs . . . ah ha. Indeed, in among the test tubes was a package with half a sandwich and a large, if bruised, pear. He handed them to Taura. She looked vastly impressed, as if he'd conjured them from his sleeve by magic, and devoured them at once, and grew less pale.

Miles foraged further for his troop. Alas, the only other organics in the fridge were little covered dishes of gelatinous stuff with unpleasant multi-colored fuzz growing in them. But there were three big shiny walk-in wall freezers lined up in a row. Miles peered through a glass square in one thick door, and risked pressing the wall pad that turned on the light inside. Within were row on row on row of labeled drawers, full of clear plastic trays. Frozen samples of some kind. Thousands—Miles looked again, and calculated more carefully—hundreds of thousands. He glanced at the lighted control panel by the freezer drawer. The temperature inside was that of liquid nitrogen. Three freezers ... *millions* of ... Miles sat down abruptly on the floor himself. "Taura, do you know where we *are*?" he whispered intensely.

"Sorry, no," she whispered back, creeping over.

"That was a rhetorical question. *I* know where we are."

"Where?"

"Ryoval's treasure chamber."

"What?"

"That," Miles jerked his thumb at the freezer, "is the baron's hundred-year-old tissue collection. My God. Its value is almost incalculable. Every unique, irreplaceable, mutant bizarre bit he's begged, bought, borrowed or stolen for the last three-fourths of a century, all lined up in neat little rows, waiting to be thawed and cultured and cooked up into some poor new slave. This is the living heart of his whole human biologicals operation." Miles sprang to his feet and pored over the control panels. His heart raced, and he breathed open-mouthed, laughing silently, feeling almost like he was about to pass out. "Oh, shit. Oh, God." He stopped, swallowed. Could it be done?

These freezers had to have an alarm system, monitors surely, piped up to Security Ops at the very least. Yes, there was a complex device for opening the door—that was fine, he didn't want to open the door. He left it untouched. It was systems readout he was after. If he could bugger up just one sensor ... Was the thing broadcast-output to several outside monitor locations, or did they run an optic thread to just one? The lab benches supplied him with a small hand light, and drawers and drawers of assorted tools and supplies. Taura watched him in puzzlement as he darted here, there, taking inventory.

The freezer monitor *was* broadcast-output, inaccessible, could he hit it on the input side? He levered off a smoke-dark plastic cover as silently as he could. There, *there,* the optic thread came out of the wall, pumping continuous information about the freezer's interior environment. It fit into a simple standard receiver plug on the more daunting black box that controlled the door alarm. There'd been a whole drawer full of assorted optic threads with various ends and Y-adaptors ... Out of the spaghetti-tangle he drew what he needed, discarding several with broken ends or other damage. There were three optical data recorders in the drawer. Two didn't work. The third did.

A quick festoon of optic thread, a swift unplugging and plugging, and he had one freezer talking to two control boxes. He set the freed thread to talking to the datacorder. He simply had to chance the blip during transfer. If anyone checked they'd find all seemed well again. He gave the datacorder several minutes to develop a nice continuous replay loop, crouching very still with even the tiny hand light extinguished. Taura waited with the patience of a predator, making no noise.

One, two, three, and he set the datacorder to talking to all three control boxes. The real thread plugs hung forlornly loose. Would it work? There were no alarms going off, no thundering herd of irate security troops.

"Taura, come here."

She loomed beside him, baffled.

"Have you ever met Baron Ryoval?" asked Miles.

"Yes, once—when he came to buy me."

"Did you like him?"

She gave him an are-you-out-of-your-mind? look.

"Yeah, I didn't much care for him either." Restrained murder, in point of fact. He was now meltingly grateful for that restraint. "Would you like to rip his lungs out, if you could?"

Her clawed hands clenched. "Try me!"

"Good!" He smiled cheerily. "I want to give you your first lesson in tactics." He pointed. "See that control? The temperature in these freezers can be raised to almost 200 degrees centigrade, for heat sterilization during cleaning. Give me your finger. One finger. Gently. More gently than that." He guided her hand. "The least possible pressure you can apply to the dial, and still move. . . . Now the next," he pulled her to the next panel, "and the last." He exhaled, still not quite able to believe it.

"And the lesson is," he breathed, "it's not how much force you use. It's where you apply it."

He resisted the urge to scrawl something like *The Dwarf Strikes Back* across the front of the freezers with a flow pen. The longer the baron in his mortal rage took to figure out who to pursue, the better. It would take several hours to bring all that mass in there from liquid nitrogen temperature up to *well-done,* but if no one came in till morning shift, the destruction would be absolute.

Miles glanced at the time on the wall digital. Dear God, he'd spent a lot of time in that basement. Well-spent, but still. "Now," he said to Taura, who was still meditating on the dial, and her hand, with her gold eyes glowing, "we have to get out of here. Now we *really* have to get out of here." Lest her next tactics lesson turns out to be, Don't blow up the bridge you're standing on, Miles allowed nervously.

Contemplating the door-locking mechanism more closely, plus what lay beyond—among other things, the sound-activated wall-mounted monitors in the halls featured automatic laser fire—Miles almost went to turn the freezer temperatures back down. His chip-driven Dendarii tools, now locked in the Security Ops office, might barely have handled the complex circuitry in the pried-open control box. But of course, he couldn't get at his tools without his tools—a nice paradox. It shouldn't surprise Miles that Ryoval saved his most sophisticated alarm system for this lab's one and only door. But it made the room a much worse trap than ever the sub-basement.

He made another tour of the lab with the filched hand light, checking drawers again. No computer-keys came to hand, but he did find a big, crude pair of cutters in a drawer full of rings and clamps, and bethought him of the duct grille that had lately defeated him in the basement. So. The passage up to this lab had merely been the illusion of progress toward escape.

"There's no shame in a strategic retreat to a better position," he whispered to Taura when she balked at reentering the support column's dark tube. "This is a dead end, here. Maybe literally." The doubt in her tawny eyes was strangely unsettling, a weight in his heart. *Still don't trust me, eh? Well, maybe those who have been greatly betrayed need great proof.* "Stick with me, kid," he muttered under his breath, swinging into the tube. "We're going places." Her doubt was merely masked under lowered eyelids, but she followed him, sealing the hatch behind them.

With the hand light, the descent was slightly less nasty than the ascent into the unknown had been. There were no other exits to be found, and shortly they stood on the stone they had started from. Miles checked the progress of their ceiling waterspout, while Taura drank again. The splattering water ran off in a flat greasy trickle downslope; given the vast size of the chamber, it would be some days before the pool collecting slowly against the lower wall offered any useful strategic possibilities, though there was always the hope it might do a bit to undermine the foundations.

Taura boosted him back into the duct. "Wish me luck," he murmured over his shoulder, muffled by the close confines.

"Goodbye," she said. He could not see the expression on her face; there was none in her voice.

"See you later," he corrected this firmly.

A few minutes of vigorous wriggling brought him back to his grille. It opened onto a dark room stacked with stuff, part of the basement proper, quiet and unoccupied. The snip of his cutters, biting through the grille, seemed loud enough to bring down Ryoval's entire security force, but none appeared. Maybe the security chief was sleeping off his drug hangover. A scrabbling noise, not of Miles's own making, echoed thinly through the duct and Miles froze. He flashed his light down a side-branching tube. Twin red jewels flashed back, the eyes of a huge rat. He briefly considered trying to clout it and haul it back to Taura. No. When they got back to the *Ariel,* he'd give her a steak dinner. Two steak dinners. The rat saved itself by turning and scampering away.

The grilled parted at last, and he squeezed into the storage room. What time was it, anyway? Late, very late. The room gave onto a corridor, and on the floor at the end, one of the access hatches gleamed dully. Miles's heart rose in serious hope. Once he'd got Taura, they must next try to reach a vehicle ...

This hatch, like the first, was manual, no sophisticated electronics to disarm. It relocked automatically upon closing, however. Miles jammed it with his clippers before descending the ladder. He aimed his light around. "Taura!" he whispered. "Where are you?"

No immediate answer; no glowing gold eyes flashing in the forest of pillars. He was reluctant to shout. He slapped down the rungs and began a silent fast trot through the chamber, the cold stone draining the heat through his socks and making him long for his lost boots.

He came upon her sitting silently at the base of a pillar, her head turned sideways resting on her knees. Her face was pensive, sad. Really, it didn't take long at all to begin reading the subtleties of feeling in her wolfish features.

"Time to march, soldier girl," Miles said.

Her head lifted. "You came back!"

"What did you think I was going to do? Of course I came back. You're my recruit, aren't you?"

She scrubbed her face with the back of a big paw—hand, Miles corrected himself severely—and stood up, and up. "Guess I must be." Her outslung mouth smiled slightly. If you didn't have a clue what the expression was, it could look quite alarming.

"I've got a hatch open. We've got to try to get out of this main building, back to the utility bay. I saw several vehicles parked there earlier. What's a little theft, after—"

With a sudden whine the outside vehicle entrance, downslope to their right, began to slide upward. A rush of cold dry air swept through the dankness, and a thin shaft of yellow dawn light made the shadows blue. They shielded their eyes in the unexpected glare. Out of the bright squinting haze coalesced half-a-dozen red-clad forms, double-timing it, weapons at the ready.

Taura's hand was tight on Miles's. *Run,* he started to cry, and bit back the shout; no way could they outrun a nerve disruptor beam, a weapon which at least two of the guards now carried. Miles's breath hissed out through his teeth. He was too infuriated even to swear. They'd been so *close.* . . .

Security chief Moglia sauntered up. "What, still in one piece, Naismith?" he smirked unpleasantly. "Nine must have finally realized it's time to start cooperating, eh, Nine?"

Miles squeezed her hand hard, hoping the message would be properly understood as, *Wait.*

She lifted her chin. "Guess so," she said coldly.

"It's about time," said Moglia. "Be a good girl, and we'll take you upstairs and feed you breakfast after this."

Good, Miles's hand signaled. She was watching him closely for cues, now.

Moglia prodded Miles with his truncheon. "Time to go, dwarf. Your friends have actually made ransom. Surprised me."

Miles was surprised himself. He moved toward the exit, still towing Taura. He didn't look at her, did as little as possible to draw unwanted attention to their, er, togetherness, while still maintaining it. He let go of her hand as soon as their momentum was established.

What the hell? Miles thought as they emerged into the blinking dawn, up the ramp and onto a circle of tarmac slick with glittering rime. A most peculiar tableau was arranged there.

Bel Thorne and one Dendarii trooper, armed with stunners, shifted uneasily—not prisoners? Half a dozen armed men in the green uniform of House Fell stood at the ready. A float truck emblazoned with Fell's logo was parked at the tarmac's edge. And Nicol the quaddie, wrapped in white fur against the frost, hovered in her float chair at the stunner-point of a big green-clad guard.

The light was grey and gold and chilly as the sun, lifting over the dark mountains in the distance, broke through the clouds.

"Is that the man you want?" the green-uniformed guard captain asked Bel Thorne.

"That's him." Thorne's face was white with an odd mixture of relief and distress. "Admiral, are you all right?" Thorne called urgently. It's eyes widened, taking in Miles's tall companion. "What the hell's *that*?"

"*She* is Recruit-trainee Taura," Miles said firmly, hoping 1) Bel would unravel the several meanings packed in that sentence and 2) Ryoval's guards wouldn't. Bel looked stunned, so evidently Miles had got at least partly through; Security Chief Moglia looked suspicious, but baffled. Miles was clearly a problem Moglia thought he was about to get rid of, however, and he thrust his bafflement aside to deal with the more important person of Fell's guard captain.

"What *is* this?" Miles hissed at Bel, sidling closer until a red-clad guard lifted his nerve disruptor and shook his head. Moglia and Fell's captain were exchanging electronic data on a report panel, heads bent together, evidently the official documentation.

"When we lost you last night, I was in a panic," Bel pitched its voice low toward Miles. "A frontal assault was out of the question. So I ran to Baron Fell to ask for help. But the help I got wasn't quite what I expected. Fell and Ryoval cooked up a deal between them to exchange Nicol for you. I swear, I only found out the details an hour ago!" Bel protested at Nicol's thin-lipped glower in its direction.

"I . . . see," Miles paused. "Are we planning to refund her dollar?"

"*Sir,*" Bel's voice was anguished, "we had *no idea* what was happening to you in there. We were expecting Ryoval to start beaming up a holocast of obscene and ingenious tortures, starring you, at any minute. Like Commodore Tung says, on hemmed-in ground, use subterfuge."

Miles recognized one of Tung's favorite Sun Tzu aphorisms. On bad days Tung had a habit of quoting the

4,000-year-dead general in the original Chinese; when
Tung was feeling benign they got a translation. Miles
glanced around, adding up weapons, men, equipment.
Most of the green guards carried stunners. Thirteen to
. . . three? Four? He glanced at Nicol. Maybe five? *On
desperate ground,* Sun Tzu advised, *fight.* Could it get
much more desperate than this?

"Ah . . ." said Miles. "Just what the devil did we offer
Baron fell in exchange for this extraordinary charity? Or
is he doing it out of the goodness of his heart?"

Bel shot him an exasperated look, then cleared its
throat. "I promised you'd tell him the real truth about
the Betan rejuvenation treatment."

"Bel . . ."

Thorne shrugged unhappily. "I thought, once we'd got
you back, we'd figure something out. But I never
thought he'd offer Nicol to Ryoval, I swear!"

Down in the long valley, Miles could see a bead moving on the thin gleam of a monorail. The morning shift
of bioengineers and technicians, janitors and office clerks
and cafeteria cooks, was due to arrive soon. Miles
glanced at the white building looming above, pictured
the scene to come in that third floor lab as the guards
deactivated the alarms and let them in to work, as the
first one through the door sniffed and wrinkled his nose
and said plaintively, "What's that awful *smell*?"

"Has 'Medtech Vaughn' signed aboard the *Ariel* yet?"
Miles asked.

"Within the hour."

"Yeah, well . . . it turns out we didn't need to kill his
fatted calf after all. It comes with the package." Miles
nodded toward Taura.

Bel lowered its voice still further. *"That's* coming
with us?"

"You'd better believe it. Vaughn didn't tell us everything. To put it mildly. I'll explain later," Miles added as
the two guard captains broke up their tete-a-tete. Moglia
swung his truncheon jauntily, heading toward Miles.
"Meantime, you made a slight miscalculation. This isn't
hemmed-in ground. This is *desperate* ground. Nicol, I
want you to know, the Dendarii don't give refunds."

Nicol frowned in bewilderment. Bel's eyes widened, as it checked out the odds—calculating them thirteen to three, Miles could tell. "Truly?" Bel choked. A subtle hand signal, down by its trouser seam, brought the trooper to full alert.

"Truly desperate," Miles reiterated. He inhaled deeply. "Now! Taura, attack!"

Miles launched himself toward Moglia, not so much actually expecting to wrestle his truncheon from him as hoping to maneuver Moglia's body between himself and the fellows with the nerve disruptors. The Dendarii trooper, who had been paying attention to details, dropped one of the nerve disruptor wielders with his first stunner shot, then rolled away from the second's return fire. Bel dropped the second nerve disruptor man and leapt aside. Two red guards, aiming their stunners at the running hermaphrodite, were lifted abruptly by their necks. Taura cracked their heads together, unscientifically but hard; they fell to hands and knees, groping blindly for their lost weapons.

Fell's green guards hesitated, not certain just whom to shoot, until Nicol, her angel's face alight, suddenly shot skyward in her float chair and dropped straight down again on the head of her guard, who was distracted by the fight. He fell like an ox. Nicol flipped her floater sideways as green-guard stunner fire found her, shielding herself from its flare, and shot upwards again. Taura picked up a red guard and threw him at a green one; they both went down in a tangle of arms and legs.

The Dendarii trooper closed on a green guard hand-to-hand, to shield himself from stunner blast. Fell's captain wouldn't buy the maneuver, and ruthlessly stunned them both, a sound tactic with the numbers on his side. Moglia got his truncheon up against Miles's windpipe and started to press, while yelling into his wrist comm, calling for back-up from Security Ops. A green guard screamed as Taura yanked his arm out of its shoulder socket and swung him into the air by the dislocated joint at another one aiming his stunner at her.

Colored lights danced before Miles's eyes. Fell's captain, focusing on Taura as the biggest threat, dropped to stunner fire from Bel Thorne as Nicol whammed her float chair into the back of the last green guard left standing.

"The float truck!" Miles croaked. "Go for the float truck!" Bell cast him a desperate look and sprinted towards it. Miles fought like an eel until Moglia got a hand down to his boot, drew a sharp, thin knife, and pressed it to Miles's neck.

"Hold still!" snarled Moglia. "That's better ..." He straightened in the sudden silence, realizing he'd just pulled domination from disaster. "*Everybody* hold still." Bel froze with its hand on the float-truck's door pad. A couple of the men splayed on the tarmac twitched, and moaned.

"Now stand away from—glk," said Moglia.

Taura's voice whispered past Moglia's ear, a soft, soft growl. "Drop the knife. Or I'll rip your throat out with my bare hands."

Miles's eyes wrenched sideways, trying to see around his own clamped head, as the sharp edge sang against his skin.

"I can kill him, before you do," croaked Moglia.

"The little man is mine," Taura crooned. "You gave him to me yourself. He came *back* for me. Hurt him one little bit, and I'll tear your head off and then I'll drink your blood."

Miles felt Moglia being lifted off his feet. The knife clattered to the pavement. Miles sprang away, staggering. Taura held Moglia by his neck, her claws biting deep. "I still want to rip his head off," she growled petulantly, remembrance of abuse sparking in her eyes.

"Leave him," gasped Miles. "Believe me, in a few hours he's going to be suffering a more artistic vengeance than anything we can dream up."

Bel galloped back to stun the security chief at can't miss range while Taura held him out like a wet cat. Miles had Taura throw the unconscious Dendarii over her shoulder while he ran around to the back of the float-truck and released the doors for Nicol, who zipped her chair inside. They tumbled within, dropped the doors, and Bel at the controls shot them into the air. A siren was going off somewhere in Ryoval's.

"Wrist comm, wrist comm," Miles babbled, stripping his unconscious trooper of the device. "Bel, where is our drop shuttle parked?"

"We came in at a little commercial shuttleport just outside Ryoval's town, about forty kilometers from here."

"Anybody left manning it?"

"Anderson and Nout."

"What's their scrambled comm channel?"

"Twenty-three."

Miles slid into the seat beside Bel and opened the channel. It took a small eternity for Sergeant Anderson to answer, fully thirty or forty seconds, while the float truck streaked above the treetops and over the nearest ridge.

"Laureen, I want you to get your shuttle into the air. We need an emergency pick-up, soonest. We're in a House Fell float truck, heading—" Miles thrust his wrist under Bel's nose.

"North from Ryoval Biologicals," Bel recited. "At about 260 kilometers per hour, which is the fastest this crate will go."

"Home in on our screamer," Miles set the wrist comm emergency signal. "Don't wait for clearance from Ryoval's shuttleport traffic control, 'cause you won't get it. Have Nout patch my comm through to the *Ariel*."

"You got it, sir," Anderson's thin voice came cheerily back over his comm.

Static, and another few seconds' excruciating delay. Then an excited voice, "Murka here. I thought you were coming out right behind us last night! You all right, sir?"

"Temporarily. Is 'Medtech Vaughn' aboard?"

"Yes, sir."

"All right. Don't let him off. Assure him I have his tissue sample with me."

"Really! How'd you—"

"Never mind how. Get all the troops back aboard and break from the station into free orbit. Plan to make a flying pick-up of the drop shuttle, and tell the pilot-officer to plot a course for the Escobar wormhole jump at max acceleration as soon as we're clamped on. Don't wait for clearance."

"We're still loading cargo—"

"Abandon any that's still unloaded."

"Are we in serious shit, sir?"

"Mortal, Murka."

"Right, sir. Murka out."

"I thought we were all supposed to be as quiet as mice here on Jackson's Whole," Bel complained. "Isn't this all a bit splashy?"

"The situation's changed. There'd be no negotiating with Ryoval for Nicol, or for Taura either, after what we did last night. I struck a blow for truth and justice back there that I may live to regret, briefly. Tell you about it later. Anyway, do you really want to stick around while I explain to Baron Fell the real truth about the Betan rejuvenation treatment?"

"Oh," Thorne's eyes were alight as it concentrated on its flying, "I'd pay money to watch that, sir."

"Ha. No. For one last moment back there, all the pieces were in our hands. Potentially, anyway." Miles began exploring the readouts on the float-truck's simple control panel. "We'd never get everybody together again, never. One maneuvers to the limit, but the golden moment demands action. If you miss it, the gods damn you forever. And vice versa. Speaking of action, did you see Taura take out *seven* of those guys?" Miles chortled in memory. "What's she going to be like after basic training?"

Bel glanced uneasily over its shoulder, to where Nicol had her float chair lodged and Taura hunkered in the back along with the body of the unconscious trooper. "I was too busy to keep count."

Miles swung out of his seat, and made his way into the back to check on their precious live cargo.

"Nicol, you were great," he told her. "You fought like a falcon. I may have to give you a discount on that dollar."

Nicol was still breathless, ivory cheeks flushed. An upper hand shoved a strand of black hair out of her

sparkling eyes. "I was afraid they'd break my dulcimer."
A lower hand stroked a big box-shaped case jammed
into the float-chair's cup beside her. "Then I was afraid
they'd break Bel."

Taura sat leaning against the truck wall, a bit green.

Miles knelt beside her. "Taura dear, are you all
right?" He gently lifted one clawed hand to check her
pulse, which was bounding. Nicol gave him a rather
strange look at this tender gesture; her float chair was
wedged as far from Taura as it could get.

"Hungry," Taura gasped.

"Again? But of course, all that energy expenditure.
Anybody got a ration bar?" A quick check found an
only-slightly-nibbled rat bar in the stunned trooper's
thigh pocket, which Miles immediately liberated. Miles
smiled benignly at Taura as she wolfed it down; she
smiled back as best she could with her mouth full. *No
more rats for you after this,* Miles promised silently.
*Three steak dinners when we get back to the Ariel, and
a couple of chocolate cakes for dessert....*

The float-truck jinked. Taura, reviving somewhat, extended her feet to hold Nicol's dented cup in place
against the far wall and keep it from bouncing around.
"Thank you," said Nicol warily. Taura nodded.

"Company," Bel Thorne called over its shoulder.
Miles hastened forward.

Two aircars were coming up fast behind them. Ryoval's security. Doubtless beefed up tougher than the average civilian police car—yes. Bel jinked again as a
plasma bolt boiled past, leaving bright green streaks
across Miles's retinas. Quasi-military and seriously annoyed, their pursuers were.

"This is one of Fell's trucks, we ought to have *something* to fling back at them." There was nothing in front
of Miles that looked like any kind of weapons-control.

A *whoomp,* a scream from Nicol, and the float-truck
staggered in air, righted itself under Bel's hands. A roar
of air and vibration—Miles cranked his head around
frantically—one top back corner of the truck's cargo
area was blown away. The rear door was fused shut on
one side, whanging loose along the opposite edge. Taura

still braced the float chair, Nicol now had her upper hands wrapped around Taura's ankles. "Ah," said Thorne. "No armor."

"What did they think this was going to be, a peaceful mission?" Miles checked his wrist comm. "Laureen, are you in the air yet?"

"Coming, sir."

"Well, if you've ever itched to redline it, now's your chance. Nobody's going to complain about your abusing the equipment this time."

"*Thank* you, sir," she responded happily.

They were losing speed and altitude. "Hang on!" Bel yelled over its shoulder, and suddenly reversed thrust. Their closing pursuers shot past them, but immediately began climbing turns. Bel accelerated again; another scream from the back as their live cargo was thus shifted toward the now-dubious rear doors.

The Dendarii hand stunners were of no use at all. Miles clambered into the back again, looking for some sort of luggage compartment, gun rack, anything—surely Fell's people did not rely only on the fearsome reputation of their House for protection.

The padded benches along each side of the cargo compartment, upon which Fell's guard squad had presumably sat, swung up on storage space. The first was empty, the second contained personal luggage—Miles had a brief flash of strangling an enemy with someone's pajama pants, flinging underwear into thruster air-intakes—the third compartment was also empty. The fourth was locked.

The float-truck rocked under another blast, part of the top peeled away in the wind, Miles grabbed for Taura, and the truck plummeted downward. Miles's stomach, and the rest of him, seemed to float upward. They were all flattened to the floor again as Bel pulled up. The float-truck shivered and lurched, and all—Miles and Taura, the unconscious trooper, Nicol in her float chair—were flung forward in a tangle as the truck plowed to a tilted stop in a copse of frost-blackened scrub.

Bel, blood streaming down its face, clambered back

to them crying "Out, out, out!" Miles stretched for the new opening in the roof, jerked his hand back at the burning touch of hot slagged metal and plastics. Taura, standing up, stuck her head out through the hole, then crouched back down to boost Miles through. He slithered to the ground, looked around. They were in an unpeopled valley of native vegetation, flanked by ropy, ridgy hills. Flying up the slot toward them came the two pursuing aircars, swelling, slowing—coming in for a capture, or just taking careful aim?

The *Ariel*'s combat drop shuttle roared up over the ridge and descended like the black hand of God. The pursuing aircars looked suddenly *much* smaller. One veered off and fled, the second was smashed to the ground not by plasma fire but by a swift swat from a tractor beam. Not even a trickle of smoke marked where it went down. The drop shuttle settled demurely beside them in a deafening crackling crush of shrubbery. Its hatch extended and unfolded itself in a sort of suave, self-satisfied salute.

"Show-off," Miles muttered. He pulled the woozy Thorne's arm over his shoulder, Taura carried the stunned man, Nicol's battered cup stuttered through the air, and they all staggered gratefully to their rescue.

Subtle noises of protest emanated from the ship around him as Miles stepped into the *Ariel*'s shuttle hatch corridor. His stomach twitched queasily from an artificial gravity not quite in synch with overloaded engines. They were on their way, breaking orbit already. Miles wanted to get to Nav and Com as quickly as possible, though the evidence so far suggested that Murka was carrying on quite competently. Anderson and Nout hauled in the downed trooper, now moaning his way to consciousness, and turned him over to the medtech waiting with a float pallet. Thorne, who had acquired a temporary plas dressing for the forehead cut during the shuttle flight, sent Nicol in her damaged float chair after them and whisked off toward Nav and Com. Miles turned to encounter the man he least wanted to see. Dr.

Canaba hovered anxiously in the corridor, his tanned face strained.

"You," said Miles to Canaba, in a voice dark with rage. Canaba stepped back involuntarily. Miles wanted, but was too short, to pin Canaba to the wall by his neck, and regretfully dismissed the idea of ordering Trooper Nout to do it for him. Miles pinned Canaba with a glare instead. "You cold-blooded, double-dealing, son-of-a-bitch. You set me up to murder a sixteen-year-old girl!"

Canaba raised his hands in protest. "You don't understand—"

Taura ducked through the shuttle hatch. Her tawny eyes widened in a surprise exceeded only by Canaba's. "Why, Dr. Canaba! What are you doing here?"

Miles pointed to Canaba. "You, stay there," he ordered thickly. He tamped his anger down and turned to the shuttle pilot. "Laureen?"

"Yes, sir?"

Miles took Taura by the hand and led her to Sergeant Anderson. "Laureen. I want you to take Recruit-trainee Taura here in tow and get her a square meal. All she can eat, and I do mean all. Then help her get a bath, a uniform, and orient her to the ship."

Anderson eyed the towering Taura warily. "Er . . . yes, sir."

"She's had a hell of a time," Miles felt compelled to explain, then paused and added, "Do us proud. It's important."

"Yes, sir," said Anderson sturdily, and led off, Taura following with an uncertain backward glance to Miles and Canaba.

Miles rubbed his stubbled chin, conscious of his stains and stink, fear-driven weariness stretching his nerves taut. He turned to the stunned geneticist. "All right, doctor," he snarled, "make me understand. Try real hard."

"I couldn't leave her in Ryoval's hands!" said Canaba in agitation. "To be made a victim, or worse, an agent of his, his merchandised depravities—"

"Didn't you ever think of asking us to rescue her?"

"But," said Canaba, confused, "why should you? It wasn't in your contract—a mercenary—"

"Doctor, you've been living on Jackson's Whole too damn long."

"I knew that back when I was throwing up every morning before going to work." Canaba drew himself up with a dry dignity. "But Admiral, you don't understand." He glanced down the corridor in the direction Taura had gone. "I couldn't leave her in Ryoval's hands. But I can't possibly take her to Barrayar. They kill mutants there!"

"Er . . ." said Miles, given pause. "They're attempting to reform those prejudices. Or so I understand. But you're quite right. Barrayar is not the place for her."

"I had hoped, when you came along, not to have to do it, to kill her myself. Not an easy task. I've known her . . . too long. But to leave her down there would have been the most vile condemnation—"

"That's no lie. Well, she's out of there now. Same as you." *If we can keep it so . . .* Miles was frantic to get to Nav and Com and find out what was happening. Had Ryoval launched pursuit yet? Had Fell? Would the space station guarding the distant wormhole exit be ordered to block their escape?

"I didn't want to just abandon her," dithered Canaba, "but I couldn't take her with me!"

"I should hope not. You're totally unfit to have charge of her. I'm going to urge her to join the Dendarii Mercenaries. It would seem to be her genetic destiny. Unless you know some reason why not?"

"But she's going to die!"

Miles stopped short. "And you and I are not?" he said softly after a moment, then more loudly. "Why? How soon?"

"It's her metabolism. Another mistake, or concatenation of mistakes. I don't know when, exactly. She could go another year, or two, or five. Or ten."

"Or fifteen?"

"Or fifteen, yes, though not likely. But early, still."

"And yet you wanted to take from her what little she had? Why?"

"To spare her. The final debilitation is rapid, but very painful, to judge from what some of the other . . . prototypes, went through. The females were more complex then the males, I'm not certain. . . . But it's a ghastly death. Especially ghastly as Ryoval's slave."

"I don't recall encountering a lovely death yet. And I've seen a variety. As for duration, I tell you we could all go in the next fifteen minutes, and where is your tender mercy then?" He *had* to get to Nav and Com. "I declare your interest in her forfeit, doctor. Meanwhile, let her grab what life she can."

"But she was my project—I must answer for her—"

"No. She's a free woman now. She must answer for herself."

"How free can she ever be, in that body, driven by that metabolism, that face—a freak's life—better to die painlessly than to have all that suffering inflicted on her—"

Miles spoke through his teeth. With emphasis. "No. It's. Not."

Canaba stared at him, shaken out of the rutted circle of his unhappy reasoning at last.

That's right, doctor, Miles's thought glittered. *Get your head out of your ass and look at me. Finally.*

"Why should . . . you care?" asked Canaba.

"I like her. Rather better than I like you, I might add." Miles paused, daunted by the thought of having to explain to Taura about the gene complexes in her calf. And sooner or later they'd have to retrieve them. Unless he could fake it, pretend the biopsy was some sort of medical standard operating procedure for Dendarii induction—no. She deserved more honesty than that.

Miles was highly annoyed at Canaba for putting this false note between himself and Taura and yet—without the gene complexes, would he indeed have gone in after her as his boast implied? Extended and endangered his assigned mission just out of the goodness of his heart, yeah? Devotion to duty, or pragmatic ruthlessness, which was which? He would never know, now. His anger receded, and exhaustion washed in, the familiar post-mission down—too soon, the mission was far from over, Miles reminded himself sternly. He inhaled. "You can't save her from being alive, Dr. Canaba. Too late. Let her go. Let *go*."

Canaba's lips were unhappily tight, but, head bowing, he turned his hands palm-out.

"Page the Admiral," Miles heard Thorne say as he entered Nav and Com, then "Belay that," as heads swiveled toward the swish of the doors and they saw Miles. "Good timing, sir."

"What's up?" Miles swung into the com station chair Thorne indicated. Ensign Murka was monitoring ship's shielding and weapons systems, while their Jump pilot sat at the ready beneath the strange crown of his headset with its chemical cannulas and wires. Pilot Padget's expression was inward, controlled and meditative; his consciousness fully engaged, even merged, with the *Ariel*. Good man.

"Baron Ryoval is on the com for you," said Thorne. "Personally."

"I wonder if he's checked his freezers yet?" Miles settled in before the vid link. "How long have I kept him waiting?"

"Less than a minute," said the com officer.

"Hm. Let him wait a little longer, then. What's been launched in pursuit of us?"

"Nothing, so far," reported Murka.

Miles's brows rose at this unexpected news. He took a moment to compose himself, wishing he'd had time to clean up, shave, and put on a fresh uniform before this interview, just for the psychological edge. He scratched his itching chin and ran his hands through his hair, and wriggled his damp sock toes against the deck matting, which they barely reached. He lowered his station chair slightly, straightened his spine as much as he could, and brought his breathing under control. "All right, bring him up."

The rather blurred background to the face that formed over the vid plate seemed faintly familiar—ah yes, the Security Ops room at Ryoval Biologicals. Baron Ryoval had arrived personally on that scene as promised. It took only one glance at the dusky, contorted expression on

Ryoval's youthful face to fill in the rest of the scenario. Miles folded his hands and smiled innocently. "Good morning, Baron. What can I do for you?"

"*Die,* you little mutant!" Ryoval spat. "You! There isn't going to be a bunker deep enough for you to burrow in. I'll put a price on your head that will have every bounty hunter in the galaxy all over you like a second skin—you'll not eat or sleep—I'll have you—"

Yes, the baron had seen his freezers all right. Recently. Gone entirely was the suave contemptuous dismissal of their first encounter. Yet Miles was puzzled by the drift of his threats. It seemed the baron expected them to escape Jacksonian local space. True, House Ryoval owned no space fleet, but why not rent a dreadnought from Baron Fell and attack now? That was the ploy Miles had most expected and feared, that Ryoval and Fell, and maybe Bharaputra too, would combine against him as he attempted to carry off their prizes.

"Can you afford to hire bounty hunters now?" asked Miles mildly. "I thought your assets were somewhat reduced. Though you still have your surgical specialists, I suppose."

Ryoval, breathing heavily, wiped spittle from his mouth. "Did my dear little brother put you up to this?"

"Who?" said Miles, genuinely startled. Yet another player in the game . . . ?

"Baron Fell."

"I was . . . not aware you were related," said Miles. "*Little* brother?"

"You lie badly," sneered Ryoval. "I knew he had to be behind this."

"You'll have to ask him," Miles shot at random, his head spinning as the new datum rearranged all his estimates. *Damn* his mission briefing, which had never mentioned this connection, concentrating in detail only on House Bharaputra. Half-brothers only, surely—yes, hadn't Nicol mentioned something about "Fell's half-brother"?

"I'll have your head for this," foamed Ryoval. "Shipped back frozen in a box. I'll have it encased in plastic and hang it over my—no, better. Double the money for the man who brings you in alive. You will die slowly, after infinite degradation—"

In all, Miles was glad the distance between them was widening at high acceleration.

Ryoval interrupted his own tirade, dark brows snapping down in sudden suspicion. "Or was it Bharaputra who hired you? Trying to block me from cutting in on their biologicals monopoly at the last, not merging as they promised?"

"Why, now," drawled Miles, "would Bharaputra really mount a plot against the head of another House? Do you have personal evidence that they do that sort of thing? Or—who did kill your, ah, brother's clone?" The connections were locking into place at last. Ye gods. It seemed Miles and his mission had blundered into the middle of an on-going power struggle of Byzantine complexity. Nicol had testified that Fell had never pinned down the killer of his young duplicate ... "Shall I guess?"

"You know bloody well," snapped Ryoval. "But which of them hired you? Fell, or Bharaputra? *Which?*"

Ryoval, Miles realized, knew absolutely nothing yet of the real Dendarii mission against House Bharaputra. And with the atmosphere among the Houses being what it apparently was, it could be quite a long time before they got around to comparing notes. The longer the better, from Miles's point of view. He began to suppress, then deliberately released, a small smile. "What, can't you believe it was just my personal blow against the genetic slave trade? A deed in honor of my lady?"

This reference to Taura went straight over Ryoval's head; he had his *idée fixe* now, and its ramifications and his rage were an effective block against incoming data. Really, it should not be at all hard to convince a man who had been conspiring deeply against his rivals, that those rivals were conspiring against him in turn.

"Fell, or Bharaputra?" Ryoval reiterated furiously. "Did you think to conceal a theft for Bharaputra with that wanton destruction?"

Theft? Miles wondered intently. Not of Taura,

surely—some tissue sample Bharaputra had been dealing for, perhaps? Oh *ho*—

"Isn't it obvious?" said Miles sweetly. "You gave your brother the motive, in your sabotage of his plans to extend his life. And you wanted too much from Bharaputra, so they supplied the method, placing their super-soldier inside your facility where I could rendezvous with her. They even made you pay for the privilege of having your security screwed! You played right into our hands. The master plan, of course," Miles buffed his fingernails on his T-shirt, "was mine."

Miles glanced up through his eyelashes. Ryoval seemed to be having trouble breathing. The baron cut the vid connection with an abrupt swat of his shaking hand. Blackout.

Humming thoughtfully, Miles went to get a shower.

He was back in Nav and com in fresh grey-and-whites, full of salicylates for his aches and contusions, and with a mug of hot black coffee in his hands as antidote to his squinting red eyes, when the next call came in.

So far from breaking into a tirade like his half-brother, Baron Fell sat silent a moment in the vid, just staring at Miles. Miles, burning under his gaze, felt extremely glad he'd had the chance to clean up. So, had Baron Fell missed his quaddie at last? Had Ryoval communicated to him yet any part of the smoldering paranoid misconceptions Miles had so lately fanned to flame? No pursuit had yet been launched from Fell Station—it must come soon, or not at all, or any craft light enough to match the *Ariel*'s acceleration would be too light to match its firepower. Unless Fell planned to call in favors from the consortium of Houses that ran the Jumppoint Station. . . . One more minute of this heavy silence, Miles felt, and he would break into uncontrollable blither. Fortunately, Fell spoke at last.

"You seem, Admiral Naismith." Baron Fell rumbled, "whether accidentally or on purpose, to be carrying off something that does not belong to you."

Quite a few somethings, Miles reflected, but Fell referred only to Nicol if Miles read him right. "We were compelled to leave in rather a hurry," he said in an apologetic tone.

"So I'm told." Fell inclined his head ironically. He must have had a report from his hapless squad commander. "But you may yet save yourself some trouble. There was an agreed-upon price for my musician. It's of no great difference to me if I give her up to you or to Ryoval, as long as I get that price."

Captain Thorne, working the *Ariel*'s monitors, flinched under Miles's glance.

"The price you refer to, I take it, is the secret of the Betan rejuvenation technique," said Miles.

"Quite."

"Ah . . . hm." Miles moistened his lips. "Baron, I cannot."

Fell turned his head. "Station commander, launch pursuit ships—"

"Wait!" Miles cried.

Fell raised his brows. "You reconsider? Good."

"It's not that I *will* not tell you," said Miles desperately, "it's just that the truth would be of no use to you. None whatsoever. Still, I agree you deserve some compensation. I have another piece of information I could trade you, more immediately valuable."

"Oh?" said Fell. His voice was neutral but his expression was black.

"You suspected your half-brother Ryoval in the murder of your clone, but could not chain any evidence to him, am I right?"

Fell looked fractionally more interested. "All my agents and Bharaputra's could not turn up a connection. We tried."

"I'm not surprised. Because it was Bharaputra's agents who did the deed." Well, it was possible, anyway.

Fell's eyes narrowed. "Killed their own product?" he said slowly.

"I believe Ryoval struck a deal with House Bharaputra to betray you," said Miles rapidly. "I believe it involved the trade of some unique biological samples in Ryoval's possession; I don't think cash alone would have been worth their risk. The deal was done on the highest levels, obviously. I don't know how they figured to divide the spoils of House Fell after your eventual death—maybe they didn't mean to divide it at all. They seem to have had some ultimate plan of combining their operations for some larger monopoly of biologicals on Jackson's Whole. A corporate merger of sorts." Miles paused to let this sink in. "May I suggest you may wish to reserve your forces and favors against enemies more, er, intimate and immediate than myself? Besides, you have all our credit chit but we have only half our cargo. Will you call it even?"

Fell glowered at him for a full minute, the face of a man thinking in three different directions at once. Miles knew the feeling. He then turned his head, and grated out of the corner of his mouth, "Hold pursuit ships."

Miles breathed again.

"I thank you for this information, Admiral," said Fell coldly, "but not very much. I shall not impede your swift exit. But if you or any of your ships appear in Jacksonian space again—"

"Oh, Baron," said Miles sincerely, "staying far, far away from here is fast becoming one of my dearest ambitions."

"You're wise," Fell growled, and moved to cut the link.

"Baron Fell," Miles added impulsively. Fell paused. "For your future information—is this link secured?"

"Yes?"

"The true secret of the Betan rejuvenation technique—is that there is none. Don't be taken in again. I look the age I do, because it is the age I am. Make of it what you will."

Fell said absolutely nothing. After a moment a faint, wintry smile moved his lips. He shook his head and cut the com.

Just in case, Miles lingered on in sort of a glassy puddle in one corner of Nav and Com until the Comm Officer reported their final clearance from Jump-point Station traffic control. But Miles calculated Houses Fell, Ryoval, and Bharaputra were going to be too busy with each other to concern themselves with him, at least for a while. His late transfer of information both true and false among the combatants—to each according to his measure—had the feel of throwing one bone to three starving, rabid dogs. He almost regretted not being able to stick around and see the results. Almost.

Hours after the Jump he woke in his cabin, fully dressed but with his boots set neatly by his bed, with no memory of how he'd got there. He rather fancied Murka must have escorted him. If he'd fallen asleep while walking alone he'd surely have left the boots on.

Miles first checked with the duty officer as to the *Ariel*'s situation and status. It was refreshingly dull. They were crossing a blue star system between Jump points on the route to Escobar, unpeopled and empty of everything but a smattering of routine commercial traffic. Nothing pursued them from the direction of Jackson's Whole. Miles had a light meal, not sure if it was breakfast, lunch, or dinner, his bio-rhythm being thoroughly askew from shiptime after his downside adventures. He then sought out Thorne and Nicol. He found them in Engineering. A tech was just polishing out the last dent in Nicol's float chair.

Nicol, now wearing a white tunic and shorts trimmed with pink piping, lay sprawled on her belly on a bench, watching the repairs. It gave Miles an odd sensation to see her out of her cup, it was like looking at a hermit crab out of its shell, or a seal on the shore. She looked strangely vulnerable in one-gee, yet in null gee she'd looked so right, so clearly at ease, he'd stopped noticing the oddness of the extra arms very quickly. Thorne helped the tech fit the float cup's blue shell over its reconditioned anti-grav mechanism, and turned to greet Miles as the tech proceeded to lock it in place.

Miles sat down-bench from Nicol. "From the looks of things," he told her, "you should be free of pursuit from Baron Fell. He and his half-brother are going to be fully occupied avenging themselves on each other for a while. Makes me glad I'm an only child."

"Hm," she said pensively.

"You should be safe," Thorne offered encouragingly.

"Oh—no, it's not that." Nicol said. "I was just think-ing about my sisters. Time was I couldn't wait to get away from them. Now I can't wait to see them again."

"What are your plans now?" Miles asked.

"I'll stop at Escobar, first," she replied. "It's a good nexus crossing, from there I should be able to work my way back to Earth. From Earth I can get to Orient IV, and from there I'm sure I can get home."

"Is home your goal now?"

"There's a lot more galaxy to be seen out this way," Thorne pointed out. "I'm not sure if Dendarii rosters can be stretched to include a ship's musician, but—"

She was shaking her head. "Home," she said firmly. "I'm tired of fighting one-gee all the time. I'm tired of being alone. I'm starting to have nightmares about grow-ing legs."

Thorne sighed faintly.

"We do have a little colony of downsiders living among us now," she added suggestively to Thorne. "They've fitted out their own asteroid with artificial gravity—quite like the real thing downside, only not as drafty."

Miles was faintly alarmed—to lose a ship commander of proven loyalty—

"Ah," said Thorne in a pensive tone to match Nicol's. "A long way from my home, your asteroid belt."

"Will you return to Beta Colony, then, someday?" she asked. "Or are the Dendarii Mercenaries your home and family?"

"Not quite that passionate, for me," said Thorne. "I mainly stick around due to an overwhelming curiosity to see what happens next." Thorne favored Miles with a peculiar smile.

Thorne helped load Nicol back into her blue cup. After a brief systems check she was hovering upright again, as mobile—more mobile—than her legged com-panions. She rocked and regarded Thorne brightly.

"It's only three more days to Escobar orbit," said Thorne to Nicol rather regretfully. "Still—72 hours—4,320 minutes. How much can you do in 4,320 minutes?"

Or how often, thought Miles dryly. *Especially if you*

don't sleep. Sleep, per se, was not what Bel had in mind, if Miles recognized the signs. Good luck—to both of them.

"Meanwhile," Thorne maneuvered Nicol into the corridor, "let me show you around my ship. Illyrican-built—that's out your way a bit, I understand. It's quite a story, how the *Ariel* first fell into Dendarii hands—we were the Oseran Mercenaries, back then—"

Nicol made encouraging noises. Miles suppressed an envious grin, and turned the other way up the corridor, to search out Dr. Canaba and arrange the discharge of his last unpleasant duty.

Bemusedly, Miles set aside the hypospray he'd been turning over in his hands as the door to sickbay sighed open. He swiveled in the medtech's station chair and glanced up as Taura and Sergeant Anderson entered. "My *word*," he murmured.

Anderson sketched a salute. "Reporting as ordered, sir." Taura's hand twitched, uncertain whether to attempt to mimic this military greeting or not. Miles gazed up at Taura and his lips parted with involuntary delight. Taura's transformation was all he'd dreamed of and more.

He didn't know how Anderson had persuaded the stores computer to so exceed its normal parameters, but somehow she'd made it disgorge a complete Dendarii undress kit in Taura's size: crisp grey-and-white pocketed jacket, grey trousers, polished ankle-topping boots. Taura's face and hair were clean enough to outshine her boots. Her dark hair was now drawn back in a thick, neat, and rather mysterious braid coiling up the back of her head—Miles could not make out where the ends went—and glinting with unexpected mahogany highlights.

She looked, if not exactly well-fed, at least less rawly starving; her eyes bright and interested, not the haunted yellow flickers in bony caverns he'd first seen. Even from this distance he could tell that re-hydration and the chance to brush her teeth and fangs had cured the ketone-laced breath that several days in Ryoval's sub-basement on a diet of raw rats and nothing else had produced. The dirt-encrusted scale was smoothed away from her huge hands, and—inspired touch—her clawed nails had been, not blunted, but neatened and sharpened, and then enameled with an iridescent pearl-white polish that complemented her gray-and-whites like a flash of jewelry. The polish had to have been shared out of some personal stock of the sergeant's.

"Outstanding, Anderson," said Miles in admiration.

Anderson smirked proudly. "That about what you had in mind, sir?"

"Yes, it was." Taura's face reflected his delight straight back at him. "What did you think of your first wormhole jump?" he asked her.

Her long lips rippled—what happened when she tried to purse them, Miles guessed. "I was afraid I was getting sick, I was so dizzy all of a sudden, till Sergeant Anderson explained what it was."

"No little hallucinations, or odd time-stretching effects?"

"No, but it wasn't—well, it was quick, anyway."

"Hm. It doesn't sound like you're one of the fortunates—or unfortunates—to be screened for Jump pilot aptitudes. From the talents you demonstrated on Ryoval's landing pad yesterday morning, Tactics should be loathe to lose you to Nav and Com." Miles paused. "Thank you, Laureen. What did my page interrupt?"

"Routine systems checks on the drop shuttles, putting them to bed. I was having Taura look over my shoulder while I worked."

"Right, carry on. I'll send Taura back to you when she's done here."

Anderson exited reluctantly, clearly curious. Miles waited till the doors swished closed to speak again. "Sit down, Taura. So your first twenty-four hours with the Dendarii have been satisfactory?"

She grinned, settling herself carefully in a station chair, which creaked. "Just fine."

"Ah," He hesitated. "You understand, when we reach Escobar, you do have the option to go your own way.

You're not compelled to join us. I could see you get some kind of start, downside there."

"What?" Her eyes widened in dismay. "No! I mean . . . do I eat too much?"

"Not at all! You fight like four men, we can bloody well afford to feed you like three. But . . . I need to set a few things straight, before you make your trainee's oath." He cleared his throat. "I didn't come to Ryoval's to recruit you. A few weeks before Bharaputra sold you, do you remember Dr. Canaba injecting something into your leg? With a needle, not a hypospray."

"Oh, yes." She rubbed her calf half-consciously. "It made a knot."

"What, ah, did he tell you it was?"

"An immunization."

She'd been right, Miles reflected, when they'd first met. Humans did lie a lot. "Well, it wasn't an immunization. Canaba was using you as a live repository for some engineered biological material. Molecularly bound, dormant material," he added hastily as she twisted around and looked at her leg in disquiet. "It can't activate spontaneously, he assures me. My original mission was only to pick up Dr. Canaba. But he wouldn't leave without his gene complexes."

"He planned to take me with him?" she said in thrilled surprise. "So I should thank *him* for sending you to me!"

Miles wished he could see the look on Canaba's face if she did. "Yes and no. Specifically, no." He rushed roughly on before his nerve failed him. "You have nothing to thank him for, nor me either. He meant to take only your tissue sample, and sent me to get it."

"Would you rather have left me at—is that why Escobar—" she was still bewildered.

"It was your good luck," Miles plunged on, "that I'd lost my men and was disarmed when we finally met. Canaba lied to me, too. In his defense, he seems to have had some dim idea of saving you from a brutal life as Ryoval's slave. He sent me to kill you, Taura. He sent me to slay a monster, when he should have been begging me to rescue a princess in disguise. I'm not too pleased with Dr. Canaba. Nor with myself. I lied through my teeth to you down in Ryoval's basement, because I thought I had to, to survive and win."

Her face was confused, congealing, the light in her eyes fading. "Then you didn't . . . really think I was human—"

"On the contrary. Your choice of test was an excellent one. It's much harder to lie with your body than with your mouth. When I, er, demonstrated my belief, it had to be real." Looking at her, he still felt a twinge of lurching, lunatic joy, somatic residual from that adventure-of-the body. He supposed he always would feel something—male conditioning, no doubt. "Would you like me to demonstrate it again?" he asked half-hopefully, then bit his tongue. "No," he answered his own question. "If I am to be your commander—we have these non-fraternization rules. Mainly to protect those of lower rank from exploitation, though it can work both—ahem!" He was digressing dreadfully. He picked up the hypospray, fiddled with it nervously, and put it back down.

"Anyway, Dr. Canaba has asked me to lie to you again. He wanted me to sneak up on you with a general anesthetic, so he could biopsy back his sample. He's a coward, you may have noticed. He's outside now, shaking in his shoes for fear you'll find out what he intended for you. I think a local zap with a medical stunner would suffice. I'd sure want to be conscious and watching if he were working on *me*, anyway." He flicked the hypospray contemptuously with one finger.

She sat in silence, her strange wolfish face—though Miles was getting used to it—unreadable. "You want me to let him . . . cut into my leg?" she said at last.

"Yes."

"Then what?"

"Then nothing. That will be the last of Dr. Canaba for you, and Jackson's Whole, and all the rest of it. That, I promise. Though if you're doubtful of my promises, I can understand why."

"The last . . ." she breathed. Her face lowered, then rose, and her shoulders straightened. "Then let's get it over with." There was no smile to her long mouth now.

*   *   *

Canaba, as Miles expected, was not happy to be presented with a conscious subject. Miles truly didn't care how unhappy Canaba was about it, and after one look at his cold face, Canaba didn't argue. Canaba took his sample wordlessly, packaged it carefully in the biotainer, and fled with it back to the safety and privacy of his own cabin as soon as he decently could.

Miles sat with Taura in sickbay till the medical stun wore off enough for her to walk without stumbling. She sat without speaking for a long time. He watched her still features, wishing beyond measure he knew how to relight those gold eyes.

"When I first saw you," she said softly, "it was like a miracle. Something magic. Everything I'd wished for, longed for. Food. Water. Heat. Revenge. Escape." She gazed down at her polished claws, "Friends . . ." and glanced up at him, ". . . touching."

"What else do you wish for, Taura?" Miles asked earnestly.

Slowly she replied. "I wish I were normal."

Miles was silent, too. "I can't give you what I don't possess myself," he said at length. The words seemed to lie in inadequate lumps between them. He roused himself to a better effort. "No. Don't wish that. I have a better idea. Wish to be yourself. To the hilt. Find out what you're best at, and develop it. Hopscotch your weaknesses. There isn't time for them. Look at Nicol—"

"So beautiful," sighed Taura.

"Or look at Captain Thorne, and tell me what 'normal' is, and why I should give a damn for it. Look at me, if you will. Should I kill myself trying to overcome men twice my weight and reach in unarmed combat, or should I shift the ground to where their muscle is useless, 'cause it never gets close enough to apply its strength? I haven't got *time* to lose, and neither have you."

"Do you know how little time?" demanded Taura suddenly.

"Ah . . ." said Miles cautiously, "do you?"

"I am the last survivor of my crèche mates. How could I not know?" Her chin lifted defiantly.

"Then don't wish to be normal," said Miles passionately, rising to pace. "You'll only waste your precious time in futile frustration. Wish to be great! That at least you have a fighting chance for. Great at whatever you are. A great trooper, a great sergeant. A great quartermaster, for God's sake, if that's what comes with ease. A great musician like Nicol—only think how horrible if she were wasting her talents trying to be merely normal." Miles paused self-consciously in his pep talk, thinking, *Easier to preach than practice....*

Taura studied her polished claws, and sighed. "I suppose it's useless for me to wish to be beautiful, like Sergeant Anderson."

"It is useless for you to try to be beautiful *like* anyone but yourself," said Miles. "Be beautiful like Taura, ah, that you can do. Superbly well." He found himself gripping her hands, and ran one finger across an iridescent claw, "Though Laureen seems to have grasped the principle, you might be guided by her taste."

"Admiral," said Taura slowly, not releasing his hands, "Are you actually my commander yet? Sergeant Anderson said something about orientation, and induction tests, and an oath...."

"Yes, all that will come when we make fleet rendezvous. Till then, technically, you're our guest."

A certain sparkle was beginning to return to her gold eyes. "Then—till then—it wouldn't break any Dendarii rules, would it, if you showed me again how human I am? One more time?"

It must be, Miles thought, akin to the same drive that used to propel men to climb sheer rock faces without an antigrav belt, or jump out of ancient aircraft with nothing to stop them going splat but a wad of silk cloth. He felt the fascination rising in him, the death-defying laugh. "Slowly?" he said in a strangled voice. "Do it right this time? Have a little conversation, drink a little wine, play a little music? Without Ryoval's guard squad lurking overhead, or ice cold rock under my ..."

Her eyes were huge and gold and molten. "You did say you liked to practice what you were great at."

Miles had never realized how susceptible he was to flattery from tall women. A weakness he must guard against. Sometime.

They retired to his cabin and practiced assiduously till halfway to Escobar.

MARGARET WEIS
New York Times Bestselling Author
& DON PERRIN

"**Adventures and misadventures . . . plot twists and humor . . . sure to please Weis's many fans.**"
—*Publishers Weekly*

ROBOT BLUES

When a museum curator hires the Mag Force 7 to steal a robotic artifact from an excavation site, Xris feels this could be easy money. And when the mercenaries realize they've lost a deceptively dangerous antique, all havoc breaks loose. It's up to the Mag Force 7 to find it before the bloodthirsty Corasians aliens bent on human annihilation—can use it for ultimate destruction. (455819—$6.99)

"**Swashbuckling . . . makes one think of *Star Wars*.**"
—*Booklist*

THE KNIGHTS OF THE BLACK EARTH

They are Mag Force 7, the finest mercenary squad in the known universe. Their leader Xris is on a mission of vengeance against the comrade who betrayed him years before. Yet before Xris can claim his revenge, he and his men are recruited for a job they cannot turn down. And Xris's only hope of stopping them lies in joining forces with an old enemy.

(455142—$5.99)

from **RoC**

*Prices slightly higher in Canada.

The Roc Frequent Readers Club
BUY TWO ROC BOOKS AND GET
ONE SF/FANTASY NOVEL FREE!

Check the free title you wish to receive (subject to availability):